KT-199-132

Zoë Barnes was born and brought up on Merseyside, but now lives in Gloucestershire. She had a variety of jobs, from hearing-aid technician to French translator, before becoming a full-time writer, and is also a semi-professional singer. Zoë and her partner Dmytro share their cottage near Cheltenham with their four cats, Grizzle, Griselda, Juno and Jupiter.

Zoë is the bestselling author of *Hitched*, *Bumps* and *Hot Property*, also published by Piatkus.

Zoë Barnes loves to hear from her readers.
Write to her c/o Piatkus Books, 5 Windmill Street,
London, W1P 1HF or via e-mail at
zoebarnes@yahoo.co.uk

Also by Zoë Barnes

Bumps
Hitched
Hot Property

Bouncing Back

Zoë Barnes

PIATKUS

For more information on other books published by Piatkus,
visit our website at www.piatkus.co.uk

Copyright © 2000 by Zoë Barnes

First published in Great Britain in 2000 by
Judy Piatkus (Publishers) Ltd of
5 Windmill Street, London W1P 1HF
e-mail: info@piatkus.co.uk

This edition published 2000

The moral right of the author has been asserted

A catalogue record for this book is available from the British Library

ISBN 0 7499 3189 2

Set in Times by
Phoenix Photosetting, Chatham, Kent

Printed and bound in Great Britain by
Mackays of Chatham PLC, Chatham, Kent

To Jupiter, who chewed the manuscript to perfection.

Just when it was all going so well . . .

A fat, black, disreputable-looking cloud sneaked over the crest of the hill, homed in on a Northampton office block, and casually emptied its bladder on the roof. It was that kind of day: murky, March and monotonous. Even the pigeons looked depressed.

Inside a featureless office on the third floor, Cally Storm was getting precisely nowhere.

'Nope,' she said, trying to keep her irritation in check. 'Didn't get a word of that. Look, I'm sorry but you're just not making yourself clear.'

On the other side of the glass-topped desk, the small Italian with the sharp suit and the soft brown eyes blinked frustratedly. He looked about fourteen, had skinny ankles and ought by rights to have been smoking behind the bike sheds, not running the Human Resources division of Banco Torino (UK) plc. More important, he was definitely not old enough to be Cally's new boss. And if there'd been any justice in the world, she'd have been sitting in that chair, not him.

'You still no unnerstan'?' he repeated, rather pointlessly thought Cally, since the only words of English the new Italian management team seemed confident with were 'Hello', and 'Manchester United'.

'Maybe if you spoke more slowly,' she ventured, her jaw muscles aching with the effort of not slapping him about the head. 'Slooow-ly?'

She added hand movements for extra emphasis. A GCSE in Italian might have helped, but then she'd have missed out on double basketball at school, and you had to get your priorities right. Cally was confident that she had sorted hers out ages ago. One: aim for the top and don't stop till you get there. Two: there is no two. Number two sucks.

'Is my accent, yes?'

'Er . . . well . . .'

There was no polite answer to that. This was a man who did not so much command the English language as lie down and invite it to trample all over him. Cally fiddled restlessly with the handle of her new leather portfolio, one eye on the clock. Get to the point, get to the point, she seethed inwardly. It was all right for him, of course. He was on a nice two-week jolly from Milan; all expenses paid and nothing to do but get in people's way and tell them they were spending too much on paperclips.

Things had gone from bad to worse since the takeover. Meetings, meetings, meetings. No decisions seemed to get made any more, the canteen smelled permanently of pesto and she was already half an hour late for a meeting with the Lower Slaughter Fatstock Cooperative. Didn't these Mediterranean types realise how many other companies would be more than happy to insure Farmer Giles's Friesians against foot rot?

Still, she supposed things would settle down eventually. It wasn't the first time LBS Agri-Finance had been taken over, and it probably wouldn't be the last.

Signor Toscelli chewed his lower lip. 'Ah. *Momento.*'

From the depths of an Armani trouser pocket, he produced a dog-eared phrase book and flipped feverishly through it till he found what he was looking for.

'*Si, si*, here is what I say.' His index finger jabbed at the page. 'You. Are.' His lips struggled to frame the unfamiliar diphthong. 'Fay-aired.'

Cally's nose wrinkled. 'What?'

'Fay-aired.' In exasperation, he spun the book round so that it was facing Cally, and jabbed a triumphant finger. 'Fay-airrred. This is correct, no? You are . . .?'

Fired?

Somewhere in the pit of Cally's stomach, a lift fell fifteen storeys.

'Fired!' squeaked Cally, as everything crystallised into horrible clarity, and her lovely new executive portfolio tumbled off her lap. 'Is this some kind of sick joke?'

Unfortunately, Signor Toscelli wasn't laughing.

Well, well, fucking well, thought Cally, staring bitterly out of the snot smeared bus windows. So this is where the number forty-two goes. And just think, if I hadn't got the golden elbow off Banco Torino (UK), I'd probably never have set out on this glorious voyage of discovery. Not.

She rubbed a small patch of window clear and peered through the glass. Snow. Effing snow, every effing where. Now didn't that just make everything perfect? One minute a harmless little bit of rain, the next there's a sodding blizzard and you can't get a taxi for love or money. One minute you've got a great job with brilliant prospects, the next you're out on your ear and some bastard Italian has swiped the keys to your company car.

3

So kind of them to lend her a Banco Torino carrier bag to put her things in. Horribly overstuffed, it bounced about on her lap, threatening to spew its contents in ten different directions as the bus crested a speed bump at thirty miles an hour, swerved to avoid the world's biggest pothole, skidded on wet slush and gaily rattled across the corner of the pavement, all without changing gear.

Cally retrieved a sheep-shaped money-box as it toppled sideways, and stuffed it back into the bag. A plastic sheep, two desk tidies, twelve issues of *Farmer's Weekly* and a red sock she wasn't even sure was hers: was this dross all she had to show for ten years spent selling more lambing insurance than anybody else in the history of LBS? And all of a sudden she – little miss whizz-kid – was redundant, and she hadn't even seen it coming. Well ha bloody ha, Cally Storm, she told herself. Looks like the joke's on you.

Of course, if she forced herself to be rational about it she could just about see that there was no reason why she shouldn't be made redundant. It happened to loads of people all the time, it wasn't anything personal. Fact was, a big fat multinational like Banco Torino just couldn't figure out what to do with someone who'd once insured a pet angora goat against alopecia.

Sod that, it felt personal. Ten years she'd endured, ten long years of threatened mergers and takeovers and flotations and rationalisations, and OK, the LBS might have moved her round the country like an unclaimed parcel, but they'd never once hinted that she might actually be dispensable. Quite the reverse: there had even been whispers about promoting her to Something Big in grain silos.

Which didn't alter the fact that she was dispensable,

4

or that she hated it. Almost as much as she'd hated having to ask the way to the bus stop. Typical: you wait years to get your own numbered parking space, and the day after you do, they kick you out on your arse.

'Look Mam!' chirruped a child across the gangway. 'It's snowing again! Just like in that video about the Eskimos.'

Cally turned to look out of the window. It wasn't just snowing, it was coming down so hard you could barely see through it; like God had just punctured his duvet and emptied the whole lot over Northampton. Her head sank forward on to the back of the seat in front. Terrific. All this town needed now was a rain of venomous toads and a fleshing-eating zombie or two, and the day would be just perfect.

Still, nothing else could possibly go wrong. Could it?

Look on the bright side, Cally ordered herself as she squelched up Laburnum Walk towards the house she'd never liked, in the area that gave her the creeps. At least you've got somewhere warm and dry to live, the fridge is full of cheesecake, and the neighbours don't fill their front gardens with burned-out Ford Capris.

True, she grudgingly conceded. But it won't be warm and dry for much longer if that hole in the roof isn't fixed, will it? And you know damn well cheesecake gives you zits. And who's going to fork out for the Velux windows, now you've joined the end of the dole queue? Oh – and don't forget the collapsing garden shed, and the damp in the conservatory, and the woodworm in the window seat . . .

Pull yourself together, she urged herself sternly. Stop feeling sorry for yourself. It's not as bad as all that, at least you've still got Rob. Yes, hissed the demon on her

5

shoulder; and Rob's still got his lovely shiny company BMW.

She stood outside the gate to number thirty-one, melting snow pouring down the back of her neck, so cold and wet she didn't give a damn any more, and gazed up through falling snowflakes at the character-less, pebbledashed façade. OK so there were nicer houses, but then again there were much nastier ones too, and it wasn't everyone who got to live in a four-bedroomed semi in a sought-after area of Northampton, now was it? And anyhow, like Rob was always reminding her, it wasn't just a house, it was an invest-ment. Sometimes she suspected that was all it was.

Pushing open the gate, she stomped wearily up to the front door in her ruined mules, and slid her key in the lock. Rob would make it all better, she had already decided. He would towel her down like a wet sheepdog, bundle her up in a duvet and make her some of his special cocoa. He'd probably buy her a new pair of shoes too. That's what husbands were for.

As she stood in the hall, shedding snow on to the brand-new natural wood flooring, Cally heard Rob's voice floating out of the front room. He must be on the phone, selling another consignment of fifteen-foot palm trees to some shopping mall. She kicked off her wet shoes and padded on numb feet towards the kitchen, trying not to disturb him. Funny though. She cocked an ear as she passed the half-open door. It didn't sound like a business call. In fact, she could have sworn she just heard the word . . . 'knickers'.

Knickers?

She pushed the door soundlessly open. Mind you, even if she had made her entrance accompanied by the pipes and drums of the Royal Highland Fusiliers, Rob probably wouldn't have noticed. He was leaning casually against the chimney breast, telephone flex wound round a flirtatious index finger, receiver snuggled comfortably under his chin.

'. . . black ones again? Why aren't you wearing those lovely little red ones I got you? What's that? You . . .' He chuckled dirtily. 'Come here and say that, you naughty girl, and I'll give you a good spanki—'

Rob turned and froze as his eyes fixed on Cally, business suit plastered to her soaked and shivering body, mid-brown hair steaming limply like the winnets on a sheep's backside. He swallowed, smiled weakly and jammed the receiver back on the hook.

'Cally love, you're . . .'

'Home early? Yes I am, aren't I?'

Rob gave a nervous giggle, his face passing through at least a dozen tortured expressions as he leafed through his mental file of excuses. 'I was just . . . er . . .'

'Surprised? I bet you bloody were.'

He took a step towards her, arms stretched out. 'Cally love, I mean, it isn't . . .'

It was strange really. Cally didn't feel hurt or upset or betrayed. Suddenly and inexplicably, she felt overwhelmingly bored. Bored with life, bored with this house, and most especially bored with the utterly boring man she had had the misfortune to marry.

He reached out to put an arm round her, but she ducked aside. 'Oh give it a rest, Rob. I'm not interested in your feeble excuses.'

'They're not . . .'

'Got huge tits has she? Bigger than mine?' She thrust her 34Cs in his face. 'God you're pathetic, you know that?'

Panic entered Rob's eyes.

7

'No, no, you've got it all wrong, I was only . . .'

'Spare me the gory details, Rob, it's the oldest story in the book. Just get out of my sight.'

'Cally, don't be an idiot.'

'There's only one idiot around here, and it isn't me. I want you out of this house. Now.'

'But you can't just throw me out of my own house!'

'Oh can't I?'

Seizing him by the shoulders, and surprising both of them with her own strength, she propelled him towards the front door. Halfway along the hall, he spun round, parrying her with raised hands.

'Look, Cally, darling, I admit I've been stupid, but it was just a bit of harmless fun, OK?'

'Correction. Not OK.' She wrenched open the front door and pointed out into the arctic waste that was Northampton. 'Get out, Rob.'

'But I . . .' She shoved him in the belly and he tripped over the doormat, landing out on the step with the empty milk bottles and the hedgehog book-scraper. 'Ow!'

Slamming the door on him, she turned away. Two seconds later he was whimpering plaintively through the letter box. 'Cally, you can't do this to me! It's snowing, for Chrissakes!'

'Is it?' Opening the door, she threw an umbrella at his head. 'I suppose you'll be wanting this then. Now piss off out of my life and don't come back.'

Her heart was pounding and her head was thumping. By the time she reached the living room she was hyperventilating so fast that she felt quite faint. What now? Breathe into a brown paper bag and wait for the sky to fall in on her? No job, no bloke – what next? They said bad things always happened in threes.

There was a bottle of vintage champagne in the bottom of the kitchen dresser. She pulled it out and banged it down on the table. OK, so she and Rob had been saving it for a special occasion, but they didn't come much more special than this, did they? It wasn't every day your entire life came crashing down around your ears.

Chapter One

After what seemed like years, it had finally stopped raining.

Cally peered into a plastic water-butt. 'Dad,' she called back over her shoulder, 'is this parsnip or lentil?'

A tall, thin man emerged from the tepee and into the light, pushing his round, wire-rimmed glasses back up his bony nose. Marc Storm looked for all the world like a prep-school headmaster at a Seventies' theme party.

'Neither, it's Anglo-Saxon honey beer – a friend of mine researched the recipe for me.'

He ruffled her hair affectionately, which made her feel all of six years old. 'Dad!' She ducked away. 'Grow up.'

'Perish the thought.' Marc lowered his voice. 'So – fancy giving me your expert opinion?'

Cally pulled a face. 'No way am I tasting any more of that horrible home-brew. You know what it did to Mrs Davis's cat.'

Her father swept aside her objections. 'Ah, but this stuff is seriously good.'

'If it's vile I'm saying so.'

'Deal. But you won't.'

He dipped in an old tin mug and handed it to her. 'Well?'

'Not as bad as it looks,' she conceded, not sure whether she was disappointed or relieved. 'Probably turn out to be deadly poisonous, mind.'

'Cally.'

She looked up sharply, recognising her father's tone of voice. 'Whatever it is, the answer's no.'

'All I want is for you to tell me what's wrong.'

Too promptly, she snapped back: 'Nothing.'

Marc sighed. 'How's Rob?'

'I haven't the faintest idea.' She kicked a rotting turnip out of the way. 'And frankly I couldn't care less.'

'You've not seen him then?'

'No. Why should I?'

Hands in pockets, Marc wriggled the toe of his shoe into the boggy earth. 'Cally love, he's your husband.'

'So?' The word came out like a challenge.

'So, husbands and wives generally live in the same house.'

'You and Mum don't,' pointed out Cally, childishly pleased to have scored a point.

Marc sighed. 'Look. It's not that we don't like having you around – it's not often your mother has somebody to share the house with – but let's face it, you don't usually stay for more than a day or two, do you?'

Cally avoided her father's gaze. 'Why shouldn't I stay a bit longer if I want?'

'No reason at all. But it's been a fortnight, Cally. You've not spent that long at home since your mum grounded you when you were sixteen.'

She chose to ignore her father's probing, hating the way his questions targeted the very parts of her that hurt the most. 'Do you want me to hoe round these blue things, or dig them out?'

'Never mind the blue things.' Marc's voice took on

an unaccustomed note of firmness. 'Just tell me what's wrong with you and Rob. Have you had a row?'

Something curled up and howled at the back of Cally's wounded heart. 'I just don't want to talk about it. All right?'

'This fifty-foot fibreglass woman in a leopardskin bikini, with this, like, helter-skelter slide thing running all the way down her thigh. Now that's entertainment.' The short man with the gold earring swung round for Rob's reaction. 'Am I right, or am I right?'

Rob was doing his best to be enthusiastic about B-Movie Heaven, his client's kitsch new theme park – the contract could be worth thousands in commission over the next couple of years – but all Rob could think about was the last phone conversation he had had with Cally. It had consisted of precisely two words, and one of those was 'off'. Not a promising stage in his campaign to win her back.

'Oh God,' he groaned, 'what am I going to do?'

Greg Prince halted by the site of the Killer Tomato white-knuckle ride. 'Do? You're going to quote me for two hundred live tropical creepers for Tarzan's Jungle Dome, that's what.'

'I didn't mean about the plants, I meant about Cally. What am I going to do about her? She's walked out on me and the hamster, and now she won't even speak to me.'

'God help us, give it a rest can't you?' Greg was rapidly tiring of Rob's one-note conversation. 'Do you want this contract or what?'

'Of course I do.' Rob struggled to visualise money pouring itself into his bank account, but all he could see was Cally's face, mouthing obscenities at him as she threw the minidisc player at his head. 'It's just . . . I'm a bit distracted, that's all.'

' 'Course you are, mate.' Greg clapped him on the back in a matey sort of way. 'Women – who needs 'em, eh?'

I do, Rob moaned silently. That's what got me into this mess in the first place. He cleared his throat. 'Jungle creepers. Right.'

'Big ones, mind. No good getting little tiddly things, can't wait for 'em to grow, see? We've got to be up and running by August Bank Holiday. Big and impressive, that's what the punters want.' He jabbed his mobile phone at Rob's notebook. 'Am I right or am I right?'

Rob smiled weakly. 'Right.'

'Oh – and don't forget the date palms. Nothing under ten foot, and I want real bananas on them banana plants.'

Rob trailed Greg through the embryonic theme park, clambering over headless Martians, a giant ant and one of Cerberus's spare heads from the much-hyped Monsters of Hades ride. 'The thing is,' he panted, disentangling an ant's leg from his trousers, 'she won't believe I've changed.'

Greg groaned. 'Are you on about your ex-wife again?'

'Wife,' Rob corrected him. 'And she's staying that way if I've got anything to do with it. Only problem is, I just don't know what to do,' he finished lamely.

Defeated by Rob's relentlessness, Greg sat down on a Martian. 'Why are you telling me all this, mate?'

Rob looked sheepish. ''Cause I've got nobody else to tell it to, I s'pose.'

'You're a bit of a sad git really, aren't you?' commented Greg, not unkindly. 'So – what happened to your bit on the side? Dumped you, did she?'

14

'Leanne?' Rob's shoulders sagged. 'She left me for some muscle-bound ape from the Pexercise Health Spa. Said I never stopped going on about Cally.'

'Seems a fair enough comment,' observed Greg drily. 'So – you want your wife back. Am I right or am I right?'

'You're right.'

'Better get off your arse and do something about it then. Have you tried going round and seeing her?'

'She slammed the door in my face.' Rob indicated the swollen tip of his bruised nose. 'I've told her it's all over with Leanne, and it was just a stupid mistake, but she won't listen. I've even tried going down on my knees and begging her to come back to me, but she just says why should she.'

'Hmm.' Greg rubbed the dark stubble on his chin. 'I can see her point.'

Rob looked peeved, but had to concede that Greg was right. 'So what do I do?'

Greg shrugged. 'You're asking the wrong bloke, mate. I've been married three times and none of them understood me. But if she's got no reason to come back, why don't you give her one?'

'Give her one? She won't even let me through the front door.'

'Not that, you moron. Give her a reason. A reason to come back.'

'A reason? Oh.' Rob wrinkled his nose and stared into the middle distance, where a forest of mini-skyscrapers was being erected, girder by girder. Then he clicked his fingers. 'A reason! Of course, why didn't I think of it before? The house!'

'What about it?'

'I'll tell her if she's not coming back, I'm putting it

on the market. You know what women are like, they're all nest-builders. She's only staying away to make me feel bad. Once she thinks I'm selling the nest from under her, she'll be back like a shot.'

'Hang on a minute,' cautioned Greg. 'This is none of my business, right, but don't you think that's a bit over the top?'

'No, no, you don't understand. I won't really be selling it, I'll just pretend to.' His face shone with enthusiasm. 'Great idea, huh? It's bound to make her realise what she's giving up.'

'Yeah, yeah, terrific,' replied Greg, without enthusiasm. 'Now, about those jungle creepers.'

It was a couple of evenings later when the phone rang in Evie Storm's front hall and a head of glossy brown curls popped round the door of the living room.

'It's for you, darling.' Evie winked encouragingly and mouthed the word 'Rob'.

Cally shrank back into the sofa, suddenly petrified and angry and pleased, all at once. 'Tell him I'm not in.'

Evie smiled sweetly down the phone. 'She's just coming now, Rob, take care. Here you are, darling.'

The cordless phone found its way into Cally's hand, and Evie's neat little figure skipped off jauntily back to the kitchen, closing the door behind her. Damn you, thought Cally, tempted to drop the phone into the fish tank but reluctant to inflict Rob on her father's neon tetras. Damn everyone and everything and the whole damn world.

'What do you want?' she demanded. She'd thought she was ready for him, but her stomach turned a somersault as Rob's voice came crackling down the line from Northampton.

'Just to talk.'

Big uncomfortable pause.

'What about?'

'Oh you know.'

'Not if you don't tell me,' she snapped back. Go on, hissed the demon on her shoulder. Make him suffer. It's not as if he doesn't deserve it. 'Get to the point, Rob, I haven't got all night.'

'Are you all right?'

Anger sizzled and popped inside her. 'Is that all you rang to say? I'm fine, Rob. F-I-N-E.' Her voice rose several decibels. 'I'm out of a job, my husband's screwing a bouncy castle, why wouldn't I be fine?'

She heard Rob cough uneasily on the other end of the line. 'This is all my fault, isn't it?'

'Give that man a prize.'

'So you're not coming back home yet then?'

Cally's hand tightened around the receiver. 'Yet? What do you mean, "yet"? I'm not coming home, Rob. Full stop. When are you going to get that into your thick skull?'

'But—'

She didn't pause to let him get a word in. 'Anyway, that place isn't home any more, not since you . . . you . . . soiled it with that cheap tart.'

'Right. I see.' Rob paused for effect. 'In that case, I guess I'd better go ahead and ring round the estate agents.'

Cally caught her breath, suddenly dizzy. 'What estate agents?'

'We'll need a proper valuation before we put the house on the market, won't we?'

'What!' Cally's head whirled. 'Sell the house? Rob, what the hell are you on about?'

17

'Look Cal,' said Rob, his voice firmer and more confident now. 'I know you love this house – we both do – but, well, it's always been our house, hasn't it? Our home. It's no use to me without you, and anyway, it's far too big for one. Plus . . .'

It took Cally several seconds to stop gaping and start shouting. 'Rob, you total bastard! I'm gone five minutes and already you're putting my house on the market.'

'Your house?'

'Yes Rob, my house! It was my sodding cut-price mortgage that got us it in the first place, you can't just go selling it from under me without so much as a by-your-leave. I'll get a solicitor and make him stop you!'

'For God's sake, Cally,' protested Rob, 'be reasonable! What use have I got for a four-bedroomed house? And what's the point of you paying your share of the mortgage if you're not coming back?'

Not coming back. The rotten, heartless, cheating git made it sound so final. And maybe it was final. Cally didn't know whether to cry, scream or ask the RAF to drop a bomb on Laburnum Walk.

'Oh, I get it. You don't actually want me back. You and Leanne have decided to sell up and invest in a little love-nest. Well thanks a million, Rob. Nice of you to tell me.'

'No, it's not like that! Of course I want you back. It's just I thought . . . with the house being so big . . .'

'Over my dead body, do you hear?' she yelled down the phone, and cut him off in mid-protest. Whatever else he might have to say, she didn't want to hear it. Bloody house. Bloody Rob. Bloody love. None of it was worth all the pain and hassle.

'Did I hear raised voices, darling?' enquired Evie,

choosing that very moment to come back into the living room with a tray of decaff.

Cally snivelled and flopped into the old, misshapen armchair that still smelled of her very first dog. Suddenly she felt extremely small and empty.

'Mummy,' she said, in a voice that sounded about five years old, 'Rob doesn't love me any more.'

Chapter Two

'Cally, sweetheart, we both know I won't be able to do this if you don't lie still.' Marc Storm's younger and considerably more affluent sister contemplated her spreadeagled niece with a mixture of irritation and concern. 'So let's try a little harder, shall we?'

'It's not that I don't appreciate what you're trying to do,' replied Cally, wincing as another acupuncture needle crash-landed on her kneecap, 'but I don't think this is going to work.'

'That's not the attitude,' scolded her mother. 'You know your Auntie Samantha's doing her best to help your depression.'

Paralyse me, more like, thought Cally, trying not to remember the TV programme she'd seen about somebody who had been rendered helpless from the neck down by a bricklayer with a white coat and a packet of panel pins.

'Mum, I told you, I'm not depressed,' she said, for the umpteenth time.

'Then why have you stopped varnishing your toenails?'

'Because . . . Because I just couldn't be bothered any more. OK?'

Cally had had enough. Before you could say 'spinal injuries unit' she was off the sofa bed and halfway across the front room, needles sprouting out of her like a back-to-front hedgehog.

'Cally!' protested Evie. But she was already disappearing up the stairs. 'You can't just . . .'

A distant door slammed shut.

'Evie, dear,' confided Samantha, 'I really do think she's dreadfully depressed.'

'I can see that for myself, thank you!' snapped Evie, unusually ruffled. 'Why do you think I asked you to come over and help?'

'I'm a nurse, not an acupuncturist. Between you and me, I think she ought to see a proper doctor.'

Evie looked distinctly unimpressed. 'I hope you're not suggesting what I think you're suggesting.'

'They do say the new-generation anti-depressants are wonderful, you know, these serotonin reuptake inhibitors. Hardly any side-effects at all. In fact, my friend Ja—'

'Fill my daughter full of synthetic chemicals? Turn her into a zombie? Samantha, how could you!'

'It was only a suggestion, dear.' Samantha exchanged worried looks with her brother, who had just arrived from the allotment with a week's consignment of underpants and a box of chicken manure. 'Marc, I was just suggesting to Evie that maybe what Cally needs is a teensy bit of conventional medical help.'

'Sounds like a sensible idea,' agreed Marc. 'She does seem very down.'

'How can you!' Evie looked at him as though he had just admitted to sleeping with a Young Conservative. 'You of all people! Well, you may want to turn the poor girl into a chemical factory, but I'm her mother and I'm not going to let you!'

* * *

22

'Cally,' ventured Evie, taking a step into the room.

A subterranean voice rose from somewhere under the duvet. 'Go away.'

Evie closed the door and sat down on the end of the bed. It was broad daylight outside, but the flowery curtains were drawn tight shut, reducing Cally's bedroom to a murky green twilight.

'You can't stay in here forever,' she pointed out reasonably.

'Why not?'

'Because . . .' Evie flailed around for a sensible answer. 'Come on darling,' she pleaded, edging a little way up the duvet, 'it really upsets me to see you like this.'

'I told you, I'm all right, I just need some space.'

A hand emerged and swatted away Evie's attempt to put a hand on Cally's shoulder.

'Cally . . .'

'Just leave me alone.'

Evie sat on the edge of the bed and gazed around the room, desperate for inspiration. There must be something here that would give her a clue, something from Cally's past – a nostalgic memory of happier times? But then again, maybe not.

Evie's brow furrowed as her eyes confronted the relics of Cally's teenage years. Piles and piles of storybooks – how she'd loved losing herself in fantasies when she was younger, the more weird and wonderful the better. Sherlock Holmes, Star Wars, Narnia. Her eyes travelled along the shelves, packed with youthful dreams, and upwards to the pinboard, where a prefect's badge dangled from a drawing pin, obscuring Luke Skywalker's head. Suddenly everything had changed.

Where had it all started to go wrong? Somewhere in

Cally's early teens, it was hard to pinpoint exactly when or why, but the evidence was plain to see. No more story-books, no more fantasies. Instead there were gleaming ranks of sports trophies, certificates, glowing school reports. Overnight, Cally had gone from dreamy child to obsessive over-achiever. Bloody Thatcher, thought Evie; this is all your fault.

'Listen,' she said, this time with greater firmness. 'I'm going out on one of my farm visits later.'

Silence.

'Why don't you come with me?'

No reply.

'It'd do you the world of good to get a breath of fresh air.' She waited for a response, but none came so she changed tack. 'I know he slept with this other girl, sweetheart, but it's not the end of the world. You could just forgive and forget. I'm sure it's you Rob really loves.'

The figure in the bed slipped ever so slightly further under the duvet, so that little more than a tuft of mid-brown hair was left visible.

'Well, if that's the way you want it,' sighed Evie, giving up the fight. Bending down, she lifted the corner of the duvet, kissed the top of her daughter's head and tiptoed away, closing the door gently behind her.

'It's hopeless,' lamented Marc, coming down the stairs from Cally's room. 'I know it would do her good, but she won't touch a drop.'

'Well I'll have it if she won't.' Cally's elder brother Apollo took the tin mug from Marc's hand. 'I'm gasping for a drink, you should try cycling all the way from Bristol with a telly on the back.'

He raised the mug to his mouth, then stopped, sniffed and pulled a face that made him look more fourteen than thirty-four. 'Ugh, what the hell is this?'

'St John's Wort, pinch of sage, few boiled nettles . . .'

'Any lentils?'

'What do you think I am?' demanded Marc indignantly. 'No lentils, just a sliver of frangula bark to purify the blood.'

'I thought we were trying to cheer the poor girl up, not poison her,' commented Samantha.

Marc bridled at this. 'At least I'm not sticking needles in her.'

'Nor would I,' retorted Samantha, 'if you'd only listen to me and send her to a proper doctor.'

'I am not having my daughter filled full of mind-altering drugs!'

Marc couldn't resist a half-smile. 'Really? I seem to remember you being quite fond of them back in your student days.'

His wife turned on him. 'Oh, shut up!'

Samantha sprang to her brother's defence. 'At least he's trying to help, which is more than some people have done.'

'I brought her my spare portable TV,' protested Apollo. 'I had to bike the damn thing all the way from Bristol, remember.'

Marc sniffed. 'Spare TV indeed! What on earth does anybody need a spare TV for?'

'To lend to their depressed sister to cheer her up.'

'It's a nice thought,' commented Evie, 'but you can only get one channel on it, and between you and me I don't think it's quite up her street.'

'Well, it's the thought that counts. Besides, I'm not sure why I bothered, all she did was grunt.'

Evie sighed. 'At least a grunt is more than I got out of her.'

They stood in doleful silence at the foot of the stairs, all gazes directed towards the sound of Radiohead wailing disconsolately behind Cally's bedroom door.

'Oh my God,' groaned Apollo, 'I wish she'd shut that racket up. She's starting to make me feel depressed. Can't she go out and get herself a man or something?'

'She's got a man,' pointed out Marc. 'It's called a husband, remember?'

'But she's left him,' Samantha reminded Marc. 'And I can't say I'm surprised, either.'

'No,' conceded Marc, 'but she'll go back to him in the end, you mark my words. She thinks the world of that boy.'

'Only thing is, he's not a boy, is he? He's a grown man and he ought to know better. And so should you,' added Samantha, 'with your lentils and your frangula bark. Why you couldn't take that nice job at Porton Down I'll never know.'

Evie intervened. 'Whether or not Cally goes back to Rob, she's got to pick up the pieces and get on with her life. She can't stay locked in her room for weeks on end, can she?'

'So how exactly are we going to get her out of there?' enquired Apollo, who had never quite forgiven his parents their unconventional choice of name and had told all the other people at the PureFood wholefood cooperative that his real name was Kevin. 'With a crowbar?'

Evie ran an impatient hand through her short, neat hair, revealing just a few grey hairs among the glossy brown. 'I thought we might have a little party,' she said. 'Invite one or two new people over for her to meet.

What was the name of that boy she used to like – that trainee solicitor?'

'Oh, I get it,' said Apollo. 'You're trying to pair her off and get a discount on the divorce into the bargain. Don't you think you're jumping the gun a bit?'

'I am not trying to pair her off!' objected Evie, but without much conviction. 'And anyhow,' she added as she stomped back up the stairs, 'somebody round here has to do something.'

Cally lay face-down on her bed, plucking tufts of pink candlewick out of the bedspread.

'He loves me, he loves me not. He still doesn't love me. In fact he hates me. He's shagging her, and her tits are fourteen times the size of mine. The bitch.'

A single tear escaped from her eyelid, ran slowly down the side of her nose and dripped on to her battered old cuddly elephant, which was as old as she was and had been through the wash so many times in its thirty years of life that all its stuffing had sunk to the bottoms of its legs. She knew just how it felt. Being thirty was utter rubbish; and she had a feeling that being thirty-one was going to be even worse.

In the corner of the room, a tiny portable television babbled away to itself in a horribly cheerful monotone. Permanently stuck on Channel 6, it peddled a non-stop diet of gardening programmes, gameshow repeats and adverts for reconstituted marble headstones. Cally would have got up to turn the damned thing off, but she had a horrible feeling that the silence would make her feel even worse.

On the screen, a woman was flashing pristine dentures. 'I used to fear social situations, but now, with new StayFresh rubber pants . . .'

27

There was a knock at the door.

'Bog off.'

A head appeared: oval, with a big nose and plenty of straight brown hair, except on top where it was starting to thin. 'Hi Sis, OK if I come in?'

He didn't wait for her to throw the elephant at him, but simply took her glare for an invitation and helped himself to the chair next to the bed.

'Look, you've got mail.' He waggled a handful of envelopes.

'Big deal.' Surreptitiously, Cally wiped her wet eyes on the elephant's trunk. She might be falling apart, but she sure as hell didn't want her big brother to know that.

'Let's see.' He sorted through the envelopes. 'Oooh look, somebody wants to give you a platinum credit card.'

'Ha ha.'

'And there's a newsletter from that book club you're in. Oh, and I wonder what this is?'

He waved it in Cally's face, but she pushed his hand away. 'I suppose you're going to insist on telling me.'

Apollo pointed to the logo. 'Look, it's from Banco Torino. Your lovely big redundancy package must have come through at last.'

'Oh how sooooper. Pardon me if I don't get out the Union Jack bunting.'

He teased her with the envelope. 'Go on, open it – you know you want to.'

Cally wheeled round, taking him by surprise and nearly toppling him on to the floor. 'Oh I do, do I? Well if you're so bloody fired up about it, why don't you open it? God, you're so sodding smug sometimes I really hate you, do you know that?'

Apollo's smile faltered only slightly. 'Come on Sis, get it open, let's see how rich you are.'

This time something snapped inside Cally. 'How many times do I have to tell you?' she yelled in his face. 'I am not. Bloody. Interested!'

And with that, she threw the unopened letter at the wastepaper bin. And missed.

'Hmmmm,' mused the man in the powder-blue suit. 'Nice neo-Georgian portico.'

'Is it?' Rob regarded the front of his house with a completely different eye. 'I thought it was a front door.'

'Ah, and so it is; but there are front doors and there are front doors, Rob. And a fancy front door could mean an extra hundred or two on the price.' A couple more squiggles made their way into the notebook and he flipped over the page. 'Mind if I take a look at the low-level flush amenity with en-suite vanity unit and deluxe heated towel rail?'

'Pardon?'

'Just point me in the direction of the downstairs bog, Rob. I'm desperate for a slash.'

The last few days had been some of the most traumatic of Rob's entire life. As if it wasn't bad enough having made things even worse with Cally, Leanne had refused to ditch the fitness instructor and cushion his lonely nights with her truly gargantuan boobs. So now he was having to take a really big gamble to win Cally back: actually putting the house on the market.

He didn't want to sell the darned place at all, in fact quite the reverse; but now he'd told Cally he was going to he kind of felt obliged to go through with it. So here he was, calling in favours, getting valuations from every estate agent he knew – and he was rather dismayed to find that he knew so many.

Which was perhaps one of the dodgier side effects of

being a salesman. Birds of a feather and all that. Not that Rob minded being a salesman, in fact he positively revelled in it. Nobody sold oversized indoor plants like Rob Monk, and made the entire process look like an art form. He was pretty confident that he could sell any damn thing if he put his mind to it; in fact, once he'd met Cally and decided he was going to make her fall in love with him, he'd approached the tricky task of selling himself to her as if he'd been trying to flog a shop-soiled Volvo to the Queen Mother.

And it had worked. Trouble was, he'd blown the whole damn thing and it now it wasn't working at all. He'd tried every sales trick he knew, but Cally just wasn't taking the bait any more, and for the first time in his life he was stuck with trying to shift a product he didn't even want to sell.

Which was where the procession of estate agents came in. First there was Wanda, a blowsy forty-year-old Rob had had a brief fling with while in Bracknell to close a deal for forty-seven potted palms. There wasn't much else to do in Bracknell. He'd vaguely hoped that the minute she set eyes on the half-finished loft conversion and the untidy hole in the dining-room wall that had never quite turned into a decorative arch, Wanda would laugh in his face and tell him the house wasn't worth tuppence halfpenny. But to his dismay she'd told him to add forty grand to the figure and then hike it up another ten 'to make it look like you're willing to negotiate'.

And that was only the beginning of it. Zack ('the market's booming, mate'), Becky ('loooovely gazebo, sweetie'), Phil ('you're sitting on a goldmine') and Terry ('if it doesn't shift inside a week I'll halve my commission') sent Rob's morale plunging to unplumbed depths. Even the tweedy old fart from the snooty place in the village said that despite the fact that it was the ugliest semi he had ever seen, he was confident he could sell it for half as much again as Rob and Cally had paid for it. Rob started to panic. His imagination began to run riot. Could you could fake subsidence? Or deathwatch beetle?

He'd never have imagined the prospect of money could make him feel so bad.

It had been a finely balanced operation, but Rob had managed to get all the estate agents in and out of the house without any of them knocking over his precious plants or bumping into each other. This last achievement was fairly crucial, as he had slept with two of them (or was it three?), given a false name to another, and the other three couldn't stand the sight of each other. Rob wondered how he could ever have allowed his life to get this complicated.

And then it got even worse.

It was all his own fault. He'd miscalculated. But how was he to know that Damian would show up two hours late after too many lunchtime beers, or that Ewan would switch his mobile off so that Rob couldn't tell him not to come?

They locked horns in the conservatory, over Cally's beloved ceramic Mickey Mouse, which was now sporting several cracks. Plants aside, Rob had never been very good at looking after things. According to Cally he wasn't very good at anything else either.

'You,' hissed Ewan, his freckled Celtic knuckles whitening around the edges of his clipboard.

'What the bloody hell's he doing here?' demanded Damian, swaying belligerently and knocking his half-drunk coffee into the cheese plant. Oh shit, thought Rob, sliding the pot out of the way. My beautiful plant. God knows what that idiot's done to your root system.

'Doing my job,' replied Ewan with Highland primness. 'Which is more than you can do, the state you're in.'

Damian's Neanderthal brow sunk lower, shading his small, beady eyes like a rocky overhang above a couple of primeval caves.

'Wazzatsupposetamean?' he demanded, in a rush of alcoholic breath.

Ewan's face registered a sneer of disgust. 'You're pissed again.'

'I am not. Just 'cause I like a drink now and then . . .'

'Now and then!'

'I hate to interrupt,' said Rob, steering Damian away from the fragile bonsai maple he had grown from a seed. 'But I thought you were valuing my house.'

Eyes still fixed disapprovingly on Damian, Ewan slid the sleek gold pen out of his top pocket. 'Conservatory,' he murmured, jotting down notes, 'About sixteen-six by twelve.'

'Aren't you going to measure up?'

Ewan smiled condescendingly and patted Rob on the shoulder. 'I'm a professional, Rob. Just leave this to me.'

'Ginger git,' muttered Damian, *sotto voce*.

Ewan wheeled round. 'What did you say?'

'You heard.'

Rob nudged him out into the hallway. 'Thanks for coming Damian, why don't you go home and have a nice sleep?'

But Damian wasn't listening. He was tailing Ewan's every move.

32

'You did the right thing calling me in, Rob,' Ewan said, opening the understairs cupboard and peering inside. 'Don't you worry, Hart & Macgregor will get you top price on this little gem.'

'Don'tcha listen to him, he's a fucking liar, he fucking said they were just good friends, and all the time he was fucking—'

'My God, Damian,' said Ewan, pushing his way past. 'No wonder Mandy left you.'

The beady eyes blazed. 'She never left me! You stole her!'

'Did I fuck steal her.' The thin lips formed the word with faint distaste. 'She just saw sense, that's all.'

'You fuckin' baaaaastard!'

Damian lunged at Ewan, head down. Ewan side-stepped and he ran full-tilt into the hatstand Cally had found in a junkshop. It swayed, hovered for a split second in midair, then – just as Rob leapt to catch it – fell sideways and crashed right through the hall window.

'Shit,' said Damian, rubbing his head sheepishly.

'Moron,' sniffed Ewan. 'Shall I throw him out for you, Rob, or do you want him charged with criminal damage?'

My God, thought Rob, surveying the scene. Very gently and protectively, he picked up a fragment of red glass from the hall carpet. He'd never liked that kitsch Thirties' stained-glass crap, but suddenly it had become his favourite thing in the whole wide world.

'Right,' he seethed between clenched teeth, pointing a trembling finger at the front door. 'That's it. Get out.'

Ewan sniggered, making him look even more like a freckled weasel. 'My pleasure.'

'Both of you. Now.'

'B-but . . . What about the valuation?'

'Forget the valuation.'

Snatching the door open, he propelled Ewan through it and practically drop-kicked Damian on to the doorstep.

Ewan spun round. 'What about our no-commission single agency deal? Don't you want to get the sale underway today?'

'No I bloody well don't!' A kind of caveman instinct had taken hold of Rob and all at once he felt like building an eight-foot stockade around number thirty-one Laburnum Walk. 'This is my house, and nobody else is having it, right?'

He slammed the door with a satisfying crash. Two seconds later, the letter box opened and a single eye peered hopefully through.

'We could have the board put up this afternoon if you—'

'Piss. Off.'

Sitting at the bottom of the stairs in the wet breeze that blew through the shattered window, Rob listened to the distant sounds of two estate agents having a fist-fight on his front drive and felt strangely relieved.

At least they'd forced him to the decision he'd wanted to make all along. Selling up was definitely not the answer to his problems.

Evie and Apollo sat at the kitchen table, the house oddly silent around them.

'I'm worried sick about her,' confessed Evie, her normally sleek hair swept up into a faintly ridiculous point at the front from the constant dragging of her fingers. 'You know, I was so sure she'd buck up when she saw you.'

Apollo helped himself to another carob biscuit. They weren't very nice but he hadn't had any breakfast and the tension was making him ravenous. 'Sorry Mum,' he said. 'But I did try.'

She patted his hand. 'I know you did.' Her anxious grey eyes fixed his. 'The question is, what do we do now? We can't just leave her the way she is.'

'Don't worry, Mum,' said Apollo, licking crumbs from his chin. 'I'm not beaten yet, I've still got an ace up my sleeve.'

Evie looked at him quizzically. Her mouth was just opening to ask him what he was up to when a great scream of anger pierced the silence above their heads.

'Naaaaaaaaagh!'

Evie leapt to her feet.

'What the . . .?'

A moment later, the tinkling of broken glass preceded the sight of Apollo's portable TV, falling to earth past the kitchen window.

'Ah,' said Apollo, looking curiously unsurprised.

'What have you done?' demanded his mother sternly.

He had the good grace to look sheepish. 'I . . . er . . . sabotaged her CD player when she was in the loo.'

Chapter Three

The next time Rob phoned Cally, she decided she'd stopped loathing him. No, she'd long since gone past the loathing stage; as far as Cally was concerned, a complete waste of space like Rob didn't even deserve to exist. In fact none of it existed any more: not Rob, not the house, not any part of her old existence. It had all been soiled, and she wanted nothing more to do with any of it.

At least, that was the way she felt right now. In five minutes' time she'd probably feel completely different.

'Cally, listen,' pleaded Rob. 'You can't just keep putting the phone down on me.'

'Why not?'

'Because we have to talk.'

'I've got nothing more to say to you.'

'Look, I can tell you're upset, but—'

'Upset? Upset! And whose fucking fault is that?' The brief flare of anger died down as suddenly as it had kindled. Now all she felt was empty inside, empty and numb. 'I told you I don't want to talk to you, and I don't. Just go away and leave me alone.'

'But we need to talk about the house,' Rob persisted. 'Our house,' he added.

'Oh, it's ours now, is it? Last time you phoned me, you seemed to think it was yours.'

'Cally, I never . . .'

'I mean, if it was ours, you wouldn't be trying to sell it from under me, would you?'

There was a short, peculiarly tortured silence, broken only by the distant sound of somebody whistling the theme song from *Titanic*.

'As a matter of fact . . .' began Rob.

'Who's that?' demanded Cally.

'Who?'

'Who's that whistling? Oh, I get it. It's her, isn't it?'

'What?'

'You've moved her in already, have you? Still, I suppose you've been screwing her in our bed for months.'

'Cally,' protested Rob, not sure whether to laugh or cry, 'that's the glazier!'

Cally's eyes narrowed with sudden suspicion. 'What glazier?'

'The little window in the hall got broken. Look, I wanted to tell you about—'

'Broken? How?' For a moment, Cally forgot that she didn't care about the house any more. 'What the hell have you been doing? If you've laid one finger on my Mickey Mouse . . .'

Rob took a long, deep breath and tried again. 'About the house. I'm . . . er . . . not selling it after all.'

Cally's eyes narrowed in suspicion. 'Why?'

The lie came effortlessly. 'Well, I had a few estate agents in, but they said the market was very flat at the moment. But the house is still too big for me, and somebody's going to have to pay your half of the mortgage, so I thought – how do you feel about tenants?'

'Tenants!' A procession of students, vagrants and

amateur arsonists rampaged through Cally's imagination.

'Lots of people have them.'

'Lots of people have head-lice. That doesn't mean I'm having them too.'

She was so busy being vile to Rob that she didn't notice the slightly pleased note in his voice. Fantastic, he was thinking. I'm starting to get a reaction. If I play this right, she'll be begging to come home within a fortnight.

'I checked with the building society, it's perfectly legal. In fact . . .'

'Tenants!' repeated Cally. 'But you used to freak out when your own brother came to stay!'

'Yeah, I know, but when needs must, eh?'

'Don't give me that! You're up to something, aren't you? Aren't you!'

'Like what?' reasoned Rob.

'Like filling the house with shaggable women, like trying to get back at me . . . I don't know. But something.'

'Cally, I swear . . .'

She took the receiver from her ear and spoke into it slowly and disdainfully, as if it were something disgusting and unclean. 'Rob, listen to me. You are not, I repeat not, having tenants in my house. And that's final.'

Just as she rang off, the doorbell sounded. Shit, one of her mother's loony friends. All she bloody needed.

A disembodied voice drifted in from the kitchen. 'Get that could you, Cally? I'm up to my elbows in your father's Swiss chard.'

With very bad grace, Cally stomped to the door and opened it. On the doorstep, looking slightly louche with his shoulder-length ringlets and winkle-pickers, stood a young man with a strangely familiar face. He beamed with angelic idiocy, displaying a crooked front tooth.

'Hi Cally, remember me?'

Something clicked in Cally's memory. Something deeply embarrassing, like the pair of saggy grey knickers lurking at the back of her underwear drawer.

'My God,' she gasped, taking a step back. 'It's you! No, it can't be.'

Not Eddie Priest.

'It's me all right,' grinned Eddie. 'Can I come in?'

Quick as lightning, she slammed the door in his face.

'Mum,' said Cally, making the word sound like a threat.

'Hmm?' Evie went on slicing vegetables into a bowl. 'Did you manage to sort things out with Rob?'

Cally took a step closer and slid between her mother and the pile of organic greenery. 'Mum!'

She looked up. 'Yes, darling?'

'What on earth is Eddie Priest doing here?'

Evie's face brightened and she picked up a tea towel to dry her hands. 'Oh, Eddie's here already is he? How lovely. Go and ask him what he'll have to drink, will you?'

'You mean to say you . . .?' She put a hand to her mouth. 'Oh dear.'

Catching the look on Cally's face, Evie put down the tea towel and folded her arms.

'Cally Storm, what have you done to poor Eddie?'

Feeling like a cat thrown out for the night, Cally was forcibly ejected through her mother's front door.

Her worst fears were instantly realised. Eddie was there, talking to Apollo on the garden path. He looked more foppish than ever, she noted, though thank God he'd ditched most of the cringeworthy retro gear he'd been so fond of wearing at school. 'Byronic' was how he'd described himself then, though Cally severely doubted that Lord Byron had ever sported purple velvet loons.

'Greetings, fair Calliope,' he grinned, executing a low bow.

Apollo winked. Cally gave him the kind of look that would have turned a more sensitive soul to stone. Eddie went on grinning like a maniac, every bit as embarrassing as he'd been when they were friends at school. Back in those days, when friends had been like fashion accessories, Eddie Priest had been the Elton John hairweave on the head of a Gucci supermodel.

Oh God, thought Cally, turning up her jacket collar and wishing it would start to rain so she could retreat inside her hood. I suppose we'd better get this over with.

The phone was ringing in Evie's hallway as Apollo closed the front door behind him.

'Hello?'

'Apollo? It's me.'

'Hello Rob. You OK? You sound a bit . . . tense.'

'Tense? Tell me about it. This business with Cally and the house, I know it's all my stupid fault, but she just won't listen. If we can just sort things out, once and for all.'

'Sounds like a good plan,' agreed Apollo. 'Best of luck.'

'The thing is, you couldn't get Cally to come to the phone could you?' Rob went on. 'Only don't tell her it's me,' he added hastily.

41

'Love to, mate,' replied Apollo apologetically. 'But I can't, she's just gone out.'

A softly muttered 'shit' drifted down from the other end of the line. 'Out? Who with?'

'I dunno. Some bloke.'

The pause was so pregnant it could have given birth to quads.

'Do you want me to pass on a message?' Apollo enquired after a decent interval. 'I could get her to ring you when she gets back if you like.'

'No, don't bother. It's not important.'

A faint click announced that Rob had hung up. Apollo replaced the receiver, hung his coat on the hook by the door and sauntered into the kitchen, hands in pockets.

'Hi Mum.' He gave her a peck on the cheek. 'Anything to eat? I'm starving.'

She glanced up from her quarterly VAT return. 'Who was that on the phone?'

'Oh, nobody,' shrugged Apollo, helping himself to the end off a home-baked rye loaf. 'Just some salesman.'

The Rialto liked to describe itself as 'Cheltenham's other cinema'. Which was a fancy way of saying that there was only one screen, sometimes the projector broke down and the manager came round with the ice creams in the interval. In its previous incarnation it had been the Jasper Kendall Repertory Theatre, and before that a rather prestigious little Victorian music hall, and though its elderly bucket seats were uncomfortable and smelled funny, the place still retained a certain olde-worlde charm.

'There you go,' announced Eddie, wedging an

immense bucket of popcorn on the empty seat between him and Cally.

'Popcorn makes me fart.'

Eddie shrugged. 'Be my guest. Express yourself, that's what I always say.'

In spite of herself, Cally found herself almost smiling. Eddie had the kind of face you wanted to kick to a pulp and then kiss better.

'What are you doing here, Eddie?'

'Cheering you up.'

'Don't flatter yourself.' Cally accepted a grudging fistful of popcorn. 'I mean, what am I doing here?' She stole a furtive glance around her. 'I'm probably going to go home with fleas or something.'

'Well, everybody needs a pet.' Eddie munched. ''Course, John Donne reckoned fleas were quite erotic. He wrote that poem. You know, he's in bed with this woman, and this flea bites her on the—'

'Eddie,' said Cally, 'don't be disgusting, or I'm going home.'

He leaned over and a long black ringlet dangled in her Kia-Ora. 'What – and miss the director's cut of *The Italian Job*? With digitally enhanced stereo sound?'

Cally pouted like a sulky six-year-old. Eddie knew her far too well to believe she'd pass up a free ticket to one of her all-time favourite classic films. 'That's not fair. This is a plot, isn't it? You've cooked this up with my mother.'

'Is it bollocks, it's a trip to the pictures. Eat your popcorn.' He chuckled. 'Remember when we used to bunk off double geography to go to the Odeon?'

Cally remembered. 'Oh God, that was centuries ago. How old were we then?'

43

'Fourteen.' Eddie sprayed bits of popcorn out of the sides of his mouth. 'All acne and raging hormones.'

She brushed popcorn off her chest. 'Speak for yourself.' She sighed. 'Fourteen. And now it's next stop the big four-O, and downhill all the way to Complan and Zimmer frames.'

'Being thirty's not so bad,' said Eddie, who had passed that milestone several months before Cally. 'Well, not if you don't mind hair growing out of your ears.'

'Lovely. I'll really look forward to that.' Cally chewed morosely. 'Thirty – and what have I achieved in my life so far?'

'Loads, according to your mum.'

'Sod all, more like. You know, it's no wonder we both failed that geography exam,' she mused. 'I knew more about Robert Mitchum's eyebrows than I did about viti-culture in the San Fernando Valley.'

'Hey – what about the time your big brother got us in to see that private showing of *The Exorcist*?'

Cally snorted. 'Yeah. And you threw up all over the front row. I don't know, you give a bloke the chance to see the greatest horror flick of all time and he chucks up on your shoes. There's ingratitude for you.'

'You told me we were going to see *101 Dalmatians*!' protested Eddie.

'Ah, but if I'd told you the truth you wouldn't have come, would you?' reasoned Cally. 'And be fair – I sat through *Brief Encounter* with you three times.'

Eddie sighed nostalgically as the lights dimmed around them. 'Ah, *Brief Encounter*. Now that's what I call a good weepie. I've played the video that many times I've nearly worn it out.'

It was obvious to Cally that Eddie hadn't changed for

the better. Once a hopeless romantic, always a hopeless romantic – with the emphasis on hopeless. 'Give me a good action film any day. Or a nice violent Tarantino.'

Eddie screwed his face up in disgust. 'Cutting people's ears off, how can you watch that stuff! Ugh!'

'Eddie Priest, you are such a girlie!'

'I am not so!'

'Excuse me you two,' said a man's voice from the row behind. 'But some of us actually want to watch the film.'

Red-faced with trying not to giggle, Cally and Eddie settled down in their seats. This takes me back, thought Cally as the titles rolled and the familiar music began. Age fourteen, skirt waistband rolled over to lift it a couple of extra inches, gazing up at a big bright screen and letting it become her entire world, if only for a couple of hours.

Her mind drifted without her wanting it to. *Star Wars*. Now there was a film, they had real plots and real stories in those days, not like now, with all the fake monsters, fake scenery, fake acting. *Star Wars* . . . She was what – eight years old? Nine? God, but she'd loved that film. So much, she'd saved up all her pocket money to buy . . .

Something lurched inside her.

'Cally? Shut up Cally, you're—' Eddie's face loomed closer. 'My God, you're crying.'

'No I'm not,' she sniffed.

'Yes you are.'

'Look, I'm all right, just leave me be.'

A head appeared over the back of the empty seat. 'Will you please be quiet and watch the film!'

'It's all right,' said Cally, scrambling to her feet and grabbing her coat. 'I was going anyway.'

And the next thing she knew, she was stumbling up the darkened aisle towards the Exit sign, with Eddie cursing and tripping in her wake.

The bench at the bus stop was not really made for sitting on. If you leaned forward too suddenly the whole thing risked tipping over; and it had the added disadvantage of a queue of well-heeled pensioners, all casting suspicious glares at the long-haired weirdo and his red-eyed girlfriend. Not that Cally gave a damn what they might think. She was far too busy being utterly miserable to care about anything else.

'Go on,' said Eddie, pulling a skein of paper tissues from his sleeve like a stage magician producing a bunch of flowers. 'Have a good blow and tell me what all this is about.'

Cally buried her face in the tissues, mopped at her eyes and emptied her nose. She knew she must look a sight, but what the hell did that matter? Her life was a complete wreck, she might as well look like one too.

'I want my Princess Leia,' she sniffed.

Eddie looked baffled. 'Your what?'

'Leia. Princess Leia. Don't you remember? I saved up all my money to buy her, she was beautiful and she had this lovely long white dress and a big blaster gun that fired real caps.'

Eddie scratched his head. The pensioners shook theirs.

'You mean this is all about some doll you had?'

Cally drew herself up indignantly. 'Not just some doll, Princess Leia. I only ever saw the one, and the man in the shop kept it for me till I'd saved up enough to buy it. Then she . . she . . . '

'Who? Princess Leia?'

'No! That little bitch Stephanie Wilson. She sat behind me in maths.'

'What – the boss-eyed one with the razor cut?'

'She stole her. Cut her head off and threw the rest on the bonfire. It was all her fault. If she hadn't done that, I'd not be in this mess now.'

'Hang on, Cally.' Eddie squeezed on to the end of the bench, next to her, unwittingly sending five pounds of King Edwards rolling down the street. 'You've lost me. How do you get from Stephanie Wilson cutting Princess Leia's head off to you blubbing your eyes out in a bus shelter?'

More tears welled up in Cally's eyes but she didn't bother wiping them away. They were coming more easily now, flowing freely, and in a funny way they felt like a kind of release.

'Her doing that . . . She'd been trying to get me for months, hated me, I don't know why. And after that, of course, I hated her too – would've loved to kick her spotty arse round the playground. But you know what my folks are like – "Violence doesn't solve anything, Cally," "Turn the other cheek Cally," "Feel sorry for her Cally, think what she's doing to her karma." Karma my arse. I should've twatted her big time and got it out of my system.'

'So what did you do instead?'

'Decided to rub her nose in it by being better than she was at everything. She gets into the school athletics squad, I make it to the county trials. She goes out with the head boy, I nick him off her. She comes second in Maths, I have to come first. And when she says she's applied for a management trainee's job with LBS Agri-Finance.'

Eddie's eyes widened. 'You're never saying you only

47

went to the LBS because Stephanie Wilson wanted to?' Cally's face gave him the answer. 'Oh Cally, are you a prize banana or what?'

'I'm a prize banana. I guess.' Eddie gave her a matey hug, and Cally managed a watery smile. 'Bet you haven't made the same mistakes as I have.'

Eddie laughed hollowly. 'Wanna bet?'

'Let me guess, you're an eccentric billionaire and you've got seventeen children and a Saturday job in the Co-op.'

'Not quite. I went to art college, spent all my time messing around doing performance poetry, and got chucked out. Then I got sacked from the tax office for wearing non-regulation trousers. These days I paint things for a living.'

'What sort of things? Houses? Lines on the road?'

'Pub signs mainly. Have you seen the giant fibreglass carrot outside the Gardener's Arms? That's one of mine.' He swung his heels against the metal frame of the bus shelter. 'Not quite the Royal Academy, but it keeps me in rent money. Well, most of the time.'

'You don't own your own house then?'

'Who? Me? You're kidding – I mean, would you give me a mortgage?' Cally hesitated, then opened her mouth. 'Don't answer that. No, I share this teeny-weeny flat above Cooper's the bakers in Bath Road. Hardly room to swing a sock, and Tom – that's the guy I share with – well, let's just say you can get really tired of scraping somebody else's pubic hair off the toilet seat.'

Cally grimaced. En masse, like some blue-rinsed formation team, the pensioners took half a step backwards.

'Happy days,' said Cally with more than a hint of irony. 'Suppose Mum told you all about the bloody awful mess I've made of my life?'

'Actually it was Apollo.'

'I'll kill him.'

'If he doesn't kill you first. You totalled his TV, remember?'

They sat in companionable silence for a little while. Two buses arrived and departed, axles groaning under the weight of overstuffed shopping bags. Suddenly, Eddie snapped his fingers and sat bolt upright.

'I know!'

'You know what?'

'If you could have Princess Leia back, would it make you very, very happy?'

Cally blinked. 'I don't know. Why? What are you on about?'

Eddie seized her hand and dragged her to her feet. 'Never mind that, come with me, I've got an idea.'

Chapter Four

'Here we are,' announced Eddie, triumphantly slamming the door of his 1971 Hillman Imp with such gusto that flakes of rust showered off it like orange dandruff. 'Charlton Kings.'

'Yes, but why?' Cally peered out through the mud-speckled windscreen at a terrace of obsessively tidy cottages, a poster advertising the Parish Cream Tea (prize for best hat), and the back end of a well-populated graveyard. 'I mean, what's it got to do with Princess Leia?'

'You'll see, come on. No, second thoughts, don't move, the handle comes off if you try to open it from the inside.' Eddie vaulted over the bonnet, inserted a piece of bent wire into the lock of the passenger door and twiddled. 'There you go. Hurry up, or they'll be closed.'

Without waiting for any more questions, he seized Cally's hand and dragged her across the road, very nearly towing her under the wheels of a giant tractor.

'Eddie!' squealed Cally, scrambling on to the tiny pavement.

'Oi! Mind where you're goin'!' yelled the tractor driver, rumbling past.

Eddie executed an elegant V-sign in the rear-view mirror. 'Peasants. Think they own the road.' He rubbed his hands gleefully. 'It's round this corner, if we get a move on we should just be in time.'

They headed round the corner, past the parish hall and the ostentatiously displayed village stocks, a pillar box, a hole dug by the local water company and a huddle of disaffected youths, sharing a clandestine can of cider while they waited for night to fall so they could vandalise the vicar's sprouts. It was all go in Charlton Kings.

'Oh good! It's still open.'

'What is?'

'It is. The shop.' Cally's shoes skidded on the tarmac as Eddie dragged her across the road towards a shopfront so narrow, and set back so far from the pavement, that it was almost invisible between the houses on either side. 'See?'

Cally saw. The curly golden script painted across the window read: GOLD IN THE ATTIC: books and curioes.

'I did that,' said Eddie proudly. 'Tasteful, isn't it?'

'Very nice,' agreed Cally. 'But there's no "e" in "curios".'

Eddie's face fell. 'Isn't there? Bugger.'

Cally pressed her nose up against the glass, a bow-fronted mosaic of tiny square panes, like an old-fashioned sweet shop. In fact, that was exactly what it was – a kind of sweet shop for grown-ups with an addiction not to sherbet lemons but to nostalgia. She scanned the window display, taking in a dozen copies of Look-In; a Simon Le Bon jigsaw puzzle; the most garish Hawaiian shirt in the world; two teddy bears, a tin truck with the paint flaking off, and more old books than you could shake several sticks at.

'Ugh,' she said. 'What a load of old rubbish.'

Eddie flattened his nose against the glass. ''Spose. I

just thought there might . . . you know . . . be a Princess Leia or something.'

'Fat chance! My Princess Leia was well classy.'

'They've got some good gear in there, you know. Six rooms of books and all sorts, if you count the retro clothing upstairs.'

'And people actually buy this stuff?' She was about to make some comment about sad gits in purple loons when she turned her head and saw it. 'Oh look, Eddie. Look at that.'

'What?'

She pointed. 'That.'

Eddie craned his neck. 'What – the enema syringe?'

'Not that! The *Back To The Future* snowstorm.' She sighed. 'Remember that Noddy one I had when I was a kid? Apollo flushed it down the toilet.'

'Didn't have much luck with your toys, did you?' observed Eddie.

'I saw that film six times,' mused Cally. 'I was going to marry Michael J. Fox, you know – until I found out he was about three foot six and I'd have to stand in a hole to snog him.'

She ogled the snowstorm from ten different angles. It was tacky, it was silly, it was a lump of plastic filled with dirty water and a little model DeLorean that raced a train along a plastic track. It was nothing, but for some reason she couldn't quite explain, suddenly she really wanted it.

Just as she was wondering how much it was, an arm reached out from inside the shop and fingers closed on the snowstorm. Bloody typical, thought Cally. The minute I want something, somebody else snatches it away from me.

She looked up and suddenly she was looking into the second familiar face of the day: a small, impish face with a freckled nose, Mel G glasses and a haircut that looked like a cross between a high-fashion blunt-cut bob and a pixie hat.

The snowstorm tumbled back into the display window, bounced off Andy Pandy's head and landed upside-down in a pile of shop-soiled Tribbles.

'My God!' exclaimed Cally as the years rolled back. 'I don't believe it – it's Liddy!'

'No,' said Eddie, digging his heels into the pavement. 'I am not going in there, and that's all there is to it.'

Cally stared at him, puzzled. 'But Eddie, you brought me here, remember?'

He squirmed uncomfortably. 'So?'

'So let's go in and see Liddy!' She tugged at his sleeve. 'Come on, she's not going to eat you.'

'Cally . . .' he protested, but already she had him in an armlock and an irresistible force was propelling him through the doorway into the gloomy interior of the shop.

In point of fact, he had only just made it over the threshold when the air was filled with a sound like a sabre-toothed tiger chewing a road drill.

A ghastly, humourless grin froze on Eddie's face as he backed away and flattened himself against a bookcase. 'Ah. Stefan.' The horrible low growling stepped up several dozen decibels. 'Good boy, nice boy.'

Cally tried peering over his shoulder. 'What's going on—'

At that moment she was dimly aware of something launching itself into the air from a standing start. Something small and hairy and grizzled. Something that had more teeth than the jaws of Hell and smelled twice as bad.

The infernal grey thing was about six inches from Eddie's throat when Liddy sprang from nowhere, deftly snatched it by the collar and stuffed it headfirst into a nearby wastepaper basket.

'Eddie, is that you? Better leg it, he's not had his dinner yet.'

Eddie did not need telling twice. He was out through the door in half a second flat, leaving the bell jangling in his wake.

Liddy and Cally looked each other up and down. The imp winked and extracted the grey thing from the wastepaper basket. Cally was almost disappointed to see that it was a small, obese dog, albeit one with a squint and big yellow fangs that jutted up over its top lip.

'Cally!' beamed Liddy. 'Meet Stefan.'

'Don't remind me – white, two sugars, am I right?' Liddy stirred the coffee and handed a mug to Cally.

'Right,' she smiled, far too polite to admit that she hadn't taken sugar in her coffee for years. She turned the mug round in her hands, following the procession of Guinness toucans along the rim. 'How many years is it? I can't remember.'

'Oooh, must be . . .' Liddy absent-mindedly removed a bulldog clip from the seat of her trousers and made a second attempt at sitting down on a ten-volume *History of Taxidermy*. 'Five years?'

'Getting on for six. Weren't you at that Christmas party in Gloucester?'

'The one just before I left LBS, where Tim and Laurence came as a pantomime cow and fell in the pond?' Liddy giggled, bringing out the dimples in her cheeks and making her look more than ever like a six-year-old elf. 'Happy days. That wasn't long after you and Rob got married, was it?'

'Yeah,' said Cally, burying her face in her coffee. What the hell if the caffeine kept her up all night? It'd make a change from trying to sleep away her troubles. 'Happy bleeding days.'

Liddy leaned forward. Stefan dropped the Action Man he was busy chewing the legs off, and followed suit, long pink tongue hanging eagerly out of the side of his mouth as though all he was waiting for was the command to rip Cally's throat out.

'Life getting you down?'

'You could say.'

'Man trouble?'

'What man? Rob and I have split up.'

Liddy looked thunderstruck. 'No! I can't believe it. It only seems like five minutes since I was your bridesmaid. Oh Cally, I'm really sorry.'

'Don't be. He's a scumbag. Oh, and I've lost my job and I'm living in my mum's spare room. So yeah, I guess you could say life's not exactly a bowl of cherries right now.'

Stefan got to his feet, waddled across and sniffed Cally's trainers, then promptly lost interest and went back to chewing.

'He likes you,' commented Liddy.

Cally looked at the dog sceptically. 'How can you tell?'

'He didn't wee on your shoes. He does that to practically everybody – the ones he doesn't bite anyway. He's, er, a bit of a character.'

'I noticed. He doesn't like Eddie much, does he?'

'Ah well, that's because he mistook Stefan's favourite chewy blanket for a rag when he was painting the shop sign, and wiped his brushes on it. From that moment on it was all-out war. How did you meet Eddie anyhow? I wouldn't have thought he was your type.'

Cally laughed, for the first time in several weeks. 'Me and Eddie Priest – oh puhleeze! We were at school together, actually. I haven't seen him for years, and suddenly he turns up on my mum's doorstep. Between you and me, I think my brother's trying to set me up with him.'

'Hmm. Interesting taste, your brother.'

Cally's gaze homed in on Stefan. 'Almost as interesting as your taste in dogs.'

'Oh, Stefan's not mine, well not officially. He's my gran's. Matter of fact, so's this shop. All three mouldering floors of it. The thing is, she went into a home and there was nobody else to help out. So I gave up my job and came here. It was only supposed to be for a couple of months, but that was three years ago. Stefan sort of came as part of the deal.'

'Well, he's very . . .' Cally searched around for an appropriate euphemism.

'Vicious is the word you're looking for,' said Liddy serenely. 'Stefan's a complete and utter psychopath. We had quite a battle of wills to start off with, didn't we little fella?' The small, demonic presence cocked a much-mangled ear. 'The trick is, Know Your Enemy.'

Cally grunted. 'Perhaps you could give me some tips on dealing with Rob. I used to think I knew him, but obviously I was deluding myself.'

'Are things really that bad between you?'

'There's nothing between us, not any more. And in case you were wondering, Rob's a two-timing git.'

Her face crumpled at the exact moment Liddy put her arms round her and gave her a big, girly hug; a hug that brought back the old days when they'd been best mates, and blokes had been ditched as easily as a pair of laddered tights.

'Oh Liddy,' she snivelled into her friend's vast, knobbly cardigan, 'why did I ever want to grow up? Why can't things be simple, like they were when we were kids?'

Evie's voice followed Cally along the hall and up the stairs, as she threw off her jacket, kicked off her shoes and headed for her room.

'Cally? Cally, is that you?'

'Yes Mum, it's me.'

'Did you bring Eddie back for tea?'

'No Mum, he's gone home.'

Disappointed pause. 'Oh. Where did you go then?'

'Oh, nowhere special. Just the pictures, you know.' Cally paused on the landing and called down what she knew her mother wanted to hear. 'Don't worry, I had a nice time.'

'So you're . . .?'

'Fine? Yes Mum, I'm absolutely fine. I'm just going upstairs for a bit, all right?'

She breathed the purer air of freedom as she closed her bedroom door behind her. It wasn't that she didn't love her mum, far from it. It wasn't that she didn't enjoy her company – in small amounts. But today had been such a strange day, and she needed to get her head together; and that was something she couldn't do with anybody else around. Not Eddie, not Liddy, not even Mum.

She lay down on the bed, swinging her shoulder bag on to the duvet next to her. There was an extra weight in it that she'd noticed while she was walking back from

Eddie's car. Opening the flap, she felt inside; and her hand closed on something small and smooth and hard, something that fitted into the palm of her hand so snugly that it might have been tailor-made for her.

The *Back To The Future* snowstorm.

A little shiver ran through her, half of pleasure, half of sadness. Liddy must have known she'd wanted it and slipped it into her bag when she wasn't looking. On the one hand, it was lovely to have it; on the other, she didn't enjoy feeling like the kind of charity case who had to be cheered up with hugs and little presents.

She balanced the snowstorm on her chest and stared at it for a while. The little car and the little train sat completely still within the plastic dome, the white flakes settling into a thick white carpet around their wheels and the sky behind them a cloudless, untroubled blue. That's what my life used to be like, thought Cally. I just couldn't see the storm coming.

On a sudden whim, she upended it; and as she did, her finger found a little red button on the base.

'C'mon Doc,' piped up Michael J. Fox's perennially youthful voice. 'We've gotta get back to the future!'

The future. A wave of black cynicism dumped itself on Cally from a great height. What future? But in spite of herself she managed a wry smile. Yeah, back to the future.

Hoo-flaming-ray.

Chapter Five

Five weeks in my mother's spare room, thought Cally morosely. Sounds like the title of a prize-winning Norwegian novel. An exceptionally tedious one at that.

She lay on the lumpy single bed with the hideous quilted headboard, contemplating the Greenpeace calendar on the wall. She had counted the number of meerkats on that poster at least three hundred times, and was becoming very irritated by their constantly bright-eyed, born-again attitude to life. As if that wasn't bad enough, she'd had a peek at next month's picture, and spending the whole of April with a maniacally grinning chimpanzee was not a happy prospect.

Happy. Huh. What was that? She wriggled her toes in the pair of her dad's old socks she'd taken to wearing because they were comfy and it wasn't as if anybody else was going to see her, so why make an effort? Oh hell. Being only half-depressed was even worse than being completely depressed, because it left you loads of spare energy to think about how completely and utterly pants your life had become. Being half-depressed wasn't nearly as exciting as being suicidal, and nowhere near as dramatic; no tears, no despera-tion, no nothing. In fact it was the most horribly, crip-plingly boring state of mind that Cally had ever known; and she just couldn't shake it off, no matter how hard she tried.

She listened. Nothing. Nothing but absolute quiet.

Suddenly, an immense guitar riff shook the house. With a groan of rage, Cally grabbed her pillow and wrapped it round her ears, vainly trying to blot out the sound of 'Twentieth-Century Boy', played at maximum decibels on an ancient Dansette.

There was no escape. If she went downstairs, she'd only get that lecture from her mum about how she'd once almost spent a night of passion in a Transit van with Marc Bolan; and how amazing he was; and how he wouldn't have sat around moaning, oh no, because darling Marc always lived his life to the max. Huh, thought Cally, getting up and walking across to the window. And look where that got him. Stone dead, halfway up a tree.

Thoughtfully, she slid the sash window right up and poked her head and shoulders out. Fresh air, thank God. She swung her legs out and sat on the sill, swinging her heels against the rendering and not caring if she left black marks. It was quite a long way down really. But the air was so lovely and still and calm . . .

When Iggy Pop started bawling 'Lust for Life' in the room downstairs, Cally knew it was time to jump.

It was quite easy really, jumping out of a bedroom window. Well OK, it was easy if there was a bay window jutting out, halfway down, and you'd been captain of the school athletics team.

Cally landed lightly and stood up, stretching the stiffness out of her body. If only she could do the same for her head, get rid of this awful woolly feeling, find something to focus on. Being bored was so . . . well . . . *boring*.

She wandered aimlessly through her mother's front gate, and headed across the road, ignoring the screeching tyres and curses as a motorcyclist braked and swerved to avoid her. It was a cool day, and as she padded across the grass verge the dew was soaking through her socks, but she didn't notice. Somewhere in the back of her mind she was aware of her mother's voice, calling after her, but she didn't turn round.

The park across the road from Evie's house was little more than a triangle of grass with a couple of swings, a bench and a birdbath, but as she stepped through the gates, Cally began to feel the tension easing from her shoulders. There was no one here, just a blackbird pecking around after worms. Maybe she'd just sit herself down on this nice park bench for a while and think about nothing.

A sudden breeze rippled the surface of the water on the big stone birdbath, catching the watery sunlight. On a whim, Cally walked across and looked down at her reflection. Oh God, she thought as the water settled; I'm a complete mess. Unwashed brown hair, tipped with raggedy blonde ends she should have had cut out weeks ago; a sweater so old and horrible no self-respecting vagrant would have been seen dead in it; no makeup. The sight jolted her. Had she really changed so much in five short weeks?

'Noooooo!'

It was too much to bear. Flopping forward, she plunged her face into the murky water, only to draw it back two seconds later, spitting out a mouthful of pigeon-feathers.

'Excuse me,' said a slightly sarcastic voice behind her. 'But if you're trying to drown yourself, can I suggest the lake?'

She spun round, the word 'bastard' ready on her lips. But it never made it to the exit, because the moment the young man set eyes on her, he twitched like an electrocuted frog, turned ghastly white . . .

And passed out at her feet.

Evie was on the phone to an irate farmer when she heard the thunderous knocking at the back door. She put a hand over the mouthpiece.

'Just a minute.'

Thump, thump, thump.

'I said just a . . .'

Rat-a-tat-a-TAT.

'Yes, Mr Thorogood, I can tell you're unhappy about my report, but could you hold on a moment while I answer the door? Second thoughts, I'll call you straight back.'

Whatever Evie had been expecting when she opened the door, it definitely wasn't the sight of her bedraggled daughter dragging an unconscious man across her front garden by the ankles.

'Don't just stand there, Mum, give me a hand!'

Evie's calm grey eyes widened ever so slightly. 'Cally darling. I know I said you ought to get out and find yourself a man, but really . . .'

Cally responded with an evil stare. 'Oh ha ha Mum, I'm really splitting my sides. Look, can we get him inside? I'm wet through.' Evie's mouth opened. 'And before you ask, don't.'

They took one arm each and managed to prop him up with his back against the hall radiator. Evie peered into the still-pale, faintly disreputable, but undeniably good-looking face.

'Whatever did you do to him? He's out cold.'

'I didn't do anything! He just took one look at me and passed out.'

'Well, at least you made an impact then.'

'Oh shut up, Mum.'

The unconscious body gave a faint groan and twitched its rather cute nose.

'Oh look Cally, he's coming round. Quick, go and get him a glass of water.'

Cally remained rooted to the spot, gazing unblinkingly at the young man sprawled on her mother's Guatemalan hall runner; hoping Evie couldn't read her disappointment. She'd been rather hoping he'd stay unconscious and require immediate mouth-to-mouth resuscitation.

'Cally?' Evie snapped her fingers. 'Cally! Drink!'

A tad reluctantly, Cally disappeared into the downstairs cloakroom. The young man moaned, opened one eye and then chanced the other. They were a deep, twinkly, cloudless blue.

'W-where . . .?' He struggled to get both eyes pointing in the same direction. 'I mean what . . .?'

'I think you must have fainted,' explained Evie. 'My daughter was with you, she can explain. Ah, here she is now.'

Cally held out the glass of water. Evie couldn't help noticing she'd run a comb through her wet hair, and taken off that revolting old sweater. The pink T-shirt she was wearing underneath was almost presentable.

'Here you are, how are you feeling? I brought you some water.'

'No!' gasped the young man, trying so hard to get up that he banged his head on the radiator. He was staring at Cally as if she had just beamed down from a spaceship. 'No, I . . . I can't believe it.'

Cally sniffed the contents of the glass. 'No, honest. It's definitely water.'

'I'm fine, I'm great,' he assured them as they helped him to his feet, Cally supporting one arm and Evie the other.

'You ought to rest, you know,' said Evie. 'You could have a nice lie-down on my futon if you like.'

'Er, thanks, but honestly . . .'

Cally threw Evie a look that said, 'Mum, you are a shameless tart,' and interjected, 'I expect he'd rather I drove him to casualty. Or I could ring our doctor?'

'No need, honest.'

'But if you suffer from these sudden fainting fits,' protested Evie, 'you really ought to get them checked out – shouldn't he, Cally?'

He was starting to look like a hunted man. 'No look, really.' He eased himself tactfully but firmly free. 'You can let go now, I won't fall over, I promise. It was just . . . my . . . er . . .' Cally could almost see the cogs whirring in his brain. 'Height.'

'Your *height*?'

He tried to look taller than his scant six feet. 'You know – tallish bloke, blood runs to the feet when you've been standing around for a while. Next thing you know – splat.'

'Oh,' said Evie doubtfully. 'That's odd. Have you ever tried homeopathic arnica?'

'So why *were* you standing around?' enquired Cally, more and more intrigued by this interestingly crumpled stranger. 'It's not as if anything ever happens here.'

She tried to make eye contact, but every time she managed to hook up with those blue eyes he glanced swiftly away, as though there was something about her that fascinated him but which he couldn't bear to look at.

'I'm here to make a delivery.' He picked up his discarded canvas satchel from the floor. 'Don't suppose you could point me in the direction of number forty-seven?'

It was Evie's turn to look surprised. 'Forty-seven, that's this house. Oh, don't tell me, you've come with those samples of cruelty-free Stilton.'

The stranger looked baffled. 'Stilton? Sorry madam, no Stilton in here, only a nineteen seventy-eight limited edition Princess Leia with Space Blaster. For delivery to a Miss Calliope Storm.'

Cally clapped a hand to her mouth. 'A Princess . . . You've got a Princess Leia? For me? But how?'

He stuck out a hand and she took it. 'Inglis, Will Inglis. I'm a collectables dealer – Star Wars, Buffy, Simpsons, you name it I can get it. Your mate Liddy gave me a bell the other day, said you were looking for a Leia.' He opened the bag and gingerly took out the contents. 'Now, I have to say, it's only in extra fine condition, and there's no box or anything, but they're like hen's teeth these . . .'

The words dried in his throat as Cally snatched the doll from his hands, hugged it, smothered it in kisses and instantly knocked twenty per cent off its resale value. 'This is incredible! How much? How much do I owe you?'

'Nothing, Liddy settled up with me. Said you could owe her. Right.' Will slung his bag over his shoulder. 'I'll be off then. Thanks for the . . . er . . . water.'

A brief, almost lightning flash of a smile crossed his face as his gaze met Cally's; then a few seconds later he was halfway down Evie's front path.

'Hang on,' said Cally, getting to the front gate before him. 'Have you got a business card or something? Just in case I . . . you know . . . want to start collecting something?'

'Liddy knows where to find me. Be seeing you.'

The gate clanged shut, and he went whistling nervously off down the road, walking about as fast as a man could walk without being entered for the Olympics.

'Shame on you,' commented Evie, coming up to the gate.

'I don't know what you mean.'

'Come on – I saw you. Making eyes at that intriguing Mr Inglis. Not starting to take an interest in life again, are we?'

Cally stuck out her tongue and stalked back into the house.

Rob had spent a lot of the last five weeks sitting cross-legged on the living-room floor that had been earmarked for parquet but had somehow ended up as bare, paint-blotched boards dotted with rugs. In a funny way he was rather glad about that: a load of bare wooden planks with the wind whistling up through the gaps provided the perfect backdrop for his less than sunny mood.

His constant companion through these dark days had not, alas, been Leanne and her friendly bosoms, but a dog-eared copy of his personal guide, mentor and holy writ: Arvin J. Mahmoolian's *How to Sell Anything to Anyone, Anywhere, Anytime* (46th edition). Over the years, women had come and gone, along with shoulder-pads and ten per cent of his hair, but Mahmoolian had never let him down. And this time wasn't going to be an exception.

'. . . so I made this checklist, see?' Rob waved it enticingly under Greg Prince's nose but Greg was already off across the half-built theme park like a contestant in *It's a Knockout*.

To tell the truth, B-Movie Heaven bore more than a passing resemblance to some half-assed gameshow concocted by the bosses of a third-rate cable TV station. People in giant foam-rubber costumes waddled among the chaos of half-finished rides, mocked-up film sets and a Land-Rover imperfectly disguised as a giant tarantula with wildly waving legs.

'In here, Rob.' Greg punched open the door of a Portakabin and it bounced back on to Rob's recently recovered nose. 'I want to show you the schematics for Jungle World.'

Eyes watering from the impact, Rob followed him into the site office, where a giant squid was having one of its tentacles reattached.

'Problems?' demanded Greg, sliding a sheaf of papers out from under the end of the quivering rubber tentacle.

'Mmmmph-mmm-mmm-mph,' said the squid.

'Mishap with one of the motors on the submarine,' replied an overalled technician through a mouthful of yellow string. 'Soon have it sorted.'

'Just make sure you do. And get that squid out of here, I'm trying to have a meeting.' He turned to Rob with a jabbing finger. 'Let'em know who's boss, am I right or am I right?'

Rob smiled his best sales-floor smile. 'Oh you're right. Absolutely.' The paper in his hand sneaked its way towards the desk. 'Just one thing before we get started . . .'

Pushing Rob's arm out of the way without apparently noticing the paper at all, Greg rubbed his hands and spread out a large sheet of paper on the desk in front of them. 'Right, these schematics—'

'Before we look at the plans,' cut in Rob, 'I was wondering . . .' Half-apologetically, he slid his own sheet of paper on to the desk, half-obscuring the plan of Jungle World.

'Jesus H. Christ!' Greg stared at Rob in disbelief. 'You never bloody give up, do you? You're like the ancient bleeding mariner with that damn thing.'

'I wondered if you'd mind taking a look,' wheedled Rob.

'I would, actually.'

'It'd only take a minute.'

'Oh, all right. But I'd better get a discount out of this.'

'Yeah. Right. Well naturally I'm open to negotiation.'

'A fucking *big* discount. Got that?'

'Well, you are our most valued customer. I'm sure I can make a good case to the MD.' Rob's smile weakened only marginally. He was nothing if not the complete sales professional. 'Now, about this plan.'

'Yes, what about it?' Greg scanned Rob's *magnum opus*: a large sheet of paper covered in tiny, exquisite, indecipherable handwriting. Neat columns, neat figures, neat arrows snaking from one part of the paper to another: to Greg it looked like complete rubbish, and he said so. 'Rob, what is this bollocks?'

'It's my plan for getting Cally to come back to me. I've worked everything out, see?'

'You're crazy. What's wrong with flowers and chocolates?'

'You mean what's *right* with them. If I'm going to get her back I'll need to sell myself to her, do something really different.'

70

Greg's eyes uncrossed themselves. 'Well it's different all right, I'll give you that. But it's still bollocks.' Rolling up Rob's battle plan, he thrust it back at him. 'Face it son, she'd have to be Carol bleeding Vorderman to understand that, let alone fall for it.

'Now – do I get my thirty-foot fucking lianas, or what?'

Chapter Six

It was the little things.

Yeah, too right. Little things like being woken up at some ungodly hour by *Farming Today*, blasting out of your mother's bedside radio. Little things like squatting cross-legged on the landing for two bloody hours, while she did whatever middle-aged vegans do in the bathroom, and then coming downstairs to a breakfast of organic prunes in royal jelly. And as if it wasn't bad enough having to forgo your morning bowl of Frosties, you were expected to do it while your mother was putting a fresh stinkweed poultice on your father's rotting foot.

No doubt about it. It was the little things that made all the difference.

'Oh *God*.' Liddy gazed into the murky depths of her minestrone Cup-a-Soup, decided against drinking it, and plonked her mug atop a hillock of vintage *Reader's Digests*. 'How on earth do you put up with it? I think I'd *die* if I had to go back to living with my parents.'

Cally chuckled humourlessly. 'You think that's bad?' She leaned forward, causing a landslide of *Farmer's Weeklies*. 'Yesterday, I caught them at it on the kitchen table.'

The eyes behind Liddy's letter-box-shaped glasses registered puzzlement. 'At what?'

'It!'

'You mean . . .?' Liddy made an in-out motion with her hands. Cally nodded vigorously. 'No, surely not.'

'For heaven's sake yes, Liddy! Making the beast with two backs, getting it on, having it off – my parents were shagging!'

Liddy blinked. 'Ugh,' was all she could find to say. 'I think mine gave up that sort of thing about twenty-five years ago.'

'Yeah? Well, I wouldn't be too sure about that if I were you. I mean, can you imagine? You go into the kitchen for a quick peanut-butter sarnie, and there's your mum and dad, stark naked, going at it like they're auditioning for *The Joy of Sex*.'

'Mmm, nasty,' agreed Liddy.

'Just don't ever ask me to eat my dad's organic courgettes ever again, OK?'

An awkward silence fell as the two friends contemplated the full horror of the scene. Stefan, who considered himself the rightful proprietor of the shop and was regally ensconced on a pile of recently purchased fancy-dress costumes, abandoned a very chewed and slobbery twelve-inch model of Captain Kirk and started on Batman's batarang. It was probably priceless, but you didn't argue with Stefan unless you'd always felt over-endowed in the finger department.

'What are you going to do?' asked Liddy.

'No idea. Nothing, I expect.'

'I suppose you could always—'

Cally looked up, a warning glint in her eye. 'Don't even think about it, Liddy. I am *not* crawling back to Rob.'

'I wasn't going to suggest that,' replied Liddy rather piously. 'I was just going to say, I suppose you could always save up and get your own place.'

'What with?' Cally snapped her fingers. 'Oh yes, silly me. I was forgetting the gold bullion I've got stashed away in my Swiss bank account.'

'What about your redundancy settlement?'

This was greeted with a scowl. 'What about it?'

'Couldn't you . . .?' Liddy cocked her head on one side. 'Oh Cally! You haven't even opened the envelope yet, have you?'

'Might have.'

'No you haven't, you've stuck it at the back of a drawer somewhere, I know you. Honestly! How can anybody who's so good with other people's money be so crap with their own?'

'Easy.'

'Look, cash it in, you could rent yourself a little bedsit or something. Maybe a room in a shared house.'

Cally shredded her empty paper cup disconsolately. 'Lovely. Thirty years old and I can either live in my mum's box room or some scummy student fleapit.' She flung the bits in the air like soiled confetti. 'Oooh, I'm spoiled for choice.'

'Whatever.' Liddy didn't press the point. She could see Cally was restless, thoroughly pissed off and in no mood to be reasonable. Besides, the shop bell had just jangled and she couldn't afford to miss out on a customer. She nodded towards the door. 'Got to go and sell something. Tell you what, why don't you take Stefan for a nice walk?'

The girl and the dog contemplated each other warily, Stefan cocking one hairy, tattered ear at the sound of his name.

'That thing?' protested Cally as Liddy chucked her the extendable leash. 'It's Norman Bates with fur.'

'Only if you don't show him who's boss. Tell you what, why don't you go round and see Eddie?'

'Eddie! I can just see the headlines now: "Local fop found with throat ripped out. Police baffled".'

'No, no, you've got it all wrong.' Liddy scooped up Stefan in one hand, as though about to send him rolling down a bowling alley, and presented him to Cally. 'He only goes for Eddie when he's on his own territory. He's fine on neutral ground, honest.' She hooked on the leash and stuck the end in Cally's hand. 'Go on, it'll do you both good.'

'I've been stitched up,' sulked Cally.

'Yep. That's about the size of it.'

'And why do I want to see Eddie, anyway? Once every ten years is quite enough.'

'Because he's feeling down, and he could use a friend. Apparently his flatmate's just walked out on him.'

The can of Tango nearly flew out of Cally's hand as the lorry headed straight for her and swerved at the very last moment, setting up a miniature earthquake in Eddie's first-floor flat.

It was a smallish flat – but getting bigger all the time. With every lorry that hurtled round the roundabout at the end of Bath Road, the bricks in the flimsy walls seemed to judder a little further outwards, widening the cracks in the plaster.

'Like I said,' yelled Eddie above the deafening rumble of a Belgian eight-wheeler. 'A lovely view of the roundabout.'

'Mmm, very . . . panoramic.' She scratched around

for something nice to say about the flat, something that might cheer Eddie out of his obvious gloom. 'Bet it's great living over a cake shop,' she ventured with feigned enthusiasm.

'Great if you like rodent infestations.'

'Well, the traffic's keeping Stefan amused.' She nodded towards the small, round ball of aggression bouncing up and down under the windowsill, barking ferociously every time it caught a glimpse of a vehicle whizzing past below.

'I suppose that's one small mercy,' conceded Eddie with melodramatic moroseness. 'At least while he's heckling the lorries he's not attaching his fangs to my face.'

Everything about Eddie was over-dramatic, thought Cally. His clothes, his hair, the way he talked. Other people had minor problems, Eddie had full-blown crises. While the rest of the world was saving its pennies for a rainy day, Eddie was blowing his dole cheque on pink brocade trousers and asparagus tips. He'd always been like that, even at primary school. He just couldn't settle for half-measures. Sometimes Cally wondered if he preferred it that way, as though life just wasn't worth living without a bit of melodrama in it.

'I'm sooooo fed up,' sighed Eddie, giving a fluffy heart-shaped cushion a desultory punch.

'Tell me about it,' grunted Cally.

'But it was good of you to think of me, languishing here in my desolate garret with not a soul to comfort me.'

'Actually, it was Liddy's idea. She said if I didn't come, she'd get Stefan to wee in my trainers.'

'That's right, shatter my illusions why don't you? And there I was, thinking you'd come because you wanted to cheer me up.'

'Oh give over Eddie, I'm not in a fit state to cheer anybody up. It's like Eeyore joining the Samaritans.'

Eddie gave an even more expansive sigh. 'What is there to be cheerful about, anyway? My best velvet jacket's got mildew, and nobody loves me. Nobody in the whole wide world.' He cast eyes towards the Art Nouveau fireplace, and the photograph of a smiling brunette, propped up at one end of the mantelpiece. 'I thought somebody did, once . . . but it wasn't to be . . .'

'Who's that then?' enquired Cally.

'Who?'

'Don't give me that. The girl in the photo. The one you keep mooning over.'

Eddie walked over, picked up the photo and gazed at it for a couple of seconds before tucking it behind the clock. 'Ah, that's Gail.'

'Girlfriend?'

'Ex.'

'Ah.'

Eddie's eyes misted over. 'I really thought she was the one, you know. The great love of my life.'

Cally felt a twinge of compassion. 'Did you go out long?'

'Oh yes. Ages. It must have been nearly two . . . no, three . . . whole weeks.'

Cally was on the point of proposing a joint expedition to the nearest tall building when Eddie suddenly dropped to the floor like a stone, pulling her down with him in a confused heap.

'Ow!' gasped Cally, extracting Eddie's violin case from under her bruised ribs. 'What the hell are you doing?'

'Shhh. Keep still, don't let him see you!'

'Who?'

'The landlord.' Slowly and very gingerly, Eddie

peeped over the window ledge like an infantryman peering over the edge of a trench. 'Thank God for that, he's gone.' Apologetically, he peeled a congealed fried egg off the sleeve of Cally's mohair jumper. 'Sorry about that, it's safe now, shall I put the kettle on?'

Cally made a grab for the seat of his retreating trousers. 'Hang on a minute, what about the landlord?'

Eddie looked sheepish. 'There was a . . . bit of a misunderstanding.'

'What sort of misunderstanding?'

'With his daughter. I asked her out, only it turned out her fiancé didn't like it, and you know how jealous these Greeks can get.'

'Oh Eddie!'

'Plus there's the back rent I owe him since Tom moved out.'

'So why did he leave? Big row was there? Or did you try to pinch his girlfriend as well?'

'Hardly. He's gay. Actually he moved out because he found somewhere cheaper – said he needed the extra money.'

'What for?'

'He's setting up in business with—' Eddie's mouth snapped shut like a letter box, as though he had suddenly remembered something.

'With who?'

Eddie's grin was distinctly uneasy. 'Er . . . someone. Nobody you'd know.'

And he swore that was all there was to it. But for some reason, Cally was convinced there was something Eddie wasn't telling her.

Helping out in Liddy's shop was turning into a kind of daily ritual for Cally; and, though she didn't like to admit it to herself, it was one of the few rituals that gave any shape to her life these days.

'Ah. The nineteen sixty-seven pressing of *Great TV Theme Tunes*,' enthused Will Inglis, who was sitting cross-legged on the dusty parquet floor, leafing through a cardboard box of old LPs. 'Excellent. Hey, Lids.' He waved it in the air. 'I'll give you five for this one.'

'Ten,' replied Liddy without turning round from gift-wrapping a troll.

'Seven-fifty.'

'Nine, and I'm robbing myself.'

'Oh all right.' Will resumed his foraging. 'If you throw in that William Shatner single.'

'No chance!' retorted Liddy, looking for a suitably sized box to mail the troll to Cullacoats. 'I'm not a charity, you know!'

At that moment the phone rang, and Liddy squeezed past into the back room in a cloud of dust, knocking a Tribble into Cally's coffee.

'It's getting hard to rip anybody off these days,' commented Will drily. 'Much more of this, and she'll be forcing me out of business.'

Cally found that hard to believe, and said so. Will Inglis struck her as the kind of guy who, come the next Ice Age, could still make a good living selling fridge-freezers. He exuded a kind of sly, self-assured resilience that filled her with envy. The kind that ensured that no matter how much crap might be flying in Will's direction, none of it would stick. I could do with some of that, she thought enviously. Banco Torino wouldn't stand a chance.

'You must be making a packet,' commented Cally, getting on with rearranging the cookery books into alphabetical order.

'Oh must I?' retorted Will. 'And how do you work that one out?'

'People are going mad for collectables aren't they?' said Cally over her shoulder, just in time to catch Will's very blue eyes gazing straight at her with the strangest expression. 'Is something wrong?'

He looked away. 'Only your ideas about my bank balance.'

Liddy reappeared in the doorway to the back room. 'Who's a popular girl then?'

Cally returned her look quizzically. 'I give up. Who?'

Liddy held out the telephone receiver. 'You. It's Rob.'

Cally paled.

'Tell him to go to—'

'I already told him you're here so you'll have to speak to him. Here.' She thrust the phone in Cally's face. 'Go on, get on with it then.'

'Problems?' enquired Will, looking up from his pile of albums.

A cheesy smile forced itself on to Cally's face as she grabbed the receiver from Liddy. 'Oh, just this guy I used to share a house with.' Liddy's eyebrows rose. Cally ignored her and glared into the receiver. 'Right. What do you want this time?'

Taken aback, Rob knocked several pages of tightly written script off the telephone table. He cleared his throat 'Er . . . right.'

'Get on with it, Rob, or I'm going.' She got ready to slam the receiver down on him.

'Hang on, I haven't said anything yet!'

She relented. 'Well?'

'It's about . . . ' He fished page one out of the bin under the table. 'You remember we talked about getting a lodger?'

81

'No Rob,' she replied icily. '*You* talked about getting a lodger. *I* told you to go to hell.'

'Yes. Well. Anyway, I've got one. And I know it'll come as a bit of a shock, and you'll be pretty angry with me, but—'

'Fine,' interrupted Cally.

'Pardon?'

'I said fine. Excellent.' The words flew out of her mouth, and with them any fear that she might have to go back to Northampton, face up to the traumas that had kept her cowering in her mother's spare room for too long.

'But . . . ' Rob contemplated his prepared script in utter confusion.

''Bye Rob.'

Rob gazed into the dead telephone receiver and whimpered.

'Cally, noooo! You're not supposed to say that! You're supposed to hate the whole idea of strangers trampling over your lovely carpets. You're supposed to tell me if I don't change my mind you're getting the next train back to Northampton! Then we have an argument, and I burst into tears and tell you I only did it because I love you and I'm sorry, and I wanted to keep our little house safe for when you come back.'

Shit. He had been rather depending on Cally succumbing to his charms and coming back. You could go so far as to say it had been the linchpin of his entire strategy. Only by doing so would she spare him having to admit that actually there was no tenant; in fact there never had been. When it came to filling their lovely four-bed semi with the great unwashed, he was no more enthusiastic than she was.

82

Only he'd gone and blown it now, hadn't he? Shot his bolt and left himself devoid of ammunition. And now he was either going to have to find a tenant, or come up with Cally's share of the mortgage. Out of his own pocket.

Liddy looked at Cally in surprise. 'That was a quick one.'

Cally sniffed. 'Why should I waste time talking to Rob? It's not as if we've got anything to say to each other.'

'You're supposed to be married, remember?' Liddy reminded her, lowering her voice so that Will couldn't hear.

'Pity he didn't remember that when he started bedding half of Northamptonshire. I suppose I ought to be grateful he doesn't swing both ways, or he'd have bedded the other half as well.'

'That's a bit strong, isn't it? He's only strayed a couple of times . . . hasn't he?'

'I couldn't care less, Liddy. As far as I'm concerned he can share his duvet with a flying giraffe. It's all in the past.' She shoe-horned an early Delia Smith between *Sixty Ways with Suet* and *Swedish Custard Cookery*, and wiped her dusty hands on the seat of her saggy old jeans. 'Right,' she announced out loud. 'That's the cookbooks sorted out – what next?'

Liddy sneezed into a tissue. 'Nothing.'

'What about Princess Leia?' enquired Will, tilting *The Humblebums' Greatest Hits* to the light to count the scratches.

'All debts paid,' declared Liddy. 'Slate wiped clean – so she can run along and bother somebody else now, can't you Cal?'

Cally felt suddenly and curiously bereft. 'But . . . I need something to do, I'm so bored I'm going crazy!'

'Exactly,' said Liddy, evicting a family of spiders from an old shoe-box. 'Which is why your lovely brother is coming round to see you on Tuesday.'

'Apollo?' Cally's nose wrinkled. She'd seen him three times in the last fortnight, which was three times more than she'd seen him in the last year. It wasn't that they didn't get on, simply that he'd always been Big Brother, with his own life and his own friends and a job as Training Manager for PureFood Wholefoods that had rarely brought him much into contact with his omnivorous kid sister. 'What for?'

Liddy sat Cally down on a painted toy-box and squeezed on beside her. 'Because Auntie Liddy asked him to, that's why.'

'What! Why?'

'Because Auntie Liddy knows best.'

'Says who!'

Cally tried swatting her with an old *Radio Times*, but it was delicately prised out of her hand, dusted down and put back on the shelf.

'Don't mangle the stock, Cal,' scolded Will. 'That's the nineteen fifty-three Archers Coronation Special with two-colour pull-out supplement.'

'Sod the Archers, what's this about Apollo?'

'Look,' said Liddy reasonably, 'who's the best person to ask about fitting people into the right-shaped holes?'

'An undertaker?' suggested Will, replacing a record in the box.

'Shut up Will. Well, Cal?'

'Apollo. I suppose,' she conceded grudgingly. Out of the corner of her eye she noticed Will looking at her again, in that same, peculiarly intense way, as though he was searching her face for something, millimetre by millimetre. And then it was gone.

'Exactly,' said Liddy, glancing at Will, then turning back to Cally. 'And on Tuesday he's going to start helping you to find the right-shaped hole for you! It's about time you got up off your backside and started *doing* something with your life.'

Ah yes, it was the little things.

It was having to eat dinner with your mother's horrendous friends, and having to miss *The Simpsons* because of it. It was forcing down undercooked home-made spaghetti while your parents reminisced with your mother's lover about the first time they took magic mushrooms. It was watching a video about Amazonian pygmies while your dad's drunken best mate leered down your cleavage and told you all about the subliminals the government had been putting into *Coronation Street*.

Little things. Little things that said it was time to move on.

Chapter Seven

Cally wriggled into Eddie's ex-NHS armchair and treated him to her most flirtatious smile. 'So – how about it then?'

He swallowed hard. 'What – you mean . . . you and me? Here?'

Cally nodded vigorously. 'Right here. In this flat.'

'Living together?' Eddie's initial bemusement metamorphosed into blind panic. 'Cally, I'm really flattered and all that, and you know I've always liked you, but . . .'

'No, no, no! I don't mean living together, I mean living . . . together. Sharing this flat.'

'Oh.' Eddie's relief was palpable. 'You mean, like flatmates?'

'Exactly like flatmates!' Cally burst out laughing. 'Surely you didn't think I meant . . .'

Eddie blushed crimson. 'No, of course not. Hmm, well, yes . . . it all sounds very nice and I admit it'd be good to have the company . . . but I've got to pay off all this back rent, and you've not got a penny to your name, have you?'

'Ah, that's where you're wrong!' Cally whipped the unopened Banco Torino letter out of her mini-rucksack. 'See? Redundancy settlement. And anyway, I'll get a job soon.'

'You've changed your tune,' remarked Eddie. 'Last time I saw you, you were all for sticking your head in the gas oven.'

'Don't tell me you prefer me miserable.'

' 'Course not. I just think you shouldn't count your chickens, that's all. I mean, if it was that easy to get work I'd be rolling in it, wouldn't I? And right now the only job I've got on the books is repainting a garden shed in Prestbury.'

'Yeah, but the market in giant fibreglass carrots is a bit limited, isn't it? And I've got . . . skills, haven't I?'

'Ah, but are they skills that anybody wants?'

'Of course they are!' Now that she'd made up her mind to sort her life out, nobody was going to bring her down again. 'People always need somebody to tell them what to do with their money.'

'Supposing they've got any to start off with.'

She got up, went across to Eddie and gave him a great big hug that crushed the lace edging on his cravat. 'Come on, cheer up, it'll be great. Now – which room's mine?'

'Sugar in here, is it?' Apollo went straight to the cupboard above the cooker, opened it and pulled out one of the blue and white storage tins. 'So – how are you settling in? Eddie sick of you yet is he?'

Cally's jaw dropped as her brother opened another cupboard and took out the biscuit tin. She was starting to think he had occult powers. Either that, or he'd been in Eddie's flat before.

'How on earth did you know that was in there?'

'What?' Apollo followed her gaze to the tin in his hand. 'Oh – the tin?' He shrugged. 'Well, that's where I'd keep it if I lived here. It's the obvious place really. Spoons?'

'You tell me,' she teased.

Cally picked up her mug of tea and headed back towards the living room, where a plastic model of Blackpool Tower was salsa-ing its way along the window ledge to the rhythm of the passing juggernauts. Eddie lay draped across the battered *chaise-longue* like Elizabeth Barrett Browning in drag, reading *Men are from Mars, Women are from Venus*.

Apollo's plump features appeared in the kitchen doorway. 'Uh?'

'To the left of the sink, second drawer down. Shove over, Eddie, you're not the only one who wants to sit down.'

With feigned reluctance, Eddie shifted his long legs and Cally squeezed herself on to the end of the *chaise-longue*. It wasn't the comfiest piece of furniture in the world, in fact it was that hard it could have doubled as a park bench, but it was lovely not to be sitting on something that belonged to her parents.

'You still haven't told me how things are working out,' remarked Apollo, emerging from the kitchen with his tea balanced on top of the biscuit tin. 'Got you trained yet, has she Eddie?'

'She's a tyrant,' replied Eddie serenely.

'Hah!' retorted Cally, flicking off the tin lid and helping herself to a biscuit. 'Just because I wouldn't let you dry your trainers in the oven.'

'Well, why shouldn't I? It was on anyway.'

'Yes I know it was — I was cooking an apple crumble!'

'She keeps making me clean the toilet, too,' Eddie complained.

'Oh yes, poor darling. So who was it unblocked the vacuum cleaner when you sucked up that pork pie? And who's cooked you three-course dinners every night, and washed up all the dishes?'

'You want to watch her home cooking, Ed,' counselled Apollo. 'Lose that mean and hungry look and the women won't feel sorry for you any more.'

'I don't want them to feel sorry for me!' retorted Eddie. 'I want them to fall hopelessly in love with me.'

Apollo raised an eyebrow. 'Still getting nowhere fast with the masterplan then?'

'What masterplan?' demanded Cally through a mouthful of biscuit.

'Oh, Eddie's got this obsession with marrying the woman of his dreams before he hits thirty-five. Haven't you, Ed? Trouble is, he's got to find her yet.'

As though realising that he had said a little too much, Apollo abruptly stopped baiting Eddie and went back to drinking his tea.

Cally looked from Apollo to Eddie, and back again. 'So I take it you two know each other then?'

'Er . . .' mumbled Eddie non-committally.

'Not really,' said Apollo. 'So, Mum and Dad don't mind then? You flying the nest again.'

'Don't change the subject!' said Cally.

'I'm not. I mean, we don't know each other – well, not properly. Just met up once or twice, because of work. Look, Sis, if I'm going to help you make over your life we ought to get started.' He reached for the briefcase lying at his feet and swung it up on to his knees.

'Who says I want my life made over? Who says I can't manage perfectly well on my own?'

The lid of the case snapped open. 'Please yourself, Cal. But I thought you wanted a job.'

* * *

'You'll never get away with that!' squeaked Eddie, as Cally and Apollo set about dismantling Cally's CV, line by line.

'Of course I will.' Cally reached over, ruthlessly deleted 'Saturday job in shoe shop', and substituted 'Senior Sales Associate – retail'. 'Everybody does it.'

Eddie flailed his arms around like an incompetent dying swan. 'But it's . . . it's . . .'

'A tissue of lies?' suggested Apollo, with an ironic half-smile.

'It's not lying,' said Cally reprovingly. Now that they'd started, she was really getting into this. 'It's just making the most of the truth.'

'OK,' conceded Apollo. 'Have it your own way. What about these qualifications? Hmm, ten GCSEs, sounds brainy.'

'Yeah, except the grades are all really crap. So why don't we just take out the grades? *Et . . . voilà!*'

Apollo chuckled. 'Peter Mandelson would be proud of you.'

'Oooh, look,' observed Eddie. 'You've even put down that certificate you got for trying hard in Woodwork. How old were you when you got that?'

'Twelve,' confessed Cally. 'That letter rack was the only thing I ever made that didn't fall apart.'

'Right,' said Apollo, rubbing his hands. 'Let's make that "excellent carpentry skills".'

Cally laughed. 'You naughty boy! Where's your ethical stance, Apollo Storm?'

He winked. 'In the wash, with my ethical vest.' He typed in the correction. 'There. No one ever checks anyway, take it from me. OK. Now, on to LBS. Did they send you on any courses while you were there? Apart from the banking exams and stuff?'

91

'Er . . . Well, they did send me to Derbyshire once. To look at pig farms.' Cally's face lit up. 'Got it: "short course in agricultural management and animal husbandry".'

'Sounds impressive,' agreed Apollo.

'Ah,' cut in Eddie, 'but can you mangle wurzels, or whatever it is peasant farmers do?'

'Fill in forms and collect subsidies,' Cally corrected him.

'How about outside interests?' ventured Apollo.

'Pigging out,' said Eddie, repossessing the biscuit tin and finding it empty. 'That and ordering people around.'

'You know something?' said Cally, suddenly downcast at the realisation, 'I don't think I've got any outside interests.'

'Don't be daft, you must have,' protested Apollo, his fingers poised over the keyboard.

'I used to have, when I was at school. But then I started work, and there never seemed to be time for anything else.' She racked her brains. 'I did paper the box room with Rob once. Mind you, we had to take it off because half the pattern was upside-down.'

'Renovating period properties,' decided Apollo, keying it in. 'And weren't you in that office panto?'

'Well yes, but . . .' Cally struggled to recall her supporting role as a cucumber. She'd only had one line, and that had been obscene.

'So that's "amateur dramatics and stagecraft".'

Eddie piped up: 'Didn't you once sign up to do a bungee jump off Clifton Suspension Bridge?'

Cally waved the suggestion away. 'Yes, but I didn't actually do it, did I?'

A smile of fond recognition split Apollo's face from ear to ear. 'Oh yes, I remember. You chickened out and legged it to the nearest bus stop. They had to phone you from Bristol to get you to send the bungee rope back. Still, never mind: "extreme sports" it is.'

'Oh come on, that's a bit . . .!'

'Too late, it's done.' Apollo printed off a copy of Cally's brand-new, super-enhanced CV, copied the whole thing on to a floppy disk and presented it to her. 'There you go, young lady. You owe me one. Now, let's send it to a few people so they can see just how good you are.'

While she watched with a frisson of guilty excitement, Apollo posted Cally's CV to half a dozen websites.

'But if you get any interviews . . .' objected Eddie.

Cally rounded on him. 'What do you mean, if?'

'All right, when you get an interview, they're bound to find out it's a load of old bollocks, aren't they?'

Cally draped an arm round Eddie's shoulders. 'Sweetie dahling, if I can bullshit them the way I bull-shitted my way into this flat, the job's mine already.'

One rigorous career profiling exercise later, they came to the moment Cally had been dreading.

'Well?' said Apollo.

'Well what?'

'How much redundancy money did you cop for?'

'I'm not exactly sure,' she lied.

'Yes you are. Hand it over.'

He beckoned and reluctantly she extracted the crumpled letter from her bag.

'It's not much,' she said as he slid it out of the envelope, pre-empting the look of horror on his face.

'Bloody hell, you're telling me. And most of it's in training vouchers. What cheapskates!'

'Yeah.' Cally contemplated the useless bits of paper. 'Might as well chuck 'em in the bin.'

'Oh no you don't!' intervened Apollo, snatching them out of her hand.

'Why not? What use are they to me? I'm already trained!'

'Then you'll be even better trained, won't you?' Apollo flicked through the pages of the letter. 'Hmm, there's only one recruitment agency you can redeem them at locally. But it looks like you're in luck.'

'Oh joy. Let me guess, they're throwing in a free lobotomy.'

'Even better. The boss is a mate of mine, and she owes me a favour.' He dipped into his briefcase for his mobile. 'Go and put your glad rags on, Sis. I'm going to fix you up with an interview right now.'

'Ah, one of these.' The woman from Price Gotherington Recruitment picked up the training voucher between thumb and forefinger, suppressing the faintest of sniggers. 'A heave-ho special.'

Cally was severely tempted to smack Christina Shaw in the teeth with her own Louis Vuitton handbag, but even she could see that might not be the smartest of career moves. And if anything was going to start being right in her life again, Cally needed a new job – a good one. And soon.

She swallowed her pride. 'So I can exchange my vouchers for training here?'

Ms Shaw tucked a smooth strand of highlighted hair behind her ear, drawing Cally's attention to a rather exquisite cloisonné earring. Thirtysomething, immaculately dressed, successful . . . that was me two months ago, thought Cally bitterly, catching sight of a wisp of her own grown-out highlights out of the corner of her eye. And now look at me. Bitch.

'Certainly you can, but we can talk about that later, can't we?' Ms Shaw took a sip from her coffee cup, leaving not a trace of lipstick on the rim. 'First, I'd like you to tell me about yourself, Ms . . .'

'Storm,' Cally repeated through clenched teeth. 'Cally Storm.' Reaching into her briefcase, she withdrew the beautiful work of fiction which she and Apollo had created. 'I've brought my CV for you to look at. As you can see, I've had quite a lot of experience.'

'Your CV? Well, we shan't be needing that.' To Cally's absolute horror, Christina Shaw took the two sheets of paper and, without even glancing down at them, dropped them straight into the wastepaper bin. 'There, that's better.'

Christine Shaw's hypnotic grey eyes fixed on hers and Cally's toes curled with dread. 'Now, start TELLING me about yourself, Ms Storm. And don't leave anything out.'

'*Big Issue*, sir? Help the homeless?'

The girl on the pub steps waved a bunch of magazines under Rob's nose but he hardly seemed to notice her, or the grey-brown lurcher curled up on a blanket beside her. It opened one eye, looked him up and down as he flopped down on to the steps and loosened his tie, then settled back into an uneasy sleep.

It was early morning on Bath Road, and the pavements were bustling with early-morning shoppers, trotting alongside office workers sporting half-eaten pieces of toast and unknotted ties flapping round their shirt collars. Sprouts were on special offer at the Natural Grocery Store, but Rob's thoughts were not on sprouts. He should have been selling potted palms in Shrewsbury, but he wasn't thinking about potted palms either. In fact, there was only one thought in his mind.

'It's no use,' he groaned, raking a hand through the hair he had spent ages neatly gelling into place.

'What?' The *Big Issue* seller turned and looked at him warily. She was a small, rather delicate girl, naturally blonde with huge, soft brown eyes that made her look like an experimental mating between Cinderella and Bambi, and slender hands with skin so white and translucent that the veins showed clear blue underneath.

'It's no good. Here.' Rob thrust the bunch of flowers he was carrying at the girl. 'You might as well have these.'

The magazine-seller edged away from him. 'What's your game?'

'Game? There isn't any game. Go on, take them. She won't want them.' When the girl still refused to take the flowers, he threw them down on the step beside him. 'I had to do something, didn't I? I mean, I couldn't just let things go on like this.'

'Er . . . no. Whatever you say.' Her voice was soft and slightly quavery round the edges. The girl sold another magazine. 'It's OK, he's not with me.'

Rob went on, paying her no attention. 'So I woke up this morning and I thought, I'll go and see her, that's what I'll do. I've got to go and talk to her, face to face. Try and get her back. When she sees me things'll be all right, we'll sort something out.

'And what happens when I get here? I find out she's already got a new place and a new bloke to go with it. I even saw her give him a kiss on the cheek, for God's sake. I mean, what would you do?'

'I don't know what you're on about,' said the girl. 'Why don't you just leave me alone?'

'She was on the way out somewhere, see. This time of the morning, stands to reason, she's got a new job, she's on her way to work.' He hung his head. 'She's moved on already, what the hell am I going to do?'

'Morning sir,' said a much deeper voice. 'Janis bothering you is she?'

'Bothering me?' Rob looked up, dazed, and saw a middle-aged policeman looming over him. 'Who?'

'This young woman, sir.'

'I never did anything,' protested the girl.

'Only if she is, sir, I shall have to move her on.'

'He's the one you should be moving on!' Janis snatched up her pile of magazines and backed away into the doorway. 'Tell him to go away, he's frightening me.'

Frowning, the policeman bent down and sniffed Rob's breath. 'Been drinking have we, sir? Had a bit of a night on the tiles?'

'No, I've only had the one. To steady my nerves.'

'Hmm.' A hand levered him gently but firmly to his feet. 'Come along sir, time to go home and sleep it off. I'll bet your lady wife's worrying herself sick about you.'

Chapter Eight

Computer programmer, international supermodel, first woman on Mars ... The retraining possibilities were endless. But one that definitely hadn't occurred to Cally was learning to drive an ice-cream van.

It might not have been quite so appalling if there had actually been any ice cream in the van. Or if it hadn't been the Easter holidays. Or if the sun hadn't been blazing down on droves of children desperate for blueberry slush and a Cornetto. It might even have been almost bearable if she had been able to switch off the annoying jingle that came on every time she touched the brake. She had never been fond of 'Greensleeves'; well, from here on in, it would be the backing track to her worst nightmares.

Management trainee, my arse, thought Cally as she accelerated past the children's home and the nun with the twenty-pound note standing expectantly at the gate. What's any of this got to do with management training? Ms Shaw had described it as 'an exceptional training opportunity with the south-west's premier supplier of quality dairy products'; but then again, Ms Shaw had patently got it in for her. Just wait till I'm a branch manager and you want a mortgage, she thought with malicious glee, changing down for a red light.

'Gizza ninety-nine,' demanded an adolescent face, suddenly appearing at the window as she waited for red to turn to amber.

'Go away.'

'GIZZA NINETY-NINE!'

'Look I can't, I haven't got any ice cream.'

'All right then, gizza lolly.'

'I haven't got any of them either.'

'What have you got then?'

'Nothing.' Believe me, you don't want to know what I've got in here, thought Cally. 'And get back on the pavement, you'll get run over.'

'You're fuckin' useless you are! Fuckin' uuuuu . . .'

There was a small, dull clunk as Cally pulled away from the lights and her hearts stopped for one ghastly second, but there was no sign of anything amiss, no obvious bits of teenager smeared across the road, so she continued on her way, consoling herself that there wasn't much further to go. With luck when she got there, they'd let her swap Mr Jollywhip's Fun Van for something less unobtrusive – like a pogo stick maybe, or a lime green unicycle.

It wasn't until she turned the next corner that she noticed the man on the bicycle. She didn't normally pay much attention to men on bicycles, who tended to have knobbly legs and silly shorts, but this one was red in the face and pedalling fit to bust. What's more, he was shouting something and trying to catch up with her. Over the sound of the deafening jingle, she could just make out one word: 'Stop!'

No bloody fear, she thought. If he wants a ninety-nine, he can get it somewhere else. She put her foot down; he pedalled faster. Careered round the one-way system on two wheels; he almost caught her up at the lights. Took the road out of town; he took it too. This was some ice-cream addiction.

She wound down her window as she slowed to negotiate the corner and he came panting up alongside. 'No ice cream!' she yelled, pointing to the scrawled notice on the window. 'Can't you read?'

'No, stop! You've got to stop!' he gasped, gesturing wildly at the back doors of the van. And as she turned her head to snatch a quick look, she saw exactly why.

'She's punishing me, Eddie. This time she's really punishing me.'

'Don't be daft.' Eddie munched placidly on a chicken chimichanga. 'Of course she's not.'

'No?' Cally swept a sticky hand through the congealed air of the Cotswold Cantina. 'Eddie, just *look* at this place!'

It was a typical day at the Cantina. Diners who had even less money than sense browsed on Les Lynch's economy chilli at chipped Formica tables, under lamps shaped like Mexican sombreros, and bedecked with so many cobwebs that it looked like a set for Miss Havisham's wedding breakfast.

'I quite like it here actually,' protested Eddie.

Cally gave the counter an aggressive wipe. 'Eddie, it's dirt cheap. You like anything if it's cheap enough.'

'Special salsa, anyone?' enquired Les the proprietor, sashaying out of the kitchen with a big plastic bowl of something luminously red. He leaned over Eddie's plate, ladle dripping expectantly. 'Today's special, only 20p a shot.'

'Well, if you're offeri—' From behind the counter, Cally mimed a furious 'no'. Eddie's face fell. 'Second thoughts, maybe not. I'm a bit full actually.'

101

'I'll have some,' piped up a voice in the corner, and Les went off to minister to the poor of the parish.

'What was all that face-pulling in aid of?' demanded Eddie. 'I quite fancied a bit of that.'

Cally drew him closer. 'Believe me, you do *not* fancy Les's special salsa. Or at least, you wouldn't if you'd seen him making it. God, I hate it here.'

'It's not that bad – free meals on duty.'

'Quite.' Cally served up a dollop of something brown and dropped a jalapeño chilli on top. 'And it's all down to that bitch Christina Shaw. She's really putting the screws on me.'

'I don't see why you think that,' reasoned Eddie, helping himself to a complimentary pickled egg. 'I mean, what's so terrible about getting lost in Swindon? Even people who *live* in Swindon get lost in Swindon.'

'Eddie, you haven't been listening, have you?' Cally picked a stray kidney bean off the green salad, discovered it was a small beetle and swiftly let go, accidentally dropping it back in. 'It wasn't me getting lost, it was *what* I lost.'

'Not with you,' said Eddie, sneaking a handful of salad leaves.

'Eddie, I wouldn't,' began Cally, as he stuffed a handful of lettuce into his mouth.

'Wouldn't what?'

'Oh . . . nothing. Look, I'm sitting at the lights, right, and this bloke comes pedalling up on a mountain bike, waving his arms about and telling me to stop. Well, naturally I think he's after an ice cream, but it turns out he's telling me my back doors came open at the last junction.'

'That was decent of him,' nodded Eddie.

'Yeah, especially as it turns out there's this boy hanging off the door handle, screaming blue murder!'

'Blimey. Anything fall out of the van?'

'Yes it bloody well did! Three whole canisters of prime bulls' semen, to be precise. Headed for a romantic tryst with a herd of frustrated Friesians.'

'What?' Eddie regarded his soured cream with sudden distaste. 'Ugh, you're kidding.'

'Nope, straight up.'

'Ahem. Quite.'

'The firm didn't have any proper refrigerated vans to transport it in, and now it's defrosting all over the dual carriageway.'

'Ah,' said Eddie. 'Messy.' He started chewing again. 'Come to think of it, Cal, you could be right. Maybe she has got it in for you, after all.'

'But I don't want to go to the zoo,' protested Cally as Eddie's Hillman Imp coughed its way towards Tewkesbury. 'I'm not six years old!'

'No,' agreed Liddy, 'but you act as if you are, so you might as well be. Shove over, I'm sitting on Stefan.'

'If that beast wees on my upholstery, he's dead meat.' Eddie screwed his head round from the front seat. 'I've just had it retextured. Hey, do you think they'll have tigers? Tigers are cool.'

'A zoo's not a zoo without tigers,' decided Liddy. 'Is it, Stefan?' Stefan farted noisily. 'See? He's all excited.'

'I still say you shouldn't have brought him,' observed Eddie, winding down the window another inch. 'Just don't blame me if they shoot him with a tranquilliser dart and stick him in with the Tasmanian Devils.'

'I hate zoos,' moaned Cally.

'You hate everything,' retorted Liddy. 'Shut up and enjoy your day out.'

Cally stuck her tongue out. 'Yes, Mum.'

She wriggled down in her seat and gazed out at the fields and hedges gliding past. It wasn't that she didn't appreciate what Liddy and Eddie were trying to do, it was just that she hated being treated like a mentally defective toddler. Besides, she'd quite genuinely never liked zoos very much. She could still recall a trip to one when she was a little kid, having to stare at depressed-looking lions through the bars of some smelly cage, wanting to cry because all the animals looked so miserable and mangy. Zoos, ugh. If they were going to take her somewhere, they could at least have made it Cadbury World.

'Can't we go somewhere else?' she asked hopefully.

'Nope,' replied Eddie, grinning at her in the rearview mirror.

'Why not?'

'Because I've already bought the tickets. It was three quid off if you booked in advance. By the way Cal, you owe me a fiver.'

'Oh thanks very much I'm sure! Five quid to get into somewhere I don't even want to go.'

'Yes you do,' Liddy corrected her as the car slid through an arch made by the necks of two life-sized fibreglass giraffes. 'Look Cal, The Animal Experience. We're here!'

'You see,' explained the girl in the zebra-stripped T-shirt and matching wellies, 'Henry here has a bit of a problem. He's afraid of the water.'

'But – he's a sea lion!' exclaimed Liddy. 'Sea lions live in the water. Don't they?'

'Not our Henry.' As if he understood that he was being talked about, Henry flip-flopped his way along the concrete and nuzzled his keeper's hand apologetically.

'Henry had a nasty accident when he was a pup, and nearly drowned. After that he wouldn't go near water, which is why the circus gave him away and we took him in.'

'Oh, poor Henry,' said Cally, squatting down so that she was on eye-level with the unfortunate beast. Henry promptly shuffled nearer and proffered a flipper.

'He wants to shake hands,' explained the keeper. 'Not that we encourage our animals to do tricks, you understand, but it's something he learned in the circus and he just seems to want to keep on doing it. Go on – it's quite safe.'

Feeling rather idiotic, Cally gingerly grasped Henry's fish-scented flipper, and received a whiskery slobber on the cheek for good measure.

'What's going to happen to Henry?' asked a man in an anorak, a small child riding on his shoulders.

'We shall try to rehabilitate him gradually. But even if we don't manage to get him back with the other sea lions, he has a home here for as long as he needs it. That's our philosophy here at Animal Experience: we never turn away an animal in need.'

The Animal Experience was nothing like Cally had imagined it would be. It certainly wasn't like any zoo she'd ever seen or heard of. There were no tiny, cell-like cages, no bored-looking parrots plucking their own feathers out, no hard-sell merchandise outlets.

The Experience wasn't so much a zoo as a park, where the animals came first and the humans a very definite second. It was as if somebody had taken a run-down version of Blenheim Palace and developed it, and its grounds, as a place where animals could live in harmony with people. And if the zoo wasn't an ordinary one, neither were its occupants. There were giraffes with cricked necks, agoraphobic gazelles, three-legged tortoises, even a wallaby with such a shocking weight problem that it looked like a furry brown spacehopper.

But the thing that struck Cally most forcibly, and most immediately, was what a happy place it was. The animals were obviously loved, the keepers were relaxed and talkative, the park was chock-full of happy families, and you could get really, really close to the animals. Closer than Cally had ever seen before.

By the time they'd been round Hedgehog Heaven three times, Cally had completely forgotten how much she hated zoos.

'I'm parched,' announced Eddie. 'Who's for finding the nearest pub?'

'Sounds good,' nodded Liddy.

'In a minute,' said Cally, cradling a baby hedgehog in the palm of her hand. 'Look Lids, feel how soft its little spines are!'

'Yes, yes, they're lovely. Come on, my bladder's going to burst if I don't find the loos soon.'

'Be there in a minute,' promised Cally. But she'd forgotten her promise by the time Liddy and Eddie were out of sight. And when she caught sight of the big red arrow and the sign that said: TO DONKEY HEIGHTS, Cally forgot everything else as well.

It was meant to be a children's farm, of course. A place where they could meet pigs and sheep and chickens and cows, and get close to them. But there weren't many children about right now. What's more, there weren't any signs saying 'grown-ups keep out'; and in any case, you'd have to have a heart of stone not to fall in love with a tiny black thing with a splotch on its nose and a woolly head.

'Oh, I do like you!' Cally leaned over the gate and rubbed the minuscule donkey's shaggy forehead; it seemed to like it, or at any rate it nuzzled the sleeve of her jacket, leaving a glistening trail of dribble. 'You're lovely.'

In the distance, a big, docile grey donkey was submitting to the massed cuddles of half a dozen bright-eyed kids in return for a constant supply of carrots. They all looked pretty content with the arrangement.

Happy animals, happy people, everything on a human scale. This is just what a farm ought to be like, Cally mused, thinking back to some of the horrible, factory-like places she'd had to visit over the years; and the terrible, windswept crofts where the farmers scarcely lived any better than their sheep.

'Watch your fingers,' commented the donkey keeper, a man in his forties with thinning blond hair and the kind of inch-thick tan you only got from being outside in all weathers. 'See?' He nodded towards the notice on the fence. It read: PLEASE DO NOT STROKE ME, I BITE.

'Oh he wouldn't!' protested Cally, rubbing a velvety ear. 'He's so gentle.'

'You wouldn't say that if he'd just had your index finger off at the knuckle,' he replied, serenely displaying a missing digit.

'He did that to you?' Cally sharply withdrew her hand.

'Well no, actually it was an armadillo, but he's more than capable, aren't you Stan?' He pitched another forkful of hay over the fence. 'Matter of fact, he can be a holy terror when he wants to be, that's why we have to keep him in his own paddock. Bit of a character though.'

As if confirming what the keeper had said, the ever-so-adorable Stan drew back liquorice-black lips, revealing an impressive double row of teeth.

'Oh dear,' said Cally. 'Why does he do it? Was he mistreated?'

'Oh no, he just enjoys it. In some ways animals are like us, you see: some are born nice and some aren't. That's what the Experience is all about, providing a home for all animals in need, not just the cuddly ones everybody loves. That, and educating people so we can all get along a bit better.'

A bell sounded in the distance.

'Aha. Feeding time. Hope you're ready for the rush.'

'What rush?

A couple of seconds later, Cally was almost flattened by a stampede of small children, exiting the 'Pet-A-Pig' event in the main barn.

Small hands tugged at Cally's jacket. 'Miss!'

'Miss, can we feed the donkeys?'

'Can we, miss, can we?'

'Can I have my face painted like a pig?'

'Er . . .' Cally was tempted to reply that the little girl in question already bore more than a passing resemblance to a Gloucester Old Spot, but she was too busy struggling to stay upright in the seething swarm of ankle-biters. 'Hang on, don't pull like that, you'll make me fall ov—'

The end of the word was lost in a squeak, as Cally lost her footing on something wet and slippery, and landed arse-first in a patch of melted ice cream.

Not surprisingly, the children thought it was hilarious. Even Stan the donkey couldn't keep a straight face. Oh yeah, thought Cally. Absolutely hysterical. Why oh why did I wear these Jasper Conran trousers?

She opened her mouth to curse at the sea of small faces giggling down at her; but suddenly a wave of something most peculiar overtook her. Something she'd not experienced for so long that she'd almost forgotten how to do it.

She burst into a fit of uncontrollable giggles.

'Honestly,' tutted Liddy, turning to look at the snoring passenger on the back seat. 'Just look at the state of her.'

Eddie grinned as he took a peek in the rearview mirror. 'Sleeping like a baby. Ah, sweet.'

'Eddie love, the only face-paint a grown woman should be wearing comes from the cosmetics counter in Boots. When's the last time you saw Kate Moss with her face done up like a pig?'

'Er . . . Can I take the fifth on that one?'

'Oh ha ha.'

'Anyhow, I think it suits her,' said Eddie, humming along to the radio. 'She looks . . .'

'Silly?' ventured Liddy.

'Cute. And did you see the way she was playing with those kids at the farm? They loved her.'

'Kids love watching anybody make a fool of themselves,' Liddy reminded him. 'But you're right, she does look cute. Even if there is ice cream all over the seat of her pants.'

'The main thing is, she looks happy,' said Eddie firmly. 'Face it Lids, when's the last time you saw Cally smiling?'

Chapter Nine

The Hillman Imp drew to a halt outside Gold in the Attic, with a triumphant clanking of rusty metal as the dangling exhaust scraped along the gutter.

'Aaaaaah,' grinned Eddie, pointing at the sprawling figure on the back seat. 'Just look at that. The sleep of the innocent.'

'Better wake her up I suppose,' commented Liddy. 'She can't stay out here all night.'

Eddie caught her hand before it reached Cally's slumbering shoulder. 'No, look Lids, she's *smiling*.'

Liddy considered Cally's expression from a variety of different angles. 'It might be wind.'

'Don't talk rubbish, that only works with babies. No, if you ask me she's definitely happy. And when was the last time you saw Cally looking happy?'

'I can't remember.'

'Exactly.' Eddie consulted his watch. 'Go on, you've got ten minutes to get your glad rags on.'

'Glad rags?' Liddy's nose wrinkled. 'Eddie, what are you on about? Why would I want to dress up? I'm not going anywhere.'

'That's where you're wrong.' Eddie flicked open the glove box and whisked out the wildest, most Austin Powers lacy cravat Liddy had ever seen. 'I'm taking Cally out on the town – and you're coming too!'

In the double-glazed depths of Northampton, nobody can hear you scream.

Or sing, for that matter. Which was just as well, because Rob had never been blessed vocally. In fact, one or two people had been heard to remark that his version of 'Nessun Dorma' sounded like a camel being neutered with two half bricks. His Whigfield impression wasn't much better, either.

'Daba dadan dee,' he yodelled, 'deedee dani nana naaaaaaah . . .' His voice tailed off. Bloody hell but he hated Saturdays, especially Saturday nights.

Rob was sitting in the corner of the living room, surrounded by an arc of half-empty beer bottles, each one a different sort. He lifted the last bottle, took a swig and grimaced.

'I gave up not drinking for you bastards,' he griped. 'One of you might at least taste nice.'

Sat-ur-bleeding-day. He would have done just about anything not to spend Saturday night with Matthew Kelly and a TV dinner for one; why, he'd even take Cally out. Not that that was an option any longer. Sniff.

Rob gave the bottle a long, hard stare and let out a loud belch.

'Sod this for a game of soldiers.'

Planet Party was not the place for an intimate romantic experience. If you wanted quiet, subtle and spiritually enriching, you'd have been better off trying Over-Sixties' Flower Arranging at the public library. Though frankly, even Happy Hour at Stringfellow's would have been quieter than a night out at Planet Party.

Now, Cally could large it with the best of them. What's more, she wasn't averse to a bit of male attention. The trouble was, too many of the blokes in 'Cheltenham's premier nite-spot' reminded her of Rob, which didn't say a lot for her taste in men. And the way they were acting, you'd have thought she was the first clubber they'd ever seen in ice-cream-soaked Jasper Conrans and face-paint.

'Having fun yet?' yelled Eddie, over the thumping beat.

'Are you taking the piss?' retorted Cally, half-mesmerised by Eddie's absurd gyrations, which were irresistibly reminiscent of some obscure neurological disorder. 'You could at least have woken me up before you dragged me here.'

'I think it looks great,' volunteered Liddy, trying not to laugh at Cally's face.

'No you don't,' glared Cally. 'You tried to scrub it off in the bogs.'

'How was I to know it wasn't washable? Besides, you're the one who insisted on having your face painted like a pig.'

Right on cue, something nipped Cally hard on the backside. Letting out a shriek, she spun round, to be greeted by a grinning idiot with a shaven head and faux-snakeskin trousers.

'Oink, fancy a bit of animal passion do ya darlin'? I'm game if you are, know what I mean?'

'Oh fuck off!' she snapped, and all his mates fell about laughing. 'Right,' she said, turning back to Liddy and Eddie with arms aggressively folded. 'That's it, take me home. Right now.'

'We can't go home!' protested Eddie. 'It's free drinks till midnight.' He blushed coyly. 'Besides, I think I've pulled.'

'Pulled?' demanded Liddy. 'Who?'

Eddie nodded towards the bar, where a rather gorgeous blonde was smiling in his general direction. 'See? She fancies me.'

'No she doesn't,' scoffed Cally. 'She's wondering who that wally is in the lace cravat.'

'Actually,' chimed in Liddy, peering across the dance floor, 'I think she's a bit cross-eyed. She's probably not looking at you at all.'

'Well there's only one way to prove this,' announced Eddie, extracting a handful of change from his trouser pocket. 'I'm going to buy her a drink. You two just sit back and watch the master at work. You never know. This could be love.'

Approximately ten minutes later Eddie reappeared, pushing his way through the throng with two half-empty glasses and the contents of a third dripping down his face.

'Don't tell me,' said Cally, making room for him at the table, 'it's the latest fashion: ready-to-wear drinks.'

'Eddie love,' said Liddy,' what on earth did you *say* to that girl?'

'Nothing!' protested Eddie, sucking spilled lager off his cravat. 'Or at least, nothing she could possibly take offence at. As a matter of fact, she was thanking me for seeing off that yob with the wandering hands.'

Cally cast a sceptical eye at the human colossus propping up the bar. He appeared to have at least twice the usual complement of muscles, and a nose that looked as if it had been repeatedly jumped on. 'What – you saw off *him*?'

'Oh, absolutely.'

'What Eddie means,' cut in Liddy, 'is that Mr Atlas there got tired of slapping him and buggered off. Don't you, Eddie?'

Eddie waved away the insult. 'Puh-leeze. I had it all planned out, I was going to overcome him with the power of poetry.'

'Oh yeah? And how were you going to do it with his boot down your throat?'

This minor consideration cut no ice with Eddie. 'Anyhow, I've seen him off and the girl's thanking me, and I'm thinking, you've cracked it here Ed me boy . . .'

Cally poured the last forlorn drips out of Eddie's glass into her own. 'So what went wrong?'

'Well, she says to me, "By the way, I'm Linda," and sticks out her hand. So naturally I turn it over and kiss it. And then I remember that bit of Italian I learned at night school, and I think, hey, the language of *amore*, she'll be putty in my hands. This could be the big one, the love of my life.'

'And?' enquired Liddy.

'She hit me.' Liddy and Cally looked at Eddie's dejected spaniel expression, and collapsed into giggles. 'I can't understand it, she called me a dirty-minded bastard.'

'Eddie love,' confided Cally, laying a hand on his, 'you're a disaster, d'you know that?'

'Oh ta very much.'

'And Liddy's a scheming witch, aren't you Lids? But it's OK, I wouldn't have you any other way.' Cally gave Liddy's shoulder a squeeze. 'Thanks.'

'What for?'

'For being mates. For putting up with me while I've been a miserable cow.'

'That's OK,' replied Liddy cheerily, plonking her

empty glass down in front of Cally. 'The next round's on you.'

The trouble with authentic Mexican cuisine was that the end result was authentic Mexican bowel movements. And given that Cotswold Cantina's top seller was its Triple-X Alamo Revenge (garnished with extra chillies and innumerable bacteria), it was hardly surprising that the toilets were blocked again.

Unfortunately, ten years on a smooth upward glide at LBS had not prepared Cally for a career as a lavatory attendant, and still less for one as an amateur plumber. Nevertheless, somebody had to unblock the loos and as Les was busy serving up economy burritos to penniless students, the grim task had fallen to her.

As she took off her rubber glove and dropped it distastefully into the rubbish bin, Cally reflected that at no point in her career had she ever imagined that 'hands-on management training' would be like this. To think that she'd ever supposed driving across some benighted moor in a January blizzard was hard work. Hah! Compared to this, it was a piece of cake.

Still, she told herself firmly, this was just the beginning. The better placements would come later. All she had to do was hang in there and this time next year, she'd be handing Signor Toscelli his P45. Yeah, right, and was that a flock of flying pigs she could see through the broken skylight?

Dejectedly she set to mopping up the floor. Somewhere behind her, she heard the door squeak open.

'Toilets are out of order, sorry,' she murmured, without looking up.

'Ah, if it isn't Calliope,' said a familiar voice behind

her, unctuous yet edged with sarcasm. 'Enjoying our work are we?'

Cally turned round, quite slowly, brandishing her mop like a freshly sharpened spear. One false move from Christina Shaw, and it would be sticking out of her backside.

'Enjoying it?' she spat back, disinfectant raining from the dripping mop-head on to the recruitment consultant's shoes. 'Oh, I'm absolutely *loving* it. Sorry I can't shake hands right now, only I'm up to my elbows in shit.'

'Hmm.' Christina Shaw took a cautious peek into the nearest cubicle and shuddered soundlessly. 'So Mr Lynch has been keeping you busy, has he? Giving you plenty of training opportunities?'

'Oh yes,' replied Cally with acid enthusiasm. 'Training in how to unblock a U-bend, training in how to take out the rubbish, training in how to scrape chip-fat off the ceiling. If I play my cards right, I could be on to chopping onions by the end of the month.'

'Calliope, I . . .'

'. . . and if anybody wants an ex-financial adviser who knows how to electrocute cockroaches . . .'

'If you could just . . .'

'. . . then look no further. But as for *management* training, hah! On what I've been getting here I couldn't manage my way out of a wet paper bag.'

She paused for breath, and Christina Shaw took her chance to get a word in edgeways. 'Have you quite finished?'

Cally rubbed her chin and wished she hadn't. There were some smells you'd really rather not have that close to your nose. 'For the minute,' she admitted grudgingly.

'Good. Because I've come here to tell you you're going to be rotated.'

'What? Stuck on a spit and barbecued? Well I suppose it's a change from cleaning toilets.'

Christina Shaw's smile became more brittle. 'What I mean, Calliope, is that it is time you were moved on to the next segment of your management training programme.'

'Oh,' said Cally, irritation turning to interest. Nothing, absolutely nothing, could be quite as bad as sharing a small space with Les Lynch and his flatulent bottom. 'You mean you're sending me to work somewhere else?'

'Indeed.'

'About time too.'

'Somewhere where you can clean up after animals instead of people.'

Cally's jaw dropped. 'Animals!'

'That's right, Calliope,' smiled Ms Shaw. 'This time we're sending you to the zoo.'

Chapter Ten

The sun was shining, the birds were singing and heck, even the bus was on time.

There were definitely worse places to work than a zoo, mused Cally as the bus vanished on its way to distant Tewkesbury, leaving her standing in front of the two fibreglass giraffes that guarded the entrance to The Animal Experience. OK, she might not be what you'd call an animal person; she'd never hand-raised a newt or pawned her kitten heels to save orphan iguanas from extinction. But she'd always kind of not minded animals, in a controlled sort of way, and how difficult could it be, organising a few cuddly little donkeys and making sure small children didn't fall in the flamingo lake? A darn sight easier than cleaning out the toilets at the Cotswold Cantina, that was for sure.

Cally hummed to herself as she crossed the road to the kiosk by the zoo entrance. Only eight-fifty, excellent; she was ten minutes early for her first day, and that was bound to go down well with her new boss, whoever he might be. She admired her reflection in the side window of the kiosk; nice neat hair, sensible shoes, smart black trousers . . . they couldn't say she hadn't come prepared for anything.

Cally smiled to herself. It was no good Christina

Shaw trying to freak her out with hints about inconti-
nent rhinos; she had a good feeling about this placement. It was going to be a doss. A couple of weeks here,
honing her customer care skills, and then the agency
would whisk her swiftly on to something bigger and
better. Something that would prepare her for a
triumphant return to the management position she
deserved.

Marching confidently up to the ticket window, she
bent down and peered inside. A cardboard sign propped
up against the glass read: SORRY WE'RE CLOSED, and the
only sign of life in the little hut was a solitary woodlouse, sucking reflectively on a wilted lettuce leaf.

She knocked on the glass. 'Hello?'

No reply came, though the woodlouse wiggled its
antennae. She tried again.

'Anybody there?'

Since there wasn't, it was obvious they expected her
just to walk straight in and head for the main office.
Advancing towards the turnstile, she gave it a push. It
did not budge. Neither did the side gate marked PRIVATE,
NO ENTRY'.

Ah. So much for Plan A. Cally fished out the scrap of
paper Ms Shaw had given her. Plan B: ring the
Experience and get them to come and open the gate. She
turned round and surveyed the scene. A straight road
stretched out on either side, as far as the eye could see.
More specifically, a straight empty road, devoid of
traffic, houses . . . and telephone boxes.

Double bugger. Of course, if she'd still been with
LBS she'd have had her own mobile phone, but then
again, if she was still with LBS she wouldn't be
standing like an idiot outside a zoo at nine o'clock in the
morning.

Plan C then. Climb over the turnstile. No mean undertaking, at almost six feet high and built to withstand the most furious of toddler attacks, but not for nothing had Cally Storm been East Gloucestershire Under Fourteens' rock-climbing champion, two years running.

She had one leg over the top of the turnstile and her handbag clamped between her teeth when the little zebra-striped van coughed to a halt ten feet away.

A window wound down and a lean, blond head stuck out. 'Good God. What on earth are you doing up there?'

Cally spat out the strap of her handbag. 'Er . . . trying to get in.'

'We don't open until ten.'

'Yes, I know. But I'm supposed to start work in five minutes!' She peered at the face in sudden recognition. 'Here, don't I know you? You look after the donkeys, don't you?'

'Among other things,' he admitted. 'Don't tell me – you're the girl who fell in the ice cream! I didn't recognise you without your face-paint.'

'Gee, thanks.'

'You work here, you said?'

'I'm supposed to start today.' Cally wobbled precariously on top of the turnstile. 'But I can't get in.'

'That's because there's a different door for people who work here. You know, tradesmen's entrance.'

'Ah.' Cally reddened. 'I didn't think.' Swinging her legs back over, she dropped to the ground. 'God, how embarrassing.'

'It's not your fault, Simone should've been here to meet you.'

'Simone? Who's she?'

The passenger door of the van swung crookedly open. 'Hop in, I'll take you to the office.'

The interior of the keeper's van was an absolute mess; as the girl whose school desk had once housed forty-seven empty crisp packets and a copy of *Fanny Hill*, Cally warmed to him instinctively.

She had always felt that excessive tidiness was a sign of extreme mental dodginess, and if that was true, then this guy need never worry about men in white coats. Scrunched-up tissues, chocolate wrappers, empty plastic cups, a hot water bottle shaped like Kermit the frog, a pair of orange nylon underpants and half a packet of cream crackers littered the floor so liberally that Cally had difficulty finding anywhere to put her feet.

Something crunched ominously as she wriggled her toes through the mulch of debris. 'Oh!' Her hand flew to her mouth. 'Sorry.'

The keeper dismissed her concern. 'Oh, that'll be the freeze-dried mice, don't worry about it. Lulu won't mind them being a bit broken up, she's got hardly any teeth anyway, so we soak them for her.'

'Lulu?' enquired Cally doubtfully, edging her foot sideways.

'One of Pountney's Performing Cats.'

'Cats? As in lions and tigers?'

He grinned. 'Not exactly. As in, domestic moggies trained to play five-a-side football. Rather sad really, we got them when the circus went broke. So . . .' He glanced sideways. 'You're the new trainee then, are you?'

Cally nodded. 'I was made redundant, this is part of my retraining programme.'

'Anybody told you what you'll be doing yet?'

'Not exactly, no. I thought . . . seeing as I'm supposed to be a *management* trainee . . .'

'That you'll be working in the office?'

'Sort of. With maybe the odd stint shadowing one of the keepers.'

He chuckled. 'Well, the official job title is "trainee guide and animal carer". We don't officially have zoo-keepers, though everyone calls them that; in fact, this place isn't a zoo at all.'

'No?' puzzled Cally as the car rattled past an enclo-sure full of wildebeest. 'Then what is it?'

'What it says in the brochure – an *experience*.' Clicking open the glove compartment without looking down, he extracted a leaflet and stuffed it into Cally's hand. 'An educational centre for the whole family.'

Cally laughed and flopped back into her seat. 'Yeah, but that's all hype, isn't it? I mean, it's got zoo animals, so it's a zoo, right?'

'You think so?' There was a glint of amusement in the bright, grey eyes.

'Of course it is! Mind you, it's the most disorganised zoo I've ever been in.'

'You reckon?'

'Oh yes, it's complete chaos. Never mind me, whoever's in charge of this place could do with going on a management training course . . .' Her gaze drifted off to the right, where possibly the fattest wallaby in the entire known universe was browsing on a pile of fresh leaves. 'My God! Look at the state of that wallaby! How on earth could they let it get like that? See what I mean? Totally disorganised.'

The keeper smiled. 'Actually, Charlie has a congen-ital glandular problem. But I'll be glad to hear any suggestions you have to make.' Braking outside a gate marked PRIVATE: STAFF ONLY, he stuck out a hand. 'Suppose I ought to introduce myself really. My name's Henk.'

Cally swallowed. 'Henk . . . Thorfinn?'

'That's right. I own this place.'

'Well,' said the girl in the Stores, 'it sort of fits. Almost.'

Cally emerged from the changing room in a slither of over-stretched polyester. She hadn't been expecting a uniform in the first place, and definitely not one that was so tight in the leg that she'd lost all sensation in her knees. 'Is it *supposed* to look like this?' she enquired, daring a quick look at herself in the mirror on the back of the door.

' Er . . . no, well, not exactly,' confessed the girl.

'Thank God for that, I can hardly walk.'

'I expect Mrs Figgis can let the trousers out a few inches.' The girl flipped over the waistband and inspected the seam. 'And take in that bit of slack under the arms.'

Bit of slack? thought Cally, flapping her arms. I look like a pterodactyl. And a pterodactyl in beige polyester, at that. There's enough static coming off me to light Blackpool for a week. She gazed wistfully at her smart black trousers and comfy shoes. 'Couldn't I just wear my own clothes . . .?'

'Not unless you want them covered in shit.'

'Good grief, Stella,' said Henk, coming back up the cellar steps carrying a crate of cabbages. 'She can't go out into the park looking like that.'

'I had to make do with one of the old-style uniforms from the stockroom.' Stella twiddled a pink hair extension irritably. 'It's not my fault if Simone didn't get her measurements, is it?'

'Simone? Not Simone *again*.' Henk's even temper rippled into a brief growl of impatience. 'Look, you must have something better than that. It must have been in the stores for years.'

'Not in women's I haven't. We're right out of zebra-print T-shirts, and the only decent trousers we've got are in extra-large.'

'Then you'll have to kit her out in a man's shirt and trousers for the time being. She doesn't mind it being a big baggy, do you Cally?'

'Er . . . no,' Cally smiled weakly. 'I suppose not. But I was just wondering . . .'

Her train of thought was suddenly and violently derailed by the most hideous, most pungent stench she had ever encountered in her entire life: worse than blocked drains, worse than rancid sushi, worse even than a weightlifter's armpits in a heatwave. 'Ugh!' She staggered back, a hand clamped over her mouth. 'What on earth is *that*?'

'Hmm?' murmured Henk, absent-mindedly counting his cabbages. 'Oh, that'll be Vernon.'

Sure enough, about thirty seconds later the smell was followed in by its source: a tall man in his early twenties, with skin the colour of a double espresso and the kind of body odour that a gorgonzola cheese could only dream of. He looked distinctly at odds with the world.

'Morning Vern,' chirped Stella. 'Wearing your favourite aftershave again?'

'I almost had him that time,' said Vernon, ignoring the jibe. 'I swear, I almost had him.'

'Had who?' demanded Cally, trying hard to breathe in through her mouth.

'Colin.'

She turned to Henk. 'Who's Colin?'

'Our skunk,' explained Henk. 'Very rare species, the Javan Yellow. He's just a teensy bit highly strung though. Feeding time's always a battle of wills, isn't it, Vernon?'

Vernon gave his sleeve a cautious sniff which ended in a sneeze. 'Battle of smells more like.'

Henk smiled. 'Better have a shower before you show your face in Simone's office. Vernon, this is Cally. Cally, this is Vernon. He's going to be your boss.'

Cally blinked. 'My boss?' She wanted to protest, 'but he only looks about fourteen, I bet I've got tons more management experience than he has!' However she managed to keep her thoughts to herself. 'Oh. Hi.'

'Hi. So you're my new girl then?' He looked Cally up and down. 'They could at least have got you a proper uniform.'

'Yes, you might mention that to Simone when you see her,' said Henk pointedly. 'In fact tell her I'll see her in my office after lunch, if she's not too busy touching up her nail varnish.'

Vernon opened his mouth as though he was about to protest, then promptly closed it again.

'Actually,' said Stella, 'I heard she was having child-care problems. You know how it is, her being a single mum.'

'Then she can tell me all about it this afternoon. Vernon, time you were showing Cally the ropes.'

'Yes. Sure,' said Vernon. 'OK Cally, get yourself some wellies and follow me. Oh – and you'll need one of these.'

Grabbing a shovel from a stack in the corner, he threw it in her direction.

'Ever seen elephant shit before?'

126

'Actually, no.'

'Then you're in for a real treat.'

The General Mayberry liked to think of itself as a 'local', though the only other building within two miles was a cowshed, and that had no roof. Consequently the 'General' lurked by the roadside like a squat apology, its higgledy-piggledy construction plastered in layers of off-white rendering which almost but not quite covered the cracks opened up by decades of heavy lorries.

If it was local to anywhere, it was The Animal Experience; and sure enough, on any weekday evening you would find its public bar crammed with hairy men in muddy boots and steaming overalls. Nobody took much notice of the sign above the bar (NO WORK CLOTHES, LEAVE WELLIES IN PORCH), and since the General was well known among discerning agricultural folk for its liberal attitude to licensing laws, the over-powering aroma of exotic manure performed the useful function of discouraging both tourists and over-zealous constables.

Cally did not even notice the smell as she shuffled painfully through the front door of the pub. She had been so steeped in smells all day that her nose had given up and gone on strike. Besides, all she could think about was the fact that every screaming muscle in her over-stretched body was begging her to collapse on the floor and pass out.

'Actually,' she managed to gasp, 'I think I'll just ring for a taxi and go straight home.'

'Straight home, on your first day? No chance,' retorted Vernon. 'No, you don't get away that easily, I'm buying you a drink.'

'Oh. Oh all right then. But just the one.'

He beamed and clapped her on the back with a firmness that made her howl inwardly. 'Know something?
You may be small but you can't half shovel shit.'

'Er . . . thanks.' It was the oddest compliment Cally
had received since the day a hill-farmer had praised the
shape of her withers; but it was a compliment, nonethe-
less, and she couldn't help feeling a little gratified. If
you had to shovel elephant shit, you might as well be
good at it.

'Come on,' urged Vernon. 'I'll introduce you to the
gang.'

A middle-aged man at a table by the bar was dis-
coursing in a loud voice to a gaggle of colleagues.
''Course, everybody goes on about your lion dung, but
what you really wants is your rhino . . .'

'What about leopard?' enquired a voice to his left,
which belonged to an older man with tattoos on his
arms and several missing fingers. 'I knew this man,
used to swear by leopard.'

'Nah, rhino, that's what you want. Nothing like it for
yer herbaceous borders.'

'See him?' Vernon nodded towards the dung expert.
'That's Derek. Mind you, everybody calls him Winnie.'

'Why's that then?'

'Because there's nothing he doesn't know about poo.
There's nothing that man can't tell you about dung, he's
a real connoisseur. In fact he's in charge of selling off
our surplus to local gardeners.' He produced a ten-
pound note from his back pocket. 'What can I get you?
Pint of best?'

Before Cally had a chance to say that actually she'd
rather have a nice white wine spritzer, a pint glass of
something highly biological landed on the bar-top in
front of her. 'Er . . . What's that floating in it?'

Vernon took a long swig of his pint, then peered into it. 'Ah, this is the real stuff, the landlord has his own micro-brewery. They sling a dead rabbit in before the final fermentation, you know; gives it body.'

'A dead . . .?'

'Now, the one with the mangled fingers,' Vernon went on, 'that's Len. Bit of a character is Len, used to be a lion tamer before he saw the light.' He raised his glass in a toast. 'Could tell a few stories, couldn't you, Len?'

'Couldn't I what?' inquired Len suspiciously.

'Tell Cally here a few stories about lion taming.'

'Aye, plenty. Mind you, I wasnae much good at it.'

'Is that how you lost your fingers?' enquired Cally.

'What? Och no, that happened when I got ma hand stuck in the wife's food processor.'

'Bit accident-prone is Len,' explained Vernon.

'It was ma foot the lion chewed off.' Len waggled the right one under Cally's nose. 'You'd never know that was fibreglass, now would you?'

Cally had to admit that you wouldn't. As Vernon introduced her to the other keepers in turn, it occurred to her that she wasn't going to have much difficulty remembering who they all were; they were the oddest group of individuals she'd ever met. There was Oona, the trainee vet from South Africa who was taking a year out at the Experience to try and cure her fear of anything with more than four legs; Billy, the ex-convict with the reptile obsession; and Algernon, who had once lectured in philosophy and now spent his time chopping up mangoes for the fruit bats. Last but not least, there was an immense wobbly jelly of a man with a shock of red hair and a copy of the *Sporting Life* sticking out of his back pocket.

'That there's Bob,' said Len, chewing dry-roasted peanuts. 'Lazy Bob we call him.'

Lazy Bob scowled. 'I ain't lazy, it's a damn lie.'

'So how come you're always in the bog whenever anything wants doing?'

The scowl deepened. 'No I ain't.'

'Yeah,' chipped in Billy, 'and how come his tea break always lasts till lunchtime?'

'I suppose Vernon's told you how he got his name?' enquired Oona with a wink.

'No, how?' asked Cally. Everybody laughed.

'Go on Vern, tell her.'

Vernon pulled a face. 'Oh all right. Because I was conceived on the night my mum and dad won the Pools.'

Winnie chuckled. 'Just thank your lucky stars it wasn't Littlewood's,' he commented, downing his third lager. 'Introduced her to lover-boy, have you?' he enquired, jerking his head towards the bar.

Cally followed the direction of his nod. A youngish man was propping up the bar, his back to her, a row of empty glasses lined up on either side of him. 'Lover-boy?'

Vernon chuckled. 'You'll like him, he's on the run from his dad's duvet business. Bit of a ladies' man though, you want to watch yourself with him.' He nudged Cally in the ribs, and she winced. 'Hey, Will. Have you met our new girl?'

The figure at the bar straightened, turned and did a double-take. But nobody was more surprised than Cally.

It was Will Inglis.

Chapter Eleven

'Hello Will,' said Cally. 'Fancy seeing you here.'

A small muscle twitched in Will's cheek. 'Er . . . Hi,' he said, downing the last of his beer in one gulp. 'Good God, is it that time already?' he added, without so much as a glance at his watch. 'Sorry folks, can't stick around and chat, you know how it is.'

Cally had seldom seen anybody move so fast since her father had asked for volunteers to test a new lentil-based laxative. She gazed after Will in complete bafflement as the door shuddered back into its frame. 'Was it something I said?'

'Blimey,' said Len. 'And it wasn't even his round.'

Vernon clapped Cally on the back. 'Oh, Will's just like that sometimes. Bit of a man of mystery is our Mr Inglis. I expect he just spotted somebody he didn't want to run into.'

Yeah, me, thought Cally, wondering if she ought to change her deodorant. 'Such as?' she asked.

'Oh, I don't know,' hedged Oona. 'Somebody's husband, probably.'

'Talk about putting it about,' agreed Len. He leaned over and nudged Winnie. 'Was it you told me he had those two lassies on the go at the same time?'

Winnie laughed. 'It wasn't two, it was three. And

none of them ever found out about the others. You've got to hand it to Will, he's a smooth operator.'

Vernon tore open a bag of crisps and offered one to Oona. 'Don't suppose he's ever tried it on with you?'

Oona's ice-blue eyes glinted beneath her sun-streaked fringe. 'He's got more sense.'

'You mean he disnae fancy you,' retorted Len. 'Likes 'em with a bit more to hold on to if you know what I mean.'

A bit more to hold on to? Ugh, thought Cally, breathing in. She wondered why, despite his peculiar reaction and his apparently dodgy reputation, Will Inglis continued to exert a strange fascination over her. Was it the enigmatic blue eyes? The way his dark hair flopped lazily over one side of his face? The slight sardonic twist to that strong, full mouth? Or was it just the way his slender body filled those uniform trousers? Even the most objective observer would have noted that Will Inglis had a very nice bum.

'So,' said Vernon, munching crisps, 'you've met Will before then?'

'Only a couple of times,' replied Cally, suddenly self-conscious. 'He deals in collectables and memorabilia. In fact I thought that was what he did for a living.'

'What sort of collectables?' demanded Len. 'Antiques, you mean?'

'No, nothing like that. Old records, toys, Star Wars figures . . .'

'Ah.' Len nodded sagely. 'You mean crap.'

'Well, well, well,' said Vernon. 'So that's what he's been up to. Crafty devil.'

'Crafty?'

'Our friend Mr Inglis has been taking "worthless tat" off our hands for years. Worthless tat my backside, I bet he's been making a fortune out of us.' A slow smile spread across Vernon's face, and he raised his glass in an ironic toast. 'Here's to you, Will Inglis. You bastard.'

'Eddie . . .' said Cally at breakfast the next morning.

Eddie mumbled into his Coco Pops but didn't look up from *The Castle of Otranto*. 'Huh?'

'Eddie, you've got a black eye!'

This time he did raise his head from the page, revealing the sort of effect often achieved at parties with the aid of some black ink and a joke telescope. 'No! You don't say.'

He went back to reading and munching.

Cally tilted her head to one side, to get a better view. 'Eddie.'

'What now?'

'Does it hurt?'

'Yes thanks.'

She paused to empty another helping of cereal into her bowl. Ever since she'd started work at The Animal Experience, she seemed to be permanently ravenous.

'How did you get it?' She giggled. 'True love ways?'

Eddie sighed and closed his gothic classic with an irritable snap. 'No, flatmate's interior design.'

'Pardon?'

'Cally, what on earth were you thinking of, moving everything around like that?'

She shrugged winsomely. 'Oh you know, it just seemed to make better sense that way.'

'Terrific. Well just warn me next time, will you? Then maybe I won't walk straight into a hatstand that isn't supposed to be there.'

'Sorry. We haven't got any steak,' she added, 'but there's probably a couple of Quorn fillets in the fridge.'

133

'I think I'll just enjoy looking like the victim of a pub brawl, thanks.'

Cally wriggled on her chair, itching to be on the move and doing things. She hadn't felt this lively in ages. 'You're up nice and early,' she commented.

'Yes, well I would be, wouldn't I?' glared Eddie. 'Seeing as certain people programmed their radio alarms to go off at quarter past six.' Cally opened her mouth to defend herself. 'And before you say a word, it's bloody impossible to sleep through Tina Turner, even with two pillows wrapped round your head.'

'Sorry.' She swung her feet like a bored child, listening to the sound of Eddie crunching Coco Pops. 'Nice day though, isn't it?'

Eddie glanced out of the window at the roundabout below, where a mud-spattered milk float was aquaplaning through a stagnant puddle. 'Pure poetry darling.' He took a swig of orange juice. 'You're a happy little soul, aren't you?'

'There's no need to make it sound like an accusation,' retorted Cally, slightly hurt. 'I mean, what's wrong with being happy?'

'Nothing. Only a couple of weeks ago you were all for stuffing your head in the microwave. I can't keep up with you and your moods.'

Cally tapped her fingers on the table-top. Eddie was right, she was happy; or at least, she definitely wasn't unhappy, which was a big advance on suicidal.

'So what's got into you?' demanded Eddie. 'Spring fever?'

'Oh, you know. I expect it's working out of doors, getting all that sunshine, healthy exercise . . .'

'And lots and lots of lovely shit,' added Eddie.

Cally gave her hand a sniff. 'Oh, sorry, thought I'd

washed it all off. You know, it's funny but you sort of get used to it after a while.'

'I'm not sure I want to, thank you very much,' said Will.

'Oh – and there's something else,' Cally went on. 'A mystery!'

Eddie started to look vaguely interested. He liked mysteries, preferably ones with vampires, semi-clad virgins in distress and ruined castles, but at a pinch any mystery would do. 'Oh yes?'

'You know Will? Will Inglis?'

'What – that idiot with the satchel full of gonks?'

'The very same. But he's not an idiot. And guess what? He works at the zoo!'

Cally knew she'd scored a direct hit with that one, because Eddie's spoon sagged so low that his frilly shirt-cuff dangled in the milk. 'What! I mean, we are talking about the same Will Inglis?'

'Oh yes. Apparently he's very good with penguins.' And one or two other things, thought Cally ruefully, remembering what the other keepers had said about Will's amorous reputation.

'Well, well, well,' said Eddie, his face acquiring a smug smirk. 'Won't that be nice for you.'

Cally took a sudden interest in picking the raisins out of her muesli. 'I don't know what you mean.'

'Yes you do, you fancy him something rotten!'

To cover her embarrassment, she flicked a wet raisin down the open neck of his shirt. 'Oh . . . behave!'

But in her heart, she knew he was right.

In all probability, it would have been very nice indeed, working closely with Will at the Experience. Without ever really admitting to herself that she fancied him,

Cally had secretly rehearsed all their little encounters in her mind; that casual touch of fingers over the pig-bins, the amorous squeak of their wellies rubbing together as they hauled a sack of dead mackerel to the penguin pool. It was only a matter of time.

But it didn't happen quite like that. In fact, Will proved to be remarkably elusive, and in the next few days the only time she actually set eyes on him he was a speck in the distance and she was perched on the top of a scaffolding tower, hanging up mangoes for the fruit bats.

Cally found herself spending most of her working hours with the mighty and authoritative Vernon. Although he was several years younger than Cally, there seemed to be virtually nothing he did not know about anything. This was quite disconcerting for Cally, who had grown accustomed to bosses who were older, uglier and distinctly stupider than herself. It was also completely exhausting; for Vernon's brief was a roving one, and he never seemed to be in one place for more than a couple of hours at a time.

Still, it was a good way to get to know the Experience, and she was starting to get the hang of its layout. Little by little she'd been introduced to just about everything from the fire ants to the photophobic chameleon. Well, everything except Colin the Javan Yellow Skunk – and from the smell of Vernon, she'd no desire to go anywhere near him.

From the top of her stepladder, Cally could see the distant grassy slopes of Donkey Heights, the pink, moving blob that marked the flamingo enclosure, the large, lumbering shapes of three old circus elephants, walking trunk to tail behind their keeper along the central driveway that ran through the middle of the park.

'Bit more to the left,' instructed Vernon from the ground. 'You've missed a patch of mud.'

She paused and swung round gingerly to look down. 'I was just getting to that bit. But she seems to like it if I go slowly, don't you girl? It's more gentle.'

The giraffe did not come up with any intelligible reply, but from the contented way it was chewing it didn't seem to have any objections to having its neck brushed.

'Ah yes, but the trick is doing it gently and quickly,' replied Vernon. 'You've got three more giraffes and an okapi to do when you've done Dilys, and don't forget we're sorting out the llamas' backsides this afternoon.'

'You make it sound so inviting.'

It was just as she was scanning the horizon for any sign of Will that she spotted a familiar figure, striding up the driveway towards the office. A blonde-haired figure in a red tailored suit, like Father Christmas's foxier sister.

Oh shit. Christina Shaw. That could only mean one of two things: either somebody had complained about her . . . or the agency was going to rotate her again. And whichever it was, Cally had a sudden desire not to be around long enough to find out.

With a hurried apology to Vern, she was down the ladder, across the yard and inside the Twilight Kingdom within thirty seconds. And it was only then, sitting in the darkness with several dozen vampire bats between her and Christina Shaw, that Cally paused to ask herself why.

Cally smiled at Henry. Henry looked at Cally with the utmost suspicion.

'Oh come on,' she coaxed, an infuriated whine

137

starting to enter her voice. 'Give it here, there's a good chap.'

She took a step forward, and the sea lion shuffled back along the decking, the pot of sunscreen balanced defiantly on the tip of his nose. Several dozen mothers with toddlers in buggies giggled and pointed through the wire.

'Oh bollocks,' groaned Cally. 'This is harder than it looks. Can't we just leave him be?'

Vernon shook his head gravely. ''Fraid not. Henry needs his sunscreen, you know that. With his problem he doesn't keep his skin moist; and the more sun he gets, the more it dries out.'

'I know, but . . .'

'But nothing. You wouldn't want him getting cracked skin, now would you?'

Cally and the sea lion eyed each other, each weighing up the possibilities of the situation. 'Does he do this a lot?'

'Only when he thinks he can get away with it.'

'Oh great, so I'm a soft touch.'

'Definitely. Discipline, that's what that sea lion needs,' grinned Vernon. 'Don't you, Henry?'

'OK, so tell me how you discipline a sea lion.'

'Sorry. You're going to have to work this one out for yourself.'

Cally scratched her head. 'What about if you grab him and I grab the sunscreen?'

'No use, he's too strong. What you've got to do is make him give you the sunscreen. Remember, he's a trained circus animal, he's expecting you to tell him what to do.'

'That's what I'm doing!'

'Not in any way he can understand. Look, why don't you . . .'

'Vern!' called a voice through the side netting. It was the girl from the office.

'Oh damn, hang on a minute. Don't do anything till I get back. What is it, Jen?'

'Phone call. Some woman called Shaw?'

'Oh, that'll be for Cally. Cally?'

But when Vernon turned round, she was nowhere to be seen.

By the end of the week, Cally felt she was really getting into her stride. She'd never in her life imagined that getting filthy could be such fun. OK, she was totally knackered, but how many people could say they'd helped to clean a hippopotamus's back teeth? It might not cut much ice in the world of financial services, but at least it would look interesting on her CV. And pretty soon, when Vernon had finished with the introductory stuff, they were bound to move her on to the real management training. Hey, if she stuck around here, in a few months' time she could be Henk Thorfinn's right-hand woman.

She was humming to herself as she sat outside the aviary, scrubbing perches from the parrot house, when a tiny, red-haired girl with freckles the size of Smarties came skipping up.

'Mith,' she lisped through the gap where her front teeth ought to be.

'What is it?' Cally rubbed her itchy nose with the sleeve of her zebra-print sweatshirt. 'Are you lost?'

The small child shook her head. 'No, mith. Mith . . .'

'What?'

'Come with me, mith.'

Cally looked up, puzzled. 'Where? Why – what's happened?'

'Pleath.' She tugged at Cally's sleeve. 'Pleath, pleath, pleath!'

'But . . .' Cally looked about for other keepers, but there was no one in sight except the man who emptied the bins, and he ate children for breakfast. 'Oh all right, you'd better show me.'

Reluctantly, and wondering what on earth she was letting herself in for, Cally followed the little girl round the corner of the reptile house. It could be anything, from an urgent need for the toilet to fourteen escaped tigers.

In fact, it was worse than either. For there, in the sunny courtyard by the animal kitchens, sat a woman in a red suit.

Oh arse, thought Cally.

'Hello Calliope,' smiled Christina Shaw. 'Flushed you out, did she?'

'You little . . .' Cally turned and stuck her tongue out at the small girl, who reciprocated and ran off in a flurry of giggles and pink hair ribbon.

'My niece,' explained Ms Shaw.

'That figures,' said Cally, sitting down on the wall next to her. 'So – you wanted to see me then?'

'What on earth makes you think that? Could it be the fifteen separate messages I've left for you in the last few days?'

Cally contemplated the toes of her wellies in a rather immature manner. 'Messages?'

'Don't come the innocent with me, Calliope, you've been avoiding me.' The kitchen porter's white Persian waddled up, weighed up the available sleeping options and jumped heftily into the recruitment consultant's lap, lending her the perfect appearance of a Bond villain. 'This is only supposed to be a short-term placement, you do realise that?'

Cally nodded glumly.

'And you're due to be rotated any day now.' Ms Shaw stroked the fat Persian, and Cally noted with satisfaction that it had coated her red sleeve with a liberal application of white hair. 'Do I get the impression you're not terribly keen on being rotated?'

Cally stirred up the gravel with her toe. 'That depends. Where would I be going next?'

'A biscuit factory.'

'No thanks, I'd rather stay here.'

'Hmm. Actually, it's not that uncommon.'

'What isn't?'

'Trainees becoming attached to a particular firm or organisation, and wanting to stay on. In a way it's rather flattering – shows we've made good choices.' Christina tickled the cat under its chin and it started to purr appreciatively. 'You know, you could have come and told me this, instead of skulking around trying to avoid me.'

'Yes, yes, I know. But it wouldn't have done any good, would it?'

Christina raised an eyebrow. 'Wouldn't it?'

Cally looked at her in surprise. 'You mean there's a chance I *could* stay on here?'

The agency boss put up her hand. 'I didn't actually say that. And I'm not making any promises. But if you really want me to, I'll see what I can do.'

Chapter Twelve

The trouble with bottom-of-the-range, pre-pay mobile phones was that they seemed to be forever running out of power. Still, thought Cally as she plugged hers into the battery charger, at least she was back in the civilised world. No more tramping through the rain looking for an unvandalised phone box because Eddie had forgotten to post the cheque to BT; no more getting home in the evening to find she'd missed out on another job interview.

Not that there had been that many interviews, or that many jobs for that matter. Banks were closing branches all over the place and shedding staff right, left and centre. She might as well have applied to be an astronaut, she had just as much chance of being taken on. And at least you didn't have to wear a scratchy blue suit while you were orbiting Mars in a dustbin.

Exhausted after a hard day mopping up after the gibbons, Cally threw herself bum-first into the one and only comfy chair in Eddie's flat, the one with 'NHS Property' stamped across the back. She stank like something recently exhumed, but her bath would have to wait. Right now, all she wanted to do was sleep.

The first two bars of the *William Tell Overture* startled Cally out of a reverie in which she was floating through the Milky Way, dressed in an A-line skirt and a space helmet. Blearily, she forced her eyes open and glanced at the phone recharging on top of a pile of empty branflake boxes. A little picture of a singing envelope flashed back at her.

Voicemail; after sweet FA for days she'd finally got voicemail. Bugger, she thought, wishing she'd recharged the phone sooner; bet it's an interview and it was yesterday. Either that or it's Dad, wanting to know why I haven't got him that lion dung for the allotment.

She dialled up her mailbox and listened to the electronic voice. 'You have one new message, recorded at 13.55 hours today.'

A different voice kicked in, a human one this time. 'Hi Cally, it's me.'

Cally's stomach flipped over like a leaden pancake. Rob. She didn't know why the sound of his voice came as such a surprise; after all, he was still her husband, even if she had been trying to shove that uncomfortable thought to the back of her mind these past few weeks. But it sounded so strange and alien; like a voice at a seance, floating in from another world that didn't really exist any more, which perhaps had never existed at all.

'Got your number from your mother. Just to let you know I've found a tenant, she's called ... erm ... Selena.'

Cally's guts tensed.

'. . . I'm sure you'd like her . . .'

Cally hated her already.

'Anyhow, she ... er ... moved in a few days ago. Call you soon. 'Bye.'

'End of message.'

Cally sat in silence for a little while, breathing a little more quickly than she ought to have been, telling herself this was only to be expected, and trying to make out how she felt.

At last she decided. Relieved, that's how she felt. Now all she had to do was convince herself it was true.

Whatever Cally had been expecting, it certainly wasn't this. All in all, this was turning out to be a week positively packed with little surprises.

'Oh,' she said, when Vern told her.

'What's the problem?' he demanded, helping himself to a carrot from the bucket swinging at his hip. 'I thought you wanted to stay here.'

'I do.' She followed him past the fingerpost that pointed to the 'Children's Fun Farm and Nature Trail'.

'So what's up?'

'So . . . nothing's up. I'm pleased, honest.'

'Quite right too, some people'd give their right arms to spend all day wading around in poop.'

They climbed the path that wound up towards the paddocks, passing the garish assemblage of concrete toadstools and gnomes that marked the entrance to the children's nature trail. How could she tell Vernon that she was disappointed? After all, Christina Shaw had been as good as her word; she'd waved that magic handbag of hers, and sure enough, Cally's wish had come true: she'd been offered the chance to stay on in this pixie land of lions and tigers and overstuffed wallabies.

Only trouble was, she'd been fully expecting to get her very own hippo or leopard or failing that, at the very least a nice rainbow-coloured lizard to look after. And what had they landed her with instead? This.

'Here we are then,' said Vernon, rubbing his hands together with characteristic enthusiasm. 'Donkey

145

Heights. This here's Eric. He'll show you the ropes, won't you Eric?'

Cally eyed Eric dubiously. Thin and pimply with a chunk missing from his right ear, he looked like the sort of youth who would fail to recognise a rope even if it wrapped itself round his over-long neck and garotted him. She stuck out a hand.

'Hi Eric.'

Eric's neck flamed crimson, highlighting the pus-filled carbuncle under his mutilated ear. 'Hi,' he grunted, staring fixedly at the contents of Cally's well-filled stripy T-shirt.

'And that there is Josiah, and this is . . .'

A surly-looking woman the general colour and shape of a sandwich loaf crushed Cally's hand in a vice-like grip. 'Donna Bracewell. You're a girl,' she commented accusingly.

'Er . . . yes.'

'You were supposed to be a bloke.'

'Yes, well, plans change,' said Vernon briskly. 'We all have to be adaptable, don't we? And Cally's joining you for her trial period, so I'm expecting you all to help her find her feet. Now Cally, this here is—'

'Hello Bob,' said Cally.

Lazy Bob eyed her with supercilious contempt. 'You'll not last five seconds here,' he said confidently. 'Turn your back for one moment and they'll have you.'

'What? Donkeys?'

'You'll be replacing Bob,' Vernon went on. 'He's moving on to a different part of the Experience.'

'I am that. After I've had me tea break.' Lazy Bob picked up his jacket, stuffed his racing paper in the pocket and rolled off over the turf, turning to launch a final riposte. 'Won't last five minutes, any of you.'

146

'Oh, I think we'll manage,' laughed Josiah.

'No chance,' he retorted. 'Not without me here to carry you.' And with that, Lazy Bob disappeared.

'Right,' said Vernon. 'This is where you'll be working, alongside the donkeys.'

Cally's gaze drifted towards the line of interested-looking donkeys, nodding their woolly heads over the paddock fence. One or two of them she recognised from the time she'd visited with Eddie and Liddy. Well, they might not offer the danger-packed thrill of a hungry leopard, but at least they were cute and cuddly.

'So, where do I start?'

'Well,' said Vernon, 'so far you've only been working under close supervision, and Mr Thorfinn and I thought it was time we gave you a bit of responsibility.'

Cally's ears pricked up. Aha, responsibility at last! They'd finally spotted her management potential. Donkey Heights or not, maybe this could still turn out to be a good career move. 'What sort of responsibility?'

'Eric,' said Vernon, 'where is he?'

'Locked in his shed, out of trouble.'

'You mean you're giving me responsibility for a donkey?'

'That's right.'

Disappointment stung. 'What – just the one?'

Eric laughed. 'Reckon you'll have enough on your plate with one.' He jerked a thumb towards the line of stable doors, their top halves hanging open. 'There he is.'

'Where?' Cally peered but saw nothing.

'There – fourth stall on the right.'

Something twitched behind the stable door, and Cally caught sight of the ends of two long, black, fluff-tipped ears. Ah, she thought, how sweet. 'Is it a foal?'

This time everybody laughed, including Vernon. 'My

God no,' shuddered Josiah. 'That bloody thing wasn't born, it was bloody conjured up.'

'But . . . but I don't understand,' puzzled Cally.

'You will.'

Eric opened the door, and the smallest adult donkey Cally had ever seen sauntered out, casually manuring the toes of her wellies as it went. Its coat was the colour of pitch; in fact everything about it was black except for its eyes, which were rimmed with red, giving them the unsettling appearance of two burning coals in a spoil-heap, and a splodge of white on its muzzle.

'Stan!' exclaimed Cally, instantly recognising the adorable little black donkey she had stroked on her very first visit to the Experience.

Sure enough, a little nameplate around the donkey's neck read STAN; however someone with a dark sense of humour had chalked an extra A between the S and the T.

The beast and the rookie keeper eyed each other up, each weighing up the possibilities.

'There you go,' said Eric, handing Cally the halter-rope. 'He's all yours.'

'But what do I . . .?'

Vernon turned away. 'Right, this is where I love you and leave you. Coming down to the Stores, Eric? I could use a hand with those crates of bananas.'

'Right you are Mr Vernon.'

Eric followed Vernon out through the gate. Donna went back to forking hay over the fence into the paddock. Josiah whistled a funeral march as he set about scraping down the yard.

And Stan the donkey just grinned.

'Look Eddie,' said Cally, her mood rapidly winding up to a fever pitch of exasperation, 'I need this space!'

'So do I,' countered Eddie.

'No you don't!'

'Yes I do!'

Cally changed tack. 'All right then, what do you need it for?'

Eddie's mouth flapped slackly as he struggled to find a reason why Cally couldn't take over half the living room with her stuff. 'It's got my favourite chair in it.'

'Then move it.'

'And my easel.' He put a protective arm round the paint-spattered sheet that covered it.

'So? Move that as well.'

'I don't want to move it, I like the light here. It's good for painting.'

'Oh come on Eddie, you haven't painted anything for ages, you're just making excuses.'

Eddie whimpered. 'It's not fair, I was here first!'

Cally let out an exasperated sigh. 'Oh, so that's the bottom line, is it? It's OK for me to pay you rent, but this is your territory and you're buggered if anybody else is getting their hands on it.'

'Cal, I never said . . .'

'You didn't have to, it's written all over your face.' Cally squatted malevolently on the windowsill, feeling every rumble of the traffic below through the seat of her aching bottom. 'For God's sake Eddie, anybody'd think I was trying to turn you out of house and home. All I want is a few square feet to put my desk in. You know I have to do this management correspondence course, otherwise they won't keep me on at the Experience.'

'Why can't you work in your bedroom?'

'Where in my bedroom? Hanging from the ceiling with a pen between my teeth? Eddie, I have to breathe in if I open the sodding wardrobe door!'

149

'All right then, work in the kitchen.'

'On two foot six of gravy-stained work surface? Eddie,' snarled Cally, 'are you going to move that bloody chair of yours or not?'

Eddie folded his arms and stared her out. 'Not.'

'Right. I guess that's that then.' Cally gathered up her books and folders and headed off towards her bedroom.

Eddie caught up with her and followed her inside. 'What's what then?'

Cally grabbed her suitcase from the top of the wardrobe and flung it on to the bed. 'Go away Eddie.'

'What are you doing with that suitcase?'

'What does it look like?'

'Packing.'

'Then I must be packing. Get out of the way, Ed, I need those T-shirts.'

'Why are you packing?'

Cally threw the T-shirts into the case. 'Because I'm moving out.'

'What!' Eddie's face registered utter dismay.

'I'm going back to live with my mum.'

'But . . . but you can't!'

'Really?' Cally stuffed rolled-up socks into a pair of shoes and jammed them into the corners of the case. 'Why's that then?'

Eddie boinged down on to the elderly bedprings, seized her hand and kissed it. 'Because, my lady, Sir Eddie de Priest will not allow the Lady Calliope's delicate digestion to be martyred unto her cruel sire's plans for world flatulence.'

Cally relented at the look of earnest pleading on Eddie's face, and flopped down on the bed beside him. 'You're an old ham, Eddie.'

'Oink.' He squashed his nose into a snout with his index finger. 'Does this mean you're staying?'

'Not unless you start being reasonable.'

Eddie sighed. 'About moving my stuff so you can study, you mean?'

'Exactly.'

'Oh all right,' he capitulated. 'I'll move my easel. The thing is . . . I didn't want to tell you, only while you've been at work I've been painting something.'

'What – a pub sign?'

'No, a picture. For you.' He hung his head. 'I wanted it to be a surprise.'

'Oh, Eddie!' She flung her arms round his neck and kissed him noisily on the nose. 'You're a big old softie. Can I see it?'

Eddie blushed. 'Hang on a minute, listen – I'm drawing a line on the floor, and if your stuff creeps over it it's going straight in the bin, OK?'

'OK.' Cally bounced to her feet. 'Now can I see it?'

'Oh all right then.' Eddie turned the easel round and whisked off the old sheet he had hung over it. 'But don't laugh.'

'It's . . . it's a skunk!' squeaked Cally.

Eddie looked amazed. 'You mean you can actually tell what it is?'

'Oh yes.'

'And you like it?'

Cally grinned. 'Like it? Eddie darling, I love it!'

Cally peeked round the edge of the pig-bin, tracking her quarry like a big-game hunter. It was only a couple of yards away. Every muscle in her aching body tensed up as she got ready to spring. She was convinced that if she timed this one mighty leap just right, she would catch him. Wait . . . wait . . . wait . . . Now!

She sprang. And Stan slipped through her fingers like a greased eel, leaving Cally sliding along in the dust on her belly, to a round of applause from the watching punters.

'Go girl! Go get him!'

'Gee up, little horsey, she's on your tail!'

Cally skewed round and came to rest against the wall of the penguin pool. Pawing the ground some five yards away, Stan drew his lips back over yellow teeth and hee-hawed his amusement.

'Don't you hee-haw me, you furry little bastard,' muttered Cally, hauling herself to her feet and picking gravel out of her grazed knees. Stan watched her with glee, waited just long enough for her to pull herself upright, then kicked up his hooves and legged it at top speed across the ornamental rose garden.

'Will!' yelled Cally, as Stan raced past Will's back.

Despite her best efforts, Will kept tramping towards the penguin pool with his buckets of fish, apparently lost in a world of his own.

'Will!' gasped Cally helplessly out of breath. 'For crying out loud Will, are you bloody deaf?'

But Will must have been, because he still didn't seem to hear. And so Cally went scrambling off in hopeless pursuit of the runaway donkey, thinking unspeakable thoughts about men in general, and Will Inglis in particular.

Chapter Thirteen

The Whelk and Whippet was one of Cheltenham's newest and trendiest venues: a *nouveau-pauvre* café-bar that combined East End cuisine, live dog racing and sepia photographs of people with no teeth. It also did a passable tequila slammer, though the purists wouldn't touch anything but a pint of something tepid in a straight glass.

Cally wasn't sure how it had managed to become her and Eddie's 'local'. The prices were sky-high, the clientele was more bozo than boho, and neither of them could stand the sight of jellied eels. Nevertheless, they had regularly gravitated towards it over the past few weeks, so it must have something. Certainly it was the only bar Cally had ever been in where the cocktails came garnished with a whelk on a stick.

'Maybe we should try somewhere different tonight?' she suggested as they walked along the Promenade.

'Nah.' Eddie ruffled up his cravat as he glanced at himself in a shop window. 'I mean, why quit when I'm winning?'

'Winning what?'

Eddie threw her a lock of strained patience, more suited to a toddler with potty-training problems. 'My battle of attrition, what do you think? There are some absolutely *gorgeous* young ladies in that bar, my girl, and unless I'm *very* much mistaken, one of them has got my name written on her.'

'What – like, tattoed on her scalp or something? Six-six-six, the number of the Beast? Or should that be nine-nine-nine, the number of the Vice Squad?'

'Thou art a cynical and ungracious floozy, Mademoiselle Storm.'

'At least I'm not the object of your amorous attentions, I suppose that's one thing to be thankful for.'

'You'll be laughing on the other side of your face when I've found true love,' sniffed Eddie, flouncing past the bouncers outside the Whelk and Whippet.

'Eddie darling, I'll be drawing my pension.'

Swatting each other like squabbling schoolkids, they tumbled into the bar. Conversation halted for a millisecond, then a ripple of applause ran through the crowd round the TV screen as a dog in a gold lamé jacket romped home behind a lump of bedraggled fun fur.

Snatches of loud conversation filled the gaps in *Chas 'n' Dave's East End Party*.

'What did I tell ya?'

'Fourteen to one? Daylight bloody robbery.'

'Hand it over, that's twenty you owe me.'

A wallet appeared, accompanied by raucous cheering. 'Go on then, take yer pound of flesh.'

Cally hitched herself up on to a bar stool. The Australian barman grinned. 'Got some great eels on the menu tonight.'

'No thanks.'

'They're not chewy, not like that last lot.'

'Just a vodka and Red Bull and – what are you having, Ed, or are you already high on luuuurve?'

'What?' Eddie left off ogling a dark-haired Andrea

Corr lookalike, and dragged his attention back to Cally. 'Half of lager . . . no, second thoughts, make that something long and cool and sophisticated.'

'Tizer it is then,' said Cally drily.

'Don't you bloody dare. I'll have a . . . a . . . what's that thing James Bond always has?'

'Sex with large-breasted sheilas in swimsuits?' hazarded the barman, his grin widening.

'A dry Martini. That'll do. She'll be putty in my hands when she's seen me nibbling my maraschino cherry.'

Four dry Martinis later, the dark-haired girl had still not caved in to Eddie's irresistible charms.

'She's weakening,' he said, brushing crisp crumbs off his wide-lapelled velvet jacket.

'Eddie, she's snogging that man in the rugby shirt! If she gets any further down his throat, she'll be coming out of his arse.'

'She's only doing it to make me jealous. Right.' Eddie slid off his bar stool, causing his flares to ride up and expose several inches of pallid ankle. 'I'm going over there to chat her up.' He took a step forward, swayed a little and shook his head. 'No I'm not, I'm going for a pee. Where is it?'

Cally seized him gently by the shoulders and rotated him one hundred and eighty degrees. 'Ten paces forward and follow the smell. And mind the—'

'Ow.'

'Step.'

She swivelled back to the bar, where the barman was still washing glasses and grinning.

'Lively crowd in tonight,' commented Cally.

'Hmm?'

'All that cheering and stuff. You know, earlier on.'

'Oh, *that*.' The barman chuckled. 'Ah well, that's 'cause your friend there won somebody a bet, see.'

Cally's brow furrowed. 'A bet? What sort of bet?'

The barman leaned forward, elbows resting on the sticky bar-top. 'A sweepstake. Just a bit of harmless fun for the regulars. See, Joe over there, he reckoned your mate Eddie couldn't keep a girlfriend if she was stapled to his backside. I mean, let's face it, he's a nice enough guy but I've never seen a bloke go through so many women like he does. And the scenes we've had in here . . .'

'Scenes?'

'My God, you wouldn't believe it. Tears, tantrums, stuff flying around the bloody place – and that's just Eddie. First off, we thought it was performance art, then we twigged he just couldn't cut it with the ladies. That's when Sy thought of running a sweepstake on how long his latest girl would last.' He winked. 'Which is where you come in.'

'Hang on a minute,' said Cally. 'Me? Eddie's girl-friend?'

'Yeah, I know. Crazy.' The barman breathed on a glass and started rubbing it vigorously. 'Still, that's love for you.'

'But it's not . . . listen, I am definitely *not* Eddie's girlfriend!'

The barman stopped polishing. 'You're not?'

'Nope.'

'Are you sure?'

'I think I'd have noticed.'

'Aaaaah, shit.' The barman flicked his glass cloth over his shoulder. 'Now I'm going to have to break it to Gav. Everybody thought he was pitching it too high with three weeks.'

When Eddie returned from the toilet, sporting a wet stain down the front of his trousers, he found that Cally had moved her barstool noticeably further away from his.

'It's OK,' he said, hauling himself back on to his own stool at the third attempt. 'It's only water, the taps are a bit vicious.'

'Eddie,' said Cally, 'I don't want you to take this the wrong way, but you are one sad git.'

Eddie's eyebrows lifted and disappeared under his fringe, giving him the air of a startled Afghan hound. 'That's not very nice!'

'It may not be nice, sweetheart, but you and I both know it's true. Life's not a Barbara Cartland novel, you can't go through life proposing marriage to every woman you meet!'

'I don't! Well, not all of them. Besides, I can't help it if women find me irresistibly attractive.'

'Eddie, they're laughing at you. They think you're a complete prat. A saddo with more chance of catching rabies than getting married.'

Eddie pouted. 'You're supposed to be my friend.'

'I *am* your friend. That's why I'm telling you.'

'Well if I'm sad,' retorted Eddie, 'what does that make you?'

Ouch, thought Cally, holed below the waterline.

'Sadder and wiser,' she replied. 'And I'm telling you, young man, if you insist on finding someone to share your lonely duvet, one or two things are going to have to change.'

Who could possibly have imagined that one small donkey could weigh so much?

'Stan . . . Stan, you little ba—' Arms round Stan's

middle, tugging with all her might, Cally caught the eye of a group of small, giggling children, their innocent mouths plastered with chocolate. 'Stan, *please* . . .'

But Stan was having none of it. All four feet firmly planted in the feeding trough, he stood his ground and went on munching.

'Stan. You are being *very* naughty,' she admonished him in her best primary-school teacher voice. Stan eyed Cally briefly, then swished his smelly tail right in her face.

The children giggled and nudged each other. 'Look at the little donkey,' said their mother brightly, pointing happily at Stan's immoveable rump. 'He's a funny little donkey, isn't he?'

'Funny!' echoed the Greek chorus of small children. 'We love Stan, he's so funny!'

Come here and say that, thought Cally, her face contorted into a rictus grin of effort as she dug her heels into the grass and gave one last, herculean tug. Stan shifted briefly, then shook her off with a flick of his back legs and went back to the important business of stealing the other donkeys' food.

Stan should not have been in the feeding trough. In fact, he should not have been in this paddock at all. If Cally had not turned her back for a couple of minutes, to direct a school party to the parrot house, in all probability the equine Houdini would not have had the opportunity to wriggle his wiry little body through the fence and high-tail it to the land of unlimited carrots. She glanced around for help, and saw a mountain of lard undulating its way towards the stable block, no doubt for a crafty fag. By Cally's calculations he shouldn't have been anywhere near Donkey Heights, but there was no one else about so she yelled at him.

'Bob!'

Lazy Bob acknowledged her with a wave. 'What's that?'

'Can you give me a hand?'

He cupped a hand to his ear and adopted a mystified expression. 'Sorry, can't hear you. Can't stop, gotta see a man about a . . . skunk.' And with that, he vanished from sight.

Since there was no sign of Eric, and Donna had spent all morning telling everyone that she'd 'got the painters in' and felt 'like warmed-up shite', it looked as if Cally was going to have to dislodge Stan on her own. And if she didn't do it pretty soon there wasn't going to be much point in bothering, seeing as he'd already munched his way through more pony nuts than any donkey had a right to eat without getting terminal colic.

Cheek wedged against Stan's flank, Cally tried shifting him by pushing him forward. He just gave her a disdainful look and went on eating.

'Fun and games, Cally?' enquired a smooth voice behind her.

'Ha bloody ha,' replied Cally's muffled voice.

Vernon bent over, lifted up one of Stan's long, fuzzy ears, and whispered something into it. Half a second later, as though by the power of turbocharged Epsom Salts, the donkey sprang out of the trough, hurdled the paddock fence and headed straight back to his own shed, ears flat against his scalp.

'Good God,' panted Cally, picking herself out of a mess of donkey droppings and pony nuts, 'how did you do that?'

Vernon looked enigmatic. 'Trade secret. So, how are you getting on?'

Cally smiled weakly, only too aware that Vernon had

caught her at a bad moment. Vernon always seemed to do that. And it really bugged her that he was so young and so damned superior. Worse than that, Donkey Heights was in chaos, the animals were running her ragged and the public seemed to think she had been employed as Stan's straight woman. Perhaps she had.

'Oh, you know, . . .' she replied vaguely.

'Good, good.' Vernon clapped an arm round her shoulders and gave her a squeeze. 'That's the spirit, keep it up. Don't suppose you've seen Lazy Bob anywhere, have you?'

Still breathless, she pointed towards the stables. 'He went thattaway.'

Vernon's face set into an expression of grim determination. 'Right,' he said. 'Well I hope he's got a bloody good excuse, because according to my rota he's supposed to be mucking out Colin.'

And in a moment, before Cally had a chance to beg for a transfer to World of Woodlice, Vernon was off on the warpath.

It wasn't until several minutes later, as she was leaning over the fence giving Stan a piece of her mind, that she spotted Will. He was standing at the bottom of the hill, looking up at her, not moving, not saying anything.

She straightened up, suddenly uncomfortable with the intensity of his gaze. 'Hello Will,' she called out.

But he just turned and walked away, as if she didn't exist.

'You know what you deserve, don't you?' said Cally, leaning over the paddock fence to look her diminutive nemesis in the eye. Stan returned her gaze, nonchalantly chewing on a thistle. 'Don't you?'

The end of the thistle disappeared between Stan's alarming yellow teeth.

'Prunes, that's what you deserve. Two hundred-weight of prunes. It's about time somebody showed you who's boss.'

A few moments later, a heavily accented female voice made her start so suddenly that she hit her knee on the paling. 'I know what you are zinking.'

Rubbing her knee, Cally turned to be confronted by an extremely tall, impressively Gallic-looking woman with a long red ponytail and immaculate white trousers.

'Pardon?' said Cally, wondering why anybody would wear white trousers for a visit to the zoo.

'Zinking.' The Frenchwoman took a step closer, manicured fingernail jabbing at Cally's nose. 'I know your game, young lady.'

'Game? What game?'

'So you will watch your step. *Oui*?'

'I'm sorry, I don't quite . . .'

'*Oui* or *non*?'

'Erm . . . *oui*, I suppose,' replied Cally, turned cross-eyed by the golden fingernail. I . . . er . . . suppose so. Yeah, right.'

'Good. Then all is understood. *Au revoir*.'

The glossy red ponytail receded into the distance, swishing menacingly.

'Bloody hell,' thought Cally out loud.

'Trouble with Simone?' enquired Donna, slopping a pail of disinfectant down the drain.

'Oh, so that's Simone is it?'

'That's her, works in the office. Snotty French bint. Give you a hard time did she?'

'Actually I don't know what she was on about,'

confessed Cally. 'Something about knowing what was in my mind and watching my step.'

'Aaaah,' said Donna knowingly. 'That'd be cause she saw what you was doing with Vernon.'

'What was I doing with Vernon?'

'You know, letting him put his arm round you like that.' She shook her head. 'Oooh, bad move, you want to watch yourself.'

Cally gazed into the distance, at the rapidly diminishing dot that had been Simone. 'Oh. You mean she . . . and Vernon . . .?'

Donna laughed dirtily. 'Only in her dreams so far, but she's got him in her sights and she's not letting anybody else near him, that's for sure.' She looked Cally up and down. 'And definitely not some lumpy English tart with split ends.'

'Hang on,' said Cally, so stunned that she overlooked the insult. 'You're saying she thinks I fancy Vernon?'

'Stands to reason.'

'But . . . but that's ridiculous!' She fumed inwardly, outraged at the very idea. 'Vernon? I mean, *Vernon*!' She looked at Donna and realised she'd said the wrong thing. Round these parts, Vernon was the nearest thing to a household deity. 'I didn't mean . . . I mean, he's a nice enough bloke and all that . . .'

'You've got donkey shit in your hair,' said Donna flatly. 'Serves you bloody well right.'

'Hasn't anyone ever told you?' murmured Eddie, gazing deep into Cally's eyes.

'Told me what?'

He seized her right hand in his. 'That you have the most exquisite hands.'

'I do?' Cally glanced doubtfully at her grime-encrusted fingernails, and the dark-red indentations where Stan had wilfully mistaken her hand for a carrot.

'They're so small and white and soft.' Confident that he was on a winning streak, he laid it on with a trowel. 'A princess's hands.'

It was a hammy chat-up line, but Cally couldn't help being impressed. 'Well, if you say so.'

'Oh I do. Absolutely.' Eddie slid the sleeve of her jumper up her wrist as though it were a velvet stole. 'May I?'

'May you what?'

'Kiss you.'

Before she had time to say 'donkey droppings', Eddie was smothering Cally's work-worn hand in a flurry of moist smooches.

'Er . . . Eddie. Eddie! Just hang on there a minute.'

Eddie paused and looked up. 'What am I doing wrong now?'

Cally withdrew her hand and wiped it on the seat of her trousers. 'You're supposed to be chatting me up, Ed, not eating me alive.'

'I'm not eating you, I'm kissing you.'

'Ditch the saliva, Ed. Saliva just ain't sexy.' Cally took a sip of her drink. 'Go on, try that bit again.'

'Where from?'

'Let's skip the slobbering and cut to the chase. You've got my attention, but I'm playing hard to get. What are you going to say to persuade me you're sex on legs?'

'Tell you you've stolen my heart and I want you to be the mother of my fourteen perfect children?'

'God no! Haven't you listened to a thing I've said?' Eddie looked wounded. 'Start that kind of thing and they'll be out that door faster than snot off a slate.'

Eddie's expression turned to refined distaste. 'Darling, you have such a wonderfully visual turn of phrase.'

'*Darling*, it's called being a realist. Now, try it again, and before you say it, no you can't invite me up to see your etchings.'

'But they're real etchings!'

'I don't care. OK, ready now? And . . . action!'

Eddie cleared his throat and put on his best seduction voice. 'You know, I'd really like to get to know you better. A lot better.'

'That's good!' said Cally approvingly. 'Now you're starting to get the hang of it.'

'I've . . . er . . .' He consulted the notes scrawled in Biro on the back of his hand. '. . . never met anyone like you before.'

'Good, good. And the rest.'

'I was wondering . . . wondering if . . .'

'Yes, go on, go on!'

Suddenly Eddie's jaw went slack, and Cally felt his eyes drift away from her face to stare at something over her left shoulder.

'Eddie.'

He went on staring, his only reaction a small, puppydog whimper.

Cally snapped her fingers in front of his glazed eyeballs. 'Eddie! For crying out loud, you're supposed to be chatting me up!'

Several heads turned in their direction, but all Eddie did was smile stupidly. 'Cally,' he groaned, 'Cally, I think I'm in love.'

Cally turned and followed his gaze across the bar. 'The bottle-blonde with the big chest, or the brunette with the buck teeth?'

Eddie was indignant. 'They're not buck teeth, they're lovely. Just like . . . like . . .'

'Tombstones?'

Eddie glared. 'Like pearls from some Pacific lagoon. And those lips, so full and red. Those eyes . . .'

'Mmm,' nodded Cally. 'I especially like the one in the middle of her forehead.'

'Why do you have to cheapen everything?' sniffed Eddie. 'I'll have you know that girl standing over there is the love of my life.'

''Course she is. Only trouble is, your life's had so many loves it's standing room only. Face it Ed, a girl's only got to look at you once and you're booking the church. Slow it down, take the time to get to know the poor girl. Your trouble is, you treat them all the same, like extras in your private fantasy.'

'No I don't!'

'Oh yes you do. It's like you've got this mental checklist: got the suit, got the cake, got the vicar. Now all I need is somebody to play the bride. Eddie love, when you meet a woman you've got to make her feel special, like . . . like she's the best, no, the *only* sweetie in the whole damn shop.'

A brief, dark thought stole through Cally's mind. A thought about Rob. Had he ever made her feel special like that? Once maybe, a long time ago, when love had been all about cherubs and roses and perfect tomorrows. But that had been on their wedding day, and even then she'd had suspicions about him and the matron of honour.

'So what do I do?' wailed Eddie, showing distinct signs of demoralisation.

Cally spun him round. 'You get out there and you chat that girl up.'

165

'Can I recite her that love poem I wrote?'

'No you can't! And you remember all the things I've told you. Got that?'

'Yes, Mum.'

'One more quip like that, sunbeam, and you'll be singing soprano on your wedding night.'

As Cally watched him launch himself into the heaving throng like a love-missile, she wasn't sure whether to laugh or to cry.

Chapter Fourteen

Liddy found the whole thing quite hilarious.

'You mean you've actually been teaching Eddie how to chat up girls?'

'Well, trying to. It's not been easy.'

'I can imagine.' Liddy sat down at the pub table and pushed another vodka in Cally's direction. 'Here – I should think you need this after giving Eddie lessons in lurve.'

'Tell me about it.' Cally spread herself out on the comfy moquette bench seat, splashed a little tonic into the vodka and took a sip. 'Mind you, he wasn't quite as hopeless as I'd thought he'd be.'

'No?'

'Well, I sent him off to chat up this girl in the Whelk and Whippet, and it took a full ten minutes for her to blow him out. You know, if I persevere with him I think we might just get somewhere in . . . oooh . . . about two hundred years' time.'

'Rather you than me, love.' Liddy picked some food off her plate and tossed it to Stefan, who was salivating noisily under the table. 'Oi, fur-face, eat this and shut up, you'll get us thrown out.'

'Onion bhajis?' said Cally incredulously.

'Oh, he loves them. Mind you, you could float an

airship on what comes out the other end.' Liddy chewed off half a samosa and shared the other half with the dog. 'It's a wonder we ever get any customers in the shop.'

Cally looked up. 'Business not too good?'

Liddy laughed away the question. 'Come on Cal, when did you ever meet a shopkeeper who said trade was booming? Actually,' she went on, 'I was thinking of having a clearout of some of the older stock. There's one or two big collectors' fairs in the offing and I thought I might take a stall.' She smiled winsomely. 'Fancy helping out? Great opportunity to observe lower forms of life in their natural habitat.'

'No thanks. I had enough of that with Rob.'

'Talking of animals,' said Liddy, switching the subject, 'how's work?'

Cally sighed. 'Boring.'

This was clearly not the response Liddy had been expecting. 'You're kidding, right?'

'Nope, it's definitely boring.'

'But – you begged that stroppy blonde woman to let you stay on, I thought you loved it there!' Cally answered with an apathetic shrug. 'So what went wrong?'

'Oh, I don't know, I just don't fit in somehow. And the only animals I get to work with are flaming donkeys. God, I'm getting to hate donkeys.'

'But they're so cute!' protested Liddy. 'They've got lovely kind faces, you said so yourself.'

'Kind!' scoffed Cally. 'You don't know the half of it. All they ever do is eat, shit and play you up. I'm beginning to think I should've gone with the biscuit factory after all. At least I could scoff my weight in Double Custard Crunch.'

Liddy slid over on to the bench seat, next to Cally.

Ever the opportunist, Stefan jumped up on to her abandoned chair and helped himself to the last of the samosas.

'Ah,' said Liddy sagely, 'but if you ate all those biscuits you'd get as fat as Lazy Bob. And if you got fat, the gorgeous Mr Inglis wouldn't fancy you any more, would he?'

'Him!' Cally threw the last of the vodka down her throat, almost vaporising her tonsils. 'That arrogant, sarcastic, supercilious git? What makes you think I'd want him to fancy me?'

'But I thought you couldn't wait to get him round the back of the penguin pool and rip his clothes off.'

'Huh! He should be so lucky.' Cally pinched the very last spinach pakora from under Stefan's outraged nose. 'You know something, since I started work there he must have said all of . . . ooh . . . six whole words to me, and three of those were "'bye". And he's been absolutely no bloody help with the animals at all – every time I've tried to ask him, he does one of his disappearing acts.'

'What – you mean he's avoiding you?' Liddy's nose wrinkled.

'Worse. He acts like I don't even exist. Well, fine. See if I care.' Cally stopped chewing and extracted a dog hair from between her teeth. 'Worst thing of all is . . .' The words dried in her throat, strangled by embarrassment.

'What?'

Cally stared down at her boots. 'Rob's starting to look good.'

Liddy looked aghast. 'Cally, no! You don't mean that.'

'Actually,' confessed Cally ruefully, 'I think I do.'

* * *

169

That evening, the lights burned late at Gold in the Attic.

The evenings were the only time Liddy had to make a real mess in the shop; and if she was going to get her stock sorted out, she was going to have to make some serious mess. Of course, she should really have been doing the accounts and the monthly VAT return, but she thought of the jumble of paperwork on the desk upstairs and groaned inwardly. No, not that. Not yet. Not while there was an excuse to do something else.

'What do you reckon, Stefan?' she demanded, extracting a 1933 *Picturegoer's Annual* from one of the shelves and blowing off the dust. 'In or out?'

The dog waddled up, sniffed the book, turned his back on it and cocked a leg against the wastepaper bin.

'Hmm,' reflected Liddy, 'you could be right. The cover's half off and I don't suppose there's much call for chewed-up photos of Rin Tin Tin. Mind you . . .' Her hand hovered over the discard pile, then returned the book to the stack of better stock. 'Beggars can't be choosers, and there just might be somebody out there who wants it.'

Good-quality film and TV-related stuff, that was what she really needed. Cult stuff, things that people with more money than sense would pay double the value for, just to have them in their collections. *Avengers* annuals, Leonard Nimoy albums, rare *Star Wars* figures . . . Liddy knew that was where the profit lay right now, and profit was definitely uppermost in her mind.

As she sorted through the stock she had already accumulated, she talked things over with Stefan.

'It won't do, you know.'

The dog sat down and scratched its ear with its back leg.

'We can't let her get down again, can we? Not after all the progress she's been making lately.'

Stefan let out a small, guttural sound that might have been a mumble of agreement, or a burp.

'But what can we do with her, eh?' Liddy sneezed as she shifted a pile of Elvis fan club magazines and an ancient Flexidisc fluttered out. 'Whatever are we going to do with Cally?'

Bending down, she peeled the plastic disc carefully off the lino and picked it up.

'Love Me Tender'.

'Hmm.' Liddy sat down on the floor and heaved a protesting Stefan on to her lap. 'Love, eh? D'you reckon that's what she needs? A spot of romance?'

Stefan opened his mouth, letting out a gust of rancid doggy breath, and did something he almost never did. He licked Liddy's face.

'Right,' she smiled, 'you're on. A healthy dose of hearts and flowers it is. The question is, how are we going to arrange it?'

Things weren't getting any better for Cally at The Animal Experience. Frankly, they weren't getting any better elsewhere, either. And Cally was pretty sure she wasn't imagining it. When you had to spend Friday night on your own with Dale Winton and an Everest of ironing, you had a right to feel that your life lacked that certain sparkle.

Eddie was out on the town, putting his love lessons into practice. Cally glanced at the clock. Only nine o'clock, he wouldn't be home with his tail between his legs for at least another couple of hours, maybe three if he could keep off the subject of wedding invitations. She ought by rights to be wishing him success in his frenzied quest for the future Mrs Priest, but secretly she was hoping it all ended in tears by half-past. That way, at least she could look forward to a game of Cluedo before bed.

And that was about all she could look forward to. Her mum and dad were at a Save the Basking Shark meeting, all her job applications were filled out and posted, she'd done all her homework for the management diploma course, and Liddy's phone was permanently engaged. It was as if the entire world had got together to make sure Cally felt lonely and bored and vulnerable.

Her hand hovered over the redial button on the phone; then she thought of the only other person in the world left to talk to.

Rob.

Rob! No, no, no, she wasn't *that* crazy. Why on earth would she want to phone him? Because you used to love him? suggested a treacherous little voice inside her head. Because, no matter what a total and utter shit he is, he might just understand?

Before her rational mind had time to cut in and defuse the thought, she was already dialling the number. It wasn't difficult to remember; after all, a few short months ago it had been her number too. Hell, her name was still on the telephone bills.

A voice answered. 'Rob Monk.'

Her mouth felt suddenly and catastrophically dry. 'It's . . . me.'

She thought she heard a soft intake of breath; then: 'Cally?'

'Yeah.'

'My God, I didn't expect . . . I mean . . . it's been – how long? Three months?'

Three months, four days, sixteen hours and thirty-seven minutes, Cally recited in the silence of her thoughts.

'Near enough. I just thought . . . well, I was just ringing to see how you are really.'

The awkwardness was palpable; the words as jerky as the jumps on a scratched CD.

'I . . . fine, I'm fine. Just fine.'

'That's good.'

'And you?'

'Fine.'

There was a long, long silence, so tense that it felt like a taut length of elastic, stretched almost to the point of breaking and then held there. Please say something, Cally begged silently. Just say something, because I can't bear this and I'm counting, and when I get to ten I'm hanging up.

On the count of nine, Rob broke the silence.

'I was thinking. You know this theme park I've been doing the plants for? B-Movie Heaven?'

'What about it?'

'The owner's pleased with what I've done for him, and he's given me a couple of VIP tickets for the opening. I just wondered . . . would you like to see it? I mean – would you like to go with me?'

The question hung in the space between them like a trapeze-artist in mid-flight.

'I don't know,' said Cally.

'But you might?' There was a note of hope in Rob's voice. She could have slapped him right down again, there and then, but something stopped her.

'I might.' She felt a desperate need to change the subject. To pry into things that maybe, just maybe, she'd rather not know. 'Rob . . .'

173

'Yes?'

'Why don't you take somebody else?'

'I don't want to take somebody else, I want to take you.'

The demon inside her urged her on. 'You could take Selena.'

Rob's reply stuttered straight back. '*S-selena!*'

'That's her name, isn't it? The girl you're living with.'

'Living with? Cally, she's the . . . the . . .'

'The lodger you said.'

'Exactly, the lodger! Why would I want to take her anywhere?'

Why wouldn't you, more like, thought Cally. She's female and she's got a pulse, that's usually enough for you. 'You tell me,' she hedged.

Rob sighed. 'You want to know what she's like?' He licked his lips. 'OK, I'll tell you. She likes the occasional drink, she's a bit spiky . . .'

'And drop-dead gorgeous?' enquired Cally drily.

Rob considered for a moment, as though weighing up the pros and cons of telling the truth. 'She's not bad looking,' he admitted, 'in fact you might even say she's quite glamorous.'

'Oh.'

'But she's not you.'

The quiet desperation in Rob's voice cut through Cally's outer shell of cynicism and sent a shiver of pain through her soul. She opened her mouth but no sound came out.

'Cally? Cally, are you still there?'

'I have to go, Rob.'

'Cal.'

''Bye.'

The receiver clicked back on to the hook about half a second before the tears started spilling out of Cally's eyes, drenching her cheeks.

Oh Rob, she whispered to herself as she scrabbled for a clean tissue, why does it have to be this way? Why can't you make things easy for me?

The Swedish lady with the tribe of healthy-looking children spoke impeccable English, but Cally was still having problems getting her message across.

'I'm really sorry,' she repeated, 'but we don't allow visitors to ride on the donkeys.'

The Swedish tourist frowned. 'But the nice French lady in the office said it would be fine.'

Bloody Simone again, thought Cally bitterly. Who the hell does she think she is?

'I'm afraid she was mistaken,' she said, vaguely uncomfortable at the thought of making Simone look bad, though not at all sure why. 'We don't allow any of our animals to be ridden.'

'But the nice lady promised,' insisted the tourist. 'And you see, the children have come many miles to see the donkeys and ride on them. And it is Birgitte's birthday today.'

Six small eager faces gazed expectantly up at Cally, like baby birds in a nest.

'It would make the little ones very happy,' coaxed the children's mother.

Cally glanced round furtively, like a dodgy street trader. It was a quiet afternoon, there weren't any other keepers around, and the only other punters in sight were a couple of old ladies, feeding wisps of hay to a three-legged goat. It was strictly against the rules of course, but hey, who was going to know?

'Well,' she relented, 'we do have one or two donkeys who used to give rides at the seaside. I suppose I *might* be able to arrange something just for Birgitte, as it's her birthday.'

It was only a tiny infringement of the rules, and the donkey was so huge and placid that it scarcely noticed the tiny blonde tot balanced on its broad back. Cally was quite pleased with herself as she sent the smiling Scandinavians on their way, smelling only faintly of horse liniment.

But of course, there was always somebody determined to spoil the party.

'What the bloody hell do you think you were doing?' demanded Will, descending on the stables like the fifth horseman of the apocalypse.

'I beg your pardon?' Cally deliberately turned away from him to close the stable door.

Will immediately placed himself between her and the bin of pony nuts. 'Don't give me that, I saw you – giving donkey rides!' He spat the words out as though they were poisoned.

Cally's blood pressure started to rise. '*One* donkey ride,' she stressed.

'One donkey ride, ten donkey rides, it makes no difference! You know the rules here – no animals are to be exploited or abused. Full stop.'

'Exploited? Abused?' Cally stared at Will's flushed face in frank incredulity. 'Excuse me, are we on the same planet here? I let one little tiny girl have a five-minute ride on a seaside donkey . . .'

'*Ex*-seaside donkey.'

'. . . whatever. And suddenly I'm this . . . this *monster*!'

'You know the rules,' Will repeated, with such

pedantic, icy calm that Cally felt like screaming in his face. 'And if it happens again I'm going straight to Henk Thorfinn.'

Will's sheer self-righteousness made her want to slap him right across his infuriatingly good-looking face. Suddenly, all the resentment and frustration that had been building up inside her since she started working at the Experience escaped in one huge emotional blow-out.

'How *dare* you talk to me like that, you . . . you smug git!' she spluttered, tripping over her words in her hurry to get them out. 'You've not had a civil word for me since I got here, you've not lifted a finger to help me out, and the first time I make a mistake it's "ha, gotcha! You screwed up and I'm telling on you to the Big Chief".' Her face was about two inches from Will's nose. 'Well thanks for nothing!'

She thought Will's angry flush deepened a tone or two, but she was too angry herself to see much more than a red mist of fury.

'It wasn't a mistake, it was negligence.'

Just in the nick of time, Cally stopped herself pushing him into the horse trough. She couldn't do that, however much he might deserve it. 'What the hell's your problem, Will?' she snarled. 'Aren't I good enough for this place or something?'

His reply knocked the wind right out of her sails. 'Maybe not.'

Two seconds later he was sitting up to his waist in icy water. And for some strange reason, Cally felt suddenly better.

Chapter Fifteen

Life was, quite simply, pants.

That was the thought that kept Cally company as she sat on the paddock fence, watching the last of the day's visitors trailing away towards the main gates. What sort of pants? she wondered. Nasty old baggy ones that had gone grey in the wash. Bri-nylon Y-fronts. With skidmarks. Total and utter pants.

Well Cally, she reflected, I hope you're pleased with yourself. You really thought you knew what you were doing, didn't you? Oh Ms Shaw, I really love it at the zoo, please let me stay. And you know what they say about wishing for something too hard, don't you? Sometimes your wish comes true.

Being stuck here for the next thirty years, she thought with utter gloom, that's what I've got to look forward to. Bitten, kicked, shat on, ignored – and that's just by the keepers. Nobody likes me, I don't like my job, and the animals seem to think their only purpose is to make me look like an idiot. And as for Will Inglis . . .

Of course, there was a solution. She could just swallow her pride, ring up Christina Shaw and tell her she'd made a horrible mistake. Please Ms Shaw, she rehearsed, let me go to the lovely biscuit factory. I won't mind twelve-hour shifts sweeping broken cream crackers off the floor, honest I won't, just say you'll take me away from here!

Bollocks to that. She'd rather move in with the giant millipedes for a year than go grovelling to Ms Shaw. Even failed donkey-keepers had *some* pride. Hang on though. She scratched her bum with a muddy finger. It was pride that had got her into this mess in the first place. Come to think of it, it was her own stupid pride that had screwed up most of the good things in her life.

Her train of thought was interrupted by a peculiar sensation of hot breath on her backside, followed a moment later by a determined nuzzling that almost toppled her off the fence.

'Stan!' She looked down to find a slobbery muzzle exploring her curled-up fingers. 'Bog off.'

Far from dissuading the little black donkey, this produced a more insistent exploration.

'Stan, there's nothing there, I've already fed you! Look!'

She uncurled her fingers and showed him the flat of her empty hand – normally an instant recipe for disinterest – but to her surprise, Stan nuzzled her again, gently and rather wetly, with not even the faintest hint of teeth. When she looked down at him again, he was looking up at her with long-lashed, expectant eyes.

'Oh all right then,' she relented, and putting her arms about his woolly neck, she gave him a big soft hug.

'Where's this nineteen fifty-nine Malibu Barbie then?' demanded Will eagerly, shutting the shop door behind him and turning the sign to 'Closed'. 'I hope it's got all the accessories, they're worth nothing if half the gear's missing.'

'What Malibu Barbie?' asked Liddy airily, counting

up the last of the day's takings and slipping them into a bag.

'What do you mean, what Malibu Barbie? The Malibu Barbie you rang me to come and have a look at – or have you got another half-dozen stashed away in the cellar?'

Liddy closed the old-fashioned till with a loud 'ker-ching'. 'Actually,' she confessed, 'there is no Malibu Barbie. I made that up.'

'What! You mean you dragged me all the way here for nothing?'

'Oh no, definitely not for nothing.' Liddy scooped up Stefan from the chair behind the counter, and pointed to the seat. 'Sit.'

'I'm not a dog you know.'

Liddy's eyes narrowed. 'Sit, or I unleash this small hairy demon on you.'

Reluctantly, Will sat. 'OK, what's this all about?'

Liddy perched, pixie-like, on the end of the counter. 'You know something, Will? I've finally figured you out.'

'Oh yes?'

'Oh definitely. You just love being Will Inglis, Man of Mystery, don't you?'

'I don't know what you're on about,' laughed Will.

'Oh yes you do. You love having all these different lives going on all over the place at the same time, and never letting any of them overlap. And then along comes Cally Storm and spoils it all for you.'

Will's expression turned wary. 'What are you getting at?'

'Shut up and listen for once in your life. Cally's gone and spoiled your little game, hasn't she? And you've been taking it out on her.'

Will said nothing, just went on looking ill at ease.

'*Haven't you*?'

Will's head hung just a little. She couldn't see his expression now. He kicked his heels against the legs of his chair. 'Well I wouldn't exactly say that . . .'

'It's not fair on her and you know it,' insisted Liddy. As though registering his complete agreement, Stefan shifted his right buttock and vented a sonorous fart. 'Is it?'

'No,' he sighed. 'I know it isn't.'

'So.' Liddy folded her arms. 'Now we've agreed that, exactly what are you going to do about it?'

Nobody was more surprised than Cally when Will Inglis asked her out for a drink.

Well actually, that wasn't quite true. Her workmates were even more incredulous.

'What – her?' Donna picked her lower jaw up off the floor of the women's changing room. 'He's asked *her* out?'

Several pairs of eyes swivelled round and goggled in a mixture of disbelief and accusation. Cally instantly felt like the only freak in a roomful of two-headed aliens.

'It's only a drink,' she said, rather hot around the ears. 'And anyway, why shouldn't he ask me out?'

Sonja, a peroxide blonde ice-cream seller who looked like a 'before' advert for Clearasil, wriggled adroitly out of her nylon overall. 'He never goes out with brunettes,' she said firmly. 'Not even ones with big arses.'

Cally twisted her head to look down at her own backside, viewing it with a mixture of irritation and surprise. 'I haven't got an especially big arse,' she objected, turning sideways to get a different perspective. 'Have I?'

'Put it this way love,' interjected a scrawny cleaner, passing through with a bucket and a bottle of Toilet Duck, 'If you was to sit on his face he'd die happy, eh girls?'

Raucous laughter was still ringing in Cally's ears when she pushed her way into the lounge bar of the General Mayberry that evening. Big arse indeed. As if hers was anything out of the ordinary. For that matter, she reminded herself, I never go out with blokes who smell of penguins. Not that she was actually going out with Will Inglis, of course; it was only a harmless drink, a chance to socialise with a workmate. And anyhow, she didn't like him that much, did she?

Like him or not, her treacherous heart executed a backflip when she saw him waiting for her at a corner table, a can of low-alcohol lager and a short lined up in front of him. He even looked as if he might have run a comb through his random straggle of dark hair.

'Hi Will.' For some absurd reason, her mouth felt all dry and furry. What if her breath smelled horrible? Oh God, she knew she should have cleaned her teeth.

He half got out of his seat, shuffling his chair to one side to make room for her. For once in his life, Will Inglis was looking less than one hundred per cent sure of himself, and that intrigued Cally.

'I got you a vodka and tonic, did I guess right?'

'As a matter of fact, you did.' Trust Mr Know-It-All to have her all worked out; she was half-tempted to demand a banana daiquiri with two sparklers and a cocktail whelk, just to prove him wrong. 'Neat trick, I never knew you were psychic.'

He smiled. 'I'm not, I just asked Vern.'

Cally sipped her drink. 'Well. This is . . .' Her eyes

travelled slowly upwards over Will's unconventional yet compelling face, until their gazes locked. 'Different.'

'Yes.' Will looked away.

'Do I take it you've stopped hating my guts, or are we just taking time out before the next round?'

He riled a little. 'Oh come on Cally, that's a bit below the belt.'

'Is it?'

Will's shoulders slumped slightly. 'Yeah, OK, you're right. Look, I think I owe you an apology,' he began.

'Oh?' said Cally, not particularly inclined to make this easy for him. 'What for?'

'You know what for,' replied Will. 'I've been behaving like a total arsehole and I'm sorry.' His eyes met hers, and for the first time she noticed how much paler the right one was, as though it had faded in the sunshine. 'I mean that.'

Cally shrugged, not quite sure what to say. 'OK,' she said. 'Fine.'

'Is that all you're going to say?'

'What else would you like me to say?' she countered. 'I mean, for all I know first thing tomorrow you'll start pretending I don't exist again.'

Will shook his head. 'I think I'd better explain,' he said, taking a gulp of lager and wiping his mouth. 'The thing is – and this isn't an excuse – I was a bit, well, peeved.'

'Peeved?' Cally frowned. 'What – with me?'

'Kind of.' Now that he had started, the words came tumbling out, almost as if he had rehearsed them over and over until he was word-perfect. 'You see, when you first ran into me you saw me as a collectables dealer, right?'

'Right. So?'

'So that was fine. Only then you started work at the Experience, and found out I was a keeper as well. Two of my lives had . . . well . . . crossed over.'

'Two of your lives? How many more have you got?'

Will stared down at his knees and did not answer. There was a peculiar intensity to him that Cally hadn't seen before. 'It's the embarrassment, see. I mean – look. You go round letting slip to all the keepers about me being a dealer, naturally they think it's bloody hilarious that I can put a date on any Barbie doll's underwear since nineteen fifty-nine. Doesn't do a lot for my credibility in the penguin fraternity, if you get my drift.'

'Doesn't it?'

'Hardly. Then there's the serious collectors,' Will went on, warming to his theme. 'I mean, if you were some raving Barbie-doll nut, would you take a dealer seriously once you knew that funny smell was down to penguin guano?'

'I don't know,' admitted Cally. 'But I guess I might not.'

'Believe me, you wouldn't. I work hard to keep my lives separate, and with good reason. Then along you come and kind of burst my balloon.'

'Sorry,' said Cally.

'No, I'm sorry. It was no excuse to go taking it out on you.' He stuck out a hand, some of the tension erased from his face. 'Mates?'

She'd been planning to hold out on him for a while, make him sweat a bit; but he had such a nice, lopsided smile. She took his hand. 'Oh all right. Mates.'

Will let out a gust of breath that seemed to deflate his entire upper body. 'Thank God for that,' he said. 'I was starting to wonder how much longer I could keep it up, it was bloody knackering.'

'Then why on earth didn't you just make it up with me before?'

He grimaced. 'Oh you know. Stupid pride I guess. But you wouldn't understand about that.'

Cally grunted. 'Don't bet on it.'

When you got talking to him properly, Will was surprisingly good company. Maybe it was the three double vodkas talking, but Cally didn't seem to run out of things to say all evening. No awkward silences, no staring at the ceiling to avoid looking him in the face, no boredom. Just relaxed fun.

The hours passed so quickly that when the bell rang for time, Cally was stunned to glance out of the window and see that it was pitch-black outside.

'Oh shit, is it that late?'

'How are you getting home?' asked Will, draining the last few drops of low-alcohol lager.

She checked her watch. 'Taxi I guess, I've missed the last bus.'

'No problem, I'll give you a lift. Here.' Will reached under the table and pulled out a motorcycle helmet. 'Go on, take it – I've got a spare in the top box.'

Cally hesitated for all of half a second before grabbing the helmet and jamming it on over her head. Hey, so she'd always been petrified of motorbikes and the helmet was so snug the Fire Brigade would probably have to cut her out of it.

But hey – so what?

The following morning saw Cally up bright and early, without the merest trace of a hangover. In fact she felt so good that she was down at the railway station by seven o'clock: a time when she and Eddie were usually still arguing over who got the last helping of Coco Pops.

She shuffled her feet impatiently in the queue for the one and only ticket window, eager to get this done and dusted.

'Next?'

Gratefully she stepped forward. 'I'd like to apply for a refund, please.'

The queue behind her let out a collective groan.

'You'll have to fill a form in.' The clerk took the top off his Biro and the groan became a murmur of discontent. 'Reason for refund?'

'Sorry?'

He rattled off a long, weary list. 'Cancelled train, delayed train, operational difficulties, change in personal circumstances . . .'

'Change of plans.' Cally took the ticket to Northampton out of her purse and laid it on the counter. 'I've decided to cancel my trip this weekend. I won't be travelling there just yet.'

Chapter Sixteen

Ah, Thursday, thought Cally as she grabbed a plastic tray from the stack and joined the queue in the staff canteen. Cabbage and bean bake, followed by rhubarb and custard – the heralds of yet another weekend spent as the brunt of Eddie's intestinal jokes. For a self-proclaimed romantic, Eddie Priest had a very Teutonic sense of humour.

Armed with her laden tray, Cally pocketed her change and gazed out over the massed ranks of keepers, clerks, vets and cleaners. So, she mused gloomily; I wonder which unlucky bugger's going to cop for my unwanted company today.

'Hi Cally,' said Donna, shifting her chair a few inches so that she could squeeze past. Cally wondered what it was that looked odd about Donna's face, then realised with a start of alarm that it was smiling.

'There ain't much room here,' said Billy through a mouthful of masticated butter beans, 'but you could fetch yerself a chair an' we'll all budge up.' He leaned over and jabbed the man next to him in the ribs. 'Oi, Martin, that a spare chair by you, is it?'

Cally was so convinced she must be hallucinating that she would probably have gone on standing there, with her mouth open and the rhubarb congealing on the plate, if she hadn't spotted a hand in the distance, beckoning to her.

Will! A teenage thrill ran through her. He was pointing to an empty chair beside him, and she made her excuses and headed straight across the canteen to his table.

'Saw you come in, so I thought I'd save you a seat,' said Will as she sat down next to him.

'Thanks,' she panted. 'I was starting to think I'd have to eat standing up, with the donkeys. Actually . . .' She prodded her cabbage with her fork. 'I'm not sure I wouldn't swap this for a few pony nuts.'

'Bit institutional,' agreed Will, shovelling food into his mouth. 'Reminds me of school dinners.'

'Ugh,' said Cally, instantly transported back to a childhood world in which custard was sometimes the only way of distinguishing the pudding from the main course. 'Semolina and prunes.'

'Snake and pygmy pie.'

'Pulverised sprouts.'

Will waved his fork in the air. 'Did you ever have that horrible steamed roly-poly pudding? All grey and soggy.'

Cally nodded vigorously. 'Yup, once a week regular as clockwork. Weighed about ten tons, and all the squidgy red jam oozed out when you stabbed it with your spoon.'

' "Dead baby", we used to call it,' Will reminisced fondly.

Cally's cabbage turned to ashes in her mouth. 'Do you mind? Some of us are trying to eat our dinner.'

Will grinned. 'Sorry.' He pushed aside his plate and started on the pudding. ''Scuse me talking with my mouth full, only I've got a couple of cases of penguin colic I need to get back to.'

'Sounds nasty,' sympathised Cally.

'It is. And messy. And I don't like leaving Lee on his own too long, he's a nice lad but gormless isn't in it.' He snorted. 'Last time I went off for a couple of hours, when I got back I found out he'd only gone and *cooked* all the fish.'

'No!' giggled Cally, choking on a bean.

'I kid you not. Threw the whole lot in a metal bucket and boiled it up on the stove. Then he wondered why they wouldn't eat it!' Spotting Cally's distress, he patted her on the back. 'Something go down the wrong way, did it? Here, have some water.'

He poured her a glass and she drank. 'That's better, thanks.' She wiped her eyes. 'You really care about those penguins, don't you?'

'Of course I do. This isn't the sort of job you do unless you care. I mean, let's face it, you'd have to be crazy to do it for the money.'

'Is that why you deal in collectables too?' asked Cally. 'To help make ends meet?'

'Sort of.' Will toyed with a stringy chunk of rhubarb, and Cally had the feeling he was avoiding looking at her. 'Plus I enjoy it. It's like a cross between being a private detective and a big kid. How else could I get to play with Barbie dolls and watch *Blake's Seven* videos all the time?'

'*Blake's Seven*,' reminisced Cally, licking custard off her spoon. 'You know, I really used to fancy that Avon.'

Will gave her a meaningful look. 'Ah well, you would. Always preferred the evil Jacqueline Pearce myself – now, that was a bottom to get a young boy's pulse racing . . .' He cut off his own train of thought. 'Damn, is it that late already?'

191

Cally felt a twinge of disappointment. 'Oh – have you got to go now?'

'If I don't get back soon, Lee'll be barricaded in the penguin house with a whip and a chair. He just hasn't got the knack with penguins. Tell you what though. Will you be at the General Mayberry tomorrow night?'

She shrugged, as casually as she could manage. 'Dunno. Might be. Why?'

'We're picking a darts team to play Brockbourne Hall. Thought you might be interested.'

'Oh. Yes, OK. I'll be there.'

Will flashed her a smile. 'See you there then. 'Bye.'

''Bye.'

Darts, thought Cally, in the grip of a sudden panic. Must learn to play darts.

After a crash course in darts from Liddy, Cally's evening started well. Her first scores were double top, triple seventeen, and a bull. Unfortunately her second three were ceiling, gents' lavatory door and barmaid.

She did not make the team.

What was rather worse, she'd failed spectacularly in front of half the staff of The Animal Experience, including Will. Still, at least she hadn't actually killed anybody. And the weirdest thing of all was that she didn't really mind looking a total prat – which wasn't like her at all.

As she was balancing on the bar-top, trying to prise the second dart out of a solid oak beam and thanking her lucky stars that the third had bounced off the barmaid's underwired bra, Vernon jumped up beside her.

'Here, let me get that, I'm taller than you.' He reached up and plucked the dart out with ease. 'Congratulations, by the way.'

She stared at him in disbelief. 'Congratulations? What for?'

Vernon helped her down off the bar counter. 'Funniest thing I've seen in ages, that's what!' He clapped a large, hairy arm round her shoulders and crushed her in a big bear-hug. 'Come here, you daft donkey-keeper. Let me buy you a drink.'

Cally waited for the inevitable wave of hurt pride to kick in, but for some unaccountable reason, it didn't. Whatever's happening to you, Cal? she puzzled. Come on, have a good sulk. You're the girl who can't bear to come second, let alone last!

Then again, maybe coming last didn't really matter all that much. Well, sometimes anyway. Maybe it didn't really matter if she was utterly crap at darts. It was quite a liberating feeling.

'Thanks,' she smiled. 'Better make it a double.'

'Yeah,' interjected Will, tossing her a packet of crisps. 'Double top.'

Unfortunately, nobody had told Simone about the new policy of *détente*. And Simone's mission in life appeared to be to make Cally's existence a total misery.

'*Non, non, non!*' she declared, shaking her Titian ponytail like a temperamental thoroughbred. 'Zat ees no good at all!'

Simone was not Cally's favourite person at the best of times, and right now she was in danger of occupying the horse trough that Will had so recently vacated. Cally took a very long, very deep breath and stood back from the information board she had just set up outside the donkey stables – for the third time that morning.

'Go on. Surprise me. What's wrong with it this time?'

'It ees not ze right shape.'

'What?'

Simone responded with an irritated fluttering of her hands. 'Ze shape, it ees all wrong!'

'But this is the shape you told me to make it!'

'And ze background, it should not be black, black is so . . . depressing.'

Hands on hips, Cally advanced towards her nemesis. 'Excuse me,' she spat, her jaw clenched so tightly that it felt as though her teeth might explode at any moment, 'but *you* chose that background, not me! I told you it'd be better blue or green, but oh no, you wanted it black and that's why it's effing well black!'

Simone's drawn-on eyebrows arched like a Mcdonald's sign. 'Really, Miss Storm, zaire ees no reason to take zat tone wiz me!'

'Actually, I think there is,' retorted Cally. 'I've just wasted a whole morning putting these displays together and moving them all over the damn park. And you know what? I don't think you give a toss about information displays.'

'What! Zat is ridiculous.'

'No it isn't. I think you're only doing this because you want to mess me about.'

Simone's pretty mouth contracted into a moue of contempt. 'And why ever would I want to do zat?'

'Because you think there's something going on between me and Vernon.' The look on Simone's face told Cally that she had hit the nail squarely on the head. 'Only there *isn't*!'

'Zis ees all nonsense,' scoffed Simone. 'Why would I be interested in such a zing?'

'Because you're crazy about Vernon!'

'Eet ees you who are crazy, Mademoiselle Storm!'

'Oh come off it, it's obvious! And you have got to get

it into your head that I am not, repeat *not*, interested in having an affair with your precious Vernon!'

Simone looked doubtful. '*Non*? You and he, you are really not . . .?'

'Absolutely, definitely not.'

Doubt turned to suspicion. 'Why not?'

'What do you mean, why not? Because I don't fancy him!'

'Why? He ees very attractive man, *non*?'

Give me strength, thought Cally. Sometimes you just can't win. 'Listen,' she said wearily, 'he's there for the taking. The way's clear. For God's sake just go for it!'

The Frenchwoman still needed some convincing. 'You and Vernon, you are very close. At the General Mayberry ze other night . . .'

'For goodness' sake! I am really and truly not interested in him! Cross my heart and hope to die. He's not my type, OK? I'm just not interested. If I'm interested in anybody,' she added before her brain could censor her mouth, 'it's Will Inglis.'

This hit the mark, and Simone's dark eyes narrowed with interest. 'You and he? You are involved?'

'No!' said Cally hastily. Well, not yet, added her silent thoughts. You've as good as admitted to Simone that you fancy Will Inglis; isn't it about time you admitted it to yourself?

When Cally got home that night, still cursing the entire French nation, she found the flat empty and her mail sitting on her desk in a neat pile. On top of it lay an exquisite little hand-stencilled note: *For ye Ladye of ye House*. Hmm, thought Cally, Eddie's in a good mood – either he's picked up some signwriting work, or he's fallen in love again. Either way, he'll be a darn sight easier to live with.

Sitting down at the desk, she started sorting through her post. Bog-off letter from some snooty London bank . . . good, she didn't want to work for them anyway. Marked assignment from her management course. B-minus, what? Only B-minus? Some people just couldn't recognise talent if it hit them on the nose. Bill . . . another bill . . . bank statement . . . save that one for later. And . . . oh. A pink envelope addressed to her in Rob's familiar handwriting.

She hesitated. Did she really want to open anything from Rob, pink or otherwise? On the other hand, if she didn't open it she'd never know what was inside and it might turn out to have been something really important, like a divorce petition, or something. Her stomach lurched at the thought. Come on girl, she told herself, people don't send out divorce petitions in pink envelopes.

Not entirely convinced, she slit open the envelope. Inside was a small, folded piece of paper and a photograph.

Dear Cally,

Thought you might like to see a photo of my glamorous lodger.

Love
Rob

Apprehensively, she slid the photo out of the envelope. Bastard. Sending her photos of his fancy-women, just to taunt her. Hang on a minute though . . .

What?

A moment later, she was calling Rob's mobile.

'Rob Monk, hi.'

'Rob, it's me.'

Short silence. Then: 'Cally! You just don't know how good it is to hear your voice!'

'Never mind that. What I want to know is, why have you sent me a photograph of a five-foot cactus?'

There was an embarrassed cough at the other end of the line.

'Well, you did ask me a lot of questions about my lodger.'

'Selena? What's she got to do with anything?'

Rob paused. 'You're looking at her.'

Cally looked at the photo, laid on the desk in front of her. It showed an enormous, spiny cactus in an earthenware pot so heavy that the living-room floor seemed to be sagging beneath its weight.

'What – you're telling me your lodger is a *cactus*?'

'Yes. An epiphyllum actually. Remember: glamorous, a bit spiky, likes the occasional drink?'

'My God Rob, you're twisted, d'you know that?'

'Probably,' he admitted. 'But you see, I only did it because I love you. I couldn't bring myself to get a real lodger, you know, some horrible stranger who'd mess up our lovely home. But I reckoned if you thought I had a lodger ... well, you might get jealous, and ... and ...'

'And come back to you? I take it back, you're not twisted, you're just plain nuts.'

'Is it really so crazy, wanting you back?' Rob's voice was soft, almost coaxing. 'I need you, Cally. I love you.'

'I ...'

'When will I see you again? It's been so long.'

She almost, but only almost, regretted getting a refund on that train ticket. There was something very

sweet and curiously innocent about a man who cuck-
olded his wife with a giant cactus.

'I don't know, Rob.'

'Cally, please.'

'I said I don't know. Look, I'm sorry, there's
someone at the door. I really have to go now.'

Her cheeks burned with the lie as she clicked the
phone back on to the hook. She felt a little guilty, but
didn't know why. After all, she wasn't the one who'd
played away so often he'd got his own team bus, was
she?

She made herself a coffee, then sat down to open the
rest of the post. More bills, some adverts for double
glazing and stairlifts, and – good God. It couldn't be
true.

An interview.

Cally blinked, open-mouthed, at the letterheading.
Well, well, well. Maybe she'd be seeing Rob again
sooner than either of them had imagined.

Will's tiny office by the penguin pool was currently
witnessing the aftermath of a major domestic incident.

'Hold still, Bruno,' scolded Will, trying to get a look
at the penguin's injured wing. 'Behave yourself!'

'Sorry about this,' said Cally, fumbling to get a grip
on the slippery bird. 'He won't stop wriggling, I
suppose he's a bit scared.'

'Scared!' scoffed Will. 'Bruno's not scared of
anything. He's a little thug – aren't you, Bruno? That's
the trouble with rockhoppers. Aggressive little
buggers.'

'But he's so small!' exclaimed Cally.

'So was Hitler. And Mussolini. Oh – and Napoleon.
Never trust a short man.'

'Or a short penguin?'

'Right on, they're all power-crazy. You turn your back on them for five seconds and they're pecking lumps out of each other. Now, if you could just hold him so that his left wing is—'

'Ow!' squeaked Cally, as the bird swivelled its head through a full one hundred and eighty degrees and took a vicious peck at her fingers. It hurt so much that she let go of Bruno, and he fluttered off across the office, taking refuge inside an upturned cardboard box.

The next thing she knew, Will had grabbed her hands in his and was examining them minutely for signs of damage. 'Are you up to date with your tetanus shots?'

'Yes, I think so.'

'Hmm, doesn't seem to be too much damage.' Will turned a burning glare on the penguin, which was now happily grooming itself in the cardboard box. 'Bruno thinks fingers mean food, don't you mate? You all right, Cal?'

She nodded. 'It just smarts a bit, that's all.'

'You know, you really ought to . . .'

Their eyes met.

'. . . watch out.'

They were looking directly at each other now, with the kind of intensity that couldn't be explained away as accidental.

'Cally.'

'Hmm?'

'You're not . . .'

'What?'

'You're not, you know, involved with anyone, are you?'

For a split second, her heart stopped; then it began

199

racing away, at twice its normal speed. 'Why d'you ask?'

'I don't know really.' Their lips drew closer. She could feel his breath on her face. 'I just sort of . . . wondered.'

And then their lips met; and the wondering stopped.

Chapter Seventeen

Cally hadn't felt this uncomfortable on a first date since she'd attended the school disco with her knickers on back to front.

She and Will sat on the back row at the multiplex, a big tray of chilli dogs balanced on the empty seat between them. Cally wasn't really that keen on chilli dogs, but on the whole she was rather glad of them, simply because they maintained a discreet space between her and Will. She wasn't just uncomfortable, her mind was in complete turmoil.

It wasn't that she didn't like him. Hell, she'd been mooning after him for weeks, and suddenly she'd got what she wanted. That first kiss by the penguin pool had been dynamite, even better than she'd hoped it might be, and perhaps that was the scary thing. Now they had to decide where to go from here.

In the flickering light from the screen, she sneaked a look at Will. He caught her looking in his direction, and smiled.

'Shall I move it?' he mouthed, pointing at the tray.

'No, it's OK.' She took a chilli dog and bit into it.

'Enjoying the film?'

'Yeah.' She hoped her smile didn't look too forced.

'Great.'

It wasn't a bad film but to be honest, she'd almost lost track of the plot. As far as she could make out, it was just one more fluffy romantic comedy where the heroine had to choose between the good guy, who became instantly handsome when he took his glasses off, and the bad guy, who had hairy ears and a moustache. If only real life could be that simple.

Cally almost wished none of this had happened. She really liked Will, *really* liked him; but the timing was terrible, her feelings were so horribly complex right now. And there was Rob, who didn't know about Will; and Will, who didn't know about Rob. Maybe it was all more trouble than it was worth. Maybe she should give up men altogether and go for cacti.

Her thoughts were wandering back to Rob, when a loud and indignant shout interrupted the soundtrack.

'You bastard! You absolute bastard!'

Very slowly, Cally leaned sideways into the aisle and peered into the gloom. About halfway down the auditorium, the silhouette of a man was waving its arms about, completely obscuring half of Demi Moore's naked chest. Oh God no, it couldn't be.

'Get out of my seat and leave my girlfriend alone!' demanded the voice. 'Or I'll make you!'

'Oh yeah?' sneered the reply. 'And what if she doesn't want me to?'

'Ella! Ella, tell him to take his hand off your knee!'

Ella's reply was not recorded, because the next sound that reverberated through the cinema was the strangled 'Urrggh' of a man with a fist up his nose. Silhouetted against the screen, a lanky figure staggered back then hurled itself forward again, fists flailing.

'Ow.'

'Bastard.'

'Take that, you cad!'

'Sit down you daft buggers, I can't see a bloody thing.'

Seconds later, the film stopped in mid-reel, and the house lights came up.

'Oh shit,' groaned Cally, sliding down in her seat. 'It *is* Eddie.'

'Hmm,' commented Will, peering between the heads of interested onlookers. 'Is that blood?'

A man's head swivelled round. 'Do you know that hooligan?' it demanded accusingly.

Cally smiled feebly. 'Never seen him before in my life.'

'And if you'll believe that,' said Will, 'you'll believe anything. Oh look, he's got him in a headlock.'

Reluctantly, Cally hauled herself to her feet. 'Come on Will, I suppose we'd better rescue him.'

Eddie was not even remotely grateful for being rescued. He seemed to think he was winning his fist-fight with the Brad Pitt lookalike in the cool sportsgear, which was quite a feat of self-delusion for a man who was being held upside-down by his ankles.

'What happened?' demanded Cally as Will interposed himself between the two contenders.

'I only went out to get her a strawberry Cornetto,' complained Eddie. 'Two minutes I'm gone, and when I get back he's sat in my seat with his hands all over her and his tongue halfway down her throat!'

'Finders keepers,' leered the Brad Pitt lookalike. 'P'raps she fancies a real man for a change.'

'Just you watch it!' Eddie lunged forward like a bantam cockerel, only to be thwarted by Will's surprisingly rock-like right arm.

'Cool it.' He nodded towards an approaching police uniform. 'Or do you fancy a night in the cells?'

Meanwhile, in the middle of an inquisitive crowd of onlookers. Eddie's date for the evening was coolly lounging in her seat, nibbling on her strawberry Cornetto and apparently finding the whole thing frightfully amusing.

'Are you Ella?' demanded Cally.

The girl turned horsey features on her. 'I might be.'

'I don't suppose it actually occurred to you to tell that creep to push off?'

The horsey face smiled. 'Which one?'

'What do you mean, which one?'

She laughed, in a way that made Cally's flesh crawl. 'Darling, all men are creeps. And anyway, it's their job to fight over us, isn't it? The fighting's half the fun.'

Eddie was tremendously pleased with himself. He hummed loudly and tunelessly as he raced around the flat, plumping up cushions and flicking cobwebs off the cornice, occasionally glancing towards the kitchenette, where an immense bunch of flowers shared the sink with a single, long-stemmed red rose. Everything was going to be just perfect, he could feel it in his bones.

A key turned in the front door just as he was polishing the kettle, and he grabbed the bouquet and scooted back into the living room.

'Surprise!' His head popped out from behind the bunch of flowers. 'Like them?'

Cally stared in amazement at the flowers as he shoved them into her arms. 'Eddie, it's not my birthday for months. Besides, I'm not having any more birthdays, I'm old enough already.'

'It's not a birthday present, it's a thank-you.'

'What for?'

Eddie licked a fingertip and sleeked down his

eyebrows. 'For turning me into the ultimate love machine, what else?'

'Love machine? Eddie, are you ill?' She placed a hand on his forehead. 'You're not running a temperature are you? You haven't got concussion after that punch on the nose?'

Eddie looked mystified. 'Ill? Ill? I've never felt better! Don't you see, all that advice you gave me about how to chat up women – well, it worked!'

'Oh?' said Cally, rather warily. 'That's nice.'

'Nice? Oh Cally, it's wonderful! And it's all down to you. I did what you told me to, I said exactly what you told me to say, right down to the last word, and—'

Drrrrrrring!

At the sound of the doorbell, Eddie froze like a panic-stricken hamster; then started racing about the flat again, trying to tidy things up and knocking them over instead.

'Shall I get that?' enquired Cally, making a move towards the door.

'No!' squeaked Eddie, turning all colours of the rainbow in rapid succession.

Drrring. Drrrrrrrrrrring!

'Eddie,' began Cally, picking up a desk tidy and stuffing all the pens and pencils into it. 'What on earth's got into you?'

He spun round on his axis, arms flailing wildly. 'It's her, Cal!'

'Who?'

'Her! The girl I've just met. Quick, undo my pinny, the knot's got stuck!'

Cally fumbled the knot, failed to undo it, and managed to wriggle the whole frilly apron off over Eddie's head. 'There you are – now don't you think you

205

ought to answer the door before she gets fed up and goes away?'

Eddie clasped her hand. 'You answer it!'

'But you just . . .'

'Please!'

With a sigh, Cally plodded off to open the door. Just as Eddie had predicted, there was indeed a girl standing on the doorstep. A fragile-looking girl in a padded jacket and a faded, flowery skirt, with huge Bambi eyes, wavy dark hair . . . and a dog.

It could have been some kind of lurcher; at any rate it was large, thin, grey and as wiry as a chewed-up pan scourer. Cally didn't get a chance to take a proper look at it, because it took one sniff at her, and ran off yelping into the loo.

'Ziggy!' The girl dodged into the flat past Cally and ran after the dog. 'Ziggy, come out of there, what's got into you?'

She opened the loo door and grabbed the dog by the loop of rope that served as a collar, but the dog planted all four paws on the carpet and flatly refused to budge.

'Ziggy! Dunno what's got into him, he's never done this before. Ziggy, if you don't come out of there this minute . . .'

'Shall I give you a hand?' Cally put out a hand to grab the dog, but it promptly slunk behind the cistern and hunched there, gums bared and growling rather pathetically.

'Oh God, oh God, oh God,' wailed Eddie, almost in tears at the trail of devastation left by the dog on its way through the flat. 'It wasn't supposed to be like this, everything was supposed to be perfect!'

At last the girl emerged from the toilet, hauling the wiry grey dog behind her. 'I don't know why he did that,' she said, shaking her head. She sniffed the air around Cally. 'Have you got something funny on your clothes?'

Eddie wiped his eyes on his sleeve. 'Janis, this is Cally. She works in the zoo.'

'Hi,' said Janis, avoiding direct eye contact. Cally couldn't help noticing how the big, dark eyes seemed oddly unfocused, yet were constantly flicking around the flat from one thing to the next, taking in every detail, almost like a burglar casing the joint. And something completely irrational made her want to shout out, 'Hands off, this is my home!'

'I expect it's the smell of lion dung,' said Cally, with a certain malicious pleasure.

'Cally,' Eddie went on, 'this is Janis. She sells the *Big Issue*.'

One thing led to another. Then again, that was what life tended to be all about – one damn thing leading to another. One week Will was ignoring Cally, the next he was kissing her; and the one after that, he was sitting down to Sunday lunch with her at her parents' house. It was all quite scary really, as though their budding relationship had just taken on a momentum all of its own.

She'd tried to dissuade Will, but he'd been most insistent. 'Hey, we like each other don't we?'

'Well yes, but . . .'

'So I'll like your folks too.'

'I'm sure you will, but . . .'

'And how could they possibly not like somebody like me, now tell me that!'

'But Will, we hardly know each other.'

'And this is the best way I can think of for us to get to know each other better!'

In the end she caved in. He was probably right; if they were going to make anything of this fledgling relationship, he was going to have to meet her parents sooner or later, lovers and lentils and all. But she couldn't help feeling uneasy about it, and right from the moment they arrived she knew her father was going to be trouble.

'Have some more chargrilled vegetable couscous.' He practically thrust the bowl up Will's nose. 'Cally's not too keen on it, but it's Rob's favourite, isn't it Cally?'

Cally nearly choked on her deep-fried individual goat's cheese. 'Dad!'

'And he can't get enough of your mother's nutburgers.'

'Who's Rob?' enquired Will, spearing a chargrilled tomato.

Cally prayed for her father to shut up. Evie gave him a hard stare. 'I'm sure Cally's friend doesn't want to hear about all that,' she said firmly. 'Why don't you tell him about your lentils?'

'Lentils?' puzzled Will.

'Dad's developing the ultimate lentil,' explained Cally, glad of a change of subject. 'He's devoted his life to it.'

'Really?' Will looked suitably impressed. 'That's pretty cool. Do you run an experimental farm then? Or is it mostly lab work?'

'Actually he lives in a tepee and grows them on his allotment,' replied Cally. 'Don't you, Dad?'

'At least some of us do spend some of our time at home,' replied Marc, with a meaningful stare at his daughter. 'Been back to Northampton lately, have you?'

Cally tried to force a lump of aubergine down her throat with a gulp of wine. 'Not recently.'

'Northampton?'

'I used to work there,' she explained hastily to Will, feeling even guiltier than she had done when he first asked her if she was 'involved' with anybody. Trust her father to make things ten times worse, with his meaningful glances and his pointed remarks.

'Oh. Right.' Will chewed. 'Never been there, is it nice?'

'Not especially. As a matter of fact, I wasn't very happy there at all,' she added, for her father's benefit. 'Besides,' she went on, not really convincing herself, 'that's all behind me.'

'Still,' Marc came back, 'you can't just sweep the past to one side and forget about it, can you?'

For a few seconds, the silence was as thick and expectant as toadspawn. Then Evie broke the tension.

'Well, this is nice isn't it? Who's for gooseberry crumble and custard?'

After the dishes had been washed, and Will had insisted on drying up and been told not to be so silly, he found Cally sitting in the back garden, watching two bluetits squabbling over a piece of cheese.

'Hi,' he said, perching on the ornamental wall which was going to be finished one day, when Marc got his first big lentil contract. 'Mind if I join you?'

She did rather, but it seemed churlish to say so. 'Be my guest.'

'Nice people, your parents.'

'Yes. I suppose they are really.'

'You don't sound too convinced.'

Cally shrugged. She was thinking about her father's endless stream of hints, prods and downright insinuations. Talk about double standards: it was OK for him and Mum to have an 'open marriage', but when it came

209

to his daughter . . . Well, if he'd intended to make her feel guilty, he'd succeeded.

'Oh, you know.' She forced a smile. 'They're a bit unusual. Did you enjoy your lunch?'

'Very, um, healthy.'

Cally laughed. 'I'll make you some mint tea, that usually shifts the wind.'

They sat in silence for a little while. One of the bluetits made off with the piece of cheese, and the other one pecked disconsolately around the bird table, looking for the odd abandoned crumb.

'Cally,' began Will.

'Hmm?' She tried to sound casual, but she knew exactly what he was going to say next.

'That guy your dad kept going on about – what was his name – Rob? Who is he? I'm sure I've heard you mention him before.'

Cally hung her head, but the reflection in the goldfish pond at her feet wouldn't let her escape from herself, any more than Will or her father would. Time to face the music. It was almost a relief, really. She uncurled her spine, sat up straight and turned to look Will straight in the eye.

'I should have told you this before,' she sighed.

'Told me what?'

'You remember when we were in Liddy's shop, and I got a call from a guy in Northampton?'

'The one you shared a house with?'

She winced. 'Yeah. Well. You see, that was a bit of a white lie. We did more than share a house.'

Will raised an eyebrow. 'He was your boyfriend, you mean?'

'Actually . . .' She tried to swallow down the lump in her throat, but it just wouldn't go. 'Rob's my husband.'

All the colour drained from Will's face, leaving it grey as window-putty. 'You're *married*!'

'Yes. I'm sorry, like I said I should've told you sooner, only—'

Will was on his feet and walking away from her, like suddenly he didn't even want to be breathing the same air. 'Too damn right you should! My God Cally, what happened? Did it just slip your mind?'

'Please, Will.'

'Of course, it's so difficult to remember everything, isn't it? Somebody asks you if you're attached and you say no, and then a couple of weeks later you suddenly remember you've got a husband stashed away at home.'

'Will, let me explain, I never meant to . . .'

'No,' he said. The look on his face was one of betrayed innocence. 'I don't suppose you did. But that doesn't make it all right, does it?'

And then he turned and walked back into the house.

Rob was doing a jigsaw puzzle.

Frankly, computer games were slightly sad, and stamp collecting was positively tragic, but when you were reduced to doing jigsaw puzzles you knew your life had reached an all-time low.

Irritably, he rummaged in the box lid for the missing corner piece. Bloody sky. Why did these effing things have to have so much bloody sky in them? And why did it have to be the same shade of blue all over?

Why couldn't they make jigsaw puzzles with interesting pictures on, like semi-deciduous trees of Western Europe – or Melinda Messenger's chest?

The doorbell rang just as he was sneaking a sly peek at the picture on the underneath of the lid. It sounded so shrill and sudden in the echoey silence of the empty house that he dropped the whole damn thing, and pieces of Neuschwanstein Castle flew all over the living-room floor.

Bloody doorbell. Mind you, a visitor was a visitor. He wondered vaguely if Jehovah's Witnesses were any good at jigsaws. Probably. Everything else was a sin.

He opened the door. The girl on the doorstep didn't look like a Jehovah's Witness. For a start off there weren't two of her. And she was wearing a discreet lick of makeup that set off a pretty face and distracted the eye from a rather unadventurous dress sense.

'If it's double glazing,' he said, 'I'm not interested. I've decided to have the whole lot bricked up and live in the dark.'

'It's not double glazing,' she said earnestly.

'Opinion poll?'

'No.'

'Don't tell me, the end of the world is nigh.'

'Is it? I'd no idea,' she smiled. 'Actually, my name's Rachel Prince.'

Rob's interest rose a notch or two. 'Prince? As in Greg Prince?'

'I'm his cousin.' She set her little overnight case down on the doorstep. 'The thing is, I've just moved into the area and I'm looking for somewhere to live. I've come about the room.'

Chapter Eighteen

'But Caaaa-lly,' whined Eddie, hopping on the spot and grimacing.

'Oh piss off,' suggested Cally, rather cruelly in the circumstances.

'But I really, *really* need to go!'

She didn't look up from her homework. 'Then go.'

Eddie gazed in desperation around the tiny bathroom, as though hoping that a doorway to a parallel universe would miraculously open up, offering access to another, identical bathroom without Cally in it.

'But you're in here,' he whimpered.

Cally did not budge an inch. 'Tough,' she retorted, scribbling away furiously on her A4 pad. 'Get on with it. This is a timed essay.' When Eddie didn't move from the doorway, she glanced up. 'Look, I didn't want to come in here in the first place, but where else am I supposed to do my work while you and Janis are snogging on the sofa?'

There was no answer to that. The problem wasn't just Janis, weird though she was, it was Janis's dog. Wherever she went, Ziggy went too. And Ziggy had developed a complex of immense proportions about Cally. If he didn't feel safe he howled the place down; and the only time Ziggy felt safe was when either he or

Cally was in the toilet. On this occasion, Cally felt, she had definitely drawn the short straw.

'Cally,' pleaded Eddie, 'it's urgent!'

With a sigh of exasperation, Cally lowered her pen. 'Tell you what,' she suggested sweetly. 'We could always swap places.'

'Gordon Bennett what a weekend,' moaned Cally, as she and Liddy split a bottle of Bailey's and put the world to rights.

'Can't have been worse than mine,' Liddy assured her, dusting herself a place to sit in the tiny, cluttered flat above Gold in the Attic. It was late and they both had to work in the morning, but some nights your mind just wouldn't go to sleep. 'First I find a rat-hole under the stairs, then Stefan gets his head stuck in it. Thought I was going to have to call the fire brigade.'

'Ah,' said Cally, helping herself to another slug of creamy gloop. 'But at least you didn't have to spend your weekend listening to your father telling your new boyfriend how brilliant your husband is.'

'Oh dear,' said Liddy. 'Problems?'

'You're telling me. Especially as I hadn't got round to telling Will about Rob.'

'Cally! You mean he *still* didn't know you were married?'

'Well he does now,' replied Cally ruefully, raising her glass in an ironic toast. 'Thanks Dad.'

'So what did Will say when he found out?'

'Nothing much. I mean, what could he say? We were, like, really polite to each other for the rest of the afternoon, then, the minute we'd eaten the last of the Battenberg he couldn't get away fast enough. Neither could I, come to that.'

'Embarrassing,' agreed Liddy.

'That's not the half of it,' sighed Cally. 'To be honest, in a funny way I was sort of relieved.'

'Relieved?' Liddy looked quizzical. Stefan snored gently on his back, paws in the air, his jutting lower jaw a quivering row of crooked yellow teeth. 'Cally Storm, you are not *normal*. I thought you fancied the pants off Will.'

Cally wriggled uncomfortably on her wobbly Windsor chair. 'I do, I do. It's just . . . look, one minute the guy's making like I'm a bad smell under his nose or something, the next he's all over me – worse than Eddie. I was half expecting him to go down on one knee in my mum's front room!'

'Still, it's nice to be wanted,' commented Liddy wistfully. 'Some of us'd give our right arms to be lusted after by a hunk like Will Inglis.' She cast a sidelong glance at the unlovely round grey thing at her feet. '*Some* of us have nothing but a smelly old dog to warm our feet on at night.'

'Yes, well, *some* of us are still feeling pretty mixed up about our estranged husbands, thank you very much,' retorted Cally. 'Some of us can't make up our minds what to do for the best.'

Liddy leaned forward, intrigued. 'You're never thinking of going back to him?'

'I don't know,' Cally admitted, rolling her glass round in her hands so that the cream liqueur coated the inside like off-white emulsion. 'I don't know what I think any more.'

'He cheated on you!'

'I know.'

'And not just the once, either. He made you look like a complete idiot!'

215

'I know that too. I just don't know if I'm ready to chuck the whole marriage away.'

'Cally, Rob already did that for you. This is just your dad making you feel guilty. You know he's always had a blind spot about Rob.'

'No, it's more than that,' insisted Cally. 'I'm really not sure if I'm over him yet.'

'And what about you and Will?'

'What about us? There is no us. Anyhow, I've got to go and see Rob in a few days' time. Maybe that'll sort something out.'

'You never said you were going up to Northampton.'

'I wasn't. Then I got this.' She produced the letter from her pocket. 'I've got an interview in Milton Keynes. Rob and I are meeting up afterwards.'

'Well, well, well,' said Liddy. 'You are a dark horse. And there was I, thinking you were settling in at the zoo.'

Cally smiled. 'It's not a zoo, remember – it's an *experience*.'

'Hmm. And so is your love life, darling.' Liddy flung herself back in her chair and contemplated her friend through heavy-lidded eyes. 'Never mind, you've still got me and Eddie. At least we're nice and uncomplicated.'

This was received with an explosion of derisive laughter. 'Oh yeah. Right.'

Liddy looked quite wounded. 'What's complicated about me?'

'I wasn't thinking about you, I was thinking about Eddie.'

The eyes narrowed to small slits behind the letter-box-shaped glasses. 'Go on. What's he done now?'

'Only fallen in love. Again.'

216

'But he's always falling in love!'

'Ah, but is he always falling in love with girls who sell the *Big Issue*?'

Liddy scratched her head. 'Well, it takes all sorts. It's hardly a crime, is it?'

'True,' agreed Cally, 'except there's something not quite right about this little romance. I've got really bad vibes about Janis. For one thing, she wanders round the flat picking Eddie's stuff up and staring at it, like she's weighing up how much she could flog it for down the pub. And there's something really weird about her.'

'What kind of weird?'

'Well, for a start off she never looks at you when you talk to her, just gazes into space like she's on something. And the way Eddie's mooning about after her, he's heading for one hell of a fall.'

'Hmm.' Liddy reflected. 'Can't have that.'

'Frankly I don't see what we can do to stop him. He's crazy about her.'

'Then it's just as well I've got the very thing, isn't it?'

'What thing?' demanded Cally. 'What are you on about?'

Liddy smirked and rubbed her hands. 'Trust me, it'll work just fine. The only thing is, you're going to have to be a big brave girlie and do what Auntie Liddy tells you.'

'Am I up for this?'

'Of course you are!'

Cally leaned forward, refilled glass in her hands. 'All right Blofeld. Tell me more. . .'

For the next few days, Cally and Will made quite an impressive job of avoiding each other, without actually admitting to themselves that that was what they were doing. If it hadn't been for Stan, they could probably have kept it up indefinitely.

'Bloody hell, Will!' yelled Martin the sea lion keeper. 'There's a frigging donkey in the penguin pool!'

Will dropped his bucket with a clatter, sending dead mackerel slithering in all directions, and legged it towards the pool. Sure enough, a small crowd had gathered to laugh at the merry antics of the small black donkey which was thrashing its way through the water, in pursuit of several dozen very disgruntled penguins.

'Stan!' roared Will with uncharacteristic savagery. 'Get your fat furry arse out of my pool this minute!'

The donkey drew back its lips and gave a bray of joyful contempt.

'Oh God, I'm so sorry,' panted Cally, arriving on the scene at an ungainly gallop. 'I only turned my back to fill the water trough, and he limboed under that iffy bit in the paddock fence.'

Will put his hands round her neck as though to throttle her. 'How many times have I told Eric?'

'I know, I know. We were going to mend it yesterday, only—'

'Never mind the damn fence, get that donkey away from my pool!'

Cally gazed haplessly at Stan, who had jumped out of the water and was now speeding around the edge, scattering penguins right, left and centre.

'How?'

'Grab his halter as he goes past.'

She picked a soggy length of rope up off the floor. 'Guess what – he just slipped it.'

'Weetabix.' Martin's voice floated over the wall from the sea lions. 'Remember last time?'

Will clicked his fingers. 'Weetabix, of course.' He turned to Cally. 'Run to the kitchens and get some.'

'But . . .'

'Go on! Don't just stand there. Fetch the bloody Weetabix!'

'With or without milk and sugar?'

Will raised his eyes to heaven. 'Just bring the box!'

It was a strange scene: Cally standing at the side of the penguin pool, shaking a catering-sized box of Weetabix, while Will did his darnedest to sneak up on Stan with a halter.

'Come on Stan, get your lovely Weetabix.' Cally rattled the box, feeling like a complete prat. The donkey paddled around in the shallows, playing hard to get. 'It's no good, he's not interested.'

'He will be. Keep trying.' Trouser legs rolled up to the knees, Will waded through the water, watched with interest by the rockhoppers, who seemed to have cottoned on to the fact that they were not going to be eaten by a runaway donkey and were perched atop a rock, enjoying the show. 'Cally . . .'

'Hmm?'

'I . . . er . . . wanted to say . . .' He changed tack suddenly. 'Go on, say something to him, he's looking at the box.'

'Yummy yummy yummy,' said Cally, taking a biscuit out of the box and waving it enticingly. 'Look Stan, I'm eating mine. Wanted to say what?' she asked cautiously, half encouraged by the look on Will's face, half anxious that she might have misread it.

'I . . . um . . . look, I'm really . . . you know . . .'

'I'm sorry too,' cut in Cally, taking a chance as he floundered.

'Sorry?' Will was so startled that he almost lost his footing on the slippery tiles. 'But that was *my* line!'

'What have you got to apologise for? Quick, he's having a nibble – go for it!'

Will sprang, managed to get a grip on Stan's flanks, and then was shaken off as the donkey set off on another canter around the edge of the pool. 'Coming your way, Cal . . . oh damn. What have I got to apologise for? Well for a start off, I behaved like a caveman over that Rob thing. And I came on far too strong. I shouldn't have done that.'

'It wasn't your fault,' insisted Cally, as Stan trotted to a halt, shook himself and then walked right up to her and stuck his head in the cereal packet. 'I shouldn't have pushed you away. Will – quick!'

The halter was on the donkey in five seconds flat, and Will slapped the end of the rope into Cally's hand. '*Try* not to do that again,' he urged, shaking water out of his hair.

'Do what?' enquired Cally, rather distracted by the sudden, soft warmth in Will's blue eyes.

'I can't remember.'

'Neither can I.'

'Cally.'

'What?'

'Can we, I mean, could we maybe . . . try again?'

She was just closing her eyes in delicious anticipation of his lips touching hers when the sound of polite coughing shattered the mood completely.

'*Excusez-moi.*'

Cally and Will sprang apart, with the kind of laboured innocence that was an instant proclamation of guilt. Simone was standing by the penguin pool looking like a Paris fashion plate, her normally sober work suit exchanged for something short and slinky in a very Mediterranean shade of pink precisely matched to her lipstick.

'Did you want something?' enquired Will, self-consciously rolling down his trouser legs.

'I am looking for Vernon,' replied Simone's shimmery mouth. 'Do you know where 'e eez?'

'Well, I thought I saw him in the—' began Will, but he hadn't bargained for Stan's sense of timing.

In one almighty bound, the little black donkey jerked the halter rope out of Cally's hand and belly-flopped into the pool, landing with a colossal splur-doosh! that drenched Simone from head to foot.

Unlike the penguins, she did not see the funny side.

Chapter Nineteen

'I always did like the seaside,' said Liddy, skipping along the beach with her face in a big pink ball of candyfloss. Stefan followed behind with his nose to the ground, a small pink crab dangling from his mouth.

'This isn't the seaside,' Will corrected her, 'this is Weston-super-Mare. Mudside, more like.'

'Who cares?' Liddy pulled off a big blob of candyfloss and stuffed it into Will's open mouth. 'It's got sea, it's got a pier, it's got slot machines and rude postcards – that's good enough for me.'

'You're easily pleased.'

Liddy grinned. 'I must be, I've got you as a friend.'

They walked on together in the June sunshine, watching as a herring gull swooped down and made off with the chocolate flake from a ninety-nine.

'That's what you need to be more like,' counselled Will.

'What – a seagull?'

'Kind of. Quicker off the mark, up for anything. Ready to sneak in and grab the best stuff from under other people's noses. Otherwise, your stock'll never do you justice.'

'What's wrong with my stock?' demanded Liddy, leaning on Will's shoulder to take off one shoe and shake out a pebble.

'Nothing . . . as such.'

'Meaning?'

'Meaning, the stuff's all right in itself, but it's all over the place. Really unfocused. If you're going to drag in the big-spending customers, you'll need to develop more of a theme, tap into what people are really going crazy for right now.'

Liddy sat down cross-legged on the sand, wriggled out of her cardigan and let the June sun get to her winter-white arms. 'All right then, Mr Know-It-All, what *are* people going crazy for right now?'

Will kicked off his trainers and peeled off his socks. Seeing as half the Experience was closed for a couple of days, to install new equipment, he had acquired some unexpected holiday and he might as well make the most of it. After all, the ice creams were on Liddy.

'Well,' he began, 'don't overstock on *Star Wars* stuff – at least, not the new merchandise – the market's flooded with crap. Oh, and you can forget the *X-Files*, that's old hat. If I were you, I'd get in some really nice quality Sixties and Seventies cult stuff – and maybe some of that classy early Disney merchandise, from the Twenties and Thirties.'

'Hang on,' said Liddy, 'we're not all made of money, you know.'

'Yeah, sure, but the shop's doing OK isn't it? I mean, you always seem to have plenty of customers.'

'Well yes,' she admitted. 'But I can't buy in loads of stock, just like that.'

'Why not?'

She flailed. 'Because.'

'I'll give you a generous discount,' wheedled Will, lying down and covering his face with his hat.

Liddy whisked it away. 'Discount, eh? I wondered

when we'd get to your evil capitalist profit motive! Don't you ever think about anything but making money?'

'Penguins,' muttered Will, stifling a sun-warmed yawn. 'I think about them quite a lot.'

'Apart from penguins.'

'Dunno.'

'How about sex?'

Will opened one eye and glanced dubiously up at Liddy. 'Well it's very nice of you to offer, but I think I'd rather have an ice cream if it's all the same to you.'

'Oh ha ha, very clever. You know what I'm talking about. You and Cally.'

Will grabbed his hat back and covered his face again. His voice emerged from underneath it, somewhat muffled. 'What about me and Cally?'

'She's made a big impression on you, hasn't she?' He didn't answer, so she upended half a bottle of iced mineral water on his crotch.

He shot upright. 'Aaah!'

'Hasn't she?' repeated Liddy.

Will writhed inside his soaking shorts. 'What if she has?' he hedged.

What indeed? thought Liddy. And she felt strangely uncomfortable at the prospect, without really knowing why.

It was Wednesday, so this must be Milton Keynes. Lovely, lovely Milton Keynes, the town where every road was a boulevard, every corner was a right-angle and every pigeon had an American accent. Yeuch. Still, thought Cally, I ought at least to try and like it; after all, I may end up working here.

The idea filled her with unaccountable uneasiness. She ought to have been thrilled that a proper job was at last within her grasp, but her thoughts kept drifting back to The Animal Experience. Was Len remembering to give Stan his worm drench? Were the animals scared by the big machinery that was moving into the park to build tourist attractions for August Bank Holiday? It was pointless worrying about it, but that didn't stop her doing it.

The European Headquarters of the Fifth National Bank of Formosa stood at the intersection of Seventh Avenue and Churchill Boulevard; a peculiar, almost triangular building faced with veined white marble, making it look like a gigantic wedge of Stilton.

Cally felt unusually nervous as she pushed through the revolving door and stepped into the foyer. Perhaps she was more out of practice than she'd thought. It was only a few months since this kind of place had seemed like a second home, but it felt like ten years. It didn't help that her suit itched like crazy, and felt as if it had been made for somebody a completely different shape – someone without rhino-sized biceps and the thigh muscles of a steroid-enhanced shot-putter. Her entire physique had changed since she'd started working at the Experience. And somehow, inexplicably, she had lost the art of applying millimetre-perfect lippy in one slick swipe. It just didn't make sense.

'Good morning,' smiled the girl behind the desk. 'Can I help you?'

Cally handed across her interview letter, hoping the yellow stains on it would go unnoticed in the diffused lighting. Donkey urine was a bugger to get out.

'Ah yes, Ms Storm. If you'd like to pin on this badge and follow me . . . Mr Greenbaum thought you might like to meet some of the people you'd be working with while you're waiting for your interview.'

226

That sounded reasonable enough, at least, thought Cally as she followed the girl down a faceless, shiny corridor in which the only concessions to decoration were enormous water-cooling machines every ten yards.

'In here please,' the girl instructed her, opening an unmarked door and letting out the strains of plinky-plonky oriental music. 'You can leave your jacket and shoes in the rack in the corner.'

'Shoes?'

The girl smiled; a professional smile that had clearly seen a lot of active service. 'I'm sure you'll be much more comfortable doing the exercises barefoot.'

'Exercises?'

The girl disappeared. As Cally walked into the room, she registered the full horror of what she had just let herself in for. She had heard about it, laughed about it, even seen it on training videos, but until now she had never really believed it actually happened. Twenty sweating executives in shirtsleeves were simultane-ously balancing on one foot, eyes closed, waving their arms about to something that sounded like dried peas being dropped down the back of a piano.

'And . . . relax,' beamed an ancient Chinese lady in black silk pyjamas, turning off the music on the CD player. 'You are most welcome, my dear, please come and join us.'

'If it's all the same, I think I'll just watch,' replied Cally, edging towards a chair she had just spotted in the corner. 'I'm only visiting.'

'Nonsense, nonsense,' panted a portly middle-aged man, hitching up his sagging trousers. 'Join in, it's easy. You'll soon get the hang of it.'

Far from convinced, Cally allowed herself to be

manoeuvred into the middle of the back row, between the portly man and a woman with a Margaret Thatcher hairdo and cheekbones you could cut yourself on.

'Armstrong-Jones,' said the man, wiping sweat on to his shirtsleeve and sticking out his hand. 'Internal Auditor. Coming to work here?'

'Maybe. I'm here for an interview.'

'Good for you. Best bloody financial institution you can work for, is FNBF. Annual profits are half the GNP of Holland, but I expect you've already done your research.'

Since Cally's research had amounted to finding out how to get there from the train station, she just smiled and said nothing. The ancient Chinese woman switched the music back on again.

'Please to follow the others,' she instructed sweetly. 'And listen to the inner harmony of your soul.'

Cally's soul was anything but harmonious as she tried to follow something between a Maori haka and moon-walking. It didn't help that everybody else seemed to know exactly what to do. Left foot forward, right arm back. How could anybody lunge in slow motion? And the music was no help at all, it just kept plinking away in the background and making her want to go to the toilet. Oooh, come to think of it she really did want to go. Was there time to sneak out and find the Ladies?

Just when she thought she was starting to get the hang of the exercises, the music changed. One minute it was tinkling away, nice and slow and tranquil; the next it was galloping along like a club classic at the Ministry of Sound. It wouldn't have been so bad if the woman with the cheekbones hadn't been standing too close. That way, when she made with the Thai-style boxing kick, her foot wouldn't have hit Cally square in the backside, propelling her sideways into the auditor's marshmallow stomach.

The tangle of legs and arms hit the floor at the very moment the door opened, revealing a man with a sober blue suit, sarcastic eyebrows and no sense of humour.

'Miss Storm?'

'Er . . . yes,' she replied, hastily disentangling herself from the human ball of string.

'If you'd like to come with me. The interview panel are ready for you now.'

'It's not funny!' protested Cally, doing her best to be indignant as Rob spluttered into his cappuccino. 'It's not! I've never been so embarrassed in my whole life.'

'What about that time you fell down the escalator in Ikea, and showed everybody your Bugs Bunny knickers?' ventured Rob, stopping conversation at several adjoining tables.

'Shush!' Cally glanced around the café in embarrassment. 'People will hear.'

Undaunted, Rob continued to entertain everybody within a radius of ten feet. 'And the time you had that vindaloo . . .'

She covered her eyes in shame. 'Rob, nooo!'

'I bet you ten quid the bishop never got those stains out of his mitre.'

Cally's stern resolve crumbled, and her shoulders started to shake with laughter. 'Stop it!'

'See!' Rob declared triumphantly. 'It *is* funny.'

'You wouldn't say that if it'd been you,' retorted Cally. 'There I am, spreadeagled all over the Internal Auditor, and in comes the chairman of the interview panel.' She put on a snooty sneer. ' "We're ready for you now, Ms Storm." Talk about humiliating!'

'Still, the interview went well, didn't it?' Rob licked coffee froth off his spoon. 'Bet you had them eating out of your hand.'

Cally shrugged. 'I suppose.'

'You *suppose*?' Rob was aghast. 'What happened to "I'm the best in the business and I'm gonna prove it"?'

'As far as I'm concerned, if they don't like me they can get stuffed.'

Rob's expression was caught between amazement and admiration. 'Good God Cally. You *have* changed.'

She replied through a mouthful of caramel shortcake. 'Well, you haven't.'

Rob adjusted the knot on his tie. 'Still as loveable as ever, eh?'

He looked so hopeful, thought Cally. Like a puppy waiting for a pat on the head. She took a long, lingering sip of her hot chocolate. 'You know what we should be talking about, don't you?'

'Tell me.'

'A divorce.'

She was looking right into his eyes. To her surprise and discomfort, he did not look away.

'So why aren't we?' he asked softly.

He waited a long time for an answer. But he didn't get one.

When Rob got home that evening, at first he thought the house was empty. No one had plugged the TV in, and the answering machine was still switched on, though nobody had left him any messages. He felt faintly disappointed. Part of him had hoped he would return to find an impassioned message from Cally, admitting that she'd made a terrible mistake and pleading with him to

230

take her back. Ah well, maybe she'd ring him later on, when she got back to Cheltenham.

He threw his briefcase on to the hall table, shrugged off his jacket and wandered into the kitchen to put the kettle on. It was then that he saw Rachel, standing in the conservatory with the sleeves of her sensible librarian's blouse rolled up and one strand of glossy brown hair escaping from her neat chignon as she bent over a tray of cuttings.

His cuttings!

'Rachel!' He was tired, but he moved into that conservatory like greased lightning. 'Rachel, what the hell do you think you're doing!'

She glanced up with an apologetic smile. There was a little smear of cactus compost under one eye, giving her a faintly disreputable look which was completely at odds with her neat, competent image. It suited her.

'Oh, I'm sorry,' she said, wiping her hands on a cloth. 'I just couldn't stop myself.'

Rob surveyed the devastation with dismay: 'What have you done? They're all in different pots!'

'Yes, well, the thing is, as soon as I set eyes on them I knew the compost was far too wet.'

'It was?'

'Oh yes, you can't let it get too wet or you'll get root rot and all sorts of fungal problems. So I went out and bought a bag of compost and a few new pots – oh, and I mixed up some of my special rooting compound. I hope you don't mind.'

Rob blinked. 'You know about plants then?'

'Oh yes,' she smiled, as a coil of hair came unfastened from its pins, slid down over her shoulder and swished down her back. 'I've been into cacti ever since I was knee-high to a prickly pear.'

231

'Well whaddya know,' said Rob, brightening visibly. 'Looks like you and I have something in common after all.'

'Lids,' protested Cally, caving in and feeding Stefan half of her doughnut, 'it's a great idea in theory but it'll never work.'

'Why not?' demanded Liddy, taking a beaten-up Action Man out of the bargain box and rummaging around for some combat trousers to fit him.

'Because it's all very well fixing Eddie up with a blind date, but he won't go on it, will he? He's got Janis.' She leaned over. 'Ugh, Action Man in the nude, not a pretty sight.'

Liddy giggled. 'I bet Eddie isn't either.'

'Please. Don't make me think about it. There's been far too much of Eddie in the nude lately, what with Janis and Ziggy round every hour of the day. And I could do without the sound effects, as well.'

'Well,' said Liddy, 'in that case, what you need is my masterplan.'

'I told you, he won't go!'

'Oh yes he will,' Liddy corrected her, 'if it's a double date.'

'Uh?'

'And if he's doing a friend a favour to cheer her up,' said Liddy, with heavy emphasis.

'I'm not with you.'

Liddy sighed exasperatedly. 'A friend who's having *man trouble*?'

Cally was mystified. 'But Liddy, you haven't got a boyfriend, how can you have man trouble?' She registered the look of cunning in Liddy's eyes; a look Rasputin would have been proud of. And swallowed hard. 'Oh no.'

'Cally . . .'

'No.'

'Oh come on.'

'No! Absolutely not, no way, not ever!'

Liddy looked wounded. 'But it's all set up!'

'I don't care if you've fixed me up with Brad Pitt, I'm not going on a double date with Eddie!' Cally's annoyance turned into curiosity. 'What have you been up to, you devious little cow?'

'Oh, nothing much. I did the groundwork weeks ago,' said Liddy dismissively. 'When you were having Will trouble. I was only trying to help,' she added sniffily.

'What groundwork!'

'I signed you and Eddie up with a computer dating agency.'

'You did what! But they're for saddos and perverts!'

'Don't be silly. Anyhow, it's too late to back out now, the big double date's all set up for tomorrow night.' Liddy wriggled Action Man into a pair of pants and sat him in the display window with a price tag covering the dent in his head. 'So you'll have to go through with it, won't you?'

Chapter Twenty

The trouble with people who thought they were cool, thought Cally, was that they almost invariably weren't. And Clive the interior designer thought he was the coolest thing since refrigerated underpants.

'Must be interesting, being an interior designer,' suggested Cally as the four blind-daters sat eyeing each other up in one of Cheltenham's most chi-chi café-bars.

'Yeah,' agreed Eddie. 'And you don't have to perch up a ladder in the rain, painting slugs on lettuce leaves.'

Clive ran manicured fingers through two inches of root-lifted peroxide. 'Ah, but you're forgetting the tremendous responsibility.'

'You mean you have to be careful not to damage people's heirlooms?' asked Cally naively. 'Yes, I guess that must be quite stressful.'

Clive patted her hand with the kind of patient forbearance reserved for senile old grannies. 'Good God no! You have to make sure you *do* damage things, otherwise they'll only insist on hanging on to some ghastly G-Plan storage unit and ruin the whole effect.'

Sarah, Eddie's date for the evening, crossed legs that were long and slim, and vanished under the hem of a short red velvet number. She was gorgeous, thought

Cally. Just Eddie's type. Surely he couldn't resist her for long. 'You mean you deliberately . . .?'

'Trash the joint and then start from zero?' Clive let out a grating, equine laugh that set Cally's teeth on edge. 'Natch. Got to save the ignorant punter from his own total lack of taste. The way I see it, I'm a kind of social service to the aesthetically incompetent.'

'That doesn't sound very ethical to me,' said Sarah dubiously.

'Ethical!' Clive snorted. 'That's college students for you, always full of idealistic crap.'

She looked wounded. 'At least I don't take advantage of people's weaknesses.'

'You wait till you get a proper job, darling, you'll be ripping people off just like the rest of us.'

'I'd rather die! And I bet Eddie agrees with me, don't you Eddie?'

She darted a smile of encouragement at him, and Cally noticed that she was rubbing her thigh against his trouser-leg like a purring Siamese. Go for it Eddie, she willed him; but Eddie was edging his chair away again. Any further and he'd be out of the window.

'I haven't drunk here before,' he commented nervously. 'Have you, Clive?'

'Of course I have, I'm a regular. Matter of fact, I've got a little Regency townhouse just round the corner,' he added, for Cally's benefit. 'Use it for the odd weekend, when I'm not at my place in Notting Hill.'

'That's nice,' she said, stifling a yawn.

'Only four bedrooms plus the penthouse,' confessed Clive, 'but it's big enough for me. Everybody knows me in here – don't you, Mike?'

The man clearing away the glasses from the tables

returned his matey slap on the back with a blank stare. 'Is that finished with?'

Without waiting for a reply, he whisked Clive's half-full glass of Murphy's from under his nose and disappeared.

'Hey, wait a minute, come back!' protested Clive, vainly gesturing after the barman. Cally edged a little further from Clive's arm, which kept trying to snake its way round her shoulders. Sarah giggled and made eyes at Eddie. Eddie looked like a damned soul in eternal torment.

'So,' smiled Sarah, stroking her fingers down Eddie's arm.

He swallowed nervously, sending his Adam's apple into a frenzy. 'So.'

'You like poetry then?'

Yes! thought Cally, mentally punching the air. At last she's hit on something he's passionate about. If this doesn't have him melting into her arms, nothing will.

'Er . . . sort of,' said Eddie.

'Only that's what it said on the form,' coaxed Sarah. 'Your number one interest, along with gothic romances and the lithographs of Aubrey Beardsley.'

'Ah,' said Eddie. Cally could almost hear him silently cursing Liddy.

'I just love the English Romantics, don't you?' gushed Sarah. 'Especially Keats.'

Aha, Keats, thought Cally. Eddie's favourite. Go on Ed, get out of that one.

'Actually,' said Eddie, his face contorted with the agony of lying through his teeth, 'I think Keats is a pile of shite.'

Sarah's eyebrows shot up so far they disappeared into her hairline. 'You do?'

'Oh definitely. I much prefer the radical cutting edge, don't I Cally?' He kicked her under the table. *'Don't I, Cally?'*

'Don't you what?'

'What's that book I was reading the other week?' He clicked his fingers as though trying to dredge up the title.

'Rupert the Bear and the Big Red Balloon?' suggested Cally sweetly.

Eddie glared. 'I remember – *Neo-Marxist verse in Postwar Sheffield, with special reference to women's emancipation and the Stalinist dialectic.'*

Sarah looked as if she was about to burst into tears.

'Oh look, it's getting late,' said Cally brightly, willing the hands of the clock above the bar to spin round to eleven o'clock and liberation. Liddy was going to pay for this. In blood. 'Shouldn't we choose somewhere to eat?'

'La Giaconda's nice and cheap,' volunteered Eddie. 'Mind you, the olives always make me fart.' He turned to Sarah. 'Did I tell you I have this really embarrassing bowel problem?'

Clive waved away all suggestions. 'No worries, I've got it all sorted. I've booked a table for four at the Northern Lights.'

'Isn't that that chippy in Stroud that does jumbo black pudding and deep-fried Mars Bars?' said Eddie with studied oafishness.

'Black pudding!' Clive looked utterly disgusted. 'Northern Lights is the only place you can get authentic Icelandic cuisine in the whole of Gloucestershire, *actually. And* it's just got its second Michelin star.'

'Oh terrific,' said Eddie. 'Reindeer balls in polar-bear sauce. My favourite. You're a vegan aren't you, Sarah?'

'I'm sure they do a lovely plate of lichen,' replied Clive with calculated malice. He treated Cally to a particularly slimy smile. 'Nothing but the best for you, my darling. We're going to have a simply wonderful time.'

It was getting on for midnight by the time Cally and Eddie headed for home through the near-deserted streets.

'I feel sick,' complained Eddie, rubbing his stomach. 'What *was* that red stuff?'

'Rhubarb and halibut purée, apparently.'

'Oh God, I'm going to die.'

'Don't be silly.'

'Yes I am, it was vile.'

'Why did you eat it then?'

'Because it was either that or the cod pudding, and there is no way you are *ever* going to catch me eating something with cod *and* prunes in it.'

'Aw, c'mon,' she teased. 'I ate mine. Where's your spirit of adventure?'

'Down the toilet, along with the fifty quid I wasted.'

'Well . . . it was an experience,' Cally pointed out. 'And I did enjoy the bit where Sarah threw up all over Clive's shoes.'

A smile spread over Eddie's face. 'Maybe I won't die just yet,' he said. 'I'd like to live a bit longer, just so I can remember the look on his face.'

They strolled on a bit further, then started playing one-a-side football along the pavement, with an empty Coke can.

'You didn't like Clive much, did you?' observed Eddie with his usual acute perception.

'About as much as I like ringworm. What about you and Sarah?'

Eddie looked up anxiously. 'I did try and put her off. You do think I managed to put her off, don't you? Only I'd hate her to get the wrong idea.

'Eddie darling, the last I saw of her she was getting into a taxi with Clive. If that's not putting somebody off, I don't know what is!'

Retrieved from the shop doorway, the empty drinks can rattled along the kerb, sounding peculiarly loud in the night-time emptiness.

'Cally,' said Eddie in the tones of a well-trained social worker, 'I just want you to know I understand.'

'You do?'

'Oh yes. And I'm with you all the way.'

Puzzled, she stopped dribbling the can and turned to look at him. 'That's nice,' she said, for want of anything more sensible to say.

Eddie shoved his hands deep in his pockets and shuffled along, staring at his feet. 'The thing is, I had no idea things were so bad between you and Will . . .'

Just in time, Cally stopped herself saying that actually they weren't, not at the moment, but that any more of this double-dating nonsense and they soon might be.

'. . . and as we're mates, I want you to know I really admire the way you've been keeping your spirits up.'

'What? You admire me?'

'God, yes. If I'd been through what you've been through, I'd have been certified months ago. I was loveless and alone too, till Janis touched my heart and made it blossom. Look, Cal.' He stopped and took her by the shoulders. '*I'm* going to make sure you find a bloke.'

'Er . . .'

'And if you need me to come along on any more blind dates to protect you, you just say so, OK?' He struck a pose. 'It shall be Sir Eddie's proud duty to protect milady's honour.'

Cally burst out laughing, threw the Coke can into the air and drop-kicked it over a wall.

'What's so funny?' demanded Eddie.

'Nothing. Absolutely nothing.'

'So what's with the hyena impressions?'

'Proper food,' she announced, 'that's what we need. Chips. Big, squidgy, crispy chips.'

Eddie's ears pricked up. 'Now you come to mention it,' he admitted, 'I am starting to feel a bit peckish.'

'Come on then, I'll race you home. Last one in peels the spuds!'

Chapter Twenty-One

It wasn't every day that the donkeys went for a walk across The Animal Experience at six o'clock in the morning. Then again, it wasn't every day that somebody wanted to put up a bungee tower in their paddock.

'Come on, let's get a move on,' Vernon called down the ambling line of donkeys and keepers. 'There's the llamas and the shires to move after this lot, and the builders clock on at seven.'

'Bloody bastard tourists,' grumbled Lazy Bob, scratching himself as his too-tight T-shirt rode up over his wobbling stomach. 'What they want to go danglin' on bloody elastic ropes for, anyhow?'

'Who knows? But it brings in money.' Vernon fixed Bob with a none-too-patient stare. 'Anybody'd think you wanted this place to close down. Just get moving, it's the visitors who pay our wages, remember.'

'Not that they'd pay his if they could see the state of him,' commented Len, applying persuasion to the back end of a matronly grey who had stopped to sample a tasty clump of thistles. 'Gi' us a hand with Rosa, Bob, I cannae shift her on ma own.'

'Too busy,' Bob replied promptly. 'Got Colin to see to, catch up with you later.'

'Bone-idle bastard,' muttered Len.

Lazy Bob disappeared, not particularly missed by anybody, and the caravan of donkeys moved on. About halfway along its length was a strange *ménage à trois*, consisting of one man, one girl – and one Stan.

Cally and Will were walking on either side of the small black menace, Cally holding the halter and Will swinging a couple of buckets of dead mackerel. It wasn't going well.

'Won't they go off or something?' hinted Cally, indicating the buckets of fish.

'What, them? Oh no, no hurry. Did I tell you about that entire carton of vintage Barbies I got hold of last week?'

Only non-stop for the last fifteen minutes, thought Cally; not so much irritated by Will's early-morning perkiness but by her own muted feelings of guilt. It wasn't that she'd actually done anything she shouldn't have. After all, Rob was still her husband whether she liked it or not, and she'd only gone along with the Clive thing because of Liddy's crazy plans for Eddie. All the same, right now she could have done without Will being there to remind her just how confused she was feeling. Frankly, she wasn't sure how she felt about anything or anyone any more. And that included Will.

'Factory perfect, can you believe that?'

'Incredible,' muttered Cally.

'Absolutely unmarked! Still in the boxes, packed ready for delivery. Perfect nineteen sixty-one Barbies, six different costumes, have you any idea how marketable those things are? Collectors are crying out for quality like that. Mind you, I might hang on to them as an investment. What do you reckon I should do?'

Cally was jolted out of her glum imaginings. 'What d'you say?'

'The Barbies. Should I hang on to them or sell on now?'

'Well . . .'

He rubbed his chin. 'You're right, I should probably sleep on it. Don't want to make any rash decisions.'

'Yeah. Right.'

Stan's nose investigated one of Will's buckets of mackerel, sneezed on it and withdrew in disgust.

'Or maybe I'll talk to Liddy. By the way, is she all right, d'you think?'

'Who?'

'Liddy. Is she OK? Only she's been a bit weird lately.'

'Don't talk to me about Liddy,' replied Cally mutinously.

'Why? What's she done?'

'Oh, nothing. Take no notice, I'm just having a bad day.' She recaptured a straggle of hair and tucked it back behind her ear. 'A bad hair day.'

She stroked Stan's muzzle, and the donkey blew appreciative bubbles of fish-flavoured snot into her hand. When she looked up, Will was standing with his head on one side, contemplating her.

'Why are you staring at me like that?'

'Like what? Oh, just thinking.'

'What about?' She wished he would stop, it was making her feel nervous.

'Your hair.' Putting down one of the buckets, Will stroked Cally's hair back from her face and held it behind her head in an impromptu ponytail. 'It'd look so much nicer if you had it cut.'

She stared at him. 'What?'

'Yes, you've definitely got to get it cut.' He was looking at her with a peculiar intensity. 'Really short at

245

the back, with like a . . . a flick over one eye. Oh, and you should start parting your hair on the right.'

'Oh I should, should I?'

'Maybe a few highlights, nothing too obvious mind, you don't want to look tarty.'

That was the final straw.

'Will!' She wrenched her hair out of his hand. 'What the hell gives you the right to tell me how I should look?'

He looked taken aback, as though she had just said something incomprehensible. 'All I did was—'

Cally rounded on him, so vehemently that Stan left off investigating Will's pockets and turned to look at her quizzically. 'Do you know why I wear my hair like this?'

'No,' admitted Will, clearly surprised by the strength of her reaction.

'Not that it's any of your damn business, but I wear it like this because I *like* it this way. Plus, doing wacky things with it tends to distract men from my tits long enough for them to realise I've got a brain.'

Too late, Will realised what his eyes were focused on and lifted his gaze higher. 'Come on Cal, nobody could accuse you of not having a brain. All I did was suggest you might improve yourself a bit.'

That was a red rag to a bull.

'Improve myself! This is my hair you're talking about, Will. *My* hair, have you got that? And I'll wear it any damn way I like. Oh – and just in case you were thinking of asking me to wear fishnet stockings and red suspenders, you can bloody forget that too!'

'Now you're just being childish!'

He couldn't have said a worse thing.

'Here.' She thrust Stan's rope into Will's free hand.

'What's this for?'

'If you like dumb animals so much, why don't you have this one? It's got lovely short hair, and I bet it'd look great in red underwear!'

'What's going on here?' demanded Vernon, arriving on the scene.

'Nothing,' glowered Cally. 'Everything's fine.'

'Oh yeah,' snapped Will. 'Hunky bleeding dory.'

'Looks like it,' commented Vernon drily. 'Listen, I don't care what you're arguing about, and as far as I'm concerned you can have your lovers' tiffs until you're blue in the face, as long as—'

'It wasn't a lovers' tiff!' protested Cally, but Vernon silenced her with a glare.

'As long as they're in your own time, and out of uniform. While you're here you can behave like sensible adults. Will . . .'

'Yes?'

'Take that donkey to the farrier, it needs its feet trimming.'

'But what about my penguins?'

'Lee can sort them out. Cally, go and find Lazy Bob, he's gone off with the keys to the boiler house again.'

Oh hell, thought Cally, a horrible sense of foreboding descending on her like a cloud of something very, very smelly. 'But he's cleaning out Colin!'

'Good,' replied Vernon, picking up the buckets of mackerel. 'It's time you two were introduced. And while you're there, you can give Lazy Bob a hand.'

Being dismissed like a naughty girl, and sent off to find the odious Lazy Bob, did not make a good start to Cally's day. Considerably worse was knowing that wherever Lazy Bob was, she would also find Colin.

Colin. The very name sent shivers of apprehension through Cally's soul. Few at the Experience had actually set eyes on Colin the Javan Yellow Skunk, but absolutely everybody had smelled him. No matter what – or who – he went near, it inevitably carried his potent aroma around with it for what seemed like eternity; and a pong like that could really put you off your dinner. That was why anyone with any sense avoided the poor creature like the plague.

Which was probably how Lazy Bob had come to be appointed Colin's keeper. For one thing, he was excessively lazy. And for all his personal odour problems, Colin the skunk took a lot less cleaning out than forty-seven rockhopper penguins or a whole tribe of gibbons. Also, Lazy Bob had one other, indispensable quality that made him the perfect candidate for the job: ever since a nasty accident with the spiny anteaters, he had absolutely no sense of smell.

I wish my nose would fall off, thought Cally as she stomped gloomily towards the furthermost reaches of The Animal Experience. Few casual visitors to the park ever made it this far, to the semi-deserted borderland of empty paddocks and unused enclosures; the nearest ice-cream kiosk was a quarter of a mile away, and most people tended to get sidetracked by the cute alpine marmots. You had to be a dedicated skunk-lover to bother trekking past the Worm Zone to the little green wooden hut half-hidden in the trees.

'Bob?' called Cally. She waited for a reply, but none came. 'Come out Bob, I know you're skulking in there.' You lazy, lard-arsed git, she added under her breath.

A light breeze ruffled the foliage of the saplings planted inside the leafy little chicken-wire run. She pressed her face up to the wire, but could see nothing and nobody inside, though the padlock on the door of the run was unlocked and dangling free.

'Bob? Stop playing silly buggers and get out here. Vernon wants his keys back.'

Damn. It looked like she'd have to go in and fetch him out. Cautiously she pushed open the door of the run, but nothing rushed out to savage her ankles or spray her with Eau de Skunk. Nothing appeared to be lurking in the shrubbery either, so she walked with more confidence towards the wooden hut which comprised the living quarters. Maybe the skunk was ill and Bob had taken it over to the medical block or something.

'Anybody here?' The background smell increased by several notches as she pushed open the door and stuck her head inside. 'Bob? Oh, yeuch.'

It wasn't just that the hut smelt of skunk. The place was an absolute hovel. Bits of rotting fruit lay mouldering on the filthy floor, the bedding clearly hadn't been changed in days, and the water dish was completely empty. At first, Cally thought the hut was empty too, but as she turned to step outside for some fresh air, she saw it. A fluffy orange ball of misery, cowering in the corner.

'Colin?'

It started to tremble violently as she approached it, its tail fluffing up above its back. Softly and gently, she crouched down and extended her hand.

'It's all right Colin, nobody's going to hurt you.'

Which is more than you can say for Bob when I get my hands on him, she thought to herself with barely suppressed fury. Congenitally lazy or not, there was absolutely no excuse for this.

'Are you hungry? I bet you are, you poor little thing.' She rummaged in her pocket for the remains of the apple she'd meant to give to Stan, and bit off a chunk. It wasn't much, but it was something. 'Here you are, sweetie,' she said, trying to imagine she was seducing Brad Pitt with a chilled grape. 'Nice bit of apple for you, come and get it darling.'

The skunk shuffled nervously.

'Everything's all right, sweetie. Nobody's going to hurt you. Look, I'm putting this piece of apple down on the floor.'

A small, pointy snout emerged from the fluffy orange ball, followed by two bright, round eyes that glittered warily. Poor creature, thought Cally; it can't help it if it stinks. It took a sudden dart forward, snatched the fruit and darted back, like a recoiling spring.

'Good boy, there's a lovely little skunk.' It sounded silly but the skunk seemed to like it. 'Now, you just eat that all up, and then we'll see if we can get you some wa—'

She was sure she would have managed to gain the poor animal's confidence in the end, maybe even befriended it. But her Disneyesque fantasies of being at one with the skunk nation were abruptly shattered as the door of the hut burst open and Lazy Bob barged in, fag in one hand, shovel in the other, racing paper sticking out of his back pocket.

''Ere.' His Neanderthal brows knitted. 'Wot you doin' wiv my skunk?'

At the sight of Lazy Bob, Colin started shaking like a neurotic blancmange and tried to bury himself under his wet, smelly bedding. Cally rose slowly to her feet.

'He's not *your* skunk.'

'Yes he is,' said Bob, defending his territory with unusual energy. 'Colin's my responsibility, he's nuffing to do wiv you.'

'Then how come you can't even be bothered to feed him?' snapped Cally. 'And look at this!' She shoved a handful of filthy straw under his nose. 'You're not fit to look after animals, you're not fit to look after a . . . a cardboard box!'

'It's only a fucking skunk!'

'Only!'

'It stinks to high heaven.'

'So do you. And at least Colin doesn't wear the same T-shirt for a fortnight.'

'You snotty cow!—'

So bound up were they in slagging each other off, that Cally and Lazy Bob didn't notice how upset Colin was getting until it was much too late.

'And another thing . . . oh shit.' Lazy Bob suddenly stopped in mid-sentence, froze, then backed away, staring at something behind Cally's right shoulder.

'What?' Cally turned, following his gaze. Right behind her, tail fluffed up like the biggest feather duster in the world, was Colin. He looked deeply unhappy, to say the least. 'Calm down, there's a good boy,' she soothed. 'Everything's going to be fine.'

'You know what he's going to do, don't you?' Bob fumbled for the door latch. 'Shit, the door's jammed, I can't get out!'

'Good skunk, nice Colin,' purred Cally, reaching out another morsel of apple. And it looked as if he might even take it, until his nerves were stretched to breaking-point by the sight of Lazy Bob's hairy buttocks, jiggling above the waistband of his trousers as he fought to open the door.

'Oh God no,' squeaked Cally as the skunk started spinning round. 'I think he's going to . . .'

And sure enough, he did.

* * *

251

It was one hell of a smell. In fact, it was the smell from Hell.

'He ees not happy, you know,' said Simone, trying to keep her distance from the rank odour, which wasn't easy in a diminutive Portakabin. 'He ees not happy at all.'

'I don't care if he's suicidal,' retorted Cally. 'Lazy Bob's not fit to be in charge of that skunk.' She paced Simone's office floor, hands in pockets, long since oblivious to the miasma that dogged her every step. 'You can't let him get away with it.'

'True,' sighed Simone. 'But you see, he is upset because you have, how you say? invaded his *territoire*.'

'Tough. It's about time somebody did, he's a lazy git. I hope you're going to sack him.'

'I don't think zat will be necessary,' replied Simone.

'What!'

'Bob tells me he ees not happy looking after Colin, so I transfer him.'

'What – to look after another animal?'

Simone smiled. '*Mais non*. To cutting up bananas in ze animal kitchen.'

Grudgingly, Cally had to admit that this might be a reasonable compromise. And there was always the tantalising prospect that Bob might accidentally slice off part of himself and feed it to the vampire bats.

'So,' she said, 'shall I go and get washed now then?'

Simone put up her hand. 'One moment.' Getting up from her seat, she walked quickly across to the door, glanced outside and closed it. 'First, I wanted to have a leetle word wiz you.'

Here it comes, thought Cally. Vernon's bent her ear about me rowing in public with Will, and I'm going to get the big lecture on appropriate behaviour. 'Oh?' she said, as if she hadn't figured it out. 'What about?'

Simone coughed uncomfortably. 'Cally, you are a woman of ze world, yes?'

'Am I?' she replied. 'I suppose.'

'And you have been in love?'

Cally squirmed slightly. This was reminiscent of those birds and bees talks embarrassed parents tried to give you when you were about twelve and already knew more than they did. 'Yeees. Why?'

Simone's face deflated, sinking her chin on to her hands. 'Eet is Vernon,' she sighed.

'What about him?'

'I do everyzing, everyzing. I try always to make myself look nice. Why does he not notice me?'

This, thought Cally, was definitely not on my job description. 'Oh, I'm sure he does notice you,' she said encouragingly. 'It's obvious he likes you.'

Simone shook her head disconsolately. 'No, he does not. I try so hard and still he does not see zat I am in love wiz him.'

'Ah,' said Cally. 'In love. Right. I didn't realise you were quite so, you know, serious.'

'Ees it zat I am a leetle older? Or zat I have children?'

'Oh, I shouldn't think so. Vernon's great with kids.'

'He has a girlfriend already?'

Cally shook her head. 'He's never mentioned one, I think he's too busy with work for girlfriends.'

'Zen you think he does not like women? Zat he is . . .?'

'God no.' For some reason, the very thought of Vernon being gay struck her as ludicrous. 'I'm sure he isn't.'

'So you zink I still have a chance, yes?'

Cally moved to put an arm round Simone's shoulders, saw the Frenchwoman's face turn white as the

253

smell hit home, and hastily withdrew. 'Of course you do. But why are you asking me?'

Simone rattled her fingernails on the desktop.

'Vernon likes you. I was wondering . . . would you speak to him for me?'

'Me!'

'Just a leetle word, to tell him zat I, you know, like him very much?'

'Well,' said Cally doubtfully, 'I don't know if he'll take any notice of me.' She caught the look on Simone's face, and added hastily, 'But of course I will, if you want me to.'

'Zank you, Cally. I will not forget zis.'

'Zat – I mean that's OK.' She stood up to go.

'One more zing.'

'Yes?'

'Now zat Bob ees going to be working in ze animal kitchens, we will need someone to take on his job.' She smiled invitingly. 'How would you like to take care of ze Javan Yellow Skunk?'

'This smells really weird,' commented Cally, poking her nose into the cocktail Liddy had just thrown together for her.

'I hate to tell you,' replied Liddy, tossing in a little paper umbrella and half a kiwi fruit, 'but that funny smell isn't the cocktail.'

'But I've had three showers,' protested Cally, giving her own arm an exploratory sniff. 'And half a can of deodorant.'

'Better get used to it, kid,' said Liddy gaily, flopping down into an old stripey deckchair she had found in her grandmother's attic. 'From now on the only exclusive fragrance you're going to be wearing is Eau de Skunk.'

'You think I'm an idiot, don't you, taking on Colin? You think I should have said no.'

'Not if you like skunks.'

Cally wriggled down in her deckchair and savoured the evening sunshine. One of the few things she missed about the house in Northampton was spending lazy summer evenings in the garden. Well, she would just have to spend them in Liddy's garden instead.

A bee buzzed over Liddy's drink, had a quick sip of the bright pink concoction, and lumbered off to collapse drunkenly in the nearest hollyhock.

'I don't know if I do or not. I've only met the thing once, and it sprayed all over me.'

'Face it,' commented Liddy, 'if it carries on like that it might cramp your style a bit in the love-life department.'

Cally pulled a face. 'Who wants a love life anyway?'

'You do,' replied Liddy. She tapped her nose knowingly. 'Or at least, Eddie thinks you do.'

'Huh,' grunted Cally. 'Operation Eddie's not going very well, is it? All the ghastly double dates I've put up with for his sake, and he's still as stuck on Janis as ever. Maybe we should just let him get on with it.'

'Oh no.' Liddy waggled a disapproving finger. 'No, no, no, no, no.'

'What if he's happy the way he is?'

Liddy shook her head. 'Janis is bad news, you said so yourself. What about all that business with Eddie's paintings?'

'True.' Cally recalled the number of times she'd caught Janis going through Eddie's work when he wasn't there. It gave her the creeps. 'But I might be wrong about her.'

'Oh come on.'

'And besides, it's all very well for you, you don't have to go on the damn dates.'

'Ah, but think of all the gorgeous blokes you've met.'

'Gorgeous?' Cally snorted so hard that her drink went down the wrong way. 'Let me see, there was Kevin, with the pigeon loft and the skin disease. And James, with the genital piercings. Or did you mean Rodney the proctologist, with the open marriage and the brown fingernails?'

'All right, all right, maybe you haven't met Mr Right yet.'

'Darling, I haven't even met Mr Remotely Normal.'

'Unless you count Will.'

'Yeah, unless I count Will, and I'm not even sure about him.'

'Still having problems?' enquired Liddy.

'Put it this way. How many boyfriends have you had who tried to dictate what shade of nail varnish you should wear, and wanted you to stop plucking your eyebrows?'

'None,' she admitted. 'But I did have one who bought me a split-crotch rubber catsuit.'

'What did you do?'

'I broke his nose.'

They sat in companionable silence for a while, drinking Liddy's alcoholic concoctions and watching the dragonflies darting over the garden pond.

'Anyhow,' said Cally, 'I thought all this dating business was supposed to be for Eddie's benefit, not mine.'

'It is.' Liddy winked. 'But if there's any tasty talent about, you might as well have the benefit.'

'There isn't,' Cally replied firmly, 'and anyway, I'm thinking of becoming celibate.'

'Not till we've sorted Eddie out you're not!' Liddy replied firmly. 'But how are we going to do it? He's met all those nice girls, and he didn't like a single one of them.'

'No. Because he likes Janis.' She slumped in her chair.

'Can't think why, she sounds weird.'

'She is. You know what, she came up to me the other day and told me exactly how much you must have spent on my Princess Leia!'

'I expect it was just a wild guess.'

'Was it hell, she was right down to the last 99p. That girl *knows* things. And another thing, half the time you don't even know what planet she's on, she walks round in this kind of zonked-out trance.'

Liddy looked concerned. 'You don't think she's on something, do you?'

'God knows, but I'll tell you one thing for definite: whatever it is with her, it's not normal.'

'Hmm,' commented Liddy, 'but then neither is Eddie. Honestly, you go to all that trouble to find him nice girls who are mad enough to go out with him, and he hasn't even got the good grace to like *one* of them.'

Cally closed her eyes and let the sun warm her face. 'Maybe they were a bit *too* nice,' she said, sleepily. 'You know, too well scrubbed and respectable.'

'Too nice?' Liddy clicked her fingers. 'You know, you might just be on to something there . . .'

When Cally walked into the flat that night, Ziggy didn't just whimper, he took one sniff then flattened himself against the wall and howled.

'Oh. My. God!' gasped Janis, taking three steps back

and almost dropping one of Eddie's prized paintings on the floor. 'What's that terrible smell?'

Cally smirked. 'Javan Yellow Skunk. Do you like it?' Peeling off her jacket she walked through into the kitchen and stuffed it straight into the machine. 'Eddie not around?'

'No.'

'Worn him out already?' Cally enquired with more than a hint of malice. You could get seriously bored with sproinging noises from your flatmate's bedroom at all hours of the day and night.

Janis muttered something to herself, and went on sorting through Eddie's work. 'He's gone out,' she said, her voice a curiously flat monotone. ''Spect he'll be back soon.'

'What are you doing with Eddie's pictures?'

The big brown eyes fixed on Cally, but seemed to be looking right through her. 'Nothing.'

'Are you looking for something?'

The eyes swam in and out of focus. 'No. Just looking.'

It was probably only a minute or two, but it felt like at least ten. Making small talk with Janis was a nightmare, particularly with a counterpoint of howling dog in the background. At last Cally heard Eddie's footsteps on the stairs, heaved a sigh of relief and went to open the door.

He was standing outside with a bottle of sparkling wine clutched in his sweaty hands, and a look of radiant ecstasy on his face.

'Isn't it wonderful news?' he gasped, bouncing into the flat past Cally and rushing to deliver a fat squidgy kiss on to Janis's lips.

'News? What news?' demanded Cally.

258

'Hasn't Janis told you?' Eddie and his girlfriend exchanged blissed-out looks.

'Told me what?'

Eddie's grin grew unfeasibly wide. 'She's agreed to move in! Isn't that fantastic?'

Chapter Twenty-Two

Gold in the Attic had recently acquired a most unusual window display.

'For pity's sake, Cally!' wailed Eddie, plaintive in his frustration. 'Enough's enough.'

She turned her face away from him, folded her arms and scowled. 'Bog off.'

Eddie did precisely the opposite. Moving Liddy out of the way, he climbed into the shop window and squeezed himself between Cally and the glass.

'Please, Cal.'

'No.'

He flung himself to his knees, squashing the life out of an origami battle droid. 'Come back to the flat. Please. Look.' He emptied a dish of pot pourri over his head. 'I'm wearing sackcloth and ashes.'

Cally refused to let herself smile. Eddie was a selfish git. Worse than that, he was an idiot. 'I don't care if you're wearing ostrich feathers and a pink tutu, the answer's still no.'

Liddy groaned. 'Have you any idea what you're doing to my trade, squatting there in my shop window?'

'Yes,' replied Cally, with bloody-minded cheer-fulness. 'I'm boosting it. But it's OK, I won't charge you for the publicity.'

Cally had spent five hours in that shop window; five very uncomfortable hours, if the truth were told, but there were times when you either had to sacrifice your personal comfort or your pride, and Cally wasn't ready to give up on the last vestiges of her pride just yet.

She was sitting in a deckchair, a flask of coffee on one side and a hand-drawn notice propped up on the other:

FOR SALE—UNWANTED FLATMATE.

That just about summed it up.

Liddy extricated the remains of the battle droid from under Eddie's knee. 'For God's sake Cally, go home before I run out of saleable stock.'

'Yes, come home,' wheedled Eddie. 'Stop embarrassing Liddy. Look – people are staring.'

'Good,' retorted Cally, waving through the glass at a gaggle of young mothers with prams. 'Maybe one of them's got a room to let.' She fixed Eddie with a stony glare. 'What's the point of my coming back, anyway? I'd only get in the way.'

'No you wouldn't.'

'Oh yes I bloody well would! You, me, Janis and Ziggy? Oh yes, very cosy.'

'But I didn't think you'd mind!'

'You didn't think I'd mind? Good God Eddie, why don't you just sublet the bathroom to a family of Albanian refugees while you're at it! That'll make things even cosier.' She fumed at him, but there was no great satisfaction in it because he just knelt there and whimpered. 'Oh . . . and you can stop cringeing too, it won't do you any good.'

'I'm not cringeing.' Eddie winced and fished around on the floor of the display window. 'I think I've got a drawing pin in my knee.' With difficulty he prised it

262

out and rubbed his injured leg. 'I didn't think you'd mind, really I didn't. Otherwise I wouldn't have asked her.'

'Huh,' grunted Cally.

'It's true, I wouldn't.'

'Then why didn't you ask me?' Cally let out an explosion of exasperated breath. 'Look, that flat may be in your name but it's my home too, right?'

'Right.'

'So I deserve to be consulted before you go asking strange women to move in.'

'Janis isn't a strange woman,' said Eddie defensively. Catching the warning look on Cally's face, he added, 'But yes, I suppose I should have asked you. I'm sorry I didn't.'

'There you go,' said Liddy cheerfully. 'Better late than never.'

'Go on then,' said Cally.

'Go on what?' asked Eddie.

'Ask me if Janis can move in.'

Eddie turned his back on a small boy who was making rude gestures through the window at him. 'OK then. Is it all right with you if Janis moves in?'

'No. It isn't.'

'Cally!'

'If I've got a right to be consulted, I've got a right to say no.'

'You can't! I've already asked her. Besides, it's my name on the lease, you said so yourself.'

'Oh I see, so I can like it or lump it?'

Eddie looked uncomfortable, as well he might. 'Oh Cal, I've said I'm sorry. And it's not as if Janis has got some four-bedroom penthouse apartment to go back to, is it? All she's got is a shared room in some horrible hostel, run by a man called Dingo! And he wears a string vest.'

Cally looked at Liddy. Liddy looked away. She was on her own here.

'Oh Eddie,' groaned Cally. 'Can't you see what a terrible mistake you're making?'

'If I am,' replied Eddie, looking her squarely in the eye, 'it's my mistake to make.'

Eddie hummed to himself as he rustled up a delicious little gourmet supper for one. Well, it was gourmet by his standards anyway; and he'd always had a fondness for tinned spaghetti hoops.

The tomato sauce was just bubbling nicely when the doorbell sounded. Typical, thought Eddie, taking the pan off the gas with a wistful backward glance. They never tasted as nice when you reheated them, and the toast was bound to be cold and chewy by the time whoever it was had stopped trying to talk him into buying whatever it was they were selling.

He opened the door with a flourish. 'Before you say anything, I'm not intere— oh, hello Will.'

Will stood awkwardly on the landing, his one and only decent pair of trousers pressed to within an inch of their life, his face barely visible behind a large bunch of assorted lilies. Slowly the flowers sank to waist-level. 'Oh, it's you. I thought you were Cally.'

'In which case you need your eyes testing.' Eddie looked his visitor up and down, by no means inclined to invite him in. 'Anyhow, what makes you think she'd want to see you?'

Will, the king of cool, looked uncharacteristically edgy. 'She told you then? About the . . . er . . . row?'

Eddie folded his arms and leaned against the door-post, his spaghetti hoops forgotten. He was rather enjoying this. 'If you mean about the way you treated her the other day then yes, Cally did tell me. And I must say, you've got a nerve coming here.'

'I came to apologise actually,' volunteered Will, with just a hint of aggression. 'So – is she in?'

Eddie chose to ignore the question. 'You do realise she's all screwed up because of you?'

'Just tell her I'm here, will you?'

'Nope.'

'Why not?'

'Because she's not in.'

'Well, when will she be back?'

'No idea mate.' The two stood glowering at each other across the doormat for a few seconds.

'Look,' said Will finally. The lilies drooped sadly across his arms. 'Can I come in and wait?'

'Oh I suppose so,' conceded Eddie, standing back to let Will enter the flat. He closed the door then followed him into the living room. 'She doesn't need you any longer, you know.'

'Yeah, well, maybe I'll ask her that myself if it's all the same to you.'

'As a matter of fact,' Eddie continued airily, 'Cally's well on the way to finding herself someone else.'

Will's jaw dropped, as Eddie had secretly hoped it would. 'What?'

'Cup of tea?' enquired Eddie, heading towards the kitchen. 'I'll put a couple of sugars in it, you look like you're going to need it.'

So there they were, sitting in the canteen at The Animal Experience, looking like contestants in the world staring championships. Cally wondered what she had to do to

265

make them stop goggling at each other, let alone actually open their mouths and say something.

Well, somebody had to break the ice and it looked like the task had fallen to Cally.

'OK Vernon,' she began, trying not to sound too much like Claire Rayner. 'Simone's right here in front of you.' She could have sworn she saw Vernon's milk-chocolate complexion turn a shade paler. 'Is there anything you'd like to say to her?'

A small, distressed sound came out of Vernon's mouth, but nothing that resembled a word. Cally offered up a prayer for fortitude; it looked like Cupid was going to need all the help he could get.

'How about you, Simone?' she urged. 'Wouldn't you like to tell Vernon how you feel about him?'

Simone looked panic-stricken. 'I . . . I . . .'

Give me strength, thought Cally, more irritated than sympathetic. Animals were so much less trouble; just stick one male and one female in together and bingo, more babies than you could shake a stick at. Unless, of course, you were dealing with giant pandas.

'Right,' said Cally, rolling her sleeves up. 'Looks like we're going to have to do this the hard way. Vernon, do you like Simone?'

He nodded, swallowed and managed a strangled, 'Of course I do.'

'So how about you, Simone? Do you like Vernon?'

'*Mais . . . oui.*'

'Well thank God for that. So, just supposing Vernon had a couple of tickets for a show next Saturday night . . .'

'What kind of show?' cut in Simone.

'I don't know – what kind of show?' Cally asked Vernon.

'Céline Dion at the Bristol Hippodrome,' stammered Vernon.

266

Lord bless us and save us, thought Cally. That's not a show, that's a penance.

'There you go, say he had two tickets for Céline Dion at the Bristol Hippodrome, and he asked you to go with him. What would you say?'

A silly, bashful grin stole over Simone's face, turning her from sophisticated thirtysomething to besotted twelve-year-old in half a second flat.

'I would say, I would say yes!'

Vernon's face lit up like Blackpool Prom on a Saturday night. 'You would?'

'*Mais oui, certainement.*'

'But I thought I . . .'

'No, no, it was my fault . . .'

Cally was just contemplating giving them a sex manual and leaving them to get on with it, when someone tapped her on the shoulder. She wheeled round.

'Oh. Hi.'

Will looked drawn, a little tense. 'Can I have a word?' he asked.

She looked him up and down. 'How about "rat"?' she suggested sweetly.

He didn't rise to the bait. 'Please can we talk, Cally?' he repeated, glancing around him. 'And preferably in private.'

The skunk enclosure was about as private as you could get. Although conspicuously less smelly than when Cally took it over, the whole area was still redolent of something you wouldn't want to sit next to on a bus.

Colin leaned into Cally's legs, leaving behind a liberal coating of ginger hairs. Will looked at the animal doubtfully.

'I'm not at all sure a skunk's supposed to behave like that,' he commented.

Cally scratched Colin's flank. He seemed to like it; or at least, he didn't dislike it enough to run away or lift up his tail and squirt his displeasure. In her book, that was quite an achievement.

'How many Javan Yellow Skunks have you ever met?' she replied. 'Who knows how he's supposed to behave?'

'True.' Will watched her forking out the soiled bedding into a wheelbarrow. 'Come to that, who knows how any of us are supposed to behave?'

She frowned. 'That's a bit profound isn't it?'

He shrugged. 'Not profound, just confused.'

She put down the fork and leaned it against the wire. Colin sniffed it, nuzzled her wellingtons then returned to investigate his bowl of chopped-up fruit and minced meat. 'Go on,' she said. 'Tell me.'

'Tell you what?'

'Come on Will, you're the one who wanted a word, remember? So tell me what's on your mind.' She deliberately didn't give him time to reply. 'Actually I can guess.'

'Oh?'

'Eddie told me you called round at the flat.'

'Ah. Right.'

She wished her heart would stop beating so fast, and she wished she could look Will in the eye without feeling guilty – for what, she wasn't exactly sure. Her lips felt dry, and she moistened them with her tongue. 'The thing is, Will, I know how it must look—'

Will put up a hand to stop her. 'Let me guess. This is some kind of reverse-psychology game, yeah?'

'Pardon?'

'You want to find Eddie a girlfriend only he won't play ball, so you pretend you're looking for a man and he comes along to help you out. Am I right?'

Cally's face fell. 'You've been talking to Liddy.'

'Wouldn't you, in my place?'

'I guess.'

He looked ever so slightly sheepish. 'Steaming in heavy . . . well, it's not my style, despite what you might think. I like to get my facts right. But the thing is . . .' He twirled a piece of straw between his fingers.

She crossed the enclosure and sat down next to him, on the trunk of a fallen tree. 'What?'

'This sort of thing . . . this going out with other blokes.'

'I wasn't. I mean, I'm not. It's not really going *out*, is it?'

'No,' he agreed. 'And I'm not saying you've been two-timing me or anything. I mean, it's not as if we've really been going out either. Not seriously, anyway. Is it?'

His eyes fixed hers. She felt a lump rise in her throat. 'No,' she said quietly. 'I suppose not.'

'And this kind of thing . . . well, it's symptomatic, isn't it? And I was thinking . . .' He was talking quickly now, perhaps a little too quickly. 'I was thinking, maybe we ought to settle for just being friends.' He took her hands in his. 'What d'you say? Friends?'

She smiled back at him. 'Friends.'

At which precise moment Colin decided to scent-mark the log; which was quite useful really, since it gave Cally a chance to hide the tears in her eyes.

269

Chapter Twenty-Three

It had been a beautiful day, and the early evening sun was casting a mellow glow over the Bath Road roundabout, making the dusty concrete look almost inviting. Sparrows twittered merrily above the rattle of articulated lorries. The woodsmoke from barbecues mingled with the heady scent of burning diesel. Ah, a perfect English summer's evening.

Cally, however, was not feeling the least bit mellow. In fact, freezing rain with a side-order of thunder and lightning would have provided a more fitting backdrop to her mood. Alone in the flat, she rested her elbows on her bedroom windowsill and stared gloomily at the courting couple giggling as they dodged hand-in-hand across the traffic to the pub on the other side of the road.

Doomed, she decided. A few brainless weeks under the spell of the love virus, then the bickering would start and within six months they'd either be plunging steak knives into each other or, worse, deciding to be Just Good Friends. Love. When all was said and done, it was just another germ. And she was well and truly cured.

The sound of the doorbell interrupted her thoughts. She thought briefly about pretending not to be in, then decided it wasn't worth the effort. Hastily wiping her eyes on the hem of her T-shirt, she went to open the front door.

'Hiya!' chirruped Liddy, bouncing into the flat in cut-off denim shorts and a baggy yellow shirt. 'Fab weather, I've brought us some ice cream, put it in here shall I?' Her voice disappeared into the kitchen. 'Got any bowls?'

'In the cupboard under the sink. But I don't really want—'

The end of her sentence was lost in the clinking of spoons into bowls. 'You remember what you were saying about Eddie? About all the dates being a bit too nice? Well guess what, this time I've found somebody absolutely perfect.' Liddy's pixie nose peeked round the door jamb. 'A complete and utter slapper!'

Cally flopped down on to Eddie's *chaise-longue*. 'Liddy, I never actually said . . .'

Liddy was too busy being pleased with herself to listen. 'Just like Cerys out of Catatonia, only even rougher. And talk about man-eater! Even Eddie won't be able to resist this one, Cal.' Liddy paused, waiting for Cally to say something, but nothing filled the silence. She stepped out into the living room, dripping Häagen-Dazs on to the carpet. 'Cal?'

'What?' she replied dully.

'Aren't you going to ask me what complete jerk I've landed you with this time?'

Cally sighed. 'Do I have to?'

Liddy frowned. 'Are you all right?'

She didn't have to answer. The panda eyes said it all. 'Oh Cal, you've been crying!'

'No I haven't.' She wiped a finger across her cheek, smearing even more of her mascara.

Liddy sat down beside her and plonked the half-empty pot of Häagen-Dazs in her lap. 'Here, stuff your face in that and tell me what's happened.'

Cally dipped a reluctant finger into the ice cream. Comfort eating, it was such a pathetic cliché. Oh what the hell. She scooped out a dollop and ate it. 'It's Will,' she said.

'You've not had another row, have you?'

She shook her head.

'He's never dumped you!'

'Worse. He wants to be just friends.'

Liddy looked aghast. 'Oh Cal, that's terrible. Why?'

Cally answered with only the faintest tinge of accusation in her voice. 'He found out about the dating agency and Eddie and all that stuff.'

'But surely he didn't think you were really trying to meet someone else?'

'No, not exactly. He said it was "symptomatic", whatever that means. Anyway, it doesn't matter why, does it?' She tossed her hair back and sniffed loudly. 'Good riddance, that's what I say.'

Liddy looked profoundly uncomfortable. 'You don't mean that.'

'Yes I do,' said Cally, rather feebly.

'Oh God,' said Liddy, 'this is all my fault, isn't it?'

'No it isn't.' A single tear dripped down Cally's nose and landed in the French Vanilla. 'Oh well. Looks like the only man in my life now is a skunk. Literally.'

'Bloody hell John, what did you have for dinner last night – curried eggs?'

The man in the Dayglo orange jacket rammed his surveying pole into the sun-dried earth with an expression of absolute disgust.

'Don't look at me, mate,' retorted the other surveyor,

273

sniffing the air. 'That's not one of mine. Blimey, makes your eyes water though.'

Picking up bits of half-chewed fruit in the nearby skunk enclosure, Cally looked on in a sort of daze. Colin's pungent aroma wafted around her like a cloud of evil-smelling incense, but she didn't even notice the smell any more. In fact she hardly even noticed the two surveyors arguing, despite the fact that any glimpse of human life had become the highlight of her day.

Stuck out here, on a limb, with just a skunk for company, she only saw the other keepers on her breaks, and even then they kept their distance. Most probably they were talking behind her back. About her and Will.

She tossed a bit of orange peel into her bucket with a sigh. For a little while, this place had seemed so perfect; but now it was stacking up too many unhappy associations. Even the little nameplate for her personal locker had failed to arrive. Again. Maybe it was a sign.

Maybe the Experience didn't have anything to offer her, after all.

Cally hadn't planned to go out that evening, but then again she hadn't bargained on Apollo turning up, either.

'Hiya chubby cheeks.' He pinched them in that annoying, big-brother way that had driven her mad even when she was four years old. 'Glad to see me?'

'Ow,' she glared, catching sight of her reflection in the hall mirror, now boasting a cherry-red blob on either cheek. 'That hurt!'

'Oh, sorry, don't know my own strength.' He strode off into the living room, with Cally in his wake. 'Hi Eddie.'

'Oh, hello.' Eddie, who was kneeling on the floor,

looked up from massaging Janis's foot. 'You haven't met the lovely Lady Janis, have you? Janis, this is Apollo.'

Janis looked Apollo up and down. 'Hi.' Ziggy, whose hairy form was hogging the rest of the sofa, glanced up and started quivering. 'Don't worry about the dog, it's not you, it's her. She smells funny.'

Gee thanks, thought Cally, returning Janis's accusing stare. I love you too. 'At least I get off my backside and do a proper job,' she replied cuttingly.

Eddie leapt to his beloved's defence. 'Janis doesn't need to go out selling the magazines any more,' he said, gazing into her eyes. 'She's got me to look after her now, haven't you, snookiepuffs?'

Snookiepuffs! thought Cally, stifling a retch. Good God Eddie, you really have got it bad.

Apollo rubbed his hands together. 'I was just wondering, Cal. Fancy going out for a drink?'

She looked at him, puzzled. 'Not really. Why?'

'Oh go on.'

'Why?' she repeated.

'No special reason. Come on,' he wheedled, 'it'll be fun.'

Eddie's face registered instant enthusiasm. 'Oh yes, go on Cal, it'll do you good to get out. Won't it Janis?'

Janis didn't reply, but exchanged Eddie's meaningful look for a long, saliva-filled smooch. For his part, Ziggy whimpered and stuck his head under a cushion. The decision appeared to be unanimous.

'Oh all right,' Cally caved in with thoroughly bad grace. 'I'll just get my coat.'

'Nice evening,' commented Apollo as they walked down Bath Road towards the bar.

'Hmm,' grunted Cally, trudging along with head down and hands in her trouser pockets.

'You're looking well.'

'Yeah?'

'Is that a new jacket?'

Cally let out an explosion of breath. 'Cut the crap Apollo, why are you here?'

Apollo promptly switched on the look of a wounded kitten. 'To see my lovely sister and take her out, why else?'

'Don't give me that! You'd never bike all the way over here just to take me out for a drink. Come on, out with it.'

Her brother's expressions went through several versions of 'who, me?' before settling on 'it's a fair cop'. 'Oh all right, you win. Actually I did want to chat to you about something.'

He held open the door of the bar and she stepped inside. 'If Mum's primed you to ask me to move back in with her, you're wasting your time. I'm not that desperate.' Yet, she added silently. Since Janis's arrival, the atmosphere in the flat had gone past frosty to downright arctic.

They walked up to the bar and Apollo took out his wallet. 'Fancy a nice bottle of really good wine?'

'Depends how much it's going to cost me,' she replied drily.

'My treat.'

'I wasn't talking money. Look Apollo, I know you. The only time you come over all generous is when you want something.'

'That's a bit harsh.'

'And true.'

He grinned and stuffed a twenty-pound note into the

276

barman's hand. 'Something nice in a red, and two glasses.'

'Right you are, sir.'

'Actually,' confessed Apollo, 'I do want something.'

'Aha.'

'But only your time. I wanted to talk something over with you.'

She frowned. 'Why me? What's wrong with the thousand and one other people you know? What about Mum and Dad?'

He shook his head. 'No way, none of them would understand. The thing is, it's about money.'

Apollo consulted his watch. 'Nearly half-past, Tom should have been here by now.'

'You could have told me you were going into business with Eddie's ex-flatmate, instead of all that "ooh-we-don't-really-know-each-other" stuff.'

'But it's true,' protested Apollo, feeding bits of cheese sandwich to a passing pub cat. 'I've only met Ed a couple of times, and Tom and I aren't business partners yet. Well, not officially.'

'So.' Cally sat back and stretched out her legs. 'Go on then, spill the beans. I've got to get back to keep an eye on Janis.'

'God, you are paranoid.' Apollo took a deep breath. 'OK. Well, I met Tom at a franchise exhibition, a few months ago. I've been thinking of going into business on my own for a while now.'

'Have you? But I thought you liked it at PureFood.'

'Which just goes to show how little you know me, baby Sis. I'd have jumped ship ages ago, only I didn't want to chance it on my own. Anyhow, it turned out that

Tom and I were both interested in the same franchise opportunity.'

'Something to do with organic food, I suppose? Like where you're working now?'

'God no. We'd be offering paintball, tank driving, that kind of thing.'

Cally's jaw dropped. 'Tank driving! That's a bit of a jump from veggieburgers, isn't it?'

Apollo shrugged. 'We're not all like Dad you know. Some of us quite fancy making a bit of filthy lucre before we die. Some of us are well pissed off with eating tofu and going everywhere by bike. I've even started fantasising about mortgages, for fuck's sake!'

'Now that's what I call kinky.'

'You're telling me. Anyhow, Tom and I got talking about this franchise outlet that's for sale near Cheltenham, and we really fancy going for it, only the thing is, neither of us really understands the money side. Fact is, fifteen years in human resources doesn't teach you how to read a balance sheet.'

Cally broke a piece off her brother's sandwich and ate it. 'Now, why do I get the feeling you're about to ask me for something?'

Apollo's smile hovered between nervous and ingratiating. 'Only your brains,' he replied. 'We're having trouble weighing up the contracts and projections we've been given – I thought maybe you could tell us if we're being ripped off.'

'Well,' said Cally, 'I'm glad you didn't ask me for money; 'cause I'm skint.' A thought occurred to her. 'So you haven't mentioned this to Mum and Dad then?'

'Are you crazy?'

'I'm sure they'd give you advice if you asked them.' He laughed. 'What's so funny?'

'Shall I tell you about the last time Mum gave me some advice?' Apollo leaned back, hands clasped behind his head, eyes closed against the summer sunshine. 'I must have been what – thirteen, fourteen? Anyway, there I am in my bedroom with a dirty mag and a box of Kleenex, doing what teenage boys do, and she walks right in on me.'

Cally cringed. 'Oh no.'

'Oh yes. And what does she do? Sits down on the bed right next to me, and tells me it's absolutely fine, because masturbation is perfectly healthy and natural and I really mustn't be embarrassed!'

'As if!'

'Yeah, right. And it gets worse. The next thing I know, she starts talking to me about it at Dad's birthday party, really loudly, in front of everybody. You know, I've never been able to face birthday cake ever since.'

'Hmm,' said Cally. 'Well, I suppose you should be grateful she didn't get Dad to show you how to do it.'

'Please, Cal. Not even in jest.'

There was a pause. Then Cally broke the silence.

'Well, I can see why you might not want to ask Mum for advice,' she said. 'But that's not the only reason, is it?'

Reluctantly, Apollo shook his head. 'No,' he admitted. 'It isn't.'

Cally wandered around the skunk enclosure, trying to get a decent signal on her mobile. In her wake trailed Colin, wondering if she might have the odd bowl of chopped banana concealed about her person. In the absence of any other skunks to play with, fight or have sex with, Colin had discovered the joys of comfort eating.

'Colin . . . Colin sweetie, look, nothing, see? Only a phone. No, you can't eat the phone. Ah, great, a signal at last.'

She checked the number on the letter she had received that morning, dialled and waited, with mounting impatience.

'Fifth National Bank of Formosa, can I help you?'

'Mr Bryson, please. It's Calliope Storm.'

'One moment, I'm transferring you.'

One of the Brandenburg Concertos droned out of the phone for what seemed like hours. Colin gave up looking for food and started trying to stalk his own shadow. Cally's thoughts began drifting off to Apollo, and what he had told her the night before.

Then a voice cut through the music. 'Ms Storm?'

'Oh, Mr Bryson, I got your letter this morning.'

'Good, good. Then you'll know we're taking over LBS Agri-Finance from Banco Torino. And naturally we'll be needing able individuals to help us put the division on a secure footing.'

She licked her dry lips. 'By able individuals, I take it you mean . . . ?'

'That's right, people like you, Ms Storm. That's why we're offering you a job. We were wondering if you might like to run your old department at LBS.'

What the hell was the point of mobile phones if people didn't turn them on? Cally had been trying to reach Rob all day, but all she got was some annoying woman who offered to take yet another message, which no doubt he would never receive because he never got round to switching his bloody phone on.

She'd almost given up trying by the time she stopped off for a burger on the way home.

'Double bacon swiss with onion rings please,' she said. Bugger the diet, right now she needed the emotional support that only deep-fried saturated fats could provide.

'D'you want fries with that?' enquired the bored girl behind the counter.

Cally was just about to say, Make that double fries, when her phone rang.

'Cally?' said Rob's voice, slightly breathlessly. 'It's me.'

'At last! You got my messages then?' Cally shoved the right money across the counter and set off to the only empty table, manoeuvring her tray one-handed round the man with the mop and bucket.

'All six of them. Sorry I didn't get back to you earlier, but I forgot my mobile this morning and I've only just got back from the garden centre. What's wrong?'

'Nothing's wrong.' She sat down and dipped a chip in ketchup. 'Quite the opposite actually, I've been offered a job.'

'I thought you had a job.'

'A proper job. Running my old department at LBS.'

'Good God.' He sounded stunned, but not displeased, noted Cally. 'You mean they dropped you and now they can't manage without you, they want to take you back on?'

'Not exactly. Fifth National Bank of Formosa are taking over the company. It's not definite yet – I mean, there's going to be an extended interview in a few weeks' time, but they've told me it's a formality. The thing is . . .' She chewed and swallowed. 'I'm going to need to stay over in Northampton.'

'So the job'll still be based in the Northampton area?'

'Looks that way. I was wondering . . . I mean, it seems silly to pay out for a hotel room, and my old work clothes are still in the house. Would you mind if I stayed the night with you?'

'Mind? Are you crazy?' Rob's voice jumped an octave. 'Of course I don't mind! Stay as long as you like, why don't you make a week of it?'

'One night'll be fine, thanks.'

'Oh. OK then.'

'Well. If that's all settled then . . .'

'You'll let me know when you're coming?'

'Of course I will. 'Bye.'

''Bye.'

She ended the call and slipped the phone back into her bag. Her hand was shaking, ever so slightly, as she picked up her baconburger and took a bite. Had she done the right thing? she wondered. Well, it was too late to change her mind now; besides, he'd sounded so . . . so *pleased*.

And all at once it struck her; how much she'd missed the feeling that someone, somewhere was pleased to see her.

'Yes!' Rob punched the air and danced around the phone. 'Yes, yes, yes!'

He was still waltzing around the living room with a sofa cushion when Rachel walked in, weighed down by a twenty-six-pound bag of potting compost.

'You look pleased with yourself,' she remarked, staggering through to the conservatory and dropping the bag on to the potting bench.

'I am,' he replied, putting the cushion back on to the

sofa and following her. And he was just about to tell her why, when suddenly he realised.

Another woman. In Cally's house. Oh shit, he thought with a sinking feeling. She's never going to believe it's innocent.

I'm dogmeat.

Chapter Twenty-Four

'Hurry up,' repeated Vernon. 'He's waiting.'

'Who?'

'Henk, he wants to see you.'

Puzzled, Cally put down the dish of food. Colin promptly scrambled up on to his tree stump and helped himself to a mealworm. 'But why does Mr Thorfinn want to see me? What have I done?'

'Don't ask me, all I know is he wants to see you right now, so you'd better follow me.'

Since she had no choice in the matter, Cally locked up the skunk house and headed off across the park in Vernon's wake, his long, lean limbs making light work of the rough grass and gravel pathways.

'Where are we going?' she demanded, panting as she struggled to keep up.

'You'll see.'

'But this isn't the way to Mr Thorfinn's office!'

'We're not going to his office.' Sure enough, a few moments later they arrived at the Twilight Kingdom, and Vernon held open the door. 'In you go.'

She frowned. 'In there?'

'Go on.'

He gave her a gentle shove and she went inside, blinking in the unaccustomed darkness. Something the shape of a medium-sized garden shed loomed up in front of her.

'Donna?'

'Hi, Cally,' grinned the shed. 'All ready are we?'

Cally turned in puzzlement to Vernon, and saw that he was grinning too. 'What's going on? Where's Henk?'

Vernon took her by the shoulders and propelled her gently but firmly towards the Batcave. 'There you go, Donna. She's all yours.'

'Aaaaaaaaaaaagh!' wailed Cally, as the world spun past. 'Somebody get me doooooown!'

Cally was hurtling through the air, and she didn't feel at all well. Actually, the hurtling bit she could cope with. Even the bats whizzing past her nose didn't bother her that much. No, it was the being upside-down and thirty feet off the ground that her stomach found hard to adjust to.

Thirty feet below, a gaggle of keepers waved merrily up at her as she swung by her harness from the roof of the Batcave.

'Don't wriggle!' shouted Billy cheerfully. 'You'll fall on your head.'

'Pleeeeeeeeease,' she moaned, dangling lifelessly. 'I think I'm going to throw up.'

Vernon's voice rescued. 'Come on lads, let's bring her down, I think she's had enough.'

By the time they hauled her down and set her the right way up, so much blood had gone to Cally's head that it felt twice its normal size.

'You bastards,' she blurted out, swaying dizzily and almost knocking over Josiah. 'You absolute wank—ugh . . .'

Strong arms caught her just as she was about to topple over. Henk Thorfinn was smiling at her and holding out an official keeper's baseball cap. 'Congratulations, Cally.'

She shook herself. 'What congratulations? What's going on?'

Somebody jammed the cap on her head. 'You passed your probationary period, Cal. You're one of us now!'

People were patting her on the back and congratulating her, and telling her not to worry, they'd all been through this initiation stuff, but Cally wasn't really taking any of it in. There was only room for one thought in her mind right now.

'Oh hell.' She clapped a hand to her mouth.

'You all right, Cal?' enquired Vernon. 'You're looking a bit pale.'

That was the last thing she heard before she threw up all over the bushbaby.

'Never mind,' soothed Simone, sponging the last flecks of vomit out of Cally's hair. 'You will be feeling better soon.'

Cally groaned into the toilet bowl. 'Yes, but will the bushbaby?'

'Eet ees all right, zey said eet was just a leetle . . . surprised.'

Cally sat back on her haunches, took a damp paper towel from Simone's hand and wiped her mouth. 'Sorry about that,' she said weakly. 'But if they will dangle people from the bloody ceiling.'

Simone looked concerned. 'I was wondering. You are not afraid of heights, *non*?'

'Of course not,' lied Cally.

Simone's face relaxed. 'Ah, zat ees good, I thought

287

not. Eet say on your résumé zat you are experienced bungee jumper, *oui*?'

Cally heard a faint flutter of wings, that might just have been the sound of a chicken coming home to roost. 'Er, sort of.'

'Zat ees what I tell Vernon, and when I see zat you 'ave not put your name down for ze charity bungee jump next month, I zink, why not? So Vernon and I, we 'ave put your name on ze list. You do not mind?'

Cally smiled bravely. 'Of course I don't.' Which of course she didn't, since she wasn't going to be here in a month's time, was she? Thank God.

When she looked up at Simone, the Frenchwoman was gazing fondly into the middle distance, a vomit-stained paper towel in one hand and a can of air freshener in the other.

'Ah,' she sighed. 'My Vernon, he ees so lovely, *n'est-ce pas*? You are so clever, to bring us together.'

Will and Stefan contemplated each other like seasoned professionals, and both made a bid for the comfy chair at exactly the same moment.

'Too slow, loser,' said Will, catching the flying furball as it scudded across the carpet and scooping it into his lap. 'Shed a few tons of lard and then try that again.'

Stefan surveyed the lap on offer, grudgingly decided that it would do, and settled down in a warm fug of wet dog and halitosis.

Liddy didn't turn round. She went on making supper, boiling up pasta on the gas ring in the antiquated kitchen of her granny's flat. 'If you ask me, kid, there's only one loser round here and it's not him.'

Will addressed the unyielding curve of her back. 'I suppose you mean me.'

She glanced at him over her shoulder. 'I'm saying nothing. But if the cap fits . . .'

'OK, OK,' capitulated Will. 'Maybe you're right, maybe I've done a stupid thing.' He passed his hand over his forehead, sweeping back the fringe that stubbornly insisted on hanging in his eyes.

'Maybe?'

'All right, definitely. I should have accepted her for what she is, I know that. Not what I wanted her to be.'

Liddy drained the pasta and turned round to dump it on to the plates on the table. 'So why didn't you? Accept her, I mean?'

Will looked down at the dog. Its jutting lower jaw was moving gently up and down to the rhythm of its breathing as it slept. It wasn't a pretty sight, but then again, that was Stefan for you. You couldn't change him and maybe if you did succeed, you'd wish you hadn't.

'I don't know.'

'Are you sure?'

'Yes. No . . . I don't know. But what I do know now is that she's probably a damn sight better than what I wanted her to be.' He laughed, rather humourlessly. 'So you're right, aren't you? I am the loser round here.'

Liddy threw the pasta pan into the sink and wiped her hands on her jeans. Perching on the arm of the chair, she put a comforting arm round his shoulders. 'Not necessarily,' she said quietly.

He looked up at her, a question in his eyes.

They were still sitting like that when Cally let herself in by the back door and came up the stairs, unannounced. In one, painful second, she took in a snapshot of the scene: Liddy and Will, cosying up in the armchair, him gazing up into her eyes like a lovestruck cod.

289

As she walked into the room, they turned towards her; and Liddy tried to say something about things not being the way they looked. But Cally had heard that line too many times from Rob; besides, she had already noticed that Will couldn't look her in the eye, and drawn her own incriminating conclusions.

Guilty as charged.

A moment later, she turned tail and fled.

'Cally, come back!' pleaded Liddy, grabbing her friend's sleeve as she fumbled with the catch on the back door. 'I almost had him there, don't you see?'

Cally's lip curled. 'Oh, I bet you bloody well did!'

Liddy took a step backwards. 'Huh?'

'Go on, admit it.' Cally came out fighting. 'You engineered this whole situation, didn't you? Just to get your hands on Will.'

Liddy's eyes were round as flying saucers. 'Hang on a minute, you've got the wrong end of the st . . .'

'Oh give it a rest! Don't you see? It's OK, you don't have to make excuses. Believe me, Liddy, you're welcome to him.'

Chapter Twenty-Five

It was all-out war.

The battle of the bathroom cabinet had begun in earnest, and Cally surveyed the field of battle with murderous intent. How was her growing collection of anti-ageing skin creams ever going to break out of the retreat that Janis's eye shadows had forced them into? How was she ever going to halt the relentless advance of Ziggy's worming tablets?

She was standing there, deep in thought, wishing that the fluorescent light above the sink did not pick out her crow's-feet in quite such meticulous detail, when an idea struck her. Was it too childish? Yes. Was it worth it? Oh, definitely.

And without a second thought, she started a pincer movement on Eddie's Lion King toothbrush.

Rob picked up the gigantic blue teddy bear with the pink ribbon round its neck, and tried to stuff it headfirst into the cupboard under the stairs. The door promptly sprang open again and it fell out, landing at his feet with a protesting growl.

Oh shit oh shit oh shit, thought Rob, panic mounting as it dawned on him just how big an impression Rachel had made on the house since she moved in. Not *the* house, he reminded himself hastily; *our* house. Mine and Cally's.

Not that you'd know it, he thought, picking up the bear by its ear and dragging it back into the living room. How in hell's name was he going to explain the framed photographs of Indian steam engines? His idea of eternal torment was being locked on a slow train to Delhi with Gandhi and nothing to eat but prawn vindaloo. And even if he got that one past her, what about the fridge, suddenly packed full of bowel-enhancing yoghurt drinks and cucumber eye-masques? Not to mention the drawers filled with ... well, *drawers*. Big, functional ones, not the tiny little wispy things that Cally favoured.

He flopped down on the sofa and sat the bear on his knee. It grinned sadistically, so he garotted it with the pink ribbon; but it just kept on grinning. Oh God, he fretted. Cally's going to be here in less than a fortnight! Come on brain, think of something. Think!

And by some miracle of neurophysiology, by the time Rachel came in from the conservatory, Rob had thought of something.

Liddy was sitting on a stool behind the counter, reading the latest issue of *Book Collector*, when the shop bell went.

A familiar head appeared around the door. 'Knock, knock.'

Liddy looked up. 'Hello you.'

Will stepped inside. 'Hello me.' He paused. 'Liddy?'

'Yes?'

'What's up?'

'Nothing's up, why should it be?' Liddy jumped off her stool. 'I'll go and put the kettle on, shall I?'

Will ignored the suggestion. 'I've just been at the town hall.'

'That's nice. You should've said, you could've paid my council tax for me while you were there.'

'At the memorabilia fair. I did quite well, actually.'

'Glad to hear it. Shall I go and make that tea?'

He caught her arm. 'Why weren't you there?'

'Oh . . . you know,' she said vaguely.

'No I don't. You can't possibly have forgotten, you've had a poster in your window advertising it for weeks!' He took her by the shoulders, tilted up her pixie chin and forced her to look at him. 'I know you, Lids. Something's wrong, isn't it?'

'Nothing I can't handle,' she replied.

'Aha, so I was right. Something *is* wrong.'

'I didn't say that.'

'Yes you did. As good as. Come on, sit down and tell Uncle Will all about it.'

Reluctantly, Liddy allowed herself to be sat back down on the stool. 'Look, it's just my gran, OK?'

'She's ill?'

Liddy shook her head. 'Not ill exactly, just old and frail. You know she's been living in those sheltered flats in Prestbury?'

Will nodded. 'You said she likes it there.'

'Oh, she did. But then she had a fall and they said she couldn't stay there any more because she was "high dependency". That's when I had to find a home to move her into.'

'When did this happen?'

'A couple of months ago. It took weeks to find a place Gran was really happy with, and the thing is, good homes don't come cheap. And Gran used up her savings ages ago. The only thing that's keeping her in

Merryfields now is . . . well . . .' She gazed around the little shop. 'This place.'

'You mean, you're having to pay to keep her in the home?'

'Yeah, of course. That is, I suppose Gran's paying really, after all it is her shop.'

'Only the shop's not paying, right?'

Liddy wound up an old tinplate money-box, placed a penny on the lid and watched a hand shoot out and drag it inside. 'It's not that it's not paying – it's just not paying enough. Have you any idea how many hundreds of quid profit I have to make each week, just to keep my head above water?'

'And that's why you weren't at the memorabilia fair?'

She nodded. 'And why I haven't been buying in much lately. I just couldn't afford the couple of hundred quid to take a pitch at the fair. Chances are I wouldn't have made it back, not with my crummy stock.'

Will shook his head sadly. 'I'm really sorry Lids, I did-n't realise.'

'Sorry? What for? It's not your fault. It's not Gran's either, it's nobody's fault.' She ruffled her thick, cropped hair. 'Except maybe mine.'

'Don't talk crap,' chided Will.

'It's not crap. If I was a better businesswoman I wouldn't be in this mess, would I? Fact is, I need to generate lots of money, and I need to do it fast – other-wise the shop and the flat will have to go on the market.'

'So you need to speculate,' he reflected, rubbing his chin.

'Yes, I probably do. Only I haven't got anything to speculate with, have I? Let's be realistic about this, Will. Fairy godmothers don't exist and at fourteen million to one, I don't think I'll count on winning the Lottery.

'Face it, Will, it's looking like curtains for this place.'

Just about the last person Cally would have expected to see hanging about the skunk enclosure was Lazy Bob. But there was no mistaking his egg-shaped frame and she spotted him from halfway across the park, slouching with his hands in his pockets, face pressed up against the wire like a kid outside a cake-shop window.

Her hackles rose. 'Hey, what are you doing here?'

Lazy Bob glanced over his shoulder at her, then went back to looking at Colin through the wire. 'Nothing much.'

'If you've been laying a hand on that skunk . . .'

He sighed. 'I'm not all bad, you know,' he said, rather sadly.

Cally joined him at the wire. 'What – just lazy, you mean?'

'S'pose.' He shuffled awkwardly. 'You hear things working in the kitchens, you know. I just wanted to see the little fella again before . . .'

His voice tailed off and his shoulders sagged.

'Before what?' demanded Cally.

Bob jerked a thumb towards the distant diggers, rumbling up and down the patch of mud where the old outhouses had stood. 'Before that lot decide they need Colin's space, that's what.'

Before she could ask him what he meant, he started wobbling his way back down the path. Then, as if a sudden afterthought had struck him, he stopped and turned back.

'I'm glad you made it as a keeper, really I am.'

Cally wondered just how many surprises you could have in one day. 'You are?'

' 'Course, most everyone reckoned you wouldn't.' There was a note of bitterness in his voice. 'But you showed 'em in the end, didn't you?'

'Thanks,' she said, in spite of everything warming towards the mound of blubber she had often dreamed of harpooning and feeding to the lions.

'Just you remember,' he counselled, jabbing a finger for emphasis. 'You don't have to be like them to be a good keeper. You just be yourself, you hear?'

A voice answered on the end of the line, and Rob switched on his best telephone smile.

'Greg? Hi, it's Rob here, Rob Monk.'

Rob cupped a hand over his ear, to shut out some of the noise. He was standing in the middle of the posh new shopping mall on the edge of Cheltenham, supervising the installation of its authentic Nordic feature – all cool spruce trees and moss, with a little brook running down the middle and a couple of stuffed reindeer for extra effect. It was going to look pretty good once they'd manoeuvred the trees into place, but right now Rob had other, more pressing matters on his mind.

'Rob, you old bastard.' There was just a note of apprehension behind Greg's usual hail-fellow-well-met greeting. 'Hope you're not going to tell me there's a hitch with my lianas.'

'Wouldn't dream of it, Greg,' replied Rob. 'Everything's on schedule, just as we agreed.'

The note of apprehension lessened noticeably. 'Good, good. I mean, time is money – am I right or am I right?'

'You're right, Greg. One hundred per cent.' Rob

cleared his throat. 'I do . . . er . . . have a little problem I wanted to discuss with you though.'

'Oh yes?' The voice was wary now. 'What kind of problem?'

'A personal one.' Rob sidestepped to avoid a large sapling, swinging on the end of a crane. 'About . . . er . . . Rachel.'

He wasn't quite sure what he'd expected by way of reply, but it certainly wasn't a guffaw of raucous laughter.

'Aaaaah, the lovely Rachel is it?' The sound of Greg Prince wetting himself with mirth was not an attractive one, and Rob was forced to hold the phone at arm's length until he'd finished snorting like a hippopotamus. 'I thought it might be.'

That rather took the wind out of Rob's sails. 'Oh. So she told you then?'

'Rob mate, I think she's told half of Cheltenham. I mean, inviting her to go on holiday with you like that, are you a fast mover or what? Aren't I supposed to challenge you to a duel or something, you know, protect the family honour?'

Ha frigging ha, thought Rob, stapling the smile back on to his face though he longed to tell Greg exactly what he thought of him and his sense of humour.

'It wasn't like that,' he insisted.

'No? That's not what I heard.'

The spruce tree swung back across the mall, forcing Rob to duck so suddenly that he nearly fell backwards over the half-finished balcony. 'Oi!' he shouted, 'watch what you're doing with that thing. And mind you don't damage the bloody root system! You still there, Greg?'

'Uh-huh. But get a move on, I've got a working brunch in ten minutes.'

'Look, I'm telling you, it wasn't like that! I need to get Rachel out of the way for a few days, I can't have her around the place when Cally shows up.'

'Ah,' said Greg meaningfully. 'Hoping for a bit of marital bliss are we? Don't want the wife meeting up with the bit on the side?'

'Rachel is not my bit on the side.' Rob clenched his teeth. 'All I did was offer to pay for Rachel to go on holiday, and the next thing I know, she's got the wrong end of the stick. You've got to help me, Greg, please!'

Greg chuckled. 'Sorry mate, there's no way I'm getting involved in this one. This is your mess and you're going to have to sort it out yourself.

'Am I right, or am I right?'

Chapter Twenty-Six

'Look,' pleaded Cally, nailing the new felt on to the roof of the skunk house, 'what options have I got?'

Colin the skunk scratched his ear with his back leg, but said nothing helpful. Cally took another nail from the pouch at her waist, and comforted herself by bashing hell out of it.

'I can't stay where I'm living, and it'll be forever before I go up a grade and actually earn enough money to afford my own place.' She wielded the hammer with rhythmic irritation. 'I mean, no offence, but this job isn't exactly bursting with prospects, is it? Not to mention the fact that I bump into my recently ex-boyfriend at least twice a day.'

The skunk listened in silence.

'I don't have to do this, you know. I must be barmy, justifying myself to a skunk!'

Cally stepped down to admire her handiwork. *Ground Force* could probably have done it twice as neatly in half the time, but at least it would keep the rain out.

'On the other hand,' she went on, clearing up the mess she'd made, 'I could be living in my old house, working for my old employer, doing a better job for more money *and* have a husband who appreciates me for once in his life. Face it, Colin, there isn't even a choice here. Is there?'

Colin answered her question with an accusing stare, then slowly and deliberately turned and lifted his tail.

'Hey, don't turn your back on me! This isn't about you, it's about me. I'm sure you'll be all right.'

But Colin wasn't listening. He was stalking off across the enclosure; and as she called to his retreating back he disappeared inside his living quarters, in a final flash of ginger fluff.

Men! scowled Cally, throwing her hammer into the toolbox. It didn't matter what species they were, they were all the same underneath.

Cally had the oddest feeling that everybody was watching her. She'd had it all the way to the staff canteen, all the way through eating her cheese pie and chips, and now that she was on her way back to work she could still feel it. The sensation of several dozen pairs of eyes, following her everywhere she went.

Oh God, she thought; maybe they know. Maybe they all know that the week's holiday I've booked isn't a holiday at all.

'Miss!'

She kept on walking.

'Hey, miss, you with the stripy wellies!'

Cally glanced down at her feet, stopped, and turned to see where the voice was coming from. That was her big first mistake.

'That's right sweetheart, nice big smile for the camera!'

Camera? Good God, there *was* a camera, and not just one of your innocent little Polaroids – this was one of those shoulder-held things with the furry micro-phone, the sort they used for TV outside broadcasts. And the man in the red jumpsuit was pointing it straight at her!

Her mouth fell open. 'What the hell's going on?'

She didn't have a chance to find out what, because at that moment half a dozen keepers jumped her from behind; and the next thing she knew, she was writhing like a trapped gazelle inside an enormous camouflage net, with a semicircle of faces laughing down at her.

'Gotcha!'

Seconds later, a long black limousine slid out from behind the Worm Zone. As it stopped, yards away from Cally, the front passenger door opened and out stepped a grotesquely familiar figure. Six foot six in her sequinned stilettos, leather miniskirt and backcombed silver wig, Liz Talent was not the kind of woman you could forget in a hurry. Technically speaking, she wasn't a woman at all. Not that she was complaining. Transvestism had been kind to a certain washed-up ex-kids' TV presenter; it had landed him fame, fortune, his own gameshow and a lucrative contract advertising false eyelashes.

'Well h-h-h-h-h-hi there!' sparkled Liz Talent, thrusting a microphone through the camouflage net. 'Ready for *The Big One*?'

'Ready to ram that microphone up your arse,' snarled Cally. 'You die at dawn.'

'Excellent.' Liz chuckled and spun to camera. 'That way I won't miss *The Big One* tonight. Keep tuning in throughout the day, as I'll be surprising a shop assistant in Swindon and panicking a plumber in Pangbourne. Yes, stay with us to find out which other contestants will be joining Kayleigh Storm on *The Big One*. Tonight at eight – only on Channel Six.'

'Cut,' called a voice from behind the limo. 'That was super Liz, but on the next one could you show just a teensy bit more leg?'

'It's Cally,' seethed Cally from inside the net.

Liz Talent peered down at her. 'What?'

'It's Cally Storm, not Kayleigh.'

Liz treated her to a condescending smile. 'Well that's just wonderful, darling.'

'Let me go!'

A finger wagged. 'Sorry, no can do.'

'I said, LET ME GO.'

'And I said, no.' The TV presenter stuck a hand down 'her' bra and adjusted a false breast. 'Look,' she said wearily, 'we've got your girlfriend, sort it out with her.'

Cally's jaw dropped.

'You've got my *what*?'

Cally had never been in a TV dressing room before. In other circumstances she might have been quite excited to find herself sitting in the very chair that Terry Wogan had sat in, the night his toupé caught fire; but tonight all she could think about was what she wanted to do to Liddy.

'What the hell do you think you're playing at?' hissed Cally as a girl fluffed a very large faceful of powder at her.

The girl looked taken aback. 'This? This is just to set the—'

'Not you.' Cally swung her chair round to confront Liddy. 'You. What the hell have you been up to?'

Liddy hung her head. 'I don't know why,' she

302

lamented, 'but all these TV people seem to think we're, you know . . .' Her face blushed scarlet.

Cally supplied the words for her. 'Hot for each other?'

'Er, yes.' A ghost of Liddy's cheeky grin peeked out from behind the glum demeanour. 'Sorry.'

'Sorry? Sorry! You say sorry and you think that's all right?' Cally didn't know whether to throttle Liddy or merely hold her upside-down and shake her till all her teeth fell out. 'How could you *do* this to me!'

In fairness, Liddy did look mildly embarrassed. 'It was weeks ago,' she explained. 'I wanted to cheer you up.'

'Cheer me up. Right. You thought humiliating me in front of two million viewers would cheer me up.'

'But it wasn't meant to humiliate you!' protested Liddy. 'I thought the show was for pairs of friends, not you know *couples*.'

'Bloody hell Liddy, where have you been living – Outer Mongolia? This goes out on Channel Six, if it's not got sex in it they're not interested. And another thing—'

The other thing, whatever it was, didn't make it out of Cally's mouth, because at that moment Liz Talent flounced in, flanked by security men in silver lamé, the overall effect somewhat marred by Liz having to bend at the knees to get her beehive through the door.

'Everybody happy, darlings?'

Cally folded her arms defiantly. 'Nope. You're still going to die.'

Liz sparkled a shallow smile, and blew a kiss from her varnished fingertips. 'Excellent, darlings. Be lucky.'

* * *

303

The set was completely insane. Cally had never seen anything like it in her life before, not even in one of the Technicolor nightmares she tended to have after too many double vodkas. She stood in the hot glare of studio lights, her makeup slowly melting, and wondered what the designer must be on, to have come up with something that looked like a cross between the Mad Hatter's tea party and a seaside funfair.

Mind you, if the set was insane and the audience were baying, Liz Talent was positively barking. She strutted around the set like an oversized chicken, all trussed up in silver, feathers sticking out of her arse and her false breasts threatening to decapitate any unwary cameraman who ventured too close.

'Time to go for it, darlings! And remember – you're doing this for the one you luuuuurve . . .'

Am I fuck, thought Cally as someone pulled a mask down over her eyes. She hoped, with her last grain of dignity, that it wasn't the one that made you look like William Hague. Anything, any humiliation under the sun, but please, not that.

From somewhere up above, a squeaky, helium-enhanced voice reverberated around the studio:

'Aaaaaaaaaaand noooooooow contestants . . . on your marks fooooor . . . "Three Blind Mice"!'

Unseen hands pushed Cally into position. 'Get your pervy hands off my tits!' she snapped, instinctively jabbing an elbow into something fleshy that produced a satisfying 'uuuuurgh'.

A sudden, brilliant thought struck her. Of course. She'd seen a bit of this crappy show before, she knew exactly what she had to do to win.

Right, she told herself with a grim smirk. Let's do the absolute opposite.

* * *

304

The helium-enhanced voice was going crazy.

'Laydeez an' gennelmeeeeen . . . tonight's winner is . . . Kayleigh Storm!'

The audience were going crazy too, stamping their feet, clapping, shouting, whistling. Nobody took a blind bit of notice of the one dissenting voice bellowing 'It's *Cally*, you fucking morons!'

Music pounded, multicoloured spotlights whirled round the studio, and the three defeated contestants tried not to look as if they wanted to dance on Cally's grave. Everybody smiled until their faces cracked, except Cally, who mouthed obscenities at the camera until she twigged that the bastards had switched to a different one.

Just as she thought it couldn't get any worse, the floor manager sprinted out from behind a giant pair of pink plywood buttocks, grabbed Cally by the arm, and jerked it so suddenly that it almost shot out of the socket.

'Come on,' hissed the girl, dragging Cally towards the studio doors, 'get a move on, the commercial break's on in two minutes and forty-five seconds.'

'What?'

'Come *on*.'

The next thing Cally knew, she was being dragged headfirst through the double doors, shoved out into the corridor, and bundled into a lift, hotly pursued by a camera crew and a busty junior production assistant who kept blowing kisses at the camera and nudging down the zip on her tiny sports top.

'What's happening? Where are we going?' demanded Cally breathlessly as they all dived out of the lift at the fourteenth floor and started running along a maze of featureless corridors. For the first time ever, she began to wish she'd watched *The Big One* long enough to find out what happened at the end. 'Why are we running?'

'Come on, hurry up, they're waiting!'

'I don't give a damn who's bloody waiting,' wailed Cally, right into camera, 'Slow down, I've got a stitch.'

Nobody took a blind bit of notice. The girl in the sports top grinned cheesily at the camera, which helped itself to a long, lingering shot of her bouncing cleavage before panning back to Cally's hot, red, makeup-streaked face.

'Will somebody tell me what the fuck is going on?'

As they stumbled up the last flight of steps and popped out on to the roof of Channel Six HQ, Cally saw Liddy. And the helicopter.

Helicopter?

The look on Liddy's face said oh God I really screwed up, please forgive me, but there wasn't time for Cally to tell her that frankly, she was going to have to grovel a whole lot more if she was ever, ever going to get forgiven for this one. Within five seconds of arriving on the roof, Cally, Liddy, the camera crew and the top-heavy girl in the red sports top were all crammed into the helicopter like elephants into a telephone box.

'I can cope with this,' Cally repeated to herself as the rotor-blades whirled over her head. 'I can cope with this, I CAN COPE WITH THIS, I CAN, I CAN.'

'Next stop Paris!' chirruped the production assistant as the helicopter lurched into the air.

With a moan, Cally buried her face in Liddy's jumper.

'Aaah,' smiled the cameraman, getting a nice close-up of the two lovebirds. 'How cute.'

Liddy would have died of embarrassment if she hadn't had other things on her mind.

'Oh shit,' she said, shaking Cally by the shoulder.

Cally opened one bloodshot eye. 'Don't tell me, this is the bit where we get parachuted into a barrel of live ants.'

'Worse! Cally, I think I forgot to lock the shop!'

Chapter Twenty-Seven

The night wasn't just dark; it was a byword for black-
ness. The moon had long since given up and gone off to
sulk behind a blanket of thick cloud, and the only
visible light was the neon-blue flicker from the Insect-o-
cutor in the Chinese chippy.

A little further down the road, a shop door opened
easily and quietly, revealing the *Marie Celeste* of
speciality retail. A couple of startled-looking Action
Men witnessed the incursion, but seemed powerless to
intervene.

The solitary figure stepped into the shop, drew down
the blinds and turned on the light.

'Well, well, well. How stupid can you get?'

It was a small but noisy English invasion that hit Paris
in the early hours of Saturday morning.

Displaying supremely Gallic sang-froid, the night
porter at the Hotel Candide barely raised an eyebrow as
five dishevelled lunatics erupted into his nice
respectable foyer, making a horrible mess with their
camera cables and their furry microphones.

'Fab décor,' trilled Suki the production assistant,
clasping her clipboard to her Lara Croft bosom. 'D'you
suppose it's real, or designer-distressed? Now, don't

you lovebirds go anywhere, I'm just going to sort out the rooms.'

Go anywhere? Cally couldn't have run away if her life had depended on it. With her last ounce of energy, she made it to a Louis something-or-other *fauteuil* and flung her inert carcass into it. The fragile wooden structure creaked alarmingly underneath her. Ah well, if the chair hadn't been distressed before, it certainly was now.

'Things could be worse,' said Liddy, doing her best to sound encouraging.

Cally glared at her ex-best mate. 'And with my luck, they probably will.'

'Look, Cal, I really am sorry. About everything.'

'Save your breath, I'm not interested, OK?'

'Not even about Will?'

Cally's eyes glittered. 'Especially not about Will.'

Suki returned beaming from the reception desk, a big golden key dangling from her finger. 'All sorted.' She waved the key enticingly in Cally's face. 'Just time for a quick interview, and then it's off to bed for you two. Bet you can't wait to get between those satin sheets.'

A camera lens jammed itself up against Liddy's nose. 'Hang on a minute.' She had a horrible thought. 'The camera crew aren't coming with us, are they?'

'God no.' Suki waved away the very suggestion. 'Not since the injunction. Now, Ray, if you could just do me a sound check I'll get on with asking our lucky winners a few que—'

Suki's pre-camera preening was interrupted by a sound like the death-throes of a drowning motorcycle. Fast asleep, one leg dangling over the arm of the chair, one arm flung across her neck like a dead python, Cally was snoring fit to bust.

'No, I don't believe this!' pouted Suki. 'Cally. Cally!'

Cally snored on. The cameramen sniggered. The porter on the reception desk looked more disgusted than ever.

'Shall I film her like this?' suggested Ray, whipping off his lens cover.

'No way!' replied Suki, clearly peeved. 'This is a gameshow, not The Creature from the Deep.' She gave an ill-natured sniff, and swung her pink patent handbag on to her shoulder. 'I suppose that's that's then. I'll see you two at breakfast. And for God's sake don't let her sleep later than eight thirty, we've got a busy schedule tomorrow.'

'Hang on,' cut in Liddy as the production assistant stalked off towards the lift. 'Aren't you going to help me with her?'

'God no,' sneered Suki. 'I don't do bags. See you in the morning.'

The lift arrived and departed. The camera crew made their excuses and headed for the all-night bar on the corner. Some minutes passed, punctuated only by the rhythmic sound of Cally's snoring.

'It's all right,' said Liddy. 'They've gone.'

Cally halted in mid-snore and opened one malevolent eye. 'I've changed my mind about killing you,' she said.

Liddy looked relieved. 'Oh. Good.'

'Yeah, I'm going to kill her first, then you.'

'Single rooms, *madame*?' smirked the hall porter, relieving Liddy of the two overnight bags she had packed in haste and carrying them disdainfully into the lift.

'Yes, single rooms,' said Cally exasperatedly. 'I take it Liddy and I have single rooms?'

311

This was apparently the funniest thing the porter had heard all day. '*Mon dieu, mais non*! You are sharing ze finest room in ze entire hotel! Eet ees – how you say – very very *romantique, oui*?'

Cally opened her mouth to protest. 'Look, if you think I'm going to share a room with *her* . . .'

Liddy shut her up with a kick on the shin.

'You cow!' glared Cally, inspecting the damage.

Liddy smiled impishly. 'Belt up, darling. We're supposed to be in love, remember?'

Cally squared up to her, nose-tip to nose-tip. 'Look, *darling*, you can go along with this if you want, after all it's all your bloody fault we're here in the first place, but as far as I'm concerned you can stuff this whole fucking fiasco right up your—'

Ping.

The lift jolted to a halt on the seventh floor, the doors purred smoothly open and the porter glided out into a long, deep-carpeted hallway, an overnight bag dangling from either hand. '*Suivez-moi, mesdames.*'

They followed the hall porter round in what seemed like an ever-widening spiral until he stopped in his tracks, so suddenly that they both cannoned into the back of him.

'*Mesdames,*' he announced, peeling himself off Liddy's T-shirt as though it harboured some deadly virus. 'Welcome to ze honeymoon suite.'

Liddy stood in the middle of the immense sitting room, staring open-mouthed at the pink plaster cherubs gambolling across the ceiling.

'Oh my God, this place is *unreal*. Have you ever seen anything like it?'

Cally had not. The honeymoon suite was without

doubt the pinkest thing in the world; pinker even than Barbara Cartland's Sunday-best knickers. Pink walls, pink ceiling, pink telephone, pink brocade curtains, even the hangers in the pink wardrobe had pink silk bows on them. Naked pink nymphs danced round the bathroom walls; dusky-pink cushions in the shape of pouting lips littered the magenta sofas; even the toilet-brush had pink bristles.

'No, and it's vile. Just looking at it makes me feel sick.'

'Oh come on, look on the bright side,' urged Liddy. 'At least it's big.' Pushing open a set of glazed doors, she discovered an immense balcony, complete with table, chairs and big pink parasol. 'And I bet it's got a great view of the city.'

'Terrific. A great view of somewhere I don't want to be.'

'Come out and look – I can see the Eiffel Tower!'

'Bully for you. Why don't you go and jump off it and give us all a break?'

Liddy came back into the room. 'You don't mean that.' She looked at Cally's expression and wasn't so sure. 'Do you?'

'Wanna bet?' Cally kicked off her shoes and stomped over to the heart-shaped double bed. On it lay two pink babydoll nighties, laid out side by side and sprinkled with rose-petals. 'Oh my God, look at that!'

Liddy stifled a giggle. 'Aaaah – cute.'

'Hah. Cute my arse. That settles it, you're sleeping on the sofa.'

As she bent over to pull back the shimmery pink bedspread, Cally's elbow caught a button on the wall. Half a second later, the bed was undulating like the English Channel in a force ten gale; and the two nighties sprang into each other's arms in a cloud of fragrant rose-petals.

'Well I can't think of a more perfect end to a perfect day,' snapped Cally. 'Kidnapped and dragged off to some Parisian tart's boudoir by the TV crew from hell. Great. Terrific. And you know what's best of all? I get to spend three whole nights in the honeymoon suite with you.'

'Oh come on, you've got to see the funny side.'

'What funny side? I'm not laughing.'

Cally dropped on to the sofa and turned her back on Liddy, who pulled a despairing face. 'All right, I know you're angry,' she began.

'Angry? Why on earth would I be angry? I mean, it's not as if I've got any stress in my life, is it? I've only split up from my husband, lost my job, had my boyfriend nicked by my so-called best friend . . .'

'Cally, I didn't . . .'

'. . . had Eddie and Janis make me feel about as welcome as bubonic plague . . . Why the hell should I be angry?'

Something about Cally's petulance sparked Liddy's normally placid temperament into volatile life. 'Listen, you,' she commanded, plonking herself astride the arm of an easy chair and jabbing a finger in Cally's face. 'You think you've got problems?'

'I bloody know I have.'

'Not compared to me you haven't. Just listen to this, kid, and then tell me you're stressed out.'

Cally's face was ashen. 'All this stuff about your gran and the shop. I had no idea.'

'You never do,' replied Liddy.

There was a pause. 'And Will?'

314

Liddy gave a sigh. 'For the tenth time, Cal, he's just a mate. A damn sight more of a mate than you've been lately,' she added.

Cally hung her head. 'Ouch.'

'Sorry,' shrugged Liddy, 'but it's true.'

'I know,' admitted Cally ruefully. 'These last few months, all I've thought about is me, me, me. Me having a bad time, me getting dumped on from a great height. And when I saw you and Will like that . . .'

'Like I said, it was just a hug.'

'I know.' Cally was shamefaced. 'Sorry.'

Liddy sat down on the sofa next to her. 'It doesn't matter.' Her stomach growled loudly, filling the awkward silence. 'You know something? It must be nearly,' she consulted her watch, 'twenty hours since I've eaten, and even then it was only a Wagon Wheel.'

Now she came to think of it, Cally felt a bit peckish, too. A sly smile crept over her face. 'Hey, so neither of us wants to be here. And style-wise, this hotel stinks. Right?'

'Right.'

'But it's still a five-star hotel, and we're not paying the bill. And you know what five-star hotels have, don't you?'

'What?'

'Five-star room service.' Cally reached over the pink phone from the coffee table. 'How do you say "two of everything" in French?'

Chapter Twenty-Eight

Tears were rolling down Cally's cheeks. 'No, don't! I'll wet myself.'

'And what about when we gave Suki the slip in that lesbian nightclub?' giggled Liddy, sipping a second French beer in the airport lounge.

'Brilliant!' recalled Cally with a grin.

'Mind you, I did feel a bit guilty about going off and leaving her there.'

'Serves her right for trying to get you to cop off with that bargirl,' retorted Cally, taking a big bite of *millefeuilles*. She might not be sorry the filming in Paris was over, but she sure was going to miss the cakes. 'Talk about sleaze TV. If we'd got pissed and had a naked threesome with Vanessa Paradis she'd have been in seventh heaven.'

Liddy yawned. 'Instead of which, all she's got to show for it is a video of you and me eating ice creams on a *bateau mouche*. Poor Suki.'

'Huh. I'm not shedding any tears.'

A voice on the tannoy announced the departure of Flight RG2315 to Munich. Businessmen packed away their laptops and drifted across to Gate 14.

'Cal,' said Liddy, 'have you forgiven me yet, or am I still in the doghouse?'

Cally rummaged in her jacket pocket and extracted something small, round and covered in fluff. 'There you go.'

Liddy took it between finger and thumb. 'What is it?'

'My last Rolo. Actually it's not a Rolo, it's a Werther's Original, but the idea's the same.'

'Mates again then?'

'Natch.'

The voice on the tannoy piped up again. 'Flight SL9316 to East Midlands Airport is now boarding at . . .'

Cally threw the last chunk of cream slice into her mouth and shouldered her overnight bag. 'That'll be me, I'd better go.'

Liddy caught her sleeve. 'Are you sure you don't want to come back to Cheltenham with me first? I mean, you're a day early.'

'What's the point?' reasoned Cally. 'I've got a hire car waiting at the other end, and Rob's not exactly going to lock me out, is he?'

'S'pose not,' shrugged Liddy. 'Good luck then.'

'Thanks, I might need it. Tell you what, I get back on Friday. Let's go out for a drink and I'll tell you all the gory details.'

There was something about cleavage that always made Rob think of mangoes. And thanks to Rachel, he had been thinking about mangoes nonstop lately.

The thing was, it was an awkward situation. Rachel had started taking long baths every evening, and then wandering about the house in nothing but that flimsy white thing she laughingly called a dressing gown. Well, he was going to have to put his foot down about that. Absolutely. Definitely. Not a doubt about it. When

318

he remembered what it was he was putting his foot down about.

Mangoes. Mmm. He could really go a nice ripe pair of mangoes.

God, what kind of state had she got him into? As Rachel wafted round the conservatory, all damp and pink under her little white thing, Rob strove manfully to focus his mind on what he had to say.

'The thing is,' he began for the umpteenth time.

'What thing?' she enquired, leaning across him to help herself to the secateurs, and in doing so treating him to an uninterrupted view of her majestic foothills. 'Do you like my azaleas? They're really coming along, aren't they?'

Rob swallowed. 'Er . . . yes, very nice.' He tried again. 'You know my wife and I . . .?'

'Cally?'

'That's right. Well, you know we've been living apart for a few months now?'

Concern showed on Rachel's face. 'Has something happened?' She lifted big, soft, hopeful eyes. 'She's not asked you for a divorce, has she?'

'No! Nothing like that. She's . . . er . . . coming to stay.'

'Here?' Rachel's face fell. 'When?'

'Tomorrow.'

'Oh.'

'It's only for a couple of days. She's got an interview for a job in Milton Keynes, and there didn't seem much point in her paying out for a hotel.'

'You really don't have to explain.' Rachel started bustling around, tidying up imaginary specks of compost. 'It's nothing to do with me, I'm just the lodger.'

319

'I know, but I . . .' The dark eyes met his just as a bell rang in the distance. 'Oh bugger, there's someone at the door.'

'You'd better get it then, hadn't you?'

'Look, I'll be back in a minute, OK?' He strode off to the front door cursing under his breath. Why were these people things always so darned difficult? He was a successful salesman, he was supposed to be a star people-manipulator; so how come his life was littered with disgruntled women?

With very bad grace, he opened the door. And there on the doorstep stood a woman with an overnight bag in one hand and an Indian takeaway in the other.

'Hi Rob,' said Cally, planting a swift peck on his cheek and stepping past him into the hall. 'I bought supper. Shall I go straight through to the conservatory with it?'

Red alert! screamed a voice inside Rob's head. Not the conservatory, repeat, *not* the conservatory!

Cally was several paces in front of him before he'd even recovered sufficiently to slam the front door and lunge after her. 'It's a bit of a mess in there.' He grabbed her elbow and tried to divert her into the dining room. 'Maybe we should eat in here?'

She laughed in his face. 'Rob, it's been a mess in there as long as I can remember. And you know we never use the dining room. Why don't you go and get some plates?'

He let out a faint whimper and trailed after her, past the sitting room, through the kitchen and ever-nearer to the dreaded conservatory. Rob's brain worked overtime. Come on, come on, you can do this, he told it; you can come up with the excuse of the century, just *think*.

320

'Rob!' exclaimed Cally, disappearing inside.

His heart stopped. Any minute now . . .

'Wow, it's so *green* in here, look at all these plants, it's amazing!'

Uh? Cautiously he stuck a head round the door. Cally was standing in the middle of the conservatory, gazing in astonishment at the horticultural marvels Rachel had wrought since she came to live in the house. He gaped. Rachel. Where was Rachel? There was absolutely no sign of her, just an open back door to the garden.

'Come on,' urged Cally, unpacking the takeaway. 'Let's eat.' When Rob didn't move, she shook him by the shoulder. 'Hello? Anybody at home?'

He jolted out of his trance. 'Oh. Right. Yeah.' Walking across to the door, he closed it. 'Plates, right? Plates.'

Still dazed, he wandered over to the little antique pine cupboard he'd bought Cally the time he'd gone away to a conference in Cardiff and was feeling guilty about the blonde he'd met at the Little Chef. Opening the cupboard, he took out two plates. Rachel, where the hell was Rachel?

'Are you all right?' demanded Cally.

'Of course I am.' He straightened up and turned round, sniffing the air. 'Mind you, there's a really weird smell in here.'

It was Cally's turn to look uncomfortable. 'Oh damn, that'll be Colin, he loves this jacket.'

'Who the hell's Colin?'

'Colin the skunk. I look after him at the zoo, the smell's a bit . . . persistent. You wouldn't believe the funny looks I got in Paris.' She gave herself a tentative sniff. 'Trouble is, I hardly notice it these days. Is it bad?'

'Let's just say it's not Chanel No 5.'

Reluctantly, Cally got up. 'Keep my share warm, will you? I'll just dash up and have a quick shower.'

And she left, leaving Rob wondering what the hell was going to happen next.

Cally couldn't help noticing how different the house looked – or was it just that it felt different? As she climbed the stairs to the bathroom, she reflected on how long she'd been away. Was it five months, or six? She couldn't quite remember.

She paused on the landing to take in a row of artily framed photographs of steam engines. Odd that. Rob had never been the trainspotting type. Come to that, he'd never been very artistic either; his idea of high culture was a picture of Melinda Messenger with the nipples covered up. Still, maybe she'd misjudged him. Maybe what he said was true, and he really had changed.

Cally walked into the bathroom and closed the door. Strange, the house even smelled different. The sharp, citrusy smells she'd always favoured had almost disappeared, to be replaced by something sweeter and almost flowery. The Bugs Bunny soap dish was in the wrong place too, but then that was Rob all over. He never put anything back where he'd found it. She put it back on the corner of the bath, and that made her feel a little more at home.

Undressing quickly, she threw her clothes over an empty towel-stand by the open window. A shower and a change of clothes would put everything back into perspective. But as she turned on the water and waited for it to get nice and hot, she noticed something much odder than a misaligned soap dish.

A box of tampons.

She picked it up. Tampons? Nothing strange about that; except that these were a brand she'd never bought in her life. So unless Rob had developed some very peculiar fetish since she'd moved out . . .

Just then, a movement caught her eye and she swung round to face the window. But there was nothing there. Well, that wasn't strictly true; her jeans were there, but her T-shirt had vanished into thin air. Which was of course completely impossible.

Seconds later, Cally was staring in disbelief as an arm snaked in through the window, made a grab for her jeans and vanished with its prey. Bloody hell. She rushed over to the window and stuck her head out.

There, standing on the roof of *her* kitchen extension, was a half-naked girl holding a pair of jeans and a T-shirt.

'Er . . . hi.' The girl smiled nervously and held out the clothes. 'Sorry, I thought these were mine.'

Liddy watched Charlton Kings sliding past the taxi window. 'Just here, please.'

'Right you are, darling.' The car slid to a halt by the Chinese chippy. 'That'll be four-fifty.'

Liddy rummaged in her bag for the exact money. She'd have liked to tip the driver, but when you were as skint as she was every penny counted. 'There you go. Can I have a receipt, please?' she added, thinking of the accounts she'd been putting off doing for months. 'Thanks, 'bye.'

The taxi drew away and disappeared into the distance. Liddy felt a slight queasiness in the pit of her stomach as she walked the dozen yards or so to the shop. If only she'd put the double lock on the back door.

If only she'd remembered to switch on the burglar alarm. If only she wasn't such a dozy cow.

She stopped in her tracks as the front window of Gold in the Attic rolled into view from behind the corner of the greengrocer's. No. No, it wasn't true.

This couldn't be happening to her.

Chapter Twenty-Nine

'You could have told me,' commented Cally, dolloping chicken korma on to her plate. She passed the spoon to Rachel. 'He always was a prat.'

'I expect he meant to tell you,' said Rachel. Cally couldn't help noticing the way her eyes kept flitting back to Rob.

'Look, I would have.' Rob fidgeted with his shirt-cuffs, the way he always did when he wasn't being entirely on the level. 'Only I knew you'd take it the wrong way, after all that business with Selena.'

'Selena?' Rachel's eyes narrowed.

'She's a cactus,' said Cally. 'It's a long story, isn't it Rob? Why don't you tell Rachel all about it?'

'Anyway,' said Rob, avoiding Cally's gaze by helping himself to more rice, 'I wasn't intending to get a real lodger, but when Greg Prince's cousin turns up on your doorstep you don't have much option, do you?'

'Don't you?' Rachel looked wounded, but Rob seemed not to have noticed.

'Not a lot,' replied Rob through a mouthful of poppadom. 'Got to keep on the right side of Greg, he's my biggest client.'

'Oh,' said Rachel.

'Still,' prompted Cally, 'you wouldn't have taken her on as a tenant if you hadn't liked her, would you?'

'Well at least she's not a seventeen-stone psycho, eh Rach?' Rob gave Rachel a matey little punch on the shoulder, almost knocking her off her chair. Rachel looked mortified. 'Any more of that channa dhal in there, Cal?'

Wiping her mouth on her paper napkin, Rachel stood up. 'Thanks for the takeaway.'

'You're not going already, are you?' said Cally. 'You've not finished your meal.'

'Oh, you know . . . things to do.'

'Can I have your onion bhaji?' asked Rob, fork poised over Rachel's plate. She didn't answer. She was already halfway up the stairs.

'Rob,' said Cally, 'you know you're a moron, don't you?'

Rob looked genuinely surprised. 'What did I do?'

'Rachel's a nice girl, isn't she?'

'Suppose she is, yeah.'

'She's besotted with you, you know.' That much is bleeding obvious, thought Cally. So why aren't I seething with jealousy? It was an intriguing question but she didn't have any answers.

A sudden flash of panic shot across Rob's face. 'Hey, hang on a minute, if you think I've laid a hand on her . . .'

Cally shook her head, speared a cauliflower pakora with her fork and stuffed it into Rob's open mouth. 'I didn't say that, I just said she fancies you. Can I suggest something?'

He frowned. 'Like what? A chastity belt? 'Cause I swear to you Cal, I don't need one. I've changed. You can trust me now.'

She laid a hand on his arm. 'Rob.'

'What?'

'Sleep down here on the sofa tonight.'

Rob's brows knitted. 'On the sofa? I don't get it. If I'm being kicked out of bed, what's wrong with the spare room?'

'Rachel won't see if you sleep in the spare room, will she? She might think you're sleeping with me.'

'What's that got to do with anything?'

'Trust me, Rob. Just do it.'

Time really does lend distance, thought Cally as she made the familiar journey to the Northampton HQ of LBS Agri-Finance. At any rate, six months away had given her a whole new perspective, and not just on the house she'd shared with Rob.

She slammed the door of Rob's company car and pocketed the key. As she walked across the visitors' car park and entered the main building, it struck her how dingy the whole place looked. It was obvious that Banco Torino hadn't spent a penny on refurbishments; the sheep-shaped dot was missing off the 'i' in 'Agri', and the carpet in the foyer looked like it hadn't had a good clean in years. Had things really gone downhill, or had they been like this all along? Maybe she was just seeing it all with different eyes.

A white-haired security guard hailed her with a gleaming smile as she stepped in through the swing doors.

'Well, well! If it isn't Miss . . . er . . .' He tapped his forehead with a gnarled finger.

'Cally,' she said. 'Cally Storm. Hello Albert.'

'Miss Storm, of course! You'll have to forgive me, old brain's not what it was.' A fine set of false teeth flashed in the electric light. 'I say, you're looking absolutely lovely today.' He winked. 'All the boys will be after you in that pretty little skirt.'

Cally detached herself with difficulty. Funny, she'd always had a soft spot for old Albert, seen him as the last of the English gentlemen; now he struck her as more like the ghastly old codger in the Werther's Originals advert. And the new receptionist wasn't much better, with her squeaky-bright 'Good morning madam, how may I help you?', and a smile so brittle it threatened to split her head in two.

'I have an appointment with Mr Llewellyn.'

'Do take a seat, I'll just phone up and let him know you're here.' How did she manage to speak and maintain that fixed grin at the same time, wondered Cally. It was like some kind of weird ventriloquism.

She sat. A couple of middle managers sauntered through on their way to the car park. She recognised one of them, the tall blonde with the big earrings. What was she called? Jennifer something, glamour queen of the livestock department, and ambitious with it once upon a time. Must have been with LBS for . . . ooh, getting on for twenty years. Twenty years of striving for the top, and what did it get you? A desk next to the photocopier and roots that were starting to show grey instead of brown.

'Cally Storm?' She looked up to see a man in a rumpled grey suit looming over her, hand outstretched. 'I'm David Llewellyn.'

'Sorry, I was miles away.' She struggled to her feet and accepted his handshake. He, at least, looked clued-up as if going somewhere.

'I thought I'd start by showing you your new office,' he explained as they stepped into the lift.

'Great. Can't wait.' She watched him as he pressed the button for the third floor.

The third floor! She'd *dreamed* of having an office on the third floor ever since she started at LBS; yearned for the status, the cachet, the joy of knowing that she'd Made It. And now, suddenly, she had.

They walked along a beige corridor. I ought to be excited, thought Cally. Why aren't I excited?

'Here we are,' he beamed, pushing open the door and standing back to let her through. 'I think you'll like it.'

'It's great,' said Cally, wandering across a broad expanse of boring grey carpet, in the middle of which stood a boring grey desk and a matching chair. In fact, the only hint of colour in the entire office was a yellow Post-It note, stuck to the screen of the computer. 'Really nice.'

Cally's soon-to-be new boss led her across to the window. 'And as you can see, there's a great view of the car park.'

'Fantastic.'

'So you'll be able to keep an eye on your lovely new company car.'

Cally gazed out over the square of grey tarmac, almost obscured by row upon row of cars. Little, sad-looking cars that belonged to no-hopers. Trendy, aspirational cars for the young guns. And over in the corner, in their own personal spaces, a line of company cars in identical shades of grey.

Unease weighed in her stomach like an undigested Christmas dinner. Was she doing the right thing? Was she selling her soul? Was she about to paint herself into an office corner, never to escape?

The rest of the day didn't make Cally feel any more optimistic. Old colleagues greeted her with a mixture of indifference, envy and obsequiousness, depending on how her return to LBS was going to affect them. In one or two cases, as she walked away she could feel them mentally drawing the target on her back.

By mid-afternoon, she was heartily sick of people whose every word you had to decode because they never said what they really meant. As she sat in her empty office, waiting for her new boss to come back and wondering how to get used to all this greyness, she found herself longing for something *real*.

Donna, Vern, even Lazy Bob: they were real. Not this. Suddenly, Cally found herself thinking about Colin. That poor, cowardly, stinky little ball of tumble-weed, cowering in his run, wondering where she'd gone. Waiting for her to come back and feed him because he was scared stiff of everybody else.

A twinge of guilt, mingled with something more intangible, clutched at her insides. Was she really giving up Colin for this? A desk, a car and the chance to develop a perforated gastric ulcer before she was thirty-five?

'Ah, there you are, Cally.' David Llewellyn beamed as he walked back into the office. 'I thought you might like to meet your new assistant.'

A lumpily built woman in a blue suit stepped forward. Her red hair was razor-cut into a short style that was probably supposed to make her look young and trendy but merely reinforced the impression of an East German border guard.

'Cally, this is Stephanie Wilson. She's just trans-ferred over from our Hull office. Stephanie, this is Cally Storm.'

If five thousand volts had suddenly shot through the

office, they could not have had a more profound effect on Cally. Stephanie! she thought, her jaw dropping. Stephanie Wilson. My God, time hasn't been kind to you.

'Hello Stephanie,' she said, offering her hand.

Stephanie looked at it suspiciously. 'Haven't we met somewhere before?'

Her tone made it obvious that she knew damn well they had; in fact she'd committed to memory every moment of their childhood, every excruciating detail of those early days when they'd worked at LBS together. All at once Cally felt time shift full-circle. She was a snot-nosed kid with a Princess Leia doll; and Stephanie Wilson was a scheming little bitch who liked nothing better than making people's lives a misery.

One spiteful act, thought Cally. One spiteful, childish act by one unpleasant little girl; that was all it took to derail the whole of my life. Till now. Because this is where it stops.

'Have we met?' She smiled back at Stephanie with all the confidence she'd lacked, so many years ago. 'You know, I really don't remember.'

'Never, never, never, never, never!' shrieked Liddy.

Will took a step back. 'Whoa, hold on a minute. I only—'

Liddy's voice rose half an octave. 'Never, Will, do you hear me? I am *never* asking you to look after this shop again. My God, I call you up from Paris 'cause I'm having like a major crisis, and what happens? You create another one!'

'But—'

'Don't you "but" me! Look at this place.' Liddy

swept an arm round the shop, sending antique under-wear flying in all directions. 'How much have you spent, Will? Have you any idea how much this lot is worth?' She surveyed the newly stocked shop with mounting desperation. Top-quality collectables were squeezed on to every available inch of shelf space. 'What am I saying, of course you do. Will, what have you done!'

'Have you finished now?' asked Will calmly. 'I mean, is it all right if I get a word in edgeways?'

Liddy stopped flapping and threw herself on to a stool, arms belligerently folded. 'Be my guest. I'd like to hear you talk your way out of this one.'

He shrugged. 'Easy. All this new stock is mine.'

'Well it sure as hell isn't mine!'

'Look, you've got no decent stock worth selling, and I've got too much. I just thought you might like to, you know, sell it for me.'

Liddy gave a mocking laugh. 'Oh I get it, this is one of your scams, isn't it?'

'Nope.'

She ignored him. 'What is it – tax dodge? VAT fiddle? Listen Will, if you think for one minute I'm getting myself into the shit for you . . .'

He shook his head. 'No Lids, *you* listen.' He shot a sideways glance at Stefan, whose drooling jaws were homing in on a twelve-inch Betty Boop. 'Do that and you die. Horribly.' Crestfallen, the dog backed off and lay down. 'No scam, no nothing. You pay me for the stuff as and when you sell it, and the rest is your profit.'

'What? Why?'

'Come here.' Taking her by the shoulder, he practically frog-marched her over to the ancient till and

332

opened the cash drawer. 'See? That's my invoice, and those are the takings.'

Liddy stared at the neat pile of cash. 'How on earth did you manage that?'

'I put the word around, then opened the shop on Sunday for a collectors' viewing,' he explained, by now looking positively smug. 'See these?' He waved a handful of handwritten cards. 'These are the advance orders. You're going to be quids in.'

Liddy raised a hand, dazed. 'Hang on a minute, where's the catch?'

'There isn't one.'

'But where's the payoff for you?' She picked up the invoice. 'These prices are barely above cost, you're robbing yourself blind.'

'I'll still be making a profit,' he demurred. 'Besides, it's all stuff I wanted to get rid of.' He put his fingers on the corners of her mouth and pushed them upwards. 'Smile, Lids! Everything's going to be just fine.'

'I've got this feeling,' said Rob as Cally walked down the stairs towards him with her suitcase.

'What feeling?'

'The feeling that this time you're not coming back.' Their eyes met. 'I'm right, aren't I?'

Cally sat down on the stairs. 'We've got to make a decision, Rob.'

'But I thought . . .'

She shook her head. 'I think we both know it's over. If we can just admit it and move on, maybe we'll both feel a whole lot better.'

Rob sat down beside her. 'But what about the job at LBS?'

'I'm not taking it.'

'Ah. I had a feeling about that, too.'

Cally managed a half-smile. 'Don't tell me you're actually turning sensitive in your old age.'

He laughed. 'I think that's probably a bit much to ask for, don't you?' He fiddled with the end of his tie. 'So what happens now? I've never got divorced before.'

'We sort out the mortgage and stuff, I suppose.'

'I could buy you out if you want. That'd give you something to put towards a new place.'

'Whatever, we'll sort something out. And then I guess we go our separate ways.'

'Cally,' he said softly. She looked at him, and his eyes were big and moist, like a puppy's. 'I don't want to lose you.'

Oh shit, not this, she thought. Not when I'm being all grown-up and strong. 'Rob, I've just told you . . .'

'No, not that, I mean as a friend. I don't want us to lose touch. We had some good times, didn't we?'

She squeezed his hand. 'Great times. But like I said, we have to move on.' She paused. 'What are you going to do with your life?'

'Dunno. Stay where I am, I guess. Keep on raking in lots of lovely commission, courtesy of Prince Parks and Leisure.'

'Hmm,' said Cally.

'What's that mean?'

'It means, remember that invitation you got to the opening of B-Movie Heaven?'

'What about it? You still want to come?'

She shook her head. 'Why don't you take Rachel?'

Rob looked doubtful, then brightened. 'You really think so? Her and me?'

'Who knows? Ask her out and see.'

'What about you? What are you going to do?'

She got to her feet and picked up her suitcase. 'Go out and get myself a dose of reality. I think we could both do with a bit of that right now.'

Chapter Thirty

The next time Cally visited Gold in the Attic, she hardly recognised the place.

'Liddy! Where on earth did you get all this stuff?'

Liddy finished counting out change and watched her latest customer walk out of the shop with a couple of well-stuffed carrier bags. 'Isn't it brilliant?'

'It must have cost you a fortune.'

'Not yet.'

'How do you mean, not yet?'

Liddy dusted a couple of Tribbles and put them back on their shelf. 'I didn't do any of this, Will did.'

'Will!'

'Have a seat.' Liddy headed off towards the back room. 'I'll put the kettle on, then I'll tell you all about it.'

Liddy didn't look the least bit shocked, or even surprised. 'So you've finally done it then? You've really left Rob for good?'

Cally nodded.

'And you're sure? You're not having second thoughts?'

'Hell no. It's for the best, Lids, I'm not the woman he thought I was. Come to that, I'm not the woman *I* thought I was.'

'That's a bit deep,' commented Liddy.

'Not deep. Just confusing. It took me a while to get my head round it. Comes as a bit of a shock to the system when you suddenly realise you're not bothered if your husband's shagging other women.' She looked at Liddy over the top of her coffee mug. 'I suppose you think I'm mad, leaving him.'

Liddy was silent for a moment. 'Cally.'

'Hmm?'

'As a matter of fact, I'm glad. Not that I want you to be miserable or anything,' she added hastily, 'but it kind of makes things less complicated.'

'What things?'

Liddy reached into the pouch she wore slung over her combats and took out a photograph. 'Take a look at this.'

There were two people in the picture. One was a very young-looking Will, laughing at the camera in a way she'd never seen him laugh, a pint of beer in one hand and the other round a girl's waist. The girl was laughing too. Her face was at an angle to the camera, but even so the resemblance hit Cally like a speeding truck.

She looked up, eyes wide. 'Liddy . . . who *is* this?'

'It's a long story,' said Liddy, propping the photo up against the coffee jar. 'And it starts right here.'

Cally's head was spinning. She felt hyperactive, high, dizzy as a dervish on speed. The past was gone and buried, the confusion of the present suddenly clearing, beginning to make sense. Perhaps that was why she felt such an overwhelming urge to clear up every scrap of unfinished business.

Like Janis. Janis had been a thorn in her side for too long, and it was time to pull it out. Cally had rehearsed what she was going to say over and over again. 'Janis,' she would begin, in a tone that conveyed just the right degree of menace, 'I want you to go away and leave Eddie alone.' And when Janis opened her mouth to protest, Cally would leap straight down her throat with: 'It's no good, Janis, I know your game, trying to take poor Eddie for what you can get. And I won't have it, I'm not standing by while you hurt my best mate. Got that?'

Of course she'd get it, thought Cally with a glow of righteous satisfaction. A few well-chosen words, an oblique mention of a cosy little chat with the local constabulary, and Janis would soon be on her way with her scabby dog on a string. Sorted.

Only it wasn't quite that simple.

'Janis?' Cally marched straight into the flat, all guns primed and ready for action. 'Janis, where are you?'

The only answer was the rhythmic gurgling of Eddie's tropical fish tank, and another sound, curiously muffled as though it was ashamed to be heard.

Cally took a few steps towards the sound. It was coming from Eddie's room, but it wasn't Eddie making it. The door was ajar. Without knocking, she edged it further open. Janis was sitting curled up inside the deep well of the window, knees up to her chin, a sodden paper tissue crumpled in her hand. On the floor beneath the sill lay Ziggy, big eyes fixed on his mistress, whimpering in sympathy with her sobs.

The sight of Janis's tear-stained face took the wind right out of Cally's sails. 'What's the matter? Has something happened?'

Janis sniffed snot back up her dripping nose. 'I-it's E-eddie,' she sobbed, her shoulders heaving.

'Eddie! What's wrong with him?'

'H-he's g-gone.'

Cally's heart leapt momentarily, then submitted to a belated twinge of guilt. 'Gone? You mean he's left you?'

Janis's shoulders shook, making her look more than ever like a rag doll with a porcelain face. 'He w-went to the s-s-supermarket,' she sobbed. 'A-ages ago, and . . .' sniff '. . . h-he's not back yet . . .' swallow '. . . a-and I just can't manage without him.'

The last few words came out in a rush, as Janis buried her face in her skirt and dissolved into hacking sobs of utter misery. Dumbstruck, Cally wondered what on earth was going on. People didn't usually go to pieces just because their boyfriend was a bit late getting back from Tesco's.

Hesitantly, she put an arm round Janis's shoulders. 'I don't understand why you're so upset,' she confessed. 'Do you want to tell me about it?'

Janis wiped a hand across her dripping face, and took a deep breath. 'I-I'm just having one of my bad days.'

'Bad days?'

Thrusting a shaking hand into the pocket of her skirt, Janis brought out a packet of pills. 'Paroxetine 20mg, take one a day after breakfast,' read Cally. 'What are these?'

'Anti-depressants. I . . . I get down. Ever since what happened.' Janis stared into space, as though some particularly painful memory was projecting itself on to the wall in front of her. 'You don't want to know.'

Maybe that's true, thought Cally, but you obviously want to tell me. 'Yes I do,' she said, sitting on the end of the bed. 'Who knows, maybe I can help.'

Janis looked at her warily. 'Why would you want to help me? You hate me.'

'I don't hate you.' Cally was beginning to wish she'd never started this. 'I just don't understand, that's all.'

'I used to work at Pearman and Bradshawe,' said Janis.

'The auctioneers?'

'Yeah. I was a porter there, showing off the lots, learning the trade.'

An auction house, thought Cally. Of course. 'So that's how come you know so much about art and stuff?'

'I wanted to know everything about everything. I thought, one day I'm going to be someone. Really someone. An expert.' A tear traced an uneven path down her swollen cheek. 'It was all going great. Then one day this really rich guy comes into the place, he's auctioning off all this amazing Art Deco stuff. Anyhow, he makes a move on me, tries to get me into bed, and when I knock him back he goes crazy, absolutely crazy. Screams at me that I'm a prick-teasing slut. Next thing I know, some of his stuff's gone missing from the warehouse and he makes it look like I took it.'

'That's terrible. But they didn't just take his word for it, surely?'

'What do you think? He was the one with all the money so obviously he was telling the truth, wasn't he? Lost my job, lost my boyfriend, lost my flat, started drinking too much, fetched up out on the street.'

'My God,' murmured Cally. 'No wonder you're depressed.'

'Pull yourself together and straighten out your life, that's what they tell you down the social security, get yourself a job then you can get a place to live. Only they won't give you a job if you've not got an address, will they? Catch bleeding twenty-two.'

This could have been me, thought Cally with a shiver of empathy. This could so nearly have been me. 'I didn't realise,' she said lamely.

'Then I met Eddie.' Janis's face brightened. 'And he just *understood*. Straight away, like he'd been there himself. Knew what to say, knew what to do to make me feel better about myself. Even made me laugh, God knows how.'

Cally thought back to her own dark days. 'Yeah,' she said. 'Eddie's a pretty special guy.' She wanted to add, 'Even if he did learn everything he knows from me', but that would have been a cheap shot.

'He's such a good painter,' Janis went on. 'So talented. He could make really good money selling his pictures, I've tried to tell him but he's just too modest. Maybe he'd listen if it came from you.'

Cally felt suddenly ashamed. 'Actually, I was meaning to talk to you about Eddie.'

A glint of panic hardened the soft brown of Janis's huge, baby-faun eyes. 'You're not jealous?' A hand clutched at her arm. 'Don't say that, please don't say you're jealous. You're not, are you?'

'No, of course not.' She patted Janis's hand and the fingers relaxed a little. 'I was just wondering . . . about you and Eddie. Is it serious?'

The Bambi eyes softened again, and the lower lip started to quiver. 'I . . . I think so.'

'And you do want it to be?'

'Oh yes.'

For a split second, Cally felt a malicious impulse to tell Janis, 'Well forget it, because Eddie's my best mate and he deserves better than you'; then something higher kicked in and she knew what she had to say.

'I just wanted to tell you I'm moving out.'

Janis looked poleaxed. 'Why? Because of me?'

'Because you and Eddie need space, and you aren't going to get it while I'm around, are you?'

'But where will you go?'

Cally shrugged off the question. 'Oh I'll think of something, don't you worry.'

The penguin pool was never very crowded on a Monday morning, if you didn't count the penguins. And Cally had become curiously accustomed to sharing her intimate conversations with them.

'I've seen the photo,' said Cally as Will hosed down the rocks, watched with interest by his rockhoppers.

She saw his back stiffen. 'What photo?'

'Liddy showed it to me, the one of you and Emma.'

'Oh,' said Will, but he didn't turn round.

'She looks a lot like me.'

Will let out a long, slow breath and Cally had the feeling he was struggling to gain control of his emotions before he faced her. Turning off the water, he sat down on a rock, the hose across his knees. 'Looked,' he corrected her. 'And that's all. She wasn't like you in any other way, that was where I made my first big mistake.'

Cally knew the story now, from Liddy, but she let him tell it to her in his own words because he wanted to, maybe needed to. 'She was eighteen when we met,' he began, 'and I was nineteen. I fell head over heels for her the first time I saw her. The night we got engaged I remember thinking this can't be true, you're just this boring git and this incredibly beautiful girl wants to marry you. Something's got to go wrong with this, something always goes wrong for you.' He hung his head.

'And it did?'

'And how. She was a week off her twentieth birthday when her car came off that road. Nobody could tell me how it had happened, the weather wasn't bad, it was a good road, she hadn't been drinking. It simply ... happened. Just one of those things, they said at the inquest. Just one of those things! It broke my life apart. I thought, that's it Will; never get that involved ever again, that way they can't break your heart. And then I met you.'

'And I reminded you of Emma. And all the pain came back.'

'It was a total shock.' He was looking at Cally with the same intensity she'd seen in his eyes the first time they met. 'I couldn't believe how much you looked like her; it was like she was suddenly walking back into my life, turning everything upside-down again just when I thought I was learning to survive without her. And do you know how that made me feel?'

'Tell me.'

'Terrified. Elated. Resentful – God I resented you, I was terrified of what you were doing to my mind. And then ... well, the old feelings took over. I couldn't get enough of you, I wanted to be with you for all the wrong reasons.'

'Because you wanted me to be Emma?' He nodded. 'Was that why you kept trying to tell me how to do my hair, what clothes I ought to be wearing?'

'Christ Cally, you must think I'm some kind of mental case. Maybe I am.'

She shook her head. 'Not mental. Just hurting.'

'And so were you. But I was so crazy about turning you into a carbon copy of Emma, I never gave that a thought, did I? Just blundered on until you told me to piss off, and no wonder. I ruined everything.'

Cally smiled at his crestfallen face. 'And that's when we started being friends.'

He laughed. 'Yeah. Do everything arse-about-face, that's me. The thing is, Cal, once the pressure was off and I actually started getting to know you . . . well, it was obvious you were nothing like her. She was . . .' He struggled to find the right words. 'Actually it doesn't matter what she was like, all that matters is that you're different, you're you.'

'Is that good or bad?'

He took her hand. 'The best. The past's the past, Cally, I don't know why I couldn't see that before. You helped me grieve, you forced me to realise that just because something was good once, it doesn't mean something else can't be better.'

Cally shrugged. 'These things can take time, I know that.'

Will contemplated the teenage rockhopper that was assiduously attacking the toe of his boot with its beak. 'Yeah, and sometimes they want a kick up the arse. But I'm getting there, Cal. Selling off my stuff through Liddy's shop is part of saying goodbye to the past.'

'I don't understand. I thought you were just doing it to help Liddy out.'

'I am. But she's helping me out, too. The collectables business was always Emma's big thing. She started it off, and when she died it came to me. I guess I thought if I carried it on . . .' He shook his head. 'Fact is, I was wrong.'

'We all make mistakes,' Cally said softly. 'After all, I married Rob.'

'Liddy told me you're getting a divorce. Am I allowed to be glad?'

She felt his hand tighten around hers. 'Actually, I'd be really disappointed if you weren't.'

Chapter Thirty-One

Cally had stopped getting nervous about being summoned to Henk Thorfinn's office. While it often seemed that something dreadful was about to happen, it never ever did. So when she stepped inside his office on that particular Tuesday afternoon, she wasn't in the least prepared for the bad news.

'Leaving?' The smile slid off her face. 'What do you mean, Colin's leaving?'

Henk Thorfinn, never a man of many words, did not like having to repeat himself. 'Colin is leaving the Experience,' he repeated, 'and that's all there is to it.'

'But he belongs here!'

'I don't agree, and neither does the vet. You of all people should know what a difficult animal he is to manage. And besides, it's not natural for him to be on his own. We've had an offer for him to join a breeding project in Italy.'

For some completely illogical reason, Cally knew instinctively that this was absolutely, definitely not what Colin would have wanted. 'You can't!'

'I can, and I'm going to.'

'But where does that leave me?'

Henk flipped over a sheet of paper on his desk. 'Looking

after the Galapagos banded turtles. I'm sure you'll make a good job of it.'

Things were turning from bad to worse. 'Oh no, not the banded turtles!' she protested.

'What's wrong with the banded turtles?'

'You mean, apart from the fact that they only move once a fortnight, and even then it's only to hiss at a rock they've mistaken for an intruder?'

Henk folded his arms and sat back in his chair. 'Cally, I think there may be a small misunderstanding here. This is not a discussion. It's either the turtles, or nothing.'

'Nothing! As in . . .?'

'As in, P45.'

He might just as well have told her he was going to roast Colin over an open fire and serve him up in sandwiches.

'What!' she squeaked, spittle flying all over Henk Thorfinn's desk. 'Get rid of Colin *and* give me the push? We'll see about that!'

With a certain amount of trepidation, Eddie stuck his nose up against the wire of Colin's enclosure. On the other side of the padlocked gate sat Cally, bloody-mindedly refusing to budge from her upturned box.

'What's to stop them just darting you with an air rifle?' he reasoned.

'Bad PR, that's what!' Cally had no intention of letting Eddie psych her into submission. 'I can make them look really bad.'

'And make yourself look even sillier,' he ventured. ' "Kooky Keeper in Skunk Sit-In"? The local paper's going to love this.'

'It's no good, Eddie, I'm not coming out. Tell Henk Thorfinn he's going to have to reason with me.'

'You tell him, I'm keeping well out of this.'

'Collaborator.'

Eddie reminded himself that strangling Cally would probably only make things worse. Besides, he couldn't do it unless she opened the gate, and right now Cally wasn't opening Colin's gate for anybody.

'Locking yourself in things doesn't solve anything, Cal.'

'Says who?'

'Says me. Your mum's spare room, Liddy's shop window, now this. You can't keep shutting yourself off every time something goes wrong.'

Cally defrosted slightly. 'All right, you suggest something then. But I've got to do something, I can't just let them stuff Colin in a box and send him away. You know how phobic he is.'

Eddie scratched his ear. 'Hmm, I don't know what the answer is. I guess you need to do some lateral thinking.'

'Lateral thinking?' snorted Cally. 'Like you and Janis, you mean? Oh no, sorry, that's horizontal, isn't it? I always did get those two mixed up.'

'Give it a rest will you?' Eddie's placid exterior was starting to crack. 'This jealousy kick of yours is starting to get really boring.'

'I'm not jealous!' protested Cally.

'Just because you don't like Janis . . .'

'I never said I didn't like Janis.'

'You don't though, do you?'

'I didn't used to,' Cally admitted. 'But that was before. Matter of fact I think you and Janis are just right for each other.'

'Is that a compliment or an insult?' enquired Eddie.

'Neither. It's the truth.'

349

'Hmm. You're not my mum you know. I don't actually need your approval.'

'Fine.' Cally shrugged in a downcast kind of way.

'I'm still glad I've got it though.' His eyes followed the fluffy orange banner of Colin's tail as the skunk moved around his enclosure, rooting out forgotten bits of dinner. 'It was good of you to offer to move out. Mind you, that was before I knew you had this in mind.'

Things were not going well for Cally.

It wasn't that the basic idea was a bad one, quite the reverse. If she was going to be sitting here protesting anyway, she might as well make use of the time. So she'd contrived to make sure that Mum and Dad and Apollo all turned up to see her at the same time.

That far, at least, everything had gone according to plan. It wasn't until she casually slipped Apollo's business plans into the conversation that things had started to go seriously pear-shaped. And in all fairness, that wasn't really Cally's fault. Was it any wonder things went wrong when your halfwitted elder brother only gave you half the facts?

'Business!' Marc Storm was aghast. 'You want to go into *business*? After what happened last time?'

'Last time?' Cally stared through the wire at her brother, who was looking more and more uncomfortable. 'What last time?'

'You mean he hasn't told you?' Evie fixed Cally's elder brother with the kind of look elderly spinsters used on queue-jumping teenagers.

'Told me what!' Cally looked from her mother to her father to no avail, and finally opted for her brother himself, who was standing with his hands deep in his pockets and his eyes fixed on the ground at his feet. 'Apollo, what are they talking about?'

He groaned. 'I knew this was going to be a disaster, why couldn't you have waited a bit before you told them?'

'Waited a bit?' Marc folded his arms and peered over the top of his small, round spectacles. 'Like you waited before you told us you'd been arrested and hauled up in court?'

Cally's jaw hit the ground, bounced back up and nearly shattered her teeth. 'You? In court? What for?'

Apollo flopped down on a red and white concrete toadstool. 'It was a long time ago, I was only a kid.' He ran a hand through his untidy brown thatch. 'You remember that time I was backpacking in Africa? You were still at school.'

Cally cast her thoughts back. 'What about it?'

'I wasn't backpacking.'

'So what were you doing?'

'Six months for fraud.'

Cally stared at him in stunned silence. Fraud? Her big brother, in prison? The idea was so crazy it was laughable. She looked at her mother, then her father, half-expecting them to burst out laughing. Nobody did.

'Dad? Dad, this isn't true is it?'

Marc's face was stony. 'It pains me to say this, Cally, but your brother's an idiot.'

Apollo's head jerked up. 'Now hang on a minute . . .'

'You must be an idiot if you want to risk going into business again!'

'Come on Dad, you know as well as I do I had nothing to do with stealing that money.'

'No, but your partners did, didn't they? They were ripping the company off right, left and centre, and you couldn't see what was happening right in front of your eyes. The minute the shit hit the fan, they were off to the Costa del Crime, leaving you to face the music. If that doesn't make you an idiot, I don't know what does.'

'Marc,' intervened Evie.

'It's OK, Mum, I can stand up for myself. In any case, Dad's talking out of his arse.'

'At least he hasn't got a criminal record!' snapped back his mother. 'Where would you be today if he hadn't helped you out and found you a job with PureFood?'

'Where would I be?' Apollo rounded on his mother. 'A bloody long way from you lot, that's for sure!'

Oh bugger, thought Cally, listening helplessly to the happy sounds of a family at war. Three days locked in a skunk enclosure, and now this. Possibly the very last thing in the world she wanted was to watch her family tearing lumps out of each other. And it's all down to you kid, she thought glumly. Three cheers for Cally, one-woman disaster area. Try a bit harder and you could start World War Three.

'Pssssst!'

She turned to see a face peering furtively through the trees behind the enclosure. Leaving the rest of the Storm family living up to their name, Cally sneaked across to unlock the back gate.

'Brought you some food.' Will whipped a lunchbox out from under his jacket.

She grabbed the plastic box and peeled off the lid. 'Cheese and ham, Will you're an angel.'

'What's going on?' asked Will as she bit into a sandwich. 'And why is your mother trying to strangle your father?'

'Don't ask,' sighed Cally. 'Are your family mad too?'

'Which one?'

'Why, how many have you got?'

'Let's see . . . two dads, a stepmum, God knows how many uncles. Most of them are a bit crazy.' He sat down next to her while she ate. 'Talking of crazy, when are you going to give this up?'

She munched. 'I'm not.'

'Come on Cal,' he coaxed, 'you've made your point. It's going to piss down this weekend, the forecast's terrible.'

'So I'll get wet.'

'Knowing your luck you'll get struck by lightning and all we'll find are your smoking wellies.' When he spoke again, he framed the words slowly and carefully, weighing up everything before he said it. 'Look, I know what this is all about.'

'It's about Colin, that's all.'

'Don't give me that. This is about trying to hold on to something for more than five minutes, isn't it? I've been there, I know. You're desperate to cling to something *fixed* when everything else in the world seems to be changing. Go on, tell me I'm wrong.'

She popped the last crust into her mouth. 'You're a smartarse, I'll tell you that for free.'

On the other side of the enclosure, battle was well and truly joined. Evie looked infuriated; Marc looked like thunder; Apollo looked like he wished he was dead.

'And another thing,' thundered Marc, really getting into his stride now that the barriers were down and he didn't have to be Mr Reasonable any more. 'I'm sick to death of your mother parading her lovers through *my* house as if—'

'*Your* house!' exclaimed Evie.

'Yes, *my* house, if I hadn't had that job at ICI we'd never have got the mortgage.'

'No, and if I hadn't gone back to work when you jacked it in, we'd have had no money to pay it back!'

Will got to his feet. 'Best of luck sorting that lot out.'

Cally smiled savagely. 'Seeing as you're so clever, why don't you sort them out for me?'

'Eef you ask me,' said Simone as Cally came out and locked the enclosure door behind her, 'Mistair Thorfinn has been very, very *raisonnable* about ze skunk.'

'And he really is going to try and keep Colin here?' demanded Cally, still slightly reluctant to give up her protest.

'*Bien sûr, si c'est possible*. If zere is space to build him another house in ze park when all ze building work is done. But you must understand, Cally, zere are very few of ze yellow skunks in England, and Colin, he ees a lonely skunk. He need a lady skunk to keep him company, *non*?'

'*Oui*, I mean, yes. Of course he does. But . . .'

'We will keep looking for a mate for him, but if zere is no female for him here, we must send him to Italy to ze breeding programme. If zat happen, you will travel wiz him and make sure he ees happy.'

Cally had to concede that it was the best compromise she could have hoped for. And now that she had cooled down, she did feel a bit guilty about poor lonely-heart Colin, pining away with not so much as a sniff of romance.

'Well, all right,' she conceded. 'I suppose that's fair.'

'Mistair Thorfinn, he ees a very nice man,' stressed Simone reprovingly. 'Eet is not kind to take advantage of him. Still, zere is no harm done and we have sorted everything out in time for ze Bank Holiday open day. So zat is good.'

Of course, Bank Holiday Monday, thought Cally. The biggest money-spinner of the year for the Experience – and it would need to be, with all the money that had been spent on new rides and educational displays. With all the fuss about Colin, she'd put the whole thing to the back of her mind.

'I suppose we'll all be working that day,' mused Cally, who'd rather been looking forward to having Monday off.

'Of course you will be here, you must be here!' Simone looked at her rather strangely. 'You are not having ze second thoughts, no?'

'About what?'

'About ze bungee jump, what else?'

Bungee jump?

BUNGEE JUMP! The words plummeted, screaming, through Cally's mind and vanished into a fathomless black sea of panic. How could she possibly have forgotten? How could she possibly have allowed herself to imagine, even for a split second, that she could ever hurl herself off the top of a crane on the end of a length of elastic?

'Well, I . . . the thing is . . .' she stammered.

'Mistair Thorfinn, he is so counting on you,' went on Simone.

Cally let out a tiny whimper of desperation. 'He isn't really, is he?'

'Oh yes. You see, we 'ave many keepers off sick. You are ze only one we have left who is fit enough to make ze jump.'

Chapter Thirty-Two

'There's an awful lot of people here,' commented Janis, clinging to the sleeve of Eddie's velvet jacket. 'I'm not sure I like it.'

He patted her hand, for all the world like Rolf Harris reassuring a nervous greyhound. 'They're only people, don't worry. Sir Edward de Priest will protect his fair damsel.'

'Hmm,' said Cally, trying not to watch as the Cotswolds' very own formation bungee team dangled gracefully from a scaffolding rig, on the end of electric-orange bungee ropes. In ten minutes' time, she told herself, it'll be you upside-down on the end of one of those. 'But will Sir Eddie protect me, too?'

'Of course he will,' said Janis, gazing adoringly at her white knight. 'He's lovely.'

Eddie chuckled. 'I should watch out for Apollo though, if I were you.'

'Why?' enquired Cally.

'He's got five quid on you bottling out.'

Behind Eddie, Janis and Cally, the Bank Holiday crowd surged around The Animal Experience in a noisy riot of novelty deely-boppers (available in Antelope, Giraffe or Reindeer style from the gift shop), animal-print T-shirts and ice-cream cornets.

Nobody was paying much attention to the formation bungee jumpers; they were much more interested in the main event: the sponsored jump in aid of the Experience's captive breeding programme.

'Oh God,' said Cally, 'just look at the faces on them, they're all hoping the rope snaps!'

'No they're not,' soothed Janis. 'Are they, Eddie?'

'Yes they are,' she insisted. 'Look, everybody's staring at me.'

'What do you expect?' pointed out Eddie. 'If you will wear a tiger costume.'

'Nothing to do with me. It was Simone, she insisted.'

Simone's voice came across on the PA system. *'Keepers to ze bungee rig please, keepers to ze bungee rig.'*

Something screamed inside Cally's head. Sweat trickled down the side of her nose. 'I can't do this.'

Eddie grabbed her by the orange scruff of her costume. 'Oh yes you can. You're doing this for Colin, remember?'

'Am I?'

'You know you are. Every penny the Experience makes from this is another penny towards keeping Colin here.' Eddie picked up Cally's head and rammed it on over her ears. 'Now – go throw yourself off a crane.'

It was tall. Oh, but it was tall. The huge red crane towered over the Experience, its top so high that even the birds that sat on it had vertigo. A little lift shuttled up and down it, ready to carry unwary keepers to their doom.

It's no good, Cally repeated to herself as she stared up into the sky; I just can't do this, I really can't. Horrible memories of Clifton Suspension Bridge were spilling out of all the dusty cupboards in her memory; her stomach was reprising that awful moment when she'd peeped over the edge and seen just how far down it was to the bottom of the gorge. The moment when she'd legged it for the nearest phone box, with the bungee rope wriggling after her like an escaped python.

That was it. No way was she doing this. Bugger the sponsorship, bugger all the endangered species on the planet, she was heading straight for the toilets and locking herself in.

As she swung round to make her escape, she collided with a woman in an Amnesty International T-shirt.

'Cally?' Evie peered in through the jaws of the tiger-head. 'Cally, is it you in there?'

'Yes, Mum, it's me. Look, I was just . . .'

'I'm glad I caught up with you,' Evie went on, standing between Cally and freedom, 'only your dad and I just wanted to wish you good luck and tell you how proud of you we are.'

Nooooo, please don't say that, Cally willed her. For God's sake don't be proud. Tell me that jumping off a crane is a stupid idea and you think I should call the whole thing off. 'Actually Mum, I was having second tho—'

Evie rattled on regardless. 'Especially as you used to have that terrible phobia about heights.' She broke off as a thought struck her. 'You don't still have that, do you dear?'

'No,' lied Cally, giving up the fight. 'Of course not. Would I be doing this if I did?'

Evie beamed. 'Well I think it's wonderful what you're doing anyway, helping animal conservation like this. Apollo was only saying so to your father just now.'

This was news to Cally. 'Apollo and Dad? You mean they're on speaking terms again?'

'Oh yes, dear. Getting on like a house on fire, ever since your friend Will persuaded them to go into business together.' She lowered her voice. 'Now, I'm not suggesting for a moment that anything's going to go wrong, I mean, perish the thought, but you are wearing clean knickers, aren't you?'

'Ladies and gentlemen, ze sponsored bungee jump will be taking place in ze South Paddock in five minutes.'

Amid the general hullaballoo, three odd-looking figures hung around the base of the big red crane, looking for all the world like characters out of a cartoon strip.

'Did I hear Vernon say you're an old hand at this?' beamed Robyn, an athletic twentysomething who spent her days hanging from the access harness in the Twilight Kingdom. She was the only person Cally knew who could dress up in a sea-lion costume and still look sexy.

'Well . . . I think he might have been exaggerating a bit,' confessed Cally, standing at the bottom of the crane with her neck bent back and her eyes fixed on the far-distant platform at the top. The only thing distracting her from the abject terror which had gripped her was a sudden and urgent need for the toilet.

'This is my first,' confided Robyn, eyes sparkling with excitement. She waggled the plaster cast which encased her right arm to the elbow. 'I just had to sign myself out of the hospital, there was no way I was going to miss out just because of some stupid compound fracture.'

'Yeah. I bet,' said Cally, with as much enthusiasm as she could muster.

'And what's a touch of septicaemia? The ambulance'll have me back on the drip in no time.'

A loud sneeze wobbled the head of the six-foot cockroach to Cally's right. She couldn't help feeling a pang of sympathy for her colleague Ayub, who had the worst head-cold she had ever seen and who really ought to have been in bed with a nice warm Lemsip. Hurling yourself off a crane was a pretty desperate way to cure blocked sinuses.

'Urgggh, sorry,' spluttered Ayub, then promptly sneezed again, sending a fresh wave of slime dribbling out of the mouth-parts of his costume. 'Don'd subbose adybody's godda tissue?'

Cally grimaced and wiped Ayub's nose on her tail. 'He's not going to do much for sales of those beanie cockroaches in the gift shop, is he?'

Robyn laughed. 'Not even Rentokil could shift those roaches. Oh look, Cal, Simone's waving us over. Do you want to go first, or shall I?'

The man in the hard hat and climbing gear made his final adjustments, checked the tension and stood up.

'There you are. All ready to go.'

Cally flattened herself against the wire cage that enclosed the platform on three sides, closed her eyes and shook her head vigorously. 'Uh-huh, no way.'

'What's that?'

'*I'm* not ready. And you can't make me, so there!'

The bungee operator switched on his most reassuring smile. 'Look,' he reasoned, taking a step nearer.

Cally shuffled away. 'No, you look. I don't have to do anything, I can . . . I can just walk away if I want.'

The man in the hard hat turned away, thinking hard. He'd seen them like this often enough to have a dozen

361

different strategies to choose from. It was just a matter of finding the right way of pushing them off without anybody realising you'd done it deliberately. Now, if he was to just . . .

He never reached the end of that particular train of thought. Suddenly the cord jerked out from under his feet, and he fell smack on his face on the platform.

When he looked up, Cally was gone.

Chapter Thirty-Three

Cally watched her head overtake her and speed away.

The tiger's head had fallen off almost as soon as she jumped. And suddenly she was living through one of those really peculiar, disconnected moments, like when you're travelling along on a train and another one speeds past in the opposite direction; and for a split second it feels as though you're standing still.

But you're not standing still, she told herself. You're bouncing back. It's not the end of the world, in fact nothing's the end of the world any more. You can do anything you want.

A-N-Y-T-H-I-I-I-I-N-G!

And, though the G-force was crushing all the air out of her lungs, Cally let out a yell of pure, unfettered delight.

When they hauled her back up on to the platform, she was giggling like an imbecile and grinning all over her face. Which was more than you could say for Ayub, who was still sneezing and dribbling as the man in the hard hat attached the bungee rope to his ankles.

'You all right there?'

'Aaaaaaaa-tchoo!'

'Know what you're doing?'

'Squuuuurgle.'

'Ready to go?'

Ayub's reply was lost in a spray of snot as he launched himself off the platform and into the blue, to a chorus of cheers from below. Still on a high, Cally gazed out dreamily across the green expanses of the Experience; past the Regency squareness of the Big House to the ultra-modern Twilight Kingdom, and the homely little scattering of old stable buildings around the visitors' centre.

She shaded her eyes to pick out the skunk enclosure from the woodland trail behind it. It was a silly idea, waving to a skunk; but somehow she felt Colin would appreciate her thinking about him as he chewed on his afternoon mealworms.

And he might have done. Only he wasn't there. He couldn't be, because the whole of the skunk enclosure had vanished into thin air.

Cally's heart was thumping as she forcibly evicted Robyn from the lift and hijacked it down to ground level.

'Nice jump,' commented the operator as she punched open the door of the cage and leapt out. 'Very stylish.'

'Well done Cal,' said Vernon, patting her on the back. 'You're a star.'

Friendly faces swarmed round her, intent on saying nice things about her; and a couple of minutes earlier, Cally would have been only too pleased to listen to Lazy Bob and Donna singing her praises. Instead of which, she positively wrestled people out of the way and forced a path through the crowd.

The skunk enclosure. Gone. There had to be some mistake, she told herself as she ran. She'd been looking in the wrong place, or the sun had been in her eyes and it had all been some kind of weird optical illusion. Anything but what she dreaded seeing.

She kicked off her tiger feet and ran the rest of the way in her socks, scarcely noticing the sharp stones underfoot. Stan the donkey brayed a friendly hello as she passed his new paddock, but she had no time to stop. She had to know the truth.

But not this truth. Cally stood gasping, hands on hips, staring in horror and disbelief at the rectangle of earth that had been the skunk enclosure. The wire had gone, the wooden living quarters had gone, everything had gone except the two trees that had grown up through the middle; the ones with the specially nurtured low branches, that Colin sometimes climbed up on when he was feeling adventurous.

'Colin?'

The word disappeared into the empty air, unanswered. Far behind her, the sounds of cheering mocked the sudden emptiness in Cally's heart.

'Colin, where are you?'

She stopped herself. This was silly. As if a skunk was going to come running at the sound of his name, like Lassie. There was only one way to find Colin, and that was by following her nose.

When Liddy caught up with her, Cally had her face pressed up against the slats of a wooden crate, sobbing her heart out.

'Cal?' Liddy walked across the courtyard towards the crate. 'Cal, what's the matter?'

Cally turned her tear-stained face towards Liddy. 'Look – look what they've done to him. They lied to me, they said he was staying.'

Liddy crouched down and peered between the slats. 'Colin?' The orange ball of fluff quivered gently but did not wake. 'What's he doing in there?'

Cally swallowed down a sob. 'It's obvious – have you seen his enclosure?'

'No, why?'

'It's gone, that's why! They knew I'd raise hell if they told me, so they wait till I'm out of the way, then they demolish the whole place, dart Colin and stick him in a box.'

'But why would they do that?'

'To send him away and get rid of him, why do you think? Just because he smells a bit and doesn't like people.' Cally sniffed back tears of righteous anger. 'And have you seen this?' She picked up the docket lying on the top of the crate. 'Aberdeen, Liddy. They're sending Colin to Aberdeen!'

Liddy scratched her head. 'But I thought . . .'

'Yeah, so did I,' snapped Cally. 'Which just goes to show how stupid I am, doesn't it? "Don't worry about a thing, Cally, Colin's staying here. And even if he isn't staying, he's going to a lovely new skunk centre in sunny Italy, he'll be much happier there." Yeah, and I'm Pavarotti's jockstrap.'

'Perhaps it's for the best,' ventured Liddy, somewhat lamely. 'Perhaps they've got a really sexy lady skunk in Aberdeen.'

'Liddy, there are only two other Javan Yellow Skunks in the whole country, both of them are male, and they definitely aren't in Aberdeen!' Cally reached a hand between the slats and stroked the end of the sedated skunk's nose. 'I'm not going to let them, Liddy, I'm not!'

'I don't see what you can do about it,' objected Liddy. 'If Henk Thorfinn's already made up his mind.'

'Then I'll unmake it for him! There's thousands of people here today, Liddy. I-I'll climb up to the top of the crane and tell everybody what a lying bastard he is.'

'Are you sure that's wise?'

'Wise? *Wise*? I don't give a toss, I've got to do something!'

'Not the crane, Cal. Promise me you won't climb the crane.' Liddy placed a restraining hand on the shoulder of the tiger costume. 'If you fall on your head all your brains'll fall out and you know I never could stand the sight of giblets.'

'Well what then?' challenged Cally. 'Come on, help me think of something!'

Henk Thorfinn's little black and white van zipped along the dual carriageway like a turbo-charged zebra, galloping back towards Cheltenham.

Cally wasn't sure she'd wanted to know how Liddy had learned to hot-wire a van, still less that she had learned it from Will. And now that she was on the road, with a full tank of petrol and a sedated skunk in the back, she was even less sure that she was doing the right thing.

She stole a glance at herself in the rearview mirror. She looked flushed, dishevelled, her mascara was running and from the neck down she was still dressed as a tiger. Maybe, just maybe, she and Liddy hadn't really thought this through.

But it was too late to change her mind now. She and Colin were on the run.

The more Cally thought about it, the less she wanted to implicate Liddy in this whole sorry business. OK, so it had been Liddy's idea to hijack the skunk as a publicity stunt, and it had been Liddy who'd suggested hiding out at Gold in the Attic; but she wouldn't have suggested either if Cally hadn't been hell-bent on handcuffing herself to the top of the bungee crane. As far as Liddy was concerned, this was the lesser of the two evils.

As she unlocked the door of the shop, it occurred to Cally that trying to look unobtrusive was a bloody silly idea. It simply could not be done while wearing a tiger costume and carrying an orange skunk in a wooden crate. On the other hand, she could hardly take the costume off, could she? She'd turn even more heads dressed in nothing but a crop-top and a g-string. And seeing as Liddy was about half her size, she could forget raiding her wardrobe too.

She put down the heavy crate and flopped amid the dusty books. I can't stay here, she told herself. I just can't. But where else can I go? Then Cally remembered that Liddy didn't just sell books and collectables. She sold old clothes too.

Maybe she wasn't completely stuffed after all.

The Victorian pram squeaked protestingly as Cally pushed it through the lych gate and up the path to the church porch. Inside, cunningly concealed by a frilly cot blanket, slumbered Colin the skunk, blissfully unaware of all the fuss he was causing.

The Fifties' sundress wasn't really Cally's style; it itched, and had padded conical bosoms so protruberant that she couldn't even see her feet. But it was the only thing in the shop she could get on, if you didn't count the Darth Maul mask and cape.

She wheeled the pram into the church, closing the heavy door behind her. It was nice and cool in here, a huge relief after the blazing sunshine outside, and the scent from the flower arrangements was soothing and sweet. This was what she needed; somewhere quiet where she could get her head together and decide what to do next.

Options flitted in and out of her head. Was it too late to go back, and hope they hadn't noticed Colin was gone? Of course it was, the driver had only left him for ten minutes to go for a pee. Besides, how could she take the poor beast back and see him exiled to Aberdeen? It just wasn't right. On the other hand, was it right to kidnap somebody else's skunk just because they hadn't let her get her own way?

Funny how tired she felt after all this stress. Her head drooped on to her hands, until her chin was resting on the handle of the pram. It's no good Cally, she told herself just before her eyes closed; as soon as you've had a little rest you're going to have to drive Colin right back to the Experience and face the music.

She and Colin were sleeping so peacefully on the bench at the back of the church that neither of them noticed the church beginning to fill up. In fact, Cally knew nothing more about anything until someone jogged her arm and a voice woke her with a start.

'Hello, dear. Are you with the bride or the groom?'

AND THEY ALL LIVED . . .

'You were lucky Henk didn't press charges,' commented Will, sitting down on the end of Evie's spare bed.

Cally threw another pair of jeans into her suitcase. 'All right, all right, there's no need to rub it in. And I did have to fork out for the biggest dry-cleaning bill in history.'

369

'I mean, taking a skunk to a wedding . . .'

'I didn't know it was a wedding!'

'. . . and then, when that old dear looked in the pram and he jumped on her head and sprayed all over the . . .'

'Yes, thank you Will, I do remember. I was there, *actually*.'

They looked at each other, po-faced, for a moment, then burst into simultaneous laughter.

'Cally Storm, you're a muppet.'

'And you're worse than a muppet. You could've told me they were only transferring Colin to Aberdeen until they'd built the new skunk house!'

'But it was supposed to be a surprise! Henk was going to make an announcement after the bungee jumping, only you put two and two together and made five. And don't pout,' he added reprovingly.

'I'm not pouting!'

'Yes you are. And it makes you look like a penguin. Mind you, you know how fond I am of penguins.'

His lips hovered near hers. But at that moment, Marc Storm's voice boomed up the stairs. 'Are you ready yet? You're supposed to check in at the airport in half an hour.'

'Nearly,' Cally called down the stairs. She went back to stuffing socks into trainers and ramming them into the corners of her case.

'You know, you could have slept at my place these past few days,' commented Will, picking up a lacy bra, looking at it wistfully and dropping it into the suitcase. 'On the sofa, of course. I mean, you know I'm the perfect gentleman.'

Cally smirked. 'Oh, of course. But if I hadn't commandeered my dad's tepee he wouldn't have had to move back into the house with Mum, would he? And then they wouldn't have got all cosy again, like they used to be.'

'Bit of a success then?'

'Oh definitely. Between you and me, Mum's even given her boyfriend the push. Both of them, actually.'

Will sat in silence on the end of the bed, watching each item of clothing disappear into the suitcase. 'Cally.'

'Hmm?'

'Are you giving me the push, too?'

She stared at him. 'Why would I do that?'

'Because you're going away. I mean, you might not want to . . . you know.'

Cally threw down a book about captive skunk-rearing, and sat down next to him. 'I'm only going to Java for three months, to learn about Yellow Skunks. In three months' time, I'll be back with two gorgeous lady skunks and Colin will be in seventh heaven.'

'So will I,' said Will.

Cally's heart did a little skip in her chest. 'Does that mean you'll be waiting for me?'

He smiled, and kissed her. 'Oh, I'll be waiting for you,' he promised. 'No matter how bad you smell.'

Bumps
The bestselling novel by
Zoë Barnes

Sexy, single, succesful...and pregnant!

Bump number one... Just when Taz Norton's life is on a smooth upward glide – youngest sales manager at a flagship department store, own flat, cat and vintage motorbike – her lover leaves her for her ex-best friend.

Bump number two... is finding out she is pregnant the same day she is asked to handle the biggest store promotion in the company's history.

Bump number three... is the one in front of her. Goodbye toes and glamour, hello heartburn, morning sickness and support tights.

Typically, Taz decides to be Superwoman. No one is going to tell her she can't get to the top and be a single mum as well. But no one told her it was going to be so damned hard...

"A brilliant sense of comic timing; the ability to create believable characters and a touching sense of the trickiness of family relationships...an enjoyable and moving read"
Maeve Haran, *Daily Mail*

"An entertaining and light-hearted story of parenthood"
Observer

"Great read"
Prima

Hitched
Zoë Barnes

For better, for worse... *But for ever?*

Hitch number one... A quick jaunt to the registry office and off to the pub with a few friends to celebrate. That's all Gemma wants for her wedding to Rory. But then the parents hear the news.

Hitch number two... Suddenly her little wedding is hijacked and turned into a Hollywood-style extravaganza. Before she knows what's hit her, Gemma is stampeded into yards of frothing tulle, fork buffets for five hundred, kilted page boys and an all-inclusive honeymoon in the Maldives ...

Hitch number three... And while the dress may be a perfect fit, Gemma and Rory's relationship is coming apart at the seams...

An irresistible look at wedding fever from the bestselling author of *Bumps*.

Praise for *Hitched:*

"lively and compulsive"   *The Mirror*

"A great book for anyone who likes their romance laced with a healthy dose of real life"   *Options*

"A good giggle"   *Essentials*

Hot Property
Zoë Barnes

From the bestselling author of
Bumps and *Hitched*

Dream home? Dream man? *Dream on!*

When Claire inherits a house out of the blue, she thinks she's struck it rich! But while the word 'cottage' inspires images of romantic idylls and roses round the door, there's nothing remotely heavenly about Paradise Cottage. It's a tumble-down wreck in the middle of nowhere – more in need of a demolition expert than a decorator.

Still, Claire's not one to shirk a challenge. Much to the amusement of her hunky new neighbour, Aidan, she decides to renovate the cottage herself. After all problem-solving, trouble-shooting – it's what Claire does best. She's used to planning events for thousands of people. She can sort out one little cottage ... can't she?

Praise for Zoë Barnes:

'Zoë Barnes writes wonderfully escapist novels, firmly based in reality'   *Express*

'Romance and DIY – what more could you want?'
Woman's Own

Pride, Prejudice & Jasmin Field
Melissa Nathan

'Tremendous fun – an ingenious update of the greatest
love story of all time'
Jilly Cooper

Witty Jasmin Field has her own column in a national magazine
and has just landed the coveted role of Elizabeth Bennet in
a one-off fundraising adaptation of *Pride and Prejudice*.
Better yet, the play's director, Hollywood heartthrob Harry
Noble, is truly obnoxious, meaning a lot of material for her
column – and a lot of fun in rehearsals.

But then disaster strikes. Jazz's best friend abandons her
for a man not worthy to buy her chocolate, her family starts
to crumble before her eyes and her award-winning column
hits the skids. Worse still, as the lights dim, the audience
hush and Jazz awaits her cue, she realises two very
important things, one: she can't remember her lines, and
two: Harry Noble looks amazing in breeches...

"A memorable read – funny, warm and intelligent"
Woman's Own

"A witty spin on the nation's favourite novel...with a
lovable, contemporary heroine at its heart"
Good Housekeeping

"engaging debut novel"   *The Good Book Guide*

Good Husband Material
Trisha Ashley

She's settled for Mr Right...just as Mr Wrong comes along!

James is everything Tish has ever wanted in a husband –
she's married a man who even her mother approves of. He's
handsome, dependable, and will make an excellent father –
unlike Tish's first love the disreputable Fergal. Her teenage
sweetheart abandoned her for a music career and now lives
a typical celebrity lifestyle. Fergal broke her heart – James
helped mend it.

Now, they've bought a cottage in the country. The next
step – kids and a lifetime of domestic bliss. Well, that's the
plan anyway. So why is marriage to Mr Right making her
long for Mr Wrong?

Intelligent, warm and funny, Trisha Ashley is a fresh and
imaginative new voice in women's fiction.

"Trisha Ashley writes with remarkable wit and originality
and has created a deliciously acerbic heroine"

Katie Fforde

Moving On
Emma Lee-Potter

There's a first time for everything...

Kate and Laura Hollingberry are sisters. But whilst they have a close relationship, they couldn't be more different. While Laura is happy to get an undemanding little job to pass the time until she finds Mr Right, Kate wants more out of life than just a suitable husband.

Kate wants a career too. Determined to make her own way in life and not rely on her tycoon father's money or influence, she's taken a position at a local newspaper far away from home. But it's her first job, her first bid for independence, and anything can happen...

Praise for *Moving On*:

"A fresh, contemporary women's read"

Publishing News

Praise for *Hard Copy*:

"pacy exposé...tightly written, with snappy dialogue"

Daily Mail

"fast and furious"

The Mirror

"An authentic witty insight into life behind the headlines"

Books Magazine

The very best of Piatkus fiction is now available in paperback as well as hardcover. Piatkus paperbacks, where *every* book is special.

☐ 0 7499 3030 6	Bumps	Zoë Barnes	£5.99
☐ 0 7499 3072 1	Hitched	Zoë Barnes	£5.99
☐ 0 7499 3111 6	Hot Property	Zoë Barnes	£5.99
☐ 0 7499 3152 3	Pride, Prejudice & Jasmin Field	Melissa Nathan	£5.99
☐ 0 7499 3182 5	Good Husband Material	Trisha Ashley	£5.99
☐ 0 7499 3193 0	Moving On	Emma Lee-Potter	£5.99

The prices shown above were correct at the time of going to press. However, Piatkus Books reserve the right to show new retail prices on covers which may differ from those previously advertised in the text or elsewhere.

Piatkus Books will be available from your bookshop or newsagent, or can be ordered from the following address:
Piatkus Paperbacks, PO Box 11, Falmouth, TR10 9EN
Alternatively you can fax your order to this address on 01326 374 888 or e-mail us at books@barni.avel.co.uk

Payments can be made as follows: Sterling cheque, Eurocheque, postal order (payable to Piatkus Books) or by credit card, Visa/Mastercard. Do not send cash or currency. UK and B.F.P.O. customers should allow £1.00 postage and packing for the first book, 50p for the second and 30p for each additional book ordered to a maximum of £3.00 (7 books plus).

Overseas customers, including Eire, allow £2.00 for postage and packing for the first book, plus £1.00 for the second and 50p for each subsequent title ordered.

NAME (block letters) _____

ADDRESS _____

_____

I enclose my remittance for £ _____

I wish to pay by Visa/Mastercard   Expiry Date: _____
